PRAISE

The Shear

'An incredibly gripping read ... the two stories meld together beautifully and each kept me riveted.'

All the Books I Can Read

'The perfect weekend read!'

Beauty and Lace

'*The Shearer's Wife* displays McDonald's implicit understanding of the true challenges of rural life ... another great book that kept me engaged from cover to cover. A thoroughly engaging outback mystery novel.'

Mrs B's Books Reviews

'A solid story, intriguing mystery and unforgettable characters ... the best of an Aussie outback novel.'

Sam Still Reading

'A riveting rural crime story ... Fleur McDonald brings country South Australia straight into my home.'

The Burgeoning Bookshelf

Fleur McDonald has lived and worked on farms for much of her life. After growing up in the small town of Orroroo in South Australia, she went jillarooing, eventually co-owning an 8000-acre property in regional Western Australia.

Fleur likes to write about strong women overcoming adversity, drawing inspiration from her own experiences in rural Australia. She has two children, an energetic kelpie and a Jack Russell terrier.

Website: www.fleurmcdonald.com
Facebook: FleurMcDonaldAuthor
Instagram: fleurmcdonald

FLEUR
McDONALD

The Shearer's Wife

ALLEN&UNWIN
SYDNEY · MELBOURNE · AUCKLAND · LONDON

This edition published in 2021
First published in 2020

Allen & Unwin
83 Alexander Street
Crows Nest NSW 2065
Australia
Phone: (61 2) 8425 0100
Email: info@allenandunwin.com
Web: www.allenandunwin.com

 A catalogue record for this
book is available from the
National Library of Australia

ISBN 978 1 76106 556 9

Set in Sabon LT Pro by Bookhouse, Sydney
Printed in Australia by McPherson's Printing Group

10 9 8 7 6 5 4 3 2 1

 The paper in this book is FSC® certified.
FSC® promotes environmentally responsible,
socially beneficial and economically viable
management of the world's forests.

To those who are precious

Author's note

Detective Dave Burrows appeared in my first novel, *Red Dust*. I had no idea he was going to become such a much-loved character and it was in response to readers' enthusiasm for Dave that I chose to write more about him. Since then Dave has appeared as a secondary character in eleven contemporary novels and four novels (set in the early 2000s), where he stars in the lead role.

Fool's Gold, *Without a Doubt*, *Red Dirt Country* and *Something to Hide* are my novels that feature Detective Dave Burrows as he begins his career.

In these novels, set in the late 1990s and early 2000s, Dave is married to his first wife, Melinda, a paediatric nurse, and they're having troubles balancing their careers and family life. No spoilers here because if you've read my contemporary rural novels you'll know that Dave and Melinda separate and Dave is currently very happily married to his second wife, Kim.

Dave is one of my favourite characters and I hope he will become one of yours, too.

Chapter 1

1980

The beige Holden Kingswood wagon pulled to a stop next to the fuel pump at the Golden Fleece roadhouse.

Rose Kelly breathed a sigh of relief and rubbed her hands over her pregnant belly. She felt as big as an elephant and was desperate to get out of the confines of the car.

'All right then, sweet Rosie?' Ian, her husband, asked as he reached for his wallet sitting on the bench seat between them.

Rose smiled; she liked when Ian called her 'sweet Rosie'. His Irish lilt made her sound as if she were an exotic flower. His Irish rose.

'Not really. I'm really uncomfortable. How long until we get there?'

Ian threw the heavy door open. 'I'm not sure. Probably

half an hour. You'll be right. You're only pregnant, not sick. Many women have given birth in the back of a car.'

Rose groaned as she felt a solid kick from inside her, and reached for the door handle. 'That'd better not be me. I don't see *you* hauling around a stomach larger than the Opera House and getting kicked from inside!'

'Reckon I drag heavier wethers, though.' Ian grinned and leaned over, patting her leg. 'You'll be right, love.'

'Hmm. You only have to drag one sheep at a time. I've got two babies in here, Ian. Two! Could we stay here the night?' Rose asked, as she hauled herself out of the car. 'Barker looks like a nice little town. Surely they'd have a room at the pub. I'm really tired.'

Leafy trees lined the quiet street. Only two cars sat parked in front of the local shop. The voices of unseen men rose on the hot, still air: 'Catch! Catch!'

A cricket match on the oval, on Saturday afternoon, she thought. *Maybe there's a tennis club here.* Rose remembered playing tennis when she was at school. A sense of displacement hit her again. The nagging feeling of wanting to stay in one place had started a few months ago, as she'd felt her body swell. Travelling was increasingly awkward and the roads rough as her twin babies bounced inside her.

What she wouldn't do for a house and a garden, somewhere she could walk, potter and cook in a kitchen, instead of being pulled from one shed to the next. They hadn't been home since they were married twelve months before, on her nineteenth birthday, and it had been longer since she'd seen her family. Not that she was convinced they wanted to see her.

The irony of the situation was not lost on her: when she'd left her hometown, it had been to escape the confines of her strict, religious family, needing to taste freedom and space, and now all she wanted was a home. Somewhere to build a life. To raise her babies.

Her babies. Twins. She hadn't even known twins were possible. She hadn't known anything, so every part of this pregnancy was new and frightening. Ian had been so proud when she'd told him she was expecting.

'A baby! Well, it'll be a boy, for sure.'

Then there had been a bit of spotting and Ian had agreed to stop in a small town so she could visit the hospital. There, they'd found out she was having twins.

They'd driven in shell-shocked silence to the next shed. The next lot of shearers' quarters. The next lot of shearers. The shearing team—usually a dozen of them and all blokes—camped close to each other. She was sick of the constant travel, the weary men and the stench of sheep.

Their accommodation was the same as all the others: one small room for the two of them, nowhere private for a moment's peace. Rose had to share her new husband with everyone else and there were very few people for her to talk to. Sometimes she wondered how she'd ended up pregnant and on the road at twenty. But she loved and trusted Ian, and was still happy to sit beside him in the passenger seat.

She sighed, turning towards him as he spoke.

'Surely they do,' Ian nodded. 'But . . .'

The fuel attendant came out. 'How much would you like?' he asked, unscrewing the fuel cap.

'Fill her up. Thanks, mate.'

'Just passing through?' the man asked, as the smell of fuel rose into the air.

'Nah, be around for a few weeks. Got a bit of work out at a shed just north of here.' Ian walked away from the car and stretched. 'Out at Jacksonville.'

'Oh, yeah? Shearer?'

'Ian Kelly, at your service.' He held out his hand and the other man shook it.

'Stuart Martin. Good people out there at Jacksonville.' He glanced across at Rose. 'Long way to the hospital from there though. Nearly an hour's drive when the road's good. Get a thunderstorm and you'll be stuck for a while.'

'An hour, you say?' Ian answered. 'Thanks, I'll keep that in mind. Haven't been there before. Good to hear they're nice.'

'Can't go wrong with Ross and Ali Barton. Top shelf.' He looked over at Rose. 'Long to go?'

'A month or so yet. I wish they would arrive sooner,' Rose said, pushing her red hair away from her forehead. 'I'm sick of being fat and beaten up from the inside.' She paused. 'That sun's got some bite in it.' She fanned her face. Another kick and she clutched her belly, unable to stop from groaning aloud.

'Rose?' Ian took a step towards her.

An older woman, dressed in jeans and a shirt, walked out of the roadhouse, her blonde ponytail bouncing behind her. 'Hello! Oh, are you all right there?' She glanced at Ian as he put his hand on Rose's shoulder. 'Take some deep breaths now. That's right, in and out.'

Rose focused on the woman's voice and did what she was told.

The woman squatted down in front of her and smiled encouragingly. 'Well done. Keep breathing.' She turned to look up at Ian. 'Is she having contractions?'

'How the hell do I know? She was fine in the car a minute ago.' Ian took a couple of steps back, looking shaken.

Rose flapped her hands and shook her head. 'No,' she said when the pain receded. 'No, I'm fine. I get these cramps occasionally, and they go again.' She stood upright and looked at Ian. 'I'm fine, honest.'

'Come on, let's get you inside, out of the sun. I think a cold drink will do you wonders.'

'That would be wonderful, thank you,' Rose said, as the woman turned to walk inside. Rose planted her hand on her lower back as she plodded beside her, still marvelling at the change in her centre of gravity; her belly leading the way. 'I'm Rose.'

'I'm Evie,' the older woman smiled as she ushered Rose inside. 'How long to go?'

'Not soon enough! Twins, if you can believe it. Baptism by fire!'

'I can,' Evie replied. 'You're big enough. Those cramps you're getting are probably Braxton Hicks. And you're right, they come and go a bit.'

'Braxton what?'

'Hicks. It means your body is getting ready for labour.' Evie was silent for a moment while she opened the fridge and brought out an enamel jug. 'Haven't you heard about them before?'

Rose shook her head and tried to swallow the lump in her throat. 'We didn't talk much about this sort of thing in my family.'

Evie nodded with a kind smile. 'Did I hear you're on your way to Jacksonville?'

'Yeah, Ian has a stand at the shearing shed for a few weeks.'

'You're brave, going to stay out there. Away from the hospital.' She poured a glassful and handed it to Rose. 'Homemade lemonade. Sit down.'

Rose shook her head. 'I've been sitting all day. I need to stretch, but thank you.' She took a sip of the cold, sweet drink and smiled. 'This is just like my grandmother's. Lemon juice and sugar topped up with water?' she asked.

'Sure is!' Evie filled up her glass. 'Good old-fashioned, thirst-quenching drink. Plenty more where that came from.' She eyed Rose curiously. 'How long have you been on the road?'

'Feels like forever! Especially since I've got bigger. The car isn't as comfortable as it used to be. Every time we hit a pothole, I feel like the seat is coming up through my stomach!' She took another sip. 'We've come from Lucindale and before that Mount Gambier. I've forgotten where we were earlier.'

'Yep, I imagine the bubs are giving you a good kicking. Where are you from?'

'Ballarat.' She paused, suddenly and inexplicably wanting to pour out her heart to this woman. It had been so long since Rose had seen her mother, and there weren't many women to talk to on the farms and stations Ian worked. Sometimes the loneliness crept in. 'I'm a bit scared,' she said, the words tumbling out before she could stop them.

'Why's that, Rose?' Evie fixed her with such a sympathetic look, Rose thought she might cry.

'I don't know anything about this. Ian keeps saying I'll be fine. Women have had babies for generations.'

'And so they have.' Evie nodded.

'I don't even know if I'll realise when I'm in labour! I don't know anything, not even about these Braxtons— whatever you just said.' The anxiety that had been building in Rose over the months finally came to the surface.

'Oh, you'll know, all right,' Evie said dryly as she moved over to the bookshelf and started looking through the battered paperbacks and recipe books. 'How old are you?'

'Twenty.'

'Young and healthy. If you were having one baby, I'd say your Ian is right and you'd be fine. But having two is a whole different thing. You should be close to a hospital. Hasn't a doctor told you that already?'

'Last time I saw a doctor was three months ago.'

Selecting the book she was looking for, Evie handed it over to Rose. 'Here you go, have a read of this.'

Rose looked at the title: *All You Need To Know About Being Pregnant.*

'That'll give you a bit of an idea about what to expect.' Evie paused. 'I'd really have a hard think about going out to Jacksonville, Rose. It's a long way, and it'll feel even longer when the bubs decide they want to come.'

'You there, love?' Ian called out before Rose could speak. 'Let's get on the road.'

Trying not to frown, Rose took a couple of final deep gulps of her drink. 'Well, I guess that's me,' she said. She glanced around longingly. 'You've got a lovely home. Who would have thought this would be out the back of a road-house?' she said. 'I'd love a couch like yours.' She nodded towards the floral-patterned sofa, then turned to the door, and Ian. 'Coming!'

Evie put her hand on Rose's arm as they walked out to the car. 'Rose, I don't know you and this is none of my business, but I'm thinking those bubs could arrive very soon. If they're early, they'll need medical help.'

'What do you mean?' Rose glanced across at her, her eyes wide.

'Sometimes if babies are born early they need help to breathe. Lungs are the last organ to develop, and if your twins arrive prematurely, they'll need to stay in hospital for a while. We've got a good hospital here in Barker.'

'Oh.' Rose looked at Ian, then down at the ground, trying to ignore the butterflies in her stomach. The ones that weren't the babies or indigestion. They were getting harder and harder to ignore. She put her hand on her belly protectively and looked over at Ian. 'I'll need time to talk to my husband about that.' Her hands fell away as she moved towards the car.

'Of course. Still, if you decide you want to stop here, let me know. I have a little house just up the street, with no one living in it. Barker is a lovely, sleepy little town. Gets pretty warm in summer, but that's just like the welcome you'd get here.' She nodded. 'Off with you, then. But take care.'

'What are you two gasbagging about?' Ian held the car door open for Rose.

'I was just saying that being so far away from the hospital with twins on the way is quite dangerous,' Evie answered, her smile softened her firm tone. 'They might need medical help when they're born. I've just been telling Rose that you're welcome to use my other house if you need it. Just nearby, and it would easily fit your new family.'

Rose looked at Ian hopefully. 'A house sounds lovely.'

'Come on, sweet Rosie.' Ian bent to kiss her. 'You know the plan.' He turned to Evie. 'I want to get her back to Adelaide before the babies are born, but I need this shed to be able to do that.'

'Well, if you change your mind, the offer's there.'

Ian looked at her. 'Why would you do that when you don't know us?'

Evie shrugged. 'I like helping people.'

'Women have babies out in the bush all the time.'

'Yes, they do.' Evie paused, looking at Rose. 'Some survive and some don't. As I just said to Rose, twins are a different story.'

Ian gave a bark of laughter. 'In this day and age, you'd have to be pretty unlucky to have something go so wrong that you die.'

'If you're close to medical help,' Evie agreed.

Rose frowned as her middle tightened. 'Come on, Ian,' she urged. 'If we're going, let's go.' She reached her hand out to Evie. 'Thank you for your kindness. Country people and their compassion is one of the reasons I can cope being on the road.'

'Go well, you two,' Evie bade them farewell, smiling through the window to Rose as Ian started the car.

'She's a bit of an old busybody,' he said, pulling the column gear into reverse.

Rose looked out the window, tears unexpectedly filling her eyes. 'She was nice,' she said unsteadily as she looked down and opened the book to the first page.

What happens in the first trimester, she read. *Bit late for that.*

Ian glanced over at her. 'What have you got there?'

'Evie gave it to me.' She flicked the cover over so he could read the title, realising her voice shook a little as she spoke.

'Hmm.' Ian looked back at the road, silent for a while. 'Don't tell me you actually want a house and to be in one place all the time? You knew you weren't going to get that with me.'

'I know. I'm fine. Probably just tired.' She squeezed her eyes shut. What she really wanted to say was: Yes! Yes, she did want a house, with a pretty sitting room and a nursery for the babies. A bathroom she didn't have to share with men she didn't know and a pillow that wasn't lumpy.

Ian reached over and put his hand on her knee. 'Sweet Rosie, are you okay? Did the pains hurt that much?'

'They're pretty scary,' Rose admitted.

'You know I love you, don't you? This life on the road, going from shed to shed—it's the way it is. You know I don't want to be confined to one town. That's why I came to Australia. You didn't want that either.'

Rose glanced over at her husband—the tall, dark-haired Irishman she had fallen in love with the first day she saw him walk into the local pub in Ballarat, two years ago. He'd been working in a shed and come into town to let off a bit of steam. She'd been working behind the bar.

Ian had ended up sitting down one end of the bar that night, talking to her as much as he could. By the time the shed was finished, two weeks later, she'd handed in her resignation and said goodbye to her parents, leaving in the passenger seat of the Kingswood.

Her mother had been horrified. 'You've only just met him.' That was the first thing she'd said.

'Think of the family name—you leaving with him and not being married.' Her father had frowned deeply. With his role as a lay preacher in the Baptist Church, Rose could only imagine what he'd think this was doing to his Christian image, and he hadn't left her in any doubt of what he thought of her decision. 'Living together and not being married is against God's law, and no daughter of mine will be seen to be involved in such sin.'

And, finally, they had both agreed: 'Rose, you'll be back here begging us to take you in within weeks. Well, my girl, if you leave, don't think that will happen.'

That had been that. Rose, the daughter who had never rebelled, against her family or society, had picked up her bag and walked away from the tidy front yard, with its lilly-pilly hedge fence and green lawn that her father mowed every Saturday afternoon.

Her parents had stood in the doorway until she climbed into Ian's car, then turned and shut their door tightly, finalising the end of their relationship.

Their marriage had come eight months later, when they'd rolled into the sleepy town of Townsville. Rose had a photo of them standing on the town hall steps, both looking uncomfortable in their Sunday best. The registry office wedding had been followed by drinks at the Shamrock Hotel, where Ian had bragged to all who would listen that his Rose was the prettiest girl around. Their bed had been tiny and Ian's drunken snores had kept her awake. As had an annoying mozzie who seemed to know exactly where her ear was. Nothing like she'd imagined her wedding day would be.

The walk on the beach the next morning, the bouquet of flowers and gentle kisses and soft praises had made up for the flop of a wedding night.

Rosie hadn't given her family much thought, although from time to time the urge to speak to her mum was overwhelming, especially since she'd become pregnant. But that was a feeling she kept to herself.

As Ian swung the car onto the road and headed out of town, she thought about their life since she'd left. At first, she'd loved the nomadic lifestyle. She'd seen more of Australia than any of the girls she'd gone to school with. They were all back in their hometown, married or studying to be a nurse or a teacher. Their lives would emulate those of their parents. Never moving out of the same postcode, and perhaps only shifting a few streets away from where they were raised.

Rose had never wanted to be like that. She'd always yearned to get out of Ballarat, and that was why she'd taken the job at the pub—to earn enough money to be able to leave and start a new life.

But she had never counted on falling in love with Ian. And she had, quickly and hard. His accent had made her knees tremble as he whispered Irish words she didn't understand. He'd seemed wild and exciting and free.

Free. That was what she wanted to be.

Out of Ballarat and away from her parents' expectations and tight rules. The ones that would see her end up just like every other young woman in town: working for a year or two until she ended up married and pregnant. Again there was the irony, because that was exactly what Rose now was—married and pregnant.

She always found a smile on her lips when she remembered what Ian had said to her a couple of days before they left.

'Come with me, sweet Rosie. Life on the road with you will be perfect. We won't have much, but we'll have each other, and I want nothing more than you. Come with me, *A chroí*.'

Oh, how she loved the Irish endearments. They sounded so mysterious. Just like their travelling life had been meant to be.

The countryside now opened up to wide red plains, covered in golden swaying grasses and low olive-coloured shrubby trees. They looked prickly to Rose. A heat mirage shimmered at the end of the road and didn't get any closer as they drove towards it. The air felt as if it were burning as she breathed in, and the sunlight hurt her eyes.

'Rosie?' Ian was looking at her, concerned. 'I love you,' he repeated.

She touched his arm and tried to smile. 'I know.'

Chapter 2

2020

A cold wind blew through the Barker police station as the door opened; the missing-persons posters and other pamphlets and brochures flapped under the force of the breeze.

Joan, the long-standing receptionist, snatched at her paperwork and looked up, her smile turning to a frown.

Three men dressed in casual clothes but each wearing identical navy blue vests now stood in front of the desk. Dark sunglasses and stern looks were on their faces.

'Can I help you?' Joan asked, trying to reorganise the documents she'd been working on.

'Looking for the sergeant,' the one closest to her said, putting his sunglasses on top of his head. He held out a badge.

Joan looked at it. *Jerry Simms.*

'I'll get Dave for you,' she said, rising and walking casually towards the back of the office. Ducking through the doorway, she glanced over her shoulder and saw all three standing to attention, their hands clasped low in front.

'Dave!' she whispered, frantically indicating towards the front desk.

Dave looked up from his computer and over the top of the glasses perched on the end of his nose. Joan's hands were pointing, and she was making all sorts of hand signals that didn't make sense. He raised an eyebrow.

'AFP!' Joan finally managed to get out.

Both his eyebrows were near his hairline now and he leaned back in his chair for a moment before getting up and walking out into the front area.

'Detective Dave Burrows,' he said, holding out his hand to the closest man, who merely fixed Dave with a stern look.

'Can we go somewhere private?' the nameless man asked, glancing at Joan.

'Right through here,' Dave answered, gesturing in the direction he'd come from.

The three men walked past him and found chairs in his office. Dave glanced over his shoulder at Joan and gave a wink, before following them through.

Settled in the office, the ringleader, his face still serious, introduced his team.

'I'm Jerry Simms and these are my colleagues, Allan Taylor and Rob Cooper.' They all shook hands this time, though the remaining stern-faced men still didn't speak.

'What can I do for you fellas?' Dave said. 'Pretty unusual to get a visit from the AFP out in a quiet country town like Barker.' He sat and crossed his legs, ready to listen.

'We're here to intercept a package that will be arriving at the post office today. I'm only letting you know out of courtesy that we're in town. Although we'd appreciate your assistance in "doing the door" when we go in to take control of the package.'

Dave was quiet for a moment. 'Whose door?'

'We won't tell you anything more until the parcel has been delivered.'

Frowning, Dave steepled his fingers as he looked at the men. 'That doesn't sound very friendly.'

'It's not a negotiation point. We can't compromise this transaction—it's integral to a larger operation,' Jerry said, as he leaned forward. 'Detective, we require your assistance. You'll have to trust us until the procedure is finished.'

Dave narrowed his eyes and thought about his answer. 'It's the local show today. I'd hope that if you're chasing someone, they won't be a local. But if they are, it would be better if I knew who the person of interest is. You forget, Jerry, that my partner and I will probably know this person. We've both been in this town a long time. We have local knowledge that might assist you.'

Jerry shook his head before Dave had finished speaking and kept it moving until there was silence. 'No. No, we're not forgetting. What you need to understand is we haven't worked with either of you before. Both you and Senior Constable Higgins come with high recommendations, and we understand you're both competent and dedicated to the police force. But you're also very entrenched in Barker. This is a small town and the walls have ears.' He looked out towards where Joan sat, then leaned back and shook his head. 'No go.'

'Have you got a time frame? I'm going to need to talk to Jack. Let him know what's going on. He's out taking a statement from a burglary victim.'

Jerry glanced at his watch. 'At zero eleven hundred.'

The office door banged shut as Jack Higgins' voice filtered through from reception.

'Perfect timing,' Dave said.

'That bloody wind!' Jack could be heard declaring to Joan. 'It's straight off the snow. Pity it hasn't got any rain in it. Whose car's out the front?'

There was a muffled answer from Joan and silence from Jack. Dave could imagine the mimed conversation as Joan tried to tell Jack who was in the office. Maybe she'd even written him a note saying who it was. He almost grinned as he envisaged the look of surprise on Jack's face when he worked out the car belonged to Feds.

'That's Jack now.' Dave nodded towards the front. 'I'll brief him and then introduce you.'

'There's no need,' Jerry said. 'I can do that.'

Dave ignored him and met Jack as he was about to walk into the offices. 'Back out here,' he said quietly, pointing towards the front door. Jack reversed out and Dave saw Joan watching them. He gave her a thumbs up. *Everything's okay.*

Dave and Jack bent their heads together. 'What the hell is going on?' Jack asked.

'The plastic police are in there. Need our help with an operation. Got some good grass on someone expecting a package. They want us to help with the door. Don't know if its drugs or what.'

'The Feds? Whose door? What package?' The words tumbled out of Jack's mouth as Dave saw his excitement rise.

'You know as much as I do. They're not exactly forth-coming with information. Come on, I'll introduce you. Guessing it's something to do with the imports who've come into town with the ag show. I certainly hope it's no one local.'

Jack sobered. 'Yeah, good point. So, no indication?'

'Nothing.' Dave stopped and looked at Jack. 'Where's Zara today?' he asked.

'Being ever the good journalist and covering the agricul-tural show, but you know she'll sniff this out quick enough. Just the strange car will be enough.'

'Let's hope she stays on the showgrounds for a while, then.'

Dave pushed open the door and went back into his office, where the three men were leaning close together, talking in hushed tones.

'This is my partner, Jack Higgins,' Dave said. He resisted the urge to introduce the three AFP coppers as Huey, Dewey and Louie, dressed as they were in an unofficial uniform of beige chino pants and pale blue shirt, open at the neck. An air of serious confidence, and perhaps arrogance, radiated from each face. Still, Dave had come across that type of attitude before.

'G'day,' Jack said, shaking hands with them all. 'Sounds like there's something interesting in the pipeline.'

'We've got intel that a parcel will be delivered today and we want to intercept it,' Jerry confirmed. 'Do you have experience on the video camera, Senior Constable?'

'Yeah, I do.'

'Good. We need everything from the moment we knock on the door until we walk out again to be filmed. You can work with Allan here, both filming from different angles. Rob, Dave and I will get the door open. Got that?'

Dave cast a glance at Jack to see how he was taking the high-handed instructions.

'Sure, whatever you need,' Jack said, to Dave's surprise.

'Right, let's move out, boys,' Simms said to his men.

'Hold on, don't you think it's going to raise some eyebrows, three strange blokes dressed in AFP vests? Let alone a different car parked in a quiet street where all the residents know everything about everyone?'

Jerry turned to Dave. 'That's why we're taking your vehicles. We'll be back in an hour and a half.'

Dave watched them leave and raised his eyebrows at Jack.

'They can be tossers, can't they? No such thing as flexibility.'

Jack laughed and rubbed his hands together. 'But they've given us some excitement for the day.'

'Hmm. Like I said before, just so long as it isn't someone local they're chasing. I would hate to charge someone who lives here.'

'Depending on who it is,' Jack replied.

∿

Dave, Jerry and Rob sat in Dave's unmarked police car, opposite the post office. There hadn't been much conversation, which suited Dave. He'd been too busy watching all the locals who weren't at the show, walking up and down the street, dressed in heavy jackets, trying to keep the biting wind from their bodies. Who were the Feds after? The only way to guess that was to see who was going to the post office, apparently.

Dave was in the front seat, while the other two were in the back behind the tinted windows. The locals would have to look closely to realise there was anyone else in the vehicle with him.

He'd seen Mrs Hunter stop and chat with the young girl, Beattie, from the chemist shop, and Jamie Flemming had pulled up in his muddy farm ute, run in to the deli and come out with an iced coffee and sausage roll.

His wife wouldn't be too happy if she knew that's what her husband was up to, Dave thought. Jamie was supposed to be on a diet—diabetes, or so he'd told Dave last time they'd run into each other.

Everyone Dave had seen was a local, and surely whoever was supposed to have this package—whatever might be inside it—was not a local. He knew his town. Or so he hoped.

'What are we waiting for?' Dave asked. 'A delivery or a pick-up?'

'The postal delivery truck,' Rob said. They were the first words he'd spoken, other than to say hello.

'The truck would have been here at ten o'clock this morning.' Dave looked at his watch. 'It's now nearly twelve-thirty.' As he said that, he saw Joan walking towards the post office, her keys in hand. She'd be getting the police station mail, and her own, he knew. 'You've missed it.'

'No, we haven't. There had to be time to sort the mail. She'll be getting it from her mailbox soon.' There was a pause. 'Look.'

The two men leaned over the seat towards the wind-screen, then Jerry muttered, 'There we go.'

Dave stared at his receptionist, Joan, as she walked towards the post office, dread filling his stomach. 'What? Who?'

'She's coming now.' Rob pointed, his hand coming from between the seats, aimed at Joan.

Not able to find any words, Dave sat and waited. No. It couldn't be Joan they were after.

'Over there, in the green coat. Behind your receptionist.'

Dave glanced away from Joan and saw Essie Carter in a green coat. The relief was instant but replaced with scepticism. 'Who? Essie?'

'Estelle Carter of 10 Fifth Street, Barker,' Rob said. He held the page with Essie's information on it, over the back seat for Dave to take.

Reaching out, Dave kept his eyes on Essie. 'You're wrong. Essie's been here in Barker forever; rarely leaves town. She goes to church every Sunday, and volunteers at the hospital and at the Red Cross op shop. Raises her granddaughter on her own. Bloody hell, Essie must be sixty-odd. I can't imagine she's doing anything illegal.'

'You don't think? Look at her. Checking out her surroundings, looking over her shoulder,' Jerry said. 'Got all the hallmarks of guilt to me.'

'What's she supposed to have done?' Dave said. 'What's in the package?'

The two men didn't answer.

Essie had stopped briefly to talk with Joan, then hurried on to the post office. As she stepped into the alcove, where the mailboxes were, she cast a glance over her shoulder. Dave got his binoculars out and watched as, with shaking hands, Essie tried to insert the key into her box, but dropped the set. Joan was next to her and bent down to pick up the keys before Essie could.

The elderly lady snatched the keys back and then gave Joan a quick smile. She said something that looked like, 'Clumsy me.'

Joan collected the mail and turned to go, putting a hand on Essie's shoulder before she left. Dave thought he could lip read through the binoculars: 'See you at church on Sunday,' and Essie nodded without smiling.

Dave continued to observe, his eyes fixed through the lenses, his heart sinking. It was like watching a slow-motion train wreck. Essie took another look around, then a deep breath. Dave had to admit Jerry was right. This wasn't the behaviour of a person without something to hide.

She inserted the key into the lock and ducked down to look inside. As she withdrew the contents, Dave got a glance of a small yellow padded envelope before she quickly stuffed it in her jacket pocket. Then she turned and walked out onto the street again, head down.

'Guilty as sin,' Rob said. 'Hope those boys got her behaviour on video.'

'What do you think, Dave?'

Dave watched Essie walk with purpose towards the corner. 'I think there's more to this than you know.'

His mind was racing. This was the Essie who had decorated the church with flowers for Dave's wedding to Kim. The Essie who was so grateful for what Dave had done to save her daughter. The Essie who was always the first to pop into the station with a birthday cake and a smile. What he was seeing here couldn't be right.

Except he knew what he'd seen: something was happening and Essie was involved.

There's got to be more to this, he thought. *I've got to find out what.*

Chapter 3

Dave felt like a traitor as he knocked loudly on the door of 10 Fifth Street.

There was no answer.

Jerry stepped forward, pushing past Dave and raising his fist to hammer quickly on the door.

'Police!'

The banging echoed through the stone home, but there was only silence from within.

'Mrs Carter,' Jerry shouted. 'We know you're inside. It's the police!'

Still no noise or movement from inside.

'Last chance, Mrs Carter. Open up or we'll smash the door in.' He turned to Dave and Allan. 'Get ready with the battering ram.'

'Geez, Simms,' Dave said. 'Are you sure that's necessary? What you've got here is a lady you're scaring the shit out of. Let alone the neighbours watching from over the fence. The gossips will go mad. What is this all about? Let me try.'

'You saw her behaviour. You know that she knows what she's got. Narcotics. Mrs Carter!' He raised his voice and banged on the door. 'Right, on three. One . . .'

'Narcotics?' Dave said disbelievingly, just as there was a noise from inside.

The latch clicked and the door opened slowly.

Immediately Jerry put his hand on the door and foot over the jamb. He pushed hard and from the inside there was the sound of backwards steps.

When the door stopped moving, they could all see Essie Carter standing in the passageway, her eyes wide, face pale and minus her green coat.

Jerry walked forward and held up his identification, while Dave stepped back to let him take the lead. More and more he was feeling like he didn't want to be here. But he had to. He was a copper, and at least he knew that Essie would trust him.

Jack and Rob were behind Jerry, the video cameras rolling.

'Are you Mrs Estelle Carter?'

'What? Yes.' Confusion mixed with defiance crossed her face.

'I'm Jerry Simms of the Australian Federal Police. I have a search warrant for these premises. Will you step aside, please?'

The men swarmed in around her, moving through the house, opening doors and exploring rooms.

Dave caught Essie's eye and raised his hands in a silent question. *What's going on?*

She looked at him and shrugged.

Drugs? he mouthed, his incredulous look clear.

Essie dropped her head but not before he saw a flash of fear cross her features.

Around them drawers opened and closed. Dave could hear one of the men in the bathroom; pill bottles were rattling as he opened and then discarded them.

Dave looked at Essie again, but she wouldn't meet his eye. *Shit.*

He watched the chaos for a moment longer, then went into the kitchen. Clean but tired benchtops looked like they had been wiped down more than a million times. Curtains that hung in the window were spotless but old, and there was a box of toys under the table. On top sat a cup with steam rising from inside, and a tea pot.

Next to a yellow padded envelope.

Which was open, and sitting on top was a plastic pouch full of white powder.

It looked to Dave like about a kilo of heroin.

No need to look further; the Feds had found what they were looking for. Dave's heart hammered against his chest, but outwardly he remained his usual calm, professional self.

Jerry stood at the table, looking down. 'Bit of smack with your tea, Mrs Carter? Nice way to have smoko. Over here, boys. Make sure you get it on video.'

He turned to Essie, who was standing in the doorway, her arms crossed over her chest. She had tears on her cheeks, and Dave wanted to go to her, tell it was going to be okay.

But he couldn't. He was a copper and there were clearly illegal substances in this house.

From the moment Essie picked up the parcel, Dave had been hoping they would find it was an order from eBay or Etsy. Prove this jumped-up, arrogant dickhead from the plastic police wrong. But he hadn't been wrong, and deep down Dave had known the AFP wouldn't have arrived here without good cause.

'Mrs Carter, I'm advising you, you are now under arrest for the importation of narcotics.'

'Over here,' Rob said, pointing inside a drawer near the telephone. 'Another three envelopes, the same as the one on the table. Empty, but the same. Right down to the postmark. Make sure you get them on video. Take them as evidence too and get them swabbed.'

'Mrs Carter, where did you buy these drugs?'

Essie didn't answer.

'Check the rest of the house with the cameras,' Jerry instructed Rob and Dave. He pulled out a chair and sat down, then said to Essie, 'I can wait you out, Mrs Carter. But you'd make things so much easier for yourself if you answered my question.'

'No comment.' Her voice wavered, but she looked at him defiantly.

'I beg your pardon?'

Essie stepped into the kitchen. 'I don't have anything to say to you.' Her hands were clasped tightly across her chest and Dave could see the whites of her knuckles.

Dave clenched his jaw as movement from the other officers made him look away from Essie. Jack took his eyes from the camera for a second and exchanged a glance with Dave. His face was solemn.

Jerry nodded and looked around. Dave saw his eyes land on the toys and a barely visible shake of his head. He could see Jerry thinking, *Just another druggie with kids.*

Dave itched to say something, but he had to stay silent.

'Hands behind your back please, Mrs Carter,' Jerry said in a weary tone. He got out his handcuffs and moved towards her.

'No.' Dave wasn't having that. He walked to Essie's side, glaring at Simms. 'We won't need to take her down that way. Come on,' he spoke to the elderly woman now. 'We need to go to the station and ask you some questions.' He turned and gently guided her to the door.

❧

In the station, Dave stood off to the side of the kitchenette and watched as Jerry made himself a coffee. Dave's feet were planted firmly on the floor, his arms crossed as he tried to get Jerry to look at him.

'Mate, you've got the wrong person,' he said.

Jerry ignored the statement.

'Simms?' Dave's tone commanded a response.

Jerry turned around and stared at Dave. 'I know this is your town and your people and it's hard to believe a little old lady like that could smuggle in drugs. A grandmother, of all people! But it happens. You wouldn't believe the people I have to arrest for drugs. Young mums with kids in the back of cars; fit, healthy men who run businesses with million-dollar turnovers.' He shook his head. 'Drugs don't discriminate. And you were there when she picked up the package. She's probably on-selling it to the local kids and making a fortune.'

'No, there's history.'

'What history? Burrows, I've heard good things about you, but I'm starting to think you've been in this town too long. You're too close to the people here and you can't see what's under your nose.' He stirred in a sugar and gave a mirthless laugh. 'I'm sorry to say you're wrong.'

'I know what Essie did. I saw it and I'm not saying she's not aware she's acting illegally, but—' he paused, before speaking slowly and carefully '—I think she might be a pawn in this matter. And I can categorically tell you she's not a dealer.'

'And what do you base that on?'

The scorn in Jerry's tone made anger flare through Dave's stomach. He took a calming breath.

'Melissa Carter left town five years ago, under a cloud. I had arrested her for possession of heroin while she was here visiting her mother. Her mother is Essie. After the arrest, Melissa was supposed to be drying out. Barker was a great place to do it because there are so few drugs here— I'm not naive enough to think there're none, but I haven't seen anything hard. About two weeks on, I found her with a tourniquet around her arm, a needle in it, unconscious in her car at the back of her mother's house.

'We saved her, but she moved on quickly, leaving her daughter, who is all of six, with Essie to raise.'

'Moved on?'

'Disappeared. Discharged herself from the hospital and vanished.'

'Unfortunate. But it still doesn't make a case not to arrest Mrs Carter. Perhaps she needs the money to help raise the child.' Jerry shrugged as if none of this were of any consequence.

'I never said you shouldn't arrest her,' Dave answered flatly. 'I'm giving you the background, so when you interview her, you've got information you otherwise wouldn't have.'

'Sure. Thanks. I'll go and question her now. See what I can find out.'

Dave watched him leave the room, a smirk on Simms's face. Clearly he thought Dave was incompetent. 'Tosser,' he muttered, knowing Jerry wouldn't give any thought to what he'd been told.

Picking up the phone, Dave sighed and ran his fingers through his hair, before dialling Kim's number.

'Hey, honey, and to what do I owe the pleasure?' Kim's soft, flirty tone came down the line after two rings.

'I need you . . .' He stopped, realising he sounded like he was issuing orders to a constable. 'Sorry. Hi, sweetie. How are you?'

'In need of you too, but by your tone you're not calling to organise a rendezvous.'

Dave laughed. Just the sound of her voice made him feel lighter inside. 'I wish I could. Got a bit on.'

'What can I help with?' Kim's voice was concerned, and Dave felt a rush of love for his wife. She was always there, helping in the background. Never once asking questions she knew he wouldn't be able to answer, just doing what he called on her to do. Her support for him and his job was something most men would envy.

'Is your registration with the Department of Child Protection still valid? Can you still be a foster carer?'

'Yes . . . ?' Kim drew the word out into a question.

'Can you ring the school and tell them you're coming to pick up Paris Carter? I'll send an email authorising it. She'll be staying with us for a while.'

'Paris?'

'Yeah.' Dave glanced at the door that Essie sat behind. 'I . . .'

'It's okay,' Kim interrupted. 'I know you can't say anything. I'll do it now.'

'Give me five minutes to email the school with the forms.'

'Okay.' Kim didn't say any more although Dave could feel her questions pinging down the line.

'I'll tell you when I get home. But if anyone asks, Essie has gone to Adelaide on family business.'

'Right-oh. I'll go and make up the bed in the spare room.'

'Kim?'

'Yeah?'

'Thanks.'

'Honey, you don't need to thank me.'

He put down the phone, opened his computer and found the forms he needed to give to the Barker Area School, all the while wondering what Jerry was asking Essie. He wished Essie had taken legal representation, but when he'd offered the service, she'd declined. Simms had glared at him when he'd mentioned it, but Dave didn't care. Still, if she had, they probably would have had to shift her to Port Augusta or Adelaide. Barker didn't come at having a lawyer on tap.

With the forms emailed to the school, Dave got up and went to the door of the interview room, hoping to hear something.

'Can you confirm your name for me?' Simms's voice carried through the thin door.

Silence.

'Is your name Estelle Carter?'

This time he heard a low murmur from Essie. 'Yes.'

'And could you confirm your address for me?'

Essie answered that question too.

The front door to the station slammed and Jack walked in. Through the open doorway into the reception area, he could see Joan hold her finger up to make sure Jack stayed quiet. Dave continued to listen, giving them both a grave smile and a thumbs up.

'Did you receive this package today?'

Dave imagined Jerry pushing the narcotics towards Essie and her recoiling from them. He knew she hated anything to do with drugs.

33

Five years ago, Essie had stood there on the pavement and watched, helpless, as Dave and the paramedics worked to save Melissa, and she'd cursed every drug and dealer while Kim had comforted her. She'd cried at her daughter being so weak—not being able to stay away from the high and escape from the world of dealers—and cursed the year that Melissa had left Barker to study in Adelaide and been introduced to drugs.

'You've got a baby!' Essie had cried.

There was no way Essie would import drugs willingly; of that, Dave was certain.

'Mrs Carter, it's in your best interest to cooperate, as I've mentioned before,' Jerry's voice filtered through the door again. 'Please answer the question.'

Silence.

'Have you received packages like this before?'

Silence.

'How do you source the drugs?'

Silence.

'What do you do with them once you've received them?'

Silence.

'Interview terminated at 3.06 p.m.' A chair scraped along the floor and Dave heard Jerry say, 'I'll be back, Mrs Carter, and I do hope you'll feel like obliging me when I return.'

Still nothing.

Dave walked to his office before Jerry came out. He heard the door slam, then lock and a low, 'Damn it!' before Jerry appeared in his doorway.

'Well, she's had the opportunity to talk. I'm going to shift her to Adelaide, and she can deal with whatever comes her way.'

Leaning back in his chair, Dave fought the anger rising in his chest. 'Let me have a go,' he said. He wasn't about to let Essie be taken to Adelaide without trying to help her.

'What do you think you're going to get out of her?' Jerry snapped, frowning.

'I don't know, but it won't hurt to let me try.' He spread his hands out beseechingly.

'You don't know enough about the case and I can't tell you anything more about it at this stage.'

'But I know what happened today.'

Jerry blew out a breath and then shrugged. 'Suit yourself. I'm going to get another coffee.'

When Dave pushed the door open he saw Essie slumped at the table, her head resting on her arms, her shoulders shaking. He heard her swallow and try to control herself, before lifting her head up. Her face crumpled as she saw him.

Quietly he pulled the chair out and sat down, resting his elbows on the desk. He pushed across a box of tissues he'd brought from his office.

'It's okay. Kim and I are going to care for Paris while this is going on. She's going to be looked after. She'll be safe.'

This made her cry harder.

'What's going on, Essie?' he asked in a low voice.

Essie shook her head against her arms. 'I can't,' she said.

'Can't what?'

'Nothing.' She sniffed and looked up to grab a tissue and blow her nose.

Dave waited for her to speak again but she didn't, just continued to shake her head.

'Essie, I'm not going to be able to help you if you don't tell me what's going on. Now, I know this isn't you. Don't forget, I was there when Melissa was in a bad way. So, how about you start at the beginning and tell me what's happened, because that's what I'm here for. To help you.'

Her voice was hiccupping as she spoke. 'I can't say anything. You don't understand.'

'Because you're frightened?'

Nodding, Essie twisted the tissue around her fingers.

'Can you tell me who you're frightened of?'

'I don't know who they are.'

Dave watched her steadily for a few heartbeats. 'Okay. But it has something to do with Melissa?'

Essie nodded again.

Dave felt his mobile phone vibrate in his pocket, but he ignored it. Carefully, he asked another question. 'Has this been going on for long?'

Dabbing at her face with the tissue, Essie stared back at him. He held her eyes, trying to convey support and strength.

The tissue was now shredded and soggy, torn apart just like Essie. Finally, she took a deep breath and the words rushed from her. 'Three weeks.'

Dave nodded. 'Okay. How did it start?'

'Dave, I can't tell you. I would if I could.' She stared at him, her eyes wide with fear. 'I can't. There're consequences if I do.'

'Okay, okay,' Dave held his hands up calmly. 'But we can help, Essie. No matter how big the problem is, we can help. I know that Federal Agent Simms is a bit highhanded, but he's here to help too. It would be beneficial if you would speak to him.'

Suddenly, Essie straightened up. When she spoke next, her voice was stronger. 'No, Dave, I can't tell you. There's too much at stake. You do what you have to do with me.'

Dave regarded her for a moment. 'What about Paris? Surely you don't want to be away from her?'

Essie's face collapsed again. 'No, I don't. I . . . don't know,' she said shakily.

'Essie, unless you help, I think what will happen is the AFP will take you to Adelaide to be charged. You'll have to go to court but the judge will probably grant you bail. Have you got anyone to post surety for you?'

'No.' She looked over at Dave, her eyes wide. 'Will it be much?'

'I can't tell you. Maybe forty or fifty thousand. Can you mortgage the house?'

'It's not mine to mortgage.'

Dave leaned back in his chair. 'Is whoever you're protecting worth all of this, Essie? Worth the time in jail, worth leaving Paris behind?'

Dropping her eyes, Essie nodded. 'Yes,' she whispered.

Chapter 4

1980

There were five other vehicles pulled up at the shearers' quarters when Rose and Ian arrived. She recognised two of them and she closed her eyes, breathing out heavily in despair.

'Look at that,' Ian said, sounding pleased. 'Muzza and Kiz are here. Better make sure that bottle of rum is close by.'

Rose wondered if she could get to the bottle first and pour out the liquid. Maybe she could say it smashed as they drove over the rough corrugations. Except they hadn't been especially rough. She knew how this evening would play out. After dinner, she would be expected to leave the men, banished to her small room alone while they set up their gear in the shed and then broke out the pannikins and rum and talked late into the night about other sheds they'd been in and women they'd managed to bed over the month since they'd seen each other.

Ian would come back to their small room, stinking of alcohol, and want sex. He'd tell her he loved her, and she'd tell him she didn't like how much he drank or his choice of friends. Ian would call her a controlling wench. Then he'd fall into a drunken sleep, snoring as if he were trying to suck the walls in, while she would lie on her side trying to get comfortable and wondering why she was still with him.

Rose pushed the car door open. 'Come on,' she said. 'Let's find where we're sleeping and get everything unpacked.'

'In a minute. I'll just say g'day to the fellas.' Ian strode over to the quarters, calling out as he went. 'Where are you two bastards? Get out here!'

A door flew open and a short, stocky man with a shock of red hair and lily-white legs stood in the entrance, wearing a blue singlet and a pair of stubby shorts. In one hand was a beer, the other a shearing comb.

'Well, well, look who you see when you haven't got a gun. Kiz, that Irish waster Paddy's back again.' Muzza plonked down his beer and they shook hands. 'How's it going, Paddy?'

'Got a spare one of those?' Ian asked, indicating the beer.

'Always one for you, mate. Kiz! Where are you?'

'Ian,' Rose called out, trying to hide the desperation in her voice. If he started drinking now, he wouldn't stop until he fell asleep. 'Can we get unpacked first?'

Ian didn't turn around. 'Later, sweet Rosie.'

Kiz arrived with a beer. 'Paddy,' he said, touching his finger to his forehead in a salute. 'See you've still got the ball 'n' chain.'

Rose slammed the car door extra hard, and a burst of laughter came from the men. She refused to look over at them; she knew what she would see. The three of them sitting on the edge of the wooden verandah, beers in hand, looking at her for a rise. She wouldn't give it to them.

Instead, she found the kitchen. Brushing the little black bush flies away from her face, then the blowies from the screen door, she let herself into the dim room.

'Hello?'

A crash sounded, then: 'Oh, no! Bugger. Hi? Come in.'

The cool of the thick-walled stone building was a relief. She waited while her eyes adjusted to the light and then walked down a small passageway into the kitchen. The cement floor was covered in peeled potatoes and a woman with long blonde hair was kneeling over the mess.

'Can I help?' Rose asked, looking around for a sponge.

The woman glanced up. 'I don't think you should be bending down! I just dropped the damn pot of potatoes I was going to mash for tea tonight. Bugger it!' The woman stood up and smiled. 'I'm Ali Barton. You must be Rose and Ian Carter?' She looked behind Rose. 'Well, the Rose part of the Carters.'

'Yep, that's me. The other half is out catching up with his mates.' Her stomach tightened again, this time a gripping pain radiating around her middle. She gasped without meaning to.

'You all right?' Ali pulled out a chair. 'Here, sit down. Breathe. I'll get you some water. How far off are you?'

Rose waited until the feeling was gone, then looked at Ali, her eyes wide. 'That was worse than earlier. Is that what it's going to feel like?'

'Nope,' Ali said cheerfully. 'It'll be a lot worse!'

Rose sat heavily on the chair. 'Sorry to make such an entrance. I only wanted to know where we're sleeping so I could unload the bags.'

'You guys are away from the others. You're the only married couple we've got. Unusual. Mostly it's single men. You must be one tough cookie to be on the road with your husband and just about to calve.' She pointed to a door on the other side of the kitchen. 'At the end of the passageway. You'll have to share the toilet and bathroom with the cook when she gets here.'

'Oh, I thought . . .'

'Nope. My husband owns the place. I'm just helping out until Faye can get here.'

Heat flooded through Rose's face. 'I'm sorry.'

'What for? Now, are you in labour or not?' Ali threw a tea-towel over her shoulder and put her hands on her hips, looking at Rose carefully.

Wanting to laugh uncontrollably, but not knowing why, Rose assessed her body. 'I don't think so.'

'But you had another one of these pains today?'

'Yeah. Only about an hour ago.'

'Nothing in between?'

'No.'

'Well, that's handy. I'd hate to think we were going to be dealing with shearing and a new baby in the same week. Why don't you go and get settled and I'll clean up this mess?'

'Oh. Well, thank you,' she said just as a loud round of laughter went up outside. Rearranging her face into a neutral expression, she left the kitchen and followed the passageway to the end, where she pushed open the door.

The room was dark and small, with a tiny window in one wall. A double bed took up most of the room and was unmade. A small wardrobe meant there would be room for their clothes and nothing else.

Where will we put the babies if they arrive while we're still here? she wondered. Then it struck her—what would the twins even sleep in? Neither Ian nor her thoughts had gone beyond the impending birth.

'Stupid girl!' she muttered, as a trickle of fear ran through her. For the second time that day, tears started to fall. 'Oh, no, no, no!'

They hadn't thought to do anything to get ready for life after the birth of their babies. Remembering her first doctor's appointment, when the pregnancy was confirmed. The doctor hadn't told her she was carrying two babies then. That news had come after she'd had a slight bleed and a second doctor had ordered an ultrasound. Each time had been a different town and a different doctor.

She remembered leaving the hospital and walking to the pub to find Ian. 'Twins,' she'd told him over a lemonade.

Ian hadn't reacted at first. Only raised his beer for another sip. Finally, he'd looked at her. 'Twins?'

'Yeah.'

It had taken him a long time to say, 'That's great news, sweet Rosie! Two little Kellys running around in the world,' before lapsing into silence again. The startled atmosphere had continued for many days.

Since then, they'd been on the road carrying on as normal, rarely speaking about the impending birth or even acknowledging Rose was pregnant.

Maybe that wasn't normal.

As she sat on the edge of the bed, her head in her hands, a memory suddenly came to her. One of her friends, at the end of high school, had gone to live with her aunt in the Northern Territory. Rose remembered her rounded belly, thinking only that she had put on weight. Now, she was positive her friend had been pregnant and hidden away from the rest of the God-fearing, small-minded community. She had broken the unwritten code and paid the price.

Why didn't they tell us anything? she had wondered in frustration so many times since she left. None of the families spoke to their daughters about pregnancy and what happened during and after, because Rose and her friends were expected to be 'good girls' and wouldn't need to know anything about it until they were married.

Looking around the bleak room, Rose sighed as Evie's words came back to her. *'Some survive and some don't.'* It suddenly hit her. This wasn't a game. She was pregnant and soon enough there would be two little babies arriving. Two! There was no guarantee they would arrive on time, or healthy. Evie had made sure she'd understood that. Now Rose was an hour from town, from a hospital, with no way of getting there unless Ian took her. How irresponsible she'd been. And Ian had been. The lives of their babies were in their hands and no one else's.

Fear gave way to terror and she started to breathe quickly. Short, sharp breaths, until it was hard to take another. She groaned and wrapped her arms around her belly.

'Oh, no, no, no,' she muttered again, visualising a screaming little bundle being born in this tiny room, the next one following soon after. They would have nowhere to sleep. No clothes to wear. No blankets. No one to help deliver them.

She would bet her last dollar that once the babies were born, Ian would bust open a bottle of rum. 'To wet the babies' heads, sweet Rosie.' He'd be drunk and she'd be left alone to care for two little ones, with no idea what to do.

The situation seemed more and more frightening, but she knew that somehow she had to get her thoughts under control. Rose's grandmother's voice echoed through her head. *'Someone else is always worse off than you,'* she used to say.

As comforting as that might be, Rose wasn't sure what could be worse. She took a couple of steadying breaths and fanned her face with her hands.

In and out, in and out. That's right, Rose. Still, no point in worrying about any of that now, she thought as her heart rate and breathing began to slow. *Make the best of a bad situation, as Grandma would say. Not much I can do about it now other than to get on. I'm about to be a mum and those little ones will be relying on me.*

44

The bed needed making. Glancing at the dirty mattress and stained pillows, she grimaced. Her babies were going to be born into this . . . Would she call it a lifestyle? Not the type of life Rose wanted for her two babies.

She managed to get herself off the bed and out to the car. The men didn't look up, so she dragged the suitcase out of the back herself. She looked at Ian's shearing gear in the box for just a moment before deciding he could get that; the combs, cutters, handpiece and other equipment were too heavy for her.

As she took the suitcase in, she wondered if she could use that as a crib for the babies. Would they both fit inside there together?

Back in the room, she took the sheets from the case and started to make the bed. Bending forward was difficult. If Ian had been there, he could have lifted the mattress to help her. Or made the bloody thing himself.

Rose gave a grim smile as she thought that. He wouldn't know how to make a bed. Before she'd come on the road with him, he'd slept in a swag. Rose had put her foot down, refusing to sleep in the dirty sleeping bag.

'How are you going?' Ali knocked gently on the open door.

'All sorted, thank you.'

'You've been crying.'

Rose didn't know what to say. She'd never had much to do with the owners.

'I had a phone call from Evie. She's a good friend of mine.'

'Evie?' Rose's mind was blank, then realisation dawned. 'Oh, Evie from the service station.'

'She told me to watch out for you, and I think she's right. Now, I've had a couple of kids, but never twins. One is hard enough, let alone two and you being away from home.'

Rose burst into tears at her gentle tone. 'I haven't got a crib, or clothes or . . .'

Ali took her hand and pushed her back onto to the bed. 'Sit down,' she murmured, rubbing her shoulder. 'Oh, you poor wee poppet. You're just following that man of yours because you love him, aren't you? No harm in that, chickie, but things are going to have to change, and soon.'

Another ripple of pain forced its way through her middle and her tears stopped immediately. She cried out and Ali shot to her feet.

'Okay, we're not waiting until tomorrow. Stay there, I'll get Ian for you.'

'Don't leave me!' Rose grabbed her at her hand. 'You can't leave me.'

'I won't be long,' Ali soothed.

Before Rose knew it, she was alone in the room with nothing but her pain. Her head swam as the pain kept coming, starting with her belly and radiating down her legs and up to her chest.

She tried to get up, but the cramps stopped her. Her need to stand was intense. Rolling over, she half fell to the floor and got onto her hands and knees, before crawling to the wall and trying to get up.

Not able to, she groaned, the pain ripping through her, making everything around her fuzzy.

'Ian,' she muttered, as she planted her hands on the wall and again tried to force her heavy body upright.

Nothing she tried worked.

Registering a wetness between her legs, she looked down and saw a sea of red running out of her. 'No,' she tried to say, but her tongue was stuck to the roof of her mouth and everything in front of her was blurring. She knew she had to stop the flow somehow . . .

The sheets. She dragged her body towards the bed, one arm outstretched in the hope of pulling the sheets towards her.

Her hands met empty air.

'Rosie?'

Ian's voice filtered through.

'Help,' she whispered.

She was dimly aware of people coming into the room and voices around her.

'Hospital, now.'

'Too much blood.'

And then there was nothing.

Chapter 5

2020

The voice of the commentator from the shearing competition was distorted and Zara was having trouble understanding what he was saying. She wrapped her hands together and looked at the sky. White fluffy clouds were racing overhead, patches of blue showing through. The forecast was rain; after the previous couple of years of drought, the seasons seemed to have changed and the start to this winter had been wet.

The mid north of South Australia had been spared the bushfires that had ravaged the rest of Australia that summer. Even if a fire had tried to take hold, there wouldn't have been any fuel in the paddocks to carry it. Now with the rains beginning to seep through, the tractors were in the paddocks and everyone had an air of optimism rather than desolation as the bitter winds brought the cold front through.

Why the Barker Agricultural Society held their local show in July was beyond Zara. The weather wasn't pleasant: there were always frosts, and the wind coated everyone in freezing air.

'Annddd . . . he's . . . the long blow . . . We . . .'

At the patter of applause, she craned her head to try to see who was on shearing, but there were too many people in her way. So, she hoisted her reporter's bag higher on her shoulder and walked towards the shearing shed in the middle of the showgrounds, smiling and nodding at people as she went.

A year ago, her brother Will would have been alongside her while she scanned the crowd for interesting people to interview. Not this year. His ashes had been spread in the creek below the homestead, as their father's had been, and she was wandering the showground alone. The longing for him never left her.

'Zara!'

Hearing her name, Zara looked around. The music from a ride started up, loud and blurry, along with a simultaneous scream from all the kids on it, tipping them upside down as Zara automatically put her hand to her stomach. She felt sick just watching.

'Zara!'

This time she felt a hand on her arm, then a smiling face came into her line of sight.

'I've been looking for you everywhere,' Courtney Tappan said, thrusting a takeaway coffee into Zara's hand.

'You're a lifesaver,' Zara said, taking a sip and looking at her friend over the rim. 'I needed something to warm me up.'

They fell into step together.

'Where are you going now?'

'Shearing competition.' Zara nodded in the direction she was headed and took another mouthful. 'Got to interview the winner of the Quick Shears.'

A pack of kids ran by, holding large stuffed toys and show bags on their arms, laughing. One of them knocked into Zara.

'Sorry, Zara,' the young girl called as they kept running.

'You will be when I see your mother, Tori Jenkins!' Zara called back, recognising the long plait of her next-door neighbour. To Courtney, she said, 'Come on, I've got to get over there otherwise I might miss the finish. Can you understand what the commentator is even saying?'

'Nope. Too loud. That's the trouble with the show-ground PA systems, trying to be heard over the noise of sideshows and music.' Courtney pushed her hair back from her face and stuck her free hand into the pocket of her coat as she walked. Both girls were dressed in jeans and jumpers with a Driza-Bone over the top. The boots were R.M. Williams and the leather souls clicked on the gravel as they walked.

Zara looked at her friend and realised they could have been twins, with their matching outfits and hair colour. She tuned in to hear Courtney's voice above the noise.

'Have you interviewed anyone else yet?'

Zara looked at the notebook as she walked. 'I still need to get to the John Deere dealership, Young Farmers competition and Prime Lamb shed. And I want to try to grab someone from a merino stud. There're a few that have come from out of town. It'll be good to get a different perspective.'

'I bet that's got some of the local studs' noses out of joint.'

Zara shrugged. 'It shouldn't. All good competition. Sheep aren't a one-size-fits-all, you know. A ram that one person likes, well, another will find fault with. Subjective.'

They stopped at the tiered seating, right in front of the raised board of the shearing shed.

Four men were crouched over, each with a ewe between his legs, sweat dripping onto the board despite the freezing wind. The names of the men competing were pinned near the shearing head, while the judge stood next to each shearer, a stopwatch in one hand and the cord to shut off the shearing head in the other.

Zara and Courtney stood watching the men expertly run their handpiece over the belly, then use their hand to open the fleece up. A blink later and they were on the long blows, making their way down towards the back legs, and suddenly they were finished.

Nodding towards the stand, which had the name *Jesse Barnett* on it, Zara said, 'That's the bloke I want to interview. He's been the winner for the past ten years. And he's held a couple of records at other shows as well. Turns up here with the same shearing team every year and has done since he was a kid. They shear at Jacksonville after the show.'

'How'd you hear about him?' Courtney asked, as she brought out a bag of donuts. She offered one to Zara. 'Sugar fix?'

'Yum.' Zara dug into the paper bag. 'Hopper down at the pub told me. And Lachie's heard of him—he's a gun. Shears down the south-east too.'

'Nice. Looks in pretty good shape for an old fella.'

Zara raised an eyebrow as she munched on the sugar-and-cinnamon donut. 'Don't think he's that old. I reckon he's in his forties. He's pretty good-looking, actually.'

'He's older than us.' Courtney bumped her shoulder into her friend just as the commentator yelled through the microphone. 'I keep forgetting you're taken now. Still can't believe you and Jack. I mean, a copper, of all people.'

Zara felt a warm glow spread through her as she thought about Jack. 'Me either,' she agreed with a smile.

The voice of the shearing commentator caught her attention.

'Ladies and gents, there you have it, Jesse Barnett is the winner for the eleventh year in a row. Come on up here, Jesse. Sunbeam have donated a heap of shearing gear to you as the winner.'

'Looks like I'm up,' Zara said, readying to get Jesse's attention and record the interview. 'Thanks for the sustenance. See you later at the bar?'

'Where else would I be? Tye's coming tonight too.'

'Okey doke. Jack and I'll see you there,' Zara said, walking towards the stage. She snapped a couple of photos of Jesse's name and shearing stand, then took a few more

of the crowd and one of the sponsors as they handed over
his prize of a new handpiece, combs and cutters.

'Congratulations, Jesse. Hope you'll be back again next
year.'

Jesse held up his hand and gave a slight bow to the crowd.

Zara watched, a half smile playing around her lips. He
was a bit of a showman, this Jesse. Tall and muscly, his
black hair was clipped short, his face open and warm.
Shearing kept his figure trim, but Zara's eyes were drawn
to his impressive biceps.

The crowd gave another cheer as he walked off the stage.

'Mr Barnett?' Zara made sure she was in his path as he
came down the steps. 'Mr Barnett, I'm Zara Ellison from
the *Farming Telegraph*. Could I have a few words with you
about your win, please?'

Jesse nodded to a couple of other shearers who had
clapped him on the back, and then looked at Zara.

'I'm not newsworthy, I don't reckon,' he said in a deep,
gravelly voice.

'Oh, I don't think that's right. This is the eleventh year
in a row that you've won here in Barker. You've had eight
wins down in the south-east . . . and you mentor young
shearers. Lots to talk about there.'

Jesse rubbed the back of his neck uncertainly.

'I won't take up too much of your time.'

'Well . . .'

'Great!' Zara hit the record button on her phone. 'Hope
you don't mind if I record the interview? It means I'll get

everything absolutely correct when I come to write the story. How long have you been shearing?'

Jesse placed his prizes on the ground and looked at her with a curious expression. He was dressed in a shearing singlet, and braces held up his custom-made shearing jeans, his feet clad in moccasins.

'Reckon it would have to be about twenty-four years. Got a stand when I was sixteen, but I'd been holding a handpiece since I was about five. The wethers were a bit too big for me back then.' He gave a chuckle and wiped his face with the towel hanging over his shoulders.

'You've been in the shearing industry ever since you started work? You must love it.'

'Like I said, I've been around sheds since I was a whipper-snapper. You wouldn't have even been a twinkle in your dad's eye when I stepped into a shearing shed for the first time.' He grinned.

'How did you start out in the sheds, then?'

'My dad started out as a station hand when I was a young bloke, but ended up in the sheds as a shearer. I'd be with him all the time. Didn't have a mum, you see, so it was just me 'n' Dad. He worked for McNamara Contracting from when I was about ten; I was raised in among the sheep and fleeces. It's in my blood.' He nodded as if to emphasise that point. 'Don't know anything different. Used to sleep in the wool while my dad shore.' His lopsided grin showed straight, white teeth and this time Zara couldn't help but smile back.

'And you're still working for McNamara Contracting? That must be some kind of record,' she said.

'Wouldn't know, but me and the boss, Codja, we grew up together. His dad was my dad's boss and now he's mine.'

'Can you tell me a bit more about your childhood?'

'Who's gonna be interested in that?' Jesse looked at her quizzically. 'It's as boring as bat shit.'

'Not at all. I wouldn't have asked the question if—'

'Jesse Barnett . . . Well, well, well. How long has it been?'

Zara turned at the familiar voice and saw the silver hair and tall frame of Oscar Porter striding towards them. Oscar owned one of the larger farms around Barker and ran only sheep.

'G'day, boss,' Jesse answered, holding out his hand. 'Too long.'

'Don't be calling me that here.' Oscar shook his head. 'Yeah, it has. How are you?'

'Good, real good. Nothing's changed. Just shearing. Few beers, then back to shearing again. How're you getting on?'

'Fine.' Oscar grinned, then looked at Zara. 'How are you, Zara? Interviewing the shearing celeb of South Australia?'

'Yep, trying to get him to tell me about his life history. Jesse's shorn in your shed?'

Oscar nodded. 'Mine was the first stand he got; wasn't it, mate? Just after your dad passed on.'

'That's right.'

'At sixteen?' Zara asked.

'Yeah, my dear old dad dropped like a tonne of rocks one day, just before smoko. Stood up to get another sheep and over he went. Heart attack in Oscar's shed. He looked out for me for a bit. Made sure I got a stand with Codja and his old man. Always would've, but Oscar paved the way. Helped me sort out all the paperwork and stuff I didn't know anything about.'

Zara's phone buzzed in her hand and she glanced at the screen. Jack. *What are you up to?*

She quickly typed out a reply. *At show.*

Her phone vibrated again and, thinking it was Jack, she frowned, ready to tell him to let her get on with her work.

Not this time. Hopper from the pub. *Something happening at the cop shop. Strange coppers in town.*

Her frown changed to a smile and adrenalin kicked in. Sounded like a story to her. Hopper was her best source: he saw everything, heard everything and let her know as soon as he did. Jack had probably only wanted to know where she was so she didn't turn up asking questions. That'd be right; when Zara had first arrived back in Barker, her relationship with the two policemen had been strained. Both Dave and Jack had been wary of journalists, as most police were, to the point of being rude, and Zara had spent a long time earning their trust. Now here she was—her boyfriend was one of those coppers.

They were both always very careful not to put each other in a position that could compromise their careers. Because of this, she would go and find Dave and see what he had to say about things.

Shoving her phone into her bag, she interrupted the conversation between Oscar and Jesse. 'Jesse, could I buy you a drink tonight or tomorrow and finish this interview?

I don't want to intrude on your time with Oscar.' She handed him her card. 'Do you have a phone number I can contact you on?'

Oscar gave a laugh. 'You'd better give it to her, mate. She's tenacious, this one. Won't stop until she gets the story she wants.'

Jesse reeled off his number. 'I'm here for a week or so. We're shearing out at Jacksonville.'

'Could I come out there and get some photos of you shearing?'

'Sure,' Jesse shrugged.

Zara threw him a brilliant smile. 'I have a feeling your story is very interesting. I'll see you then. Bye, Oscar.' She turned and walked away, phone still in hand.

Scrolling through her contacts, she brought up her editor's number and hit dial.

'Lachie Turner.'

'Don't you look at caller ID?' she asked, though she already knew that Lachie wouldn't have even looked at his phone as he'd snatched it up from alongside his keyboard.

'Well, well, it's the roaming reporter. How's things?'

'Just wondering if you've heard anything on the news about something going on at Barker? I've been covering the show and just got a call from a source saying there're strange coppers in town. Checking in with you before I do anything else.'

There was a pause, and she knew he was flicking through the channels on the TV that hung on the wall of his office in Adelaide.

'Haven't seen anything,' Lachie said finally, as Zara reached her car. 'You got a feel?'

'Just going there now. Will let you know.' Zara jiggled the keys out of her pocket and unlocked her car door.

'Everything else okay? How's that man of yours?'

'Everything is going okay, workwise. Jack is brilliant; we're going really well.'

'How's your mum?'

It was only last year that Zara had left the bustling news-room office of the *Farming Telegraph* in South Australia's capital to move to the small township of Barker so she could help her mum and brother out on their farm. Will had been diagnosed with bowel cancer and only lived a matter of weeks after she'd moved back. It was a situation Lachie understood only too well, having lost his sister to breast cancer a few years before.

'She's okay. There are good days and bad—as you know. But we're all managing, and James is very good for Mum.'

'Good things can come out of tragedies,' Lachie said. 'Nice that he was Will's doctor; they might not have met otherwise.'

'Yeah, you're right. Anyway, I gotta go, I don't want to miss anything.'

'Jack going to give you info?'

'I wouldn't ask him. I'll find Dave and see what he's got to say. Take care.' She hung up and started the car. One thing she knew for certain: Dave would not be happy to see her.

Chapter 6

Pulling open the door to the police station, Zara smiled at Joan, who was sitting behind the desk, her pen tucked behind her ear, fingers flying across the keyboard.

The cold wind, which had been following her all day, whipped in too, banging shut the door that separated the front desk from the back offices.

Zara marvelled at how Joan's tightly curled grey hair didn't move in the breeze even as her cardigan flapped around her. She knew that under the desk, Joan would be wearing a pair of navy slacks and sensible shoes. That was Joan—sensible.

'Hello, Joan. Isn't it a feral day?'

'A normal winter day in Barker,' Joan said as she placed her glasses carefully on the bench in front of her, blinking to focus. 'What can I do for you? I thought you'd be busy at the show?'

'I was there for a couple of hours. Just thought I'd swing by and see what was happening. Is he in?' Zara asked tipping her head towards the office.

'Jack? No, he's out. Not sure where.'

'No. Dave.'

Joan's face became even more deadpan than usual. 'How did you find out so quickly?'

'I've got a sense for these things.' Zara gave a winning grin, but Joan shook her head.

'He's here, but he won't see you.'

Putting her bag on the floor, Zara leaned against the counter. 'So, what's going on? Sounds like there are out-of-town coppers here. That's odd.'

Joan shook her head. 'Oh, no. You're not getting anything out of me, and you know that. I've worked here for too long and I know how you lot work. Doesn't mean I don't like you, Zara, you know I do, but I won't be giving you any information. I like working here, and I won't jeopardise my job.'

They both looked over as a tall, dark-haired man came out from the interview room, frowning. He looked at them, nodded and kept walking to the back of the station.

'Serious sort of bloke,' Zara said, once he'd disappeared.

'Yes, he certainly has that air about him,' Joan said and looked back at the work on her computer screen. 'No point in hanging around here, Zara. Dave won't speak to you.'

'Could you just try?'

'No.' Her fingernails clicked over the keys and she didn't look back up.

Zara knew she wasn't going to get anywhere, so she picked up her bag and sighed. 'Could you tell Dave I was here? And maybe ask him to call me?'

'Zara,' Joan answered, her tone patient. 'One, you know that Dave will know you've been here. He's aware of what you do and how invested you are in your job. Two, he already has your phone number. And, three, if he wants to talk to you, he will. All right?'

'Thanks, Joan.'

Zara walked out of the station and looked across the street to the pub, but instead of going straight there to talk to Hopper, she turned down the side street that ran alongside the police station. She stood under a large Kurrajong tree and peered over the fence into the station carpark. Jack's car wasn't there, but a white unmarked government-issued sedan was parked in Dave's spot. The wind whistled through the leaves, shaking loose big, heavy drops of rain onto her coat as she jotted down the numberplate in the hope that one of her contacts in Adelaide could run the plate and see which department the car belonged to.

'Damn it,' she muttered. She'd been hoping she'd see something worthwhile. Something she could write about.

Pulling her coat a little closer around her, she turned and walked back towards the warmth of the pub.

❧

The flames from the cheery fire were leaping high, spreading warmth to every corner. The TV on the wall was on, showing a replay of the last football match between the

Fremantle Dockers and the Adelaide Crows, and a lone customer, an old man nursing a beer, stared up at the screen.

Hopper was behind the bar, polishing glasses with a tea-towel. 'Knew it wouldn't take you long,' he said with a grin when he saw her.

The older man turned and gave Zara a blank stare before looking back at the TV. Zara doubted he'd even comprehended what had just been said.

'I've been across to the station already. They're tight-lipped.'

'Well, I'd reckon they'd have to be. Those out-of-town coppers looked like they're on a mission.'

'What sort of coppers are they?'

'Dunno. They're not wearing a uniform or anything I could see that said where they were from, but they sorta look like those blokes that come from the FBI or something.'

'FBI? That's America, Hopper!' Zara gave a little laugh at the thought of the FBI running around Barker. 'Someone in Barker would have to be harbouring a terrorist or something really bad for the FBI to turn up here.'

'Well, girly, you never know. One thing I've learned behind this bar for all these years, is that if anything strange is going to happen, it'll be in a country town. The city's got nothin' on us for gossip and weird things happening.'

'Maybe, Hopper, maybe.' Zara turned and looked out through the frosted-glass front door. No movement at the station. *FBI lookalikes,* she thought. *The Feds more likely, but what the hell would they be here for?*

'I'm pretty sure they were parked out the front of the post office in Dave's car,' Hopper said as he held a glass up to the light, checking for streaks. He put it down, obviously happy with what he saw, and picked up another one.

'Really? What did you see?' Zara put her bag down and sat on the bar stool, putting her chin in her hand and staring at Hopper.

'Well, I was wiping down the windowsills when I arrived this morning. Good reason to have the curtains open, you know.' He nodded towards the windows. 'Anyhow, I looked up as they drove past and there was not just Dave in the car, but another two blokes in the back. Looked a bit squeezy from where I was standing.' He put the schooner glass down and grabbed another one, before continuing with his story. 'I walked outside, just to see which direction they were headed and they only drove a block down, then parked under the big tree near the post office.

'They sat there for probably half an hour, I reckon.' He gave a cheeky grin. 'I kept going to see if they'd moved, or arrested someone, but nothing. Just sat there like they were having a conversation.

'The last time I went out to have a squiz, they'd moved on and I couldn't see the car anywhere.'

'So, how do you know these other blokes were coppers? If they didn't arrest anyone and were just sitting in Dave's car?'

Hopper considered his answer for a moment. 'Well, they just looked like them, you know? Like the FBI on the TV shows.'

'Did you see them come back to the station?'

'Nah. I know they're all back there, though, because Dave came out about three-quarters of an hour ago to get his coffee from the deli, as usual, but I didn't see when they arrived back.'

'Interesting,' Zara pondered, then she got off the stool and picked up her bag. 'Well, I'm not going to find out what's going on by sitting here, am I? Better pound the pavement. Can I grab a coffee before I go?'

'Sure.' He took a takeaway cup from the pile and started making her flat white.

'Let me know what you find,' Hopper said as he held the steaming cup out to her.

'I will when I can,' she promised. 'Thanks for your help and the brew.'

Outside in the cold again, Zara blew on her hands, before taking out her phone and dialling Dave's number. She wasn't surprised when it rang out, unanswered.

Her fingers itched to call Jack, but she knew she couldn't do that. Bloody annoying that there were only two policemen in Barker and she was dating one of them.

She sat on the wooden bench underneath the verandah, sipping her coffee. The carnival music and the screams from the people on the rides arrived on the wind. A lone tourist's car drove down the street and the passenger looked at her as they passed.

Grinning to her herself, she thought she probably looked like an old soak sitting outside the pub, this early in the day, even with a coffee cup in her hand.

Will would have said something like: '*Making the place look untidy, Zara . . .*'

At the thought of Will, her heart felt like it might squeeze out of her chest, and she swallowed the lump in her throat. Looking at the cup she was holding, she realised her hands were shaking. Putting her hand on her chest, she tried to calm her pounding heart. Why did she react this way every time she thought about him?

Oh, she missed him, his witty comments, his advice and friendship. Taking a few deep breaths, she tried to think about something else.

Her mum had called last night, inviting her and Jack to Rowberry Glen for dinner. Zara had made an excuse. She just couldn't bear to be on the farm since Will had died. The place held too many memories of him and their dad. It just wasn't the same without them there. Even driving to the farm was painful.

Taking another deep breath and closing her eyes, Zara made sure the images of finding her father in the upside-down ute, on the road to Rowberry Glen, didn't enter her mind's eye.

Stop it, stop it, stop it. Happy things only, think about Jack. Think about why the AFP would be in Barker.

She opened her eyes again and looked around. The main street remained empty, save for the trees being buffeted in the wind and old Mr Winter's dog, who usually took himself for a walk just as the meat was being delivered to the butcher's shop.

Draining the last of her coffee, she eyed the police station, but it showed no signs of life.

'Stuff it,' she said and walked back over the road and let herself into the station, sitting in one of the plastic chairs in reception.

'Zara . . .' Joan said.

'It's okay, Joan, I'm not going to cause any trouble. Just sit here for a bit. It's cold out.'

Joan pursed her lips and continued typing.

Zara got out her notebook and jotted down what Hopper had told her. As she looked at her words, her mind ticked over.

The post office. Could they have been waiting for a delivery?

That bloke she'd seen here in the cop shop had had an authoritative air about him, which fitted with what she knew of the Feds.

Well, well, that would make life interesting, she thought.

She looked up as the front door opened and Dave walked in.

He took one look at her and kept moving, all the while holding up his hand. 'Not now, Zara.'

She shot out of her seat and followed him. 'Don't tell me "not now". This is my job. The AFP is in town and you're not giving me anything. You're avoiding me.'

'I'm not avoiding you. I don't have anything I can tell you at the moment.'

'Why are they here?'

'Zara.' Dave stopped and eyeballed her, but Zara didn't back down. She took another step towards him.

'Have they arrested anyone?'

'No comment. Get out of the station, Zara. I'll talk to you when I have something to tell you. You know I will.'

'Dave.'

'No!' His voice rose angrily. 'Enough. There's nothing for you here. Go before I have someone throw you out, or I do it myself.'

'Like who? Jack? That's a bit rich.'

Dave glared at her and opened his mouth, but Zara continued, 'Back to this are we, Dave? The "no comment" bullshit? I thought we'd sorted all this out. Haven't I proved myself to you yet?'

As he leaned towards her, Zara noticed Dave's blue eyes were cold. 'You're treading on thin ice. I'm telling you to leave. I have nothing to say.'

Zara blinked a couple of times. This wasn't like Dave. Seconds later, the door to the back of the station slammed shut and Dave was gone.

Joan didn't stop typing but glanced up with an *I told you so* look on her face.

Gathering her bag, Zara stomped out of the station and headed towards the post office, texting Lachie as she went.

Not sure what it is, but something big. AFP here. Dave acting like an arse.

Keep at it, Lachie texted back.

A block down, she spotted Kim putting grocery bags in her car and hurried towards her.

'Hi, Kim!' Zara said, reaching down into the shopping trolley to hand Kim a bag.

'Zara! I haven't seen you in ages, even though you live over the road. What are you up to? Thanks for this.' She took the bag Zara handed her.

'Good. Busy!' She paused. 'You got some kids coming to visit?' She indicated the colourful yoghurt tubs stamped with cartoon characters and cheese slices with smiley faces on the packaging.

'Yeah, Paris Carter is going to stay with us for a little while. I haven't had any kids with me for years, so it will be nice to have a chatty little voice around the house again.'

'Oh, is that the little girl who lives with her grand-mother? What's her name? Bessie?'

'Essie,' Kim corrected. 'Lovely lady—she arranged the flowers for our wedding. Got a heart of gold.'

'Oh, nice. Where's she gone?'

'Adelaide, or so I understand. Family trip.' Kim gave a quick a smile, before shutting the car boot. 'I'm really sorry, Zara, I'd love to stay and chat, but I have to pick up Paris from school. Why don't you come over later and have a glass of wine and a proper catch-up?'

'Sounds great. I'll do that.'

Don't think Dave is going to like that idea, Zara thought as she watched Kim wave and back out her car. She sighed in frustration. That was the trouble when you lived in a small country town and were friends with the local constabulary. She couldn't ask questions of friends without putting them in a compromising position.

Kim had been so kind when Zara first moved back to Barker and then when Will died. She'd also been a great support to Zara's mum during that time. But she was married to Dave, which complicated, well, everything.

Yeah, being friends with the local coppers could really hamper a girl's ability to get information, she thought.

❧

In the post office, Zara looked around for Jenny, the long-standing postmistress, but instead a young woman she hadn't seen before was serving behind the counter.

'Hi, Sarah,' Zara said, glancing at the girl's name tag. 'Is Jenny around?'

'No, sorry, she's gone for the day. I can give her a message if you like?' Sarah smiled and looked enthusiastic at the prospect.

Zara shook her head. 'No, that's fine, I'll come back tomorrow. You're new here?'

'Yeah, I just started. My husband got a job at the silos, so we shifted up a couple of weeks ago.'

'That's great! We can always do with some new blood in town. I'm Zara. Do you like working here? Do you serve behind the counter, or help sort the mail or what?'

Sarah nodded. 'Yeah, all of that. I take passport photos too. I've worked in three different post offices and know how they work. Jenny needed a hand this morning, sorting, but that's easy enough. It's funny looking at all the names and not knowing anyone.'

'Anything strange come in this morning?'

'Strange as in how?'

Zara gave a casual shrug. 'Oh, I don't know. Did Jenny say anything about an odd package, or that someone had received some mail they wouldn't usually?'

A wary look came over Sarah's face. 'Why would you want to know that? There're privacy issues with mail, you know.'

Laughing, Zara said, 'I don't know! It was just a question. Look, I'll leave you to it. Welcome to Barker. I hope you settle in quickly.'

'Thanks.' A smile broke across Sarah's face. 'I'm sure we will.'

Flicking her a wave, Zara pulled open the door and walked outside. She was just in time to see three men drive past in a now familiar car. The man driving was the one she'd seen in the police station earlier.

Essie Carter was in the back seat.

Chapter 7

1980

Ian paced the floor of the shearing shed. He'd had a sleepless night even though he knew there was nothing he could do. Yesterday Rose had been taken to Barker, unconscious. Bleeding.

He should be with her now, instead of Ali. Here he was, waiting for the gong to sound so he could drag a wether from the pen and start shearing it.

Was she okay? Were the babies okay? There were no answers.

All he could see in his mind was the last sight he'd had of Rose, as she'd been loaded into the back seat of his Kingswood.

'I'll take her,' he'd said.

'Okay,' Ali had nodded. 'You'd better get going. She needs help, fast.'

Then Ian got queasy. 'What if she . . . I . . .'

'Ian, there isn't any time to waste. You drive.'

'No, it's okay. You go. Just . . . just let me know. As soon as you can. I'd better not let the boss down by not being here.'

He'd used shearing as an excuse. He hadn't wanted to see Rose in pain, any more than he wanted to get into trouble for not taking her to the doctor often enough. He'd panicked when he'd seen her writhing on the floor, blood pooling around her. He was responsible for looking after his wife, and he hadn't done a very good job.

No, better he stayed in Jacksonville and shore the sheep. He knew naught about babies and how they came into the world. Best all of that was left to the experts.

Just so long as Rosie was all right.

Now, by the light of a fresh day, he looked over into the catching pens and saw how large the wethers were.

This station was known for the good quality wool, but at a quick glance the microns on these boys were going to be a bit higher than usual. Might have something to do with the season. He could imagine the strain of dragging them to his stand already.

'Going to be a big day,' Kiz said as he dropped his kit on the floor and bent down to get out his handpiece, combs and cutters. 'You doing okay? Any news?'

'A good day for making money,' Ian said with a bravado he didn't feel, ignoring the question. He noticed Kiz watching him. 'Don't want to talk about it. Not until I know something.'

The clicking of the wethers' hooves on the grating was loud and occasionally there was a *baa*, but other than that, the shed was quiet.

'Right. I'll be back in a bit,' Kiz said, leaving Ian by himself. A shaft of sunlight landed on the board. The dust particles danced in the light and the flies buzzed against the tin roof.

Ian walked around the edge of the shed, noting the lanolin-oiled wooden boards and spiderwebs creeping across the windows. Shearing sheds calmed him. Not that he ever told anyone when he was wound up, or worried. But he was now. Being here in the silence of the world he knew well helped settle his nerves.

He loved shearing, he loved the nomadic lifestyle, the travelling. Hanging out with his mates. He didn't want to give up any of it. But he also loved Rosie. His sweet Rosie.

Maybe his resistance to change had put Rose's life in danger.

If he had, he was no better than his father. His family at home were 'good Catholics'. His older brother Coilin had told him their mother had always been pregnant. Until the last time, when Ian was born.

She'd died in childbirth after thirteen children. Coilin had always blamed their father.

'Couldn't keep it in your pants,' he'd said to his father after a night on the whiskey. 'She'd still be here if it weren't for you.' Ian remembered the words, even though he'd only been five.

Perhaps his own need to keep his life unchanged was a similar sin.

There was a fleece on the wool table, and he reached out to feel it, looking at the crimp the way he'd been taught.

Medium, he thought. *Maybe 20 or 22 micron.*

He could smell sheep, lanolin and diesel. The smells of the shearing industry.

The floor creaked and Ian looked behind him, seeing the bloke he'd shorn with two sheds ago, with his shearing kit.

'Dougie,' Ian greeted him softly.

'You've had an exciting time of it, lad,' Dougie said with a bit of a grin. 'All right?'

'Be fine. Just a bit of scare, that's all.'

In silence, Dougie brought out his handpiece and checked it over, before getting out the screwdriver and loosening the two large screws; into the gap he put first the comb, then the cutter. Ian watched as Dougie's large hands twisted the screws back into place, before he connected it to the down-tube. Placing the handpiece on the floor, he stood up and finally eyeballed Ian.

'Paddy, I hope you'll forgive an old man his words of wisdom, but I can see you're a mess. You like the booze, the travelling, being with the blokes. But you've got a pretty little wife, who's in a spot of trouble right now. She shouldn't have been out here, hey? Rose should've been tucked up in some house somewhere, with a nice garden. You're pissing everything up against the wall. Those babies are on their way and there's nothing you can do about it, except be the best dad you can. Only way to do that is pull your head in and look after their mum.'

Ian frowned and moved away. 'I don't need a lecture . . .' He broke off as Dougie stepped close and pointed a finger into his chest.

'You do. I tried to tell you last shed, but you didn't listen. The best way to raise them babies is to love their mother. Dragging her around everywhere like you are isn't doing that.'

'I . . .'

'Paddy?' Muzza called through the door. 'Boss is lookin' for ya.'

Dougie raised his eyebrows. 'Think this is your cross-roads, lad.'

❧

Leaving the shearing shed, Ian had no choice but to head up the road that led to the main house five-hundred metres away. The walk gave him a little time to get his thoughts in order. He hadn't wanted to admit it to Dougie, but he knew the old man was right. Even so, the rebel in him wanted to shout at everyone who was interfering. Tell them that none of this was their business. To stay away. He knew how to look after his own wife.

But clearly, he didn't. Today proved that. He'd always planned to be back in Adelaide before the babies came and now maybe he was too late.

He kicked a stone as he walked, trying to get rid of the pain in his stomach. Were they all okay? Glancing at his watch he realised it was nearly twelve hours since they'd left. There must be news, that was why he was being called down to the main house.

He followed the path to the office and knocked on the door.

'Come.'

'You wanted to see me, boss?' he asked as he stepped in.

'Ah, yes, Ian. Congratulations! You have a boy and girl. Both are doing okay, but they'll have to stay in hospital for a while. Sounds like despite the scare this morning, everything went well.'

Ian couldn't speak, his heart was beating so hard. A boy. A boy! To pass his name on to. And a girl. He stared at Ross dumbly.

'Rose?' The only word he could get out.

'Well, Rose isn't out of the woods yet; she's had a hard time of it, by all accounts. Seems she lost a lot of blood and had to have a transfusion, but Ali seems to think she'll be as good as new in time.'

'In time?'

'That's all I've been told. Do you want to go and see her?'

Of course he did. Those words didn't come out, though. 'But my stand . . .'

'I understand you need this shed. And I'm not an un-reasonable man, Ian. I can hold your stand for you—it'll slow us down for the day or two that'll you'd be gone, but these circumstances aren't normal. Once you've seen your family, come back, finish the shed, then you can do whatever you need to. Find a house, settle them in. Work out what you're going to do from there. I can't see this dragging on for too long. Maybe three weeks' worth of work.'

The thought of seeing two new babies without Rose being totally well scared him. Even though he was from a big family, he was the youngest. He hadn't carted toddlers around on his hip the way his older brothers and sisters had. He didn't know how to change a nappy. What if they cried? What about names?

'Have they been named?' he asked.

Ross crinkled his forehead. 'You didn't talk about that beforehand?'

Ian shook his head.

'I haven't heard of any names. Rose might not be well enough to have done that yet. Blood transfusion and all. I imagine a medical issue like that would take the stuffing out of you for a while.'

Ian shifted uncomfortably from one foot to the other. 'Are they . . . are they looked after?' he asked.

'I would think so, lad. They're in the hospital.' Ross gave him an inquisitive look.

'If they're cared for, boss, then I'll stay. I can see them when we've finished here.' Ian nodded, showing he meant what he'd just said.

'Are you sure?'

'Yeah, I think that'd be best. Thanks for the offer, though.'

Ross turned back to the books on his desk. 'Don't mention it, man.'

Clearly he was being dismissed, so Ian opened the door, but stopped when Ross spoke again in a low voice.

'It's better that the birth happened this way, Ian. I know you wanted Rose with you, but it's much better than a dead wife and two babies to raise on your own. Or even worse, all three of them dead.' His voice broke as he said the last word.

Ian stared at the man, who was bent over his account books, not looking at him and he wondered what had happened to Ross to make him react like that.

Quietly shutting the door behind him, he made his way back to the quarters and went straight to his car. He opened the boot and then, after looking around to make sure no one was watching, he took a roll of notes out from the spare wheel well and quickly counted them.

The mixture of crinkled and dirty notes amounted to four hundred dollars. The sum of his savings. People might say that he hadn't given any thought to the impending birth, but he'd thought enough to start saving money for when they were in Adelaide. Rose would need it while she was in hospital.

He took a few deep breaths to control his emotions and blinked a few times. *Not having Rose here will be a good thing*, he tried to tell himself. *Few drinks with the boys every night and there won't be any cold shoulder. No one telling me what to do. Yeah, focus on the good things. Be a free man again. Just so long as they're looked after.*

But no matter how much he repeated those words as he walked back inside, he knew he didn't mean them.

Jogging back to main house, he knocked on Ross's office door again.

'Come.'

'Ah, boss?'

Ross turned around, surprise on his face. 'Changed your mind?'

'No. No, I haven't but I wonder if you could get this to Rose somehow?' He held out the money. 'She'll need it and she hasn't got any with her.'

Ross was still for a moment, then reached out and took the money. 'Don't you worry, Ian. I'll get it to your Rose. You have my word.'

Chapter 8

Ian pushed open the catching-pen gate and grabbed a woolly wether around his neck. With a flick of his hands, he had him on his rump and was dragging the sheep out onto the board.

The noise of the generator was loud—he'd been saddled with the stand right at the end of the shed, near the engine. Not his favourite spot. He could barely hear all the smart-arse chatter from the others with the background rumble. He couldn't add his tuppence worth either.

Sweat dripped from his forehead as he ran the hand-piece and comb under the wool of the belly and tossed it out onto the board for the rousie to pick up, all the while wondering how Rose was getting on. Was she comfortable? The information Ross had given him was scant, and he craved more. He hadn't even kissed her goodbye.

Still, he reasoned with himself, *she was pretty out of it, she won't have known.*

A loud clattering bang sounded as Sam, the rousie, dropped the paddle he was using.

A chorus of jeers went up from all the shearers.

'You'll be buying a round at the next pub, if you keep that up,' Kiz yelled.

'Keep the broom in yer hand,' Muzza shouted.

Ian grinned. Poor old mate, Sam. He was new to the job and probably didn't realise that every time he dropped the paddle, it was his shout for the whole team. Just one of the rules of the shed.

The sound of one of the wethers banging their hind legs on the wooden board was followed by swearing from Dougie as he readjusted his grip on the animal.

As he finished the last blow, Ian put down his hand-piece and pushed the wether down the chute and out into the bright light outside. He pushed his counter to record shearing another one, then stretched his back.

Looking across the shed, through the open door, he saw the reflective white of the sheep in the yards. Two men wearing wide-brimmed hats had the sheep in the raceway. They were dipping a branding wand into red liquid and then painting it on the sheeps' backs, marking them as the property of Jacksonville.

'You slacking, Paddy?' Kiz said as he finished another sheep and pushed it down the chute. He stood up and grabbed his tobacco pouch from the shelf, pulled out a piece of paper and a wad of tobacco and pushed them both into the palm of his hand. He rolled them together between his thumb and index finger until the wad was long and skinny, then licked the paper to seal it.

Kiz held it out to Ian.

'You don't get to slack just 'cause you're a new dad, you know.'

Automatically, Ian shook his head. Rose hated the smell of old smoke on him when he came back. Then he remembered she wasn't there.

'Yeah, why not,' he said above the noise of the engine, reaching out. 'Not slacking either.'

'Wool away! Wool away!'

Ian lit the cigarette and looked to see that the rousie hadn't picked up the fleece Dougie had finished and now the old man was holding a wether, waiting for the wool to be picked up so he could shear the next sheep.

The rousie ran over and shuffled the fleece around, scooped it up and threw it onto the wool table for the classer to pick over. Tiny pieces floated to the floor like snowflakes.

Ian nodded towards the young man. 'Needs to be quicker,' he said loudly.

'All right, you fellas,' Jacko, the classer, yelled. 'Enough giving him a hard time. First shed and all. Give over and get back to work.'

'Sheep oh, while you're there, mate,' Muzza called to the bloke out the back who was penning up, letting him know his catching pen was empty.

'You've got three left, mate,' Sam said back as he shoved another four wethers into the catching pen for Dougie, obviously gaining confidence now that Jacko had stood up for him.

'Yeah, and with the useless job you're doing, I'll be finished those buggers before you get there.'

'Piss off, Muzza.'

Laughter rose from the shearers but Sam kept his head down and concentrated on his job.

Ian dragged on the ciggie and felt the smoke hit the back of his throat, making him want to cough. It had been a while since he'd had one, but it tasted good. Maybe next time he went to town he'd get his own pouch of Port Royal and a packet of papers. It wasn't like Rose was going to be there to complain.

Rose. A baby boy and a baby girl. He wished they'd talked about names. He wanted to name the girl after his mother, Bridget; and the boy, Alroy. Good strong Irish names for good strong Irish stock. He would write to Rose tonight and ask her to call the twins just that. Bridget and Alroy.

'I got another bottle of that rum in me car, if you want a sip tonight. Reckon we should wet those babies' heads, don't you?' Kiz said.

From where he was leaning against the swinging doors, with his hands hanging over them, Ian looked over at Kiz, who was grinning.

'Mate, you can do whatever you want now. No one at home to tell you what to do,' Kiz said.

'I'm not bloody henpecked, you know,' Ian answered, resentment building up in him. What did his mates think?

That Rose ruled the roof? He was the man of the house—or car, as it was—and the breadwinner.

'Course you were. Any bloke with a missus is henpecked.' Kiz winked and disappeared into the pen to get another sheep. 'That's why I'll never have one. Don't want to stop what I'm doing. Be worse now you've got tin lids. She'll be wanting all your money for clothes and looking after them. All downhill from here, matey.'

'Fuck off,' Ian muttered, finishing the smoke and throwing the butt down the chute into the dirt. He pushed open the gates and grabbed a sheep, this time with force. 'I was bloody not,' he muttered.

Angrily, he picked up the handpiece and pulled the cord. The cutter whirred to life and he opened up the belly.

'Yeah, I'll have a sip tonight,' he called out above the noise of the shed. 'Got to celebrate having a boy to pass my name on to, you know.'

'Good-oh. After tea, then. Muz, you in?'

Ian couldn't hear the reply, but it must have been yes, because Kiz yelled back 'Good-oh,' again.

As he finished the next wether, he looked over at Dougie who was two stands down and staring at him, a disappointed look on his face.

Dougie shook his head and disappeared into the pen to get another wether.

Chapter 9

2020

'Mate, what the fuck is going on with Zara? She's turned pushy again,' Dave said angrily to Jack as he stomped into the office.

'What?'

'She's been out there waiting for me to come in and then hits me with all these questions she knows I can't answer.' Dave threw himself into his chair, frowning.

'Whoa, Dave. Calm down. That's normal for her and you know it. It's her job.' Jack glared at his friend.

'We can't let any of this get into the press. I don't want people judging Essie or making her the talk of the town. It'll ruin her, and you and I know there's more to this than just what we've seen today.' He slammed his fist down on the table and glowered at Jack.

Jack rose and stared back at him. 'Look, I know you're worried about Essie and I would be too, but I can't stop Zara from asking questions. Don't take your shit out on me. I haven't got any answers as to why Essie has done this.'

They stared at each other and then Dave looked away.

'You're right. I'm just worried about Essie. This whole thing doesn't make sense.' He paused and looked up from his desk. 'Sorry. I shouldn't have spoken to you like that.'

'Damn straight,' Jack said and pulled his jacket from the back of the chair. 'I'm going home. Maybe tomorrow you'll be in a better mood.'

The door slammed behind him and Dave sighed. He should have known better than to take his concern out on his partner. It had been years since he'd lost his temper like that. As a younger man he'd been fiery and reactive, but over the years he'd mellowed. These days he could usually talk his way out of a hostile situation, rather than having to use force, but clearly he still wasn't immune to the occasional outburst.

Maybe it was time he went home too; it was past five-thirty and Kim would have Paris at home with her. She could probably use the help, and they needed to find a way to explain what was going on with her grandmother. It was not a task he was looking forward to.

He switched off the lights and locked the doors before striding out into the cold evening air, hoping the walk home would clear his head.

The lights from the pub cast a long light across the street. From a distance the fairground music played across the loudspeakers and he could see the blinking lights from the carnival reflecting off the clouds.

He paused, looking at the lights, then pulled out his phone and called Kim.

'Hey,' she said.

'Hey yourself. Going okay?'

'Sure am. Paris and I are cooking.'

'I hope I'll get to enjoy that.'

'Pretty sure you will.' She paused. 'Where are you?'

'I was coming home, but I'd like to go for a wander around the showgrounds, if you don't need me straightaway. Just for a quick look.'

'We're fine here,' Kim said. 'Got some questions for you, though.'

'Yeah, and I don't have a lot of answers, but I'll fill you in when I get back. That be okay?'

'Sure, sweetie. See you soon.'

He hung up and pulled his jacket a bit closer. A car drove past and beeped at him, before pulling into the pub carpark. He gave a wave, recognising Darren Moore, a local farmer. Dave had got to know most of the locals and their cars since he'd turned up in Barker five years ago to investigate the carjacking of Kim's niece, Milly.

The Milly Bennett case was the first one he'd worked with Jack, who was a junior constable then. After the case, the two men decided to stay in Barker, where together they built the trust of the community. There was a line, though, that they both knew not to cross. Between them they knew most of the townsfolk—Dave played cricket and Jack, footy—but they kept to themselves. It was always hard policing country towns where the cops knew most of the residents.

Essie's case was a prime example.

He walked the last few blocks to the showgrounds briskly, his hands in his pockets.

'G'day, Lorraine,' he said at the gate. 'What's the damage?'

'You can go in for nothing, Dave,' she answered, smiling at him.

'Got to pay my way.' His hand hovered over his wallet. 'Got a few through the gates today?'

'Oh, go on then, make it ten dollars. I haven't heard numbers yet, but it's felt busier than last year. Lot more farmers in today, and given the good start to the season, that's not surprising.'

Dave handed over a ten-dollar note. 'Hopefully good for everyone all round,' he said, going into the grounds. 'Thanks, Lorraine. Catch you later.'

He could smell donuts and hot chips, and as he looked around he saw long lines of teenagers queuing for the dodgem cars. Walking towards the bar, he saw a couple of people he knew.

'Hey, Dave!'

'G'day, Mick.' Dave stopped and shook the hand of the president. 'Going well?'

'Sure is. Best show we've had in ten years, I reckon.'

A group of teenagers walked by, huddled together and looking at Dave. One of them leaned into his friend and whispered something. Both boys looked over and Dave had the distinct impression they were talking about him.

Half listening to Mick's description of the show, Dave followed the group with his eyes as they passed. One of them looked back over their shoulder at him as they disappeared into the crowd.

Would they be the type to buy drugs from Essie?

'Anyhow, Dave, I'd best get on. Would you and Kim like to come to the president's dinner tomorrow night?'

'Very kind of you, Mick, but we're a bit tied up at the moment.' He paused. 'The carnies caused any trouble since they've been here?'

'The carnival people? Nah. Never. This lot have been coming here for years and there's never been a skerrick of trouble.' He laughed. 'Never had to call you blokes. You know that!'

'No drugs you know of?' Dave persisted.

Mick blanched. 'Not on my grounds, there won't be.'

Dave smiled, hiding his frustration. 'Excellent. Well, I'd better keep moving too. Great to see so many people here.'

Dave held out his hand to Mick again, then walked on quickly. He wanted to get to the bar and see who was there. Whoever Essie had planned to give the drugs to would have to be close by; they wouldn't have let the gear stay in her house for long.

He had no idea who or what he was looking for, he just hoped that when he saw it—them—he would know. Or he would hear something.

There hadn't been any whispering about drug rings around town or even in the surrounding areas. Dave would have known. A worried parent would have reported a change of behaviour in their child, or there would have been break-ins to fund drug habits. None of these were happening, so whoever was blackmailing Essie—and that was what was happening, he was sure—would have to be from out of town. A stranger.

❧

Jack pulled another beer from the fridge, ripping the top off with more force than was needed, and stared moodily at the TV. He was supposed to be meeting Zara, Courtney and Tye at the showground bar tonight, but Zara hadn't texted him to organise a time yet—which told him she was following her nose somewhere. He hoped it wasn't Essie, but suspected it was. No point in heading down to the show if she wasn't going to be there.

Zara was still grieving her brother, he knew, and sometimes that made her a bit forgetful. And sad. In the months after Will's death, Jack had known her to lock herself up in her house for a day and not come out. Zara had always cited deadlines, which made sense, but had that really been why? Some of her behaviour lately worried him, but there was nothing he could put his finger on. He just tried his best to be there for her, hoping that time would heal what was going on inside her.

He adored Zara, her quirkiness and fun, the way her drive and passion filtered from her work to every part of her life. She'd captivated him from the moment he'd met her in Barker twelve months ago. In the beginning he'd kept his distance, but it hadn't been long before he couldn't keep his thoughts to himself anymore.

His fingers hovered over his phone, as he contemplated texting her. No. The plan had been she would let him know when she had finished work. They didn't crowd each other.

But that was before she knew about the AFP, he argued with himself.

'Bugger it,' he said, frowning. Jack scrolled through his call log until he found Zara's number and touched the screen. He didn't want her to think he was checking on her, or that he was concerned, but he needed to know she was okay. If there was anyone who was stubborn and independent, it was Zara.

'Hey, how are you going?' he asked when she answered.

'Not bad.'

'How was your day?'

'Fine, until your boss gave me an earful,' she answered tightly.

In the background, Jack could hear music.

'Yeah, I heard about that. Sorry. He gave me one too. He's not himself at the moment.'

'What have you got to be sorry for? You didn't give me a spray.' She paused and he heard her adjust the phone. 'What's wrong with him?'

'I don't know,' Jack answered. He couldn't tell her that this case was personal for Dave; he didn't need the barrage of questions that would follow.

'Well, he was pretty horrible.'

There would be no winners in this conversation, Jack could tell. 'Where are you?'

'At the show. I saw them take her, you know. I know it's Essie Carter.'

'You're at the show? How come you haven't called?'

'I haven't got around to it yet, I'm still working.'

The music grew louder as he imagined her walking around the grounds.

'I know it's Essie,' she repeated.

'Zara,' Jack said, much more calmly than he felt, 'you know I can't talk about it.'

'Yeah, I know you can't, and I haven't asked you to, if you've noticed. All I've said is I know who was arrested. Anyway, nothing gives Dave the right to be an arse to me when I ask questions. Can I have a white wine, please?'

It took Jack a second to realise she'd spoken this last question to someone else, and that she was in the beer tent—where they were supposed to be together. What was going on with her? His gut started to churn, but with what exactly he wasn't sure.

'It's a tricky case,' he said, working to keep his voice neutral. 'Personal for Dave and that's all I'm going to say, Zara. Have you had dinner? How about I come down and we can get a burger? We're supposed to be catching up with Court and Tye, aren't we?'

'Oh, didn't I text you? I must've forgotten. Tye's been called in to work at the hospital.'

'No, you didn't.' Jack took a sip of his beer and walked to the window to look out into the darkness. 'Bugger. Why don't you come back here, then?'

'I'm looking for . . .' There was shuffling in the background and he heard Zara say, 'Oh, hi, Jesse. I was hoping to run into you. Give me five, would you? Then we can finish that interview.' Back into the phone she said, 'I've found Jesse Barnett, the shearer I've been wanting to interview. I'll catch you tomorrow.'

Jack stared at the phone when he heard the hang-up tone. *I'll catch you tomorrow.*

He threw the phone onto the couch, swallowed the rest of his beer in one gulp, then went to the fridge for another.

❧

Dave walked through the beer tent scanning each face. Some he knew and smiled at, others he committed to memory. He was making an assumption that the person he was looking for wasn't local, and plenty of people in the bar tonight fitted that bill. None jumped out at him as noteworthy or a possible person of interest.

'Dave, mate, buy you a beer?' one of the locals asked. 'Good to see you here.'

'Thanks, but I'm on duty,' he answered with a smile and a wink. 'Next time I see you in the pub, you're on, though.'

'Sure thing.'

As he got close to the bar, he stopped and took a few steps back into a dark corner. Zara was there, with three empty wine glasses on the table and her head close to a man he didn't know. He looked familiar, but Dave couldn't put his finger on who he was.

Glancing around, he looked for Jack, cursing himself for losing his temper with him, but his senior constable wasn't in sight.

Strange.

He watched as Zara giggled and wrote a few notes, before looking at the man with a flirty smile on her face.

Shit.

❧

'But where's Granny?'

Dave heard the little girl's voice as he let himself into the house.

Kim sounded tired as she answered. 'Granny had to go to Adelaide and help some people out. I've told you all I know already, Paris.'

'But when's she going to be back?' The voice sounded high and uncertain.

'Oh, sweetie, I'm not sure. But you can stay with Dave and me until she does. Here, can you stir the cake mixture for me, while I put these biscuits in the oven?'

He put his keys on the sideboard and stood a moment rubbing his temples. A headache was forming.

Somehow, he had to tell this little girl that her grandmother had to go with the police to Adelaide. Or did he?

Dave had always had a policy of honesty. '*You don't have to remember the lies if you tell the truth all the time,*' was what he'd always told his two daughters as they were growing up. Especially when they were teenagers. As a policeman talking to victims of crime, he'd had to be honest: 'No, I don't know who broke into your house, but we're working on it.' 'Your loved one has been in an accident and they've passed away.'

There was no way he could be anything but honest.

Which is why he and Mel had decided to divorce. They had to be truthful, and the truth was, they didn't love each other anymore. They'd grown apart and Dave's job had been one of the main reasons that had happened. Mel had been resentful of policing, whereas Kim did nothing but support him.

Kim would have an opinion on what and how much they told Paris, though.

Right, he thought. *Here goes.*

Striding into the kitchen, he saw Kim standing at the bench with her long curly hair pulled into a topknot. A few strands had escaped and fell around her face. Dave's heart gave an unexpected thud. She always looked beautiful, but there was something extra special about her tonight.

Smiling, he went over to kiss her. 'You look good enough to eat,' he whispered as he pulled her into a hug.

'You're not so bad yourself,' she said.

'Eewww,' said Paris as Dave dropped a kiss on Kim's mouth. He felt her smile under his lips and a surge of desire ran through him.

Kim pulled away quickly and laughed. 'Come on, Paris, it's normal for a husband to kiss his wife when he comes home from work.'

'No one kisses Granny,' she said, licking the wooden spoon.

Dave laughed at that. 'Well, she doesn't have a husband,' he said.

Paris looked at him. 'Do you know where Granny is?'

Dave nodded. 'Yes, I do.' He glanced across at Kim. 'She's in Adelaide.'

'I know that, but whyyyy?'

Dave stared at Paris. 'Can I get back to you on that?' he asked, and Kim gave a little laugh.

'You sound like you're talking to Jack, not a six-year-old girl!' Grabbing the sponge she wiped the bench in wide circles. 'You might need to try that again.'

'Not before I talk to you.' He grabbed her hand and dragged her to the lounge room. 'We'll be right back,' he called to Paris.

'Dave!' Kim said in a hushed tone as she looked over her shoulder. 'What are you doing? We can't do anything . . .'

'As much as I want to throw you onto the couch because you look beautiful tonight, I need to ask you something.' He stared at her intently. 'What do we say to this little girl? I mean, how much do we tell her?'

'I don't know what's going on yet, remember?'

After Dave had given a selective rundown of the day's events, Kim looked at him in disbelief. 'You're kidding me?'

'I wish I was,' Dave said, the thudding in his temple getting stronger.

Kim was quiet as she took in what he'd said, then she grimaced a little. 'Essie receiving drugs. That can't be right.'

'You wouldn't believe the amount of times I've thought that today. And now Zara's chasing the story.'

'What will Zara do now, do you think?'

'Surprisingly, nothing. I thought she would be following up on any leads, but I saw her at the show tonight.'

'That doesn't sound like Zara.'

'She'll probably get intel from somewhere else.'

Kim stared. 'As in, Jack? Surely he wouldn't . . .'

'No. Not a chance. More like Adelaide. She's got a lot of contacts down there.'

'So, there's every chance there will be a story in the paper, and people around Barker are going to know. We have to tell Paris the truth, but not in detail.' Kim decided quickly. 'There's something wrong with all of this, Dave.'

'You're telling me. I told Jerry Simms there was no way that Essie would willingly be involved in something to do with drugs, but he wouldn't listen. They've taken her to Adelaide to be arraigned.' He scratched his head in frustration.

'Kim?' Paris called. 'What are you doing?'

'I'd forgotten how many questions kids ask,' Kim said. Taking a breath, she said, 'Coming.' Then she shook her head at Dave. 'This is bullshit.' Without giving him time to answer, she put a smile on her face and went back into the kitchen. Dave followed her.

'How are you going there, Paris?' she asked, putting her hand over the little girl's to help her stir the cake mixture. 'You've done a great job with that. How about I put it in a cake tin now?'

'Okay.'

'How was school today, Paris?' Dave asked, pulling up a bar stool and sitting next to her.

'Good.' She didn't look at him, but watched Kim cut the baking paper to fit the cake tin and then spoon in the mixture.

'Who's your teacher?'

'Mrs Wright.'

Dave tried again. 'Do you like her?'

Paris shrugged. 'She's okay.'

Kim put the cake in the oven. She washed her hands, then sat down on the other side of Paris.

'Now, sweetie, Dave knows a bit about where Granny is and what's going on there.'

Paris turned her large blue eyes to Dave. 'Is there something wrong?'

'Well, Paris, your Granny has had to go to Adelaide to help the police with some questions they've got.'

'Like, real policemen?' Her eyes grew larger at the thought.

'Yep, just like real policemen. She's going to be there a few days. I'm not sure how long. But I promise you, she'll be back here as soon as she can be.' As soon as he said *I promise* he wished he could take the words back. He knew better than to make promises he wasn't sure he could keep, especially to a child.

'What sort of questions?'

Dave drew a breath. 'I don't know exactly what they're going to ask.' That was the truth. He looked at Kim for help.

Kim leaned forward and brushed Paris's hair away from her forehead. 'Sweetie, the police think that Granny knows about something they're investigating, so they have to ask her questions. Now, we don't know if she can help them or not, but that's why she's gone to Adelaide. You're going to stay with us until she comes home.'

Paris sat still, taking all the words in, and Dave couldn't help but think back to when his daughters Bec and Alice were six. They'd both been smart kids, talkers, and they were used to their dad going to work as a detective. They would have understood. But a child who hadn't had anything to do with the police before, other than what she'd been taught at school, would have trouble understanding what was going on.

As Paris's eyes filled with tears, though, he realised she understood one thing: her rock and safety blanket wasn't coming home tonight.

'I want Granny,' she whispered.

'Oh, sweetheart.' Kim gathered her into a hug and kissed her head. 'I'm sure you do, and she wants to be back here with you too, I know that for a fact. But we're just going to have to wait until she's able to come home.' She paused. 'We'll find some fun things to do when you're not at school. I promise.'

Above Paris's head, Dave and Kim shared a look. Who knew when Essie would be home—if ever.

❧

Creeping into Paris's bedroom that night, Kim pulled the doona up to her chin and watched the sleeping girl. Paris's tears were dry on her cheeks now, but occasionally she hiccupped in her sleep.

Kim switched on the night light and pulled the door half shut, before going into her bedroom. Dave was already in bed, reading a book. A couple of beers always helped him relax and he was mostly good at being able to leave work behind when he got into bed. His reading glasses were new and even though they made him look sexy, Kim had to do a double-take every time she saw him wearing them. Kim doubted that in all his fifty-three years he had ever looked as good.

'Look at you,' she said with a smile, flopping on the bed and putting her head on his chest.

'Hmm? What about me?'

'You and those sexy glasses.'

Dave closed his book and put his arm around her. 'You find the craziest things attractive,' he said, kissing her forehead.

'Don't be like that. I never said you were crazy,' she quipped.

Dave chuckled, then sighed. Kim sat up and pulled out the elastic band, letting her hair tumble over her shoulders. She ran her hand through the blonde curls to fluff it up, thinking how much they'd both changed since they first met when they were seventeen.

Dave's hair was now turning grey, from the dark brown he'd once had. Kim liked to think she was still blonde, but she had a very good relationship with her hairdresser.

Putting her hand on his leg, she asked, 'What's really going on?'

He sighed. 'I talked to Essie before she left, and I couldn't get anything out of her. This whole thing has something to do with her daughter and she's frightened that if she says anything, Melissa will get into trouble.' Tapping his fingers against her thigh in time to the thoughts in his head, Dave looked at her, his blue eyes grave. 'This charge is serious. She's going to be up in front of a magistrate, which is why she's been taken to Adelaide rather than being seen by a JP closer to home. She'll have to surrender her passport and unless she's got the money to post bail, she won't be coming back to Barker any time soon.'

'Do you know if she's got the money to do that?' Kim picked at a thread on the doona cover while she listened, her fear for Essie growing with Dave's every word. 'And how will she fare in prison, Dave? She's an old lady! She must be over sixty. How could they put her in a jail with young women who are up on violent charges? She wouldn't last a day in there.'

'Steady on with the "old" bit there, honey. I'm not far off sixty.' Then Dave shook his head gently. 'She hasn't got anything. The house isn't hers and she hasn't any family who can post surety for her. Essie hasn't got anything except Melissa and Paris and what's in the house.'

Sadness spread through Kim. 'Do you ever wonder how someone could get to her age and have nobody?' she asked quietly.

'Well, obviously she's had a partner at some point; she has Melissa.'

'Yeah, she was married to a really nice bloke. I only knew him as Mr Clippers. He died about ten years ago, I think. He was the barber, obviously. I don't know if she has any other family.'

'She can't have. I asked her outright if there was anyone who could help her and she said no.'

'That doesn't mean she doesn't have any other family, though,' Kim said.

'True enough,' he said finally. A slight grin spread across his face. 'Up to some detective work?'

Kim watched him. 'What, spying on Essie? I don't think so! If she's not owning up to any other family, there's a reason behind that and we shouldn't interfere.' She raised her eyebrows and with a cheeky grin said, 'I knew someone who didn't like admitting he had family elsewhere. And there would've been a time, I'm pretty sure, he wouldn't have thanked me if I'd found them and dragged them to his doorstep.'

Dave raised in hands in defeat. 'No arguments from me. Good thing I had you to change my mind then.'

'Speaking of, have you talked to your mum lately?' Kim got off the bed and walked towards the bathroom.

'Yeah, I spoke to her yesterday. She's fine.'

'Good. I'll be back in a minute.'

'Don't be too long . . .'

Chapter 10

Zara took another mouthful of wine and looked at her notes. The words blurred a little and she cursed that she'd had so much to drink already. The noise from the bar was distracting too, but she'd needed a diversion this evening.

She'd wanted to follow the car that had driven off with Essie in it. In fact, she'd rung Lachie to tell him that's what she was going to do, and he'd told her to stay where she was.

'If it's a little granny story, we'll hear about it soon enough. Can't think it's anything big. You've got bigger stories to follow where you are. Have you spoken to that shearer yet? And don't forget about the follow-up with the politicians on the drought policy. It's all anyone is talking about in Canberra.'

'Damn it, Lachie, this has got to be bigger than you think. The AFP are involved.'

'I'm hearing you, I am. But I'll get one of the others to follow it up from here. You stay put. Get onto the Minister for Agriculture and the bloke for Water as soon as you can. Much more important.'

And so Zara, pissed off with Lachie and Dave, and frustrated that she couldn't ask Jack any questions, had made her way to the beer tent to find Courtney and Tye. Instead she'd found Jesse Barnett, bought him a beer and was listening to his stories.

'Right, you and your dad headed to Wilcannia, Jesse?' she said.

'Yeah, Dad was mates with the owner up on Palcarinya Station. He loved that country. Never really felt the need to go anywhere once we got there. Just kept to ourselves and worked hard. The station owner's wife Judy, she took me under her wing, so I had my lessons with her kids.' He took a sip of his beer and lined the empty glass up next to the previous four. 'Been real lucky. Dad and me always got looked after. Think there was something about us, you know, just a boy and his father.

'Anyways, I hung around with Judy and Bob's kids, sat in the same school room and ate at the same table as all of them. All the while, Dad and Bob, they'd be out getting around the station, checkin' waters and fencing. They ran five thousand sheep on about twenty thousand hectares. Oh, she used to be a sweet sight when it was shearing time and the blokes would run the sheep in.'

Zara saw through her murky gaze that Jesse's eyes had glazed over with the memories. He was back watching the stockman and sheep, and she could observe him without him noticing.

His face is kind, she thought, propping her chin on her palm as she listened to him talk. *And so good-looking. Brown hair, brown eyes, trim and taut because of all the shearing. Wonder if he's got a girlfriend.*

'Used to climb to the top of the windmill to watch. Big mobs, more than a thousand head, moving as one.' He turned to look at her. 'You know how you see birds flitting and flying together—they seem to know what direction the next one is going to go in and they glide together?'

'Oh, yeah, like the flocks of budgies out on the Nullarbor. I've seen them. They can almost black out the sky when there's a lot.' She leaned into him as she spoke and felt his strong arm against hers.

'You're right there, little lady.' He stopped talking and Zara looked over at him to see why.

His eyes were on her face. Zara noticed the gold fleck beneath his pupil. Other than that, it would be pretty easy to get lost in the darkness of them.

Jack.

A roar of laughter went up from a table nearby. When she glanced over, she realised that one of the blokes sitting around it had led the champion bull out in the grand parade. His cheeks were glowing with alcohol-induced redness. Did her face look like that? She reached up to touch her cheeks, just as Jesse caught her eyes again. Her face was already hot, but when Jesse looked at her like that . . . like he wanted to kiss her. Well!

'Um, you were talking about bringing the sheep in,' Zara said. She had to lick her lips and repeat what she'd said because her mouth had become dry. She snatched up her wine glass and took another sip.

Jesse stayed quiet for a little longer, still watching her, then spoke. 'From up the top of the windmill, they'd swarm like the mobs of birds one way and the other. The dogs would be running from side to side, keeping them all together. Occasionally one or two would try to break away, but the dogs would have them rounded up before the rest of the mob even knew what happened. I always knew I wanted to work with sheep, when I was watching that. Poetry in motion.

'Then there were the motorbikes at the back of mob and burly stockman who'd sit on them, smoking a rollie, calling to the dogs. I could hear their short, loud, sharp whistles even from up the windmill.' He stopped and looked at Zara. 'You want another drink?'

Oh, she did. But she didn't want the headache tomorrow.

'Why not,' she said recklessly, smiling at him as he collected their glasses and took them back to the bar. She watched as he walked away, imagining a small boy at the top of a windmill watching the mobs come into the yards. She could see his windswept hair and large smile under a grubby wide-brimmed hat, fingers clenched white as he held on to the structure.

'What are you doing?' hissed a voice behind her.

Courtney.

'What do you mean?' Zara said, running her fingers through her hair and shaking it out, trying to get rid of her imaginings.

'You're all over him! I've been watching you for the last half-hour. You haven't even noticed me over there.' Her tone held excitement, judgement and worry all mixed into one.

'I am not!' Zara tried to sound horrified. She had forgotten there would be people watching, she'd got so caught up in Jesse's story and the wine. Shit. Did it look like she was trying to crack onto Jesse? The small sober, honest part of herself knew the answer.

'You are. Where's Jack?'

Zara's face darkened as she thought about the afternoon. 'At home, I guess.'

'Why is he there while you're here with Dreamy Eyes?'

'Long story. Long pissed-off story.'

'What's the go here?' Courtney leaned in closer, a look of expectation on her face. 'He *has* got gorgeous eyes, hasn't he? I told you he was pretty tidy to look at.' She wagged her finger at Zara. 'Do not take that comment as encouragement.'

'Don't be silly. I'm just getting his life story, that's all.'

Courtney raised her eyebrows at Zara. 'Sure.' Her tone didn't sound like she meant it one little bit.

'Here we go,' Jesse said, putting two drinks on the table. 'G'day, I'm Jesse.'

'Hello, Jesse,' Courtney said, putting out her hand. 'I'm Courtney, this one's friend.'

'Can I get you a drink?'

'Yeah, stay and have a drink, Court,' Zara said, suddenly needing someone alongside her.

'No, I can't, thanks. I've got to get home.' She looked back to Zara. 'You probably should too. You've got to work tomorrow.'

Her friend's message was clear.

'I'll finish this and get going,' Zara promised, hating the way everything was moving about her. She really shouldn't be having this last drink.

Courtney said goodbye and shot a warning glance at Zara as she left. Looking down at the table, Zara took a drink of the wine, trying to gather her thoughts. All she could feel was the heat coming from Jesse's body.

'Tell me more about your dad,' she said, desperate for an interruption to her thoughts. Back to why she was really here. Not gawking at some gorgeous shearer who wasn't her boyfriend.

'Well, my dad loved working with stock too. He was more of a stockhand-type fella—you know, working on the station, rather than in a shearing team.'

'I thought you told me you grew up in a shearing team?'

Before he could answer, a shout came from behind her and Zara glanced over her shoulder in time to see a young bloke stagger, beer in hand, towards one of his mates. His head was down as if he were a charging bull. The target moved aside and another roar went up as he hit the wall and slid down to the floor. He held his beer up in triumph.

'Never spilt a drop,' he yelled, his smile wide.

Zara turned back to see Jesse laughing at the incident. 'You were saying?' she asked.

'Young fellas, huh?' Jesse regrouped. 'Now, where was I? Oh yeah. We joined the team when I was about ten. Judy and Bob sold their station after the bank foreclosed on them. They stuck it out for as long as they could, but bad seasons, low prices and high interest rates, well, they're never a great mix.'

'You must've been sad to leave Palcarinya.' She stumbled over the word.

'Yeah. Yeah I was, but we hooked up with a good team. That's where I got the bug for shearing. I started off as the get-about lad. What they used to call a tar boy. If someone yelled out *black wool*, I'd run over there with the raddle and mark the sheep. If one had flies, I'd treat it while it was still on the board. Did all the small but necessary jobs.

'For a young fella I was pretty quick on my feet and didn't get in the way. The old blokes didn't like when rousies and shed staff got under foot, so they liked me around the shed. It was like having a group of dads and grandfathers around. They'd tell me stories, offer advice and tease the hell out me. 'Specially when I got old enough to be interested in girls. "*Ah, come on, Jesse, a young good-looking rooster like you,*" they used to say, "*you could have a girl in every town if you wanted.*"' He took a sip of his beer.

Dangerous territory, Zara thought fuzzily.

'And did you?' she asked.

'Have a girl in every town? Nah. I'm not like that. The nomadic lifestyle of a shearer doesn't really make for good relationships. I just keep to myself and get on with the job at hand.'

That's lucky.

Zara raised her glass to her mouth and drank the last of the wine, before gathering up her pen and paper. 'I'd better get home,' she said. 'Gotta work in the morning.'

'I'll walk you,' Jesse said. 'Can't have you out there at night by yourself.'

'I'll be fine. This is Barker, not Sydney. Nothing here that could go wrong.'

'I would've thought you knew better than that, being a journalist. Which way?' He picked up her bag and swung it over his shoulder.

Zara glanced around, grateful to not see anyone she knew. Most of the stragglers were out-of-towners.

'No, honestly, I'll be okay. I'm only down the street and around the corner.' She stumbled as she went to walk out through the tent opening and Jesse caught her arm, stopping her from falling.

'I think I'll walk you home. Don't want you taking a face plant and getting gravel rash and a black eye. That would spoil your pretty face and wouldn't look too good while you were getting around interviewing people.'

Zara giggled at the thought. 'Never done that before! A face plant, I mean.'

'Best you don't try it. I've done it a few times. Thought I'd broken my nose once. 'Nother time, I was heading home from a cut out. We'd been drinking in the shed and we walked back to the quarters. I went to brush my teeth and got all dizzy. Whacked my head on a corner of the shower on the way down. Got a couple of stitches in my cheek for my trouble.'

'Oh, no! Try not to do that again. One of the blokes who ran the tyre joint in Port Augusta had that happen to him. Fell backwards at the pub. Next bloke who went to the loo found him dead on the ground. Hit his head too hard.' Zara knew she was rambling, but she couldn't help it. The fresh air had kicked the alcohol in even harder and she could feel herself walking unsteadily alongside Jesse.

Casually, Jesse put his arm around her. 'Think you need a bit of help to stay upright.'

'I've got a boyfriend,' she blurted out.

'I know. I heard. And I also just told you I don't have a girl in every town. I'm walking you home 'cause I like to think I'm a gentleman. You're perfectly safe with me.'

❧

A noise filtered through Kim's sleep-addled brain and she woke with a start in the dark. She lay frozen in bed. Was someone trying to get into the house?

It'd happened once before. A disgruntled criminal, whom Dave had arrested for shoplifting and assault, came for a midnight visit after he'd been released from jail. He'd hammered on their door three separate times one night, but they'd never caught him in the act. Dave had known who it was, though he hadn't been able to prove it. A quick chat to him the next morning had put a stop to that.

Dave snored gently next to her, but now, other than the occasional dog bark, there was silence.

Kim rolled onto her side and put her hands underneath her cheek. She hadn't been able to stop thinking about Essie and what she must be going through. Essie in a jail cell with another two or three women, all younger, harder, crueller than the older lady could ever be. Kim had imagined one of them backing Essie against a wall, spitting at her, demanding things from her.

Sighing, Kim threw the covers back and got up, heading out into the kitchen.

Moonlight was filtering through clouds that raced across the night sky. Standing at the window, she sipped a glass of water, wondering what Essie was doing now. Curled up in a hard bed? Perhaps she was crying. Or maybe she was too scared to cry.

One thing Kim knew, was that she would be thinking about Paris.

A shadow passed under a streetlamp outside and Kim looked to see what had moved. The outline of two people, casting long shadows behind them, walked arm in arm along the pavement.

Kim frowned and moved closer to the window. Who was . . .

Zara's familiar curls blew out in the wind, and Kim relaxed. She and Jack had obviously had a late night at the show.

Then she looked again. Zara was with a man, but he wasn't the right size or shape to be Jack. This man was tall, lean and walked with longer strides.

They followed the path around the house until they stopped at Zara's front door. Kim watched as the man put the key in the lock and opened the door, letting Zara go in first and following behind her.

Kim stood stock-still, wondering what she'd just seen.

Chapter 11

The phone rang, startling Zara awake. Her first realisation was that her head hurt. Not just her head. Behind her eyes and across her nose.

Gingerly she felt her face; it felt normal. The hurt was a headache kind of pain. A hangover kind of pain. All across her head and face.

Oh, she had a doozy.

'Shut up,' she muttered to the phone as she reached out to her bedside table. Knocking the phone to the floor, she sat up, feeling her head throb even harder.

'Oh. My. God.' She lay back down again and closed her eyes, waiting for the thumping to subside.

The phone became silent and Zara lay there, turning over in her mind what had happened last night.

She remembered talking to Jesse and hearing some of his stories. She remembered him walking her home and . . .

Groaning aloud, Zara sat up again and opened the drawer of the bedside table, getting out some Panadol.

Swallowing two without water, she got up and went into the bathroom, splashed her face and looked at herself in the mirror. 'What is wrong with you?' she said.

Heat flowed through her as she remembered tripping over when she got inside and Jesse lifting her up. He had helped her to the bedroom.

The phone rang again.

She found it under her bed. 'Court,' she said in a croaky voice.

'So, what happened last night?'

'Nothing.' Zara found a glass and filled it with water before making her way to her office and switching the computer on.

'Are you sure?' Courtney said doubtfully. 'You were really flirting with him when I was there. That's why I didn't stay. Didn't think you needed any company.'

Zara was flooded with shame. 'No, he just walked me home. Made sure I got here okay. Nothing happened. I told him I had a boyfriend.'

'That doesn't stop some of them.'

'He's a real gentleman.' She clicked on her email and waited for the messages to download.

'Ha! And they all pretend that too. You're telling me he didn't even try to kiss you?'

Zara was quiet, searching her memory. His gentle hands on her body, lifting her legs onto the bed and covering her up with the doona.

'No. No kiss. No nothing. He made sure I was safe and then he left once I was in bed. God, I can't believe I did that. I haven't had a blow-out like that since Will died.'

'Are you sure?'

'Yeah,' Zara said quietly. 'I know nothing happened.'

'What about Jack?'

Tears pricked at Zara's eyes. 'I don't even know why I did what I did! I love Jack. I was just so angry with Dave and him that I blew everything out of whack.'

There was silence on the line before Courtney said, 'You never talk about Will.'

'I don't want to talk about him. It's too hard. Brings up too many memories.'

'Maybe you need to.'

Zara saw a message from Lachie and clicked to open it, answering at the same time. 'I'll talk about him when I'm ready.'

'Zara, last night was so out of character for you. There's something else going on.'

You were right. Lachie's message read. *Action on the granny front. Charged with possession of narcotics. Liz caught the story this morning.*

'Damn it!' Zara snapped, frustration coursing through her. That should have been her story. Drugs. In Barker. Her patch. 'Bloody hell.'

'What?'

'The story I wanted to write, but I couldn't get Dave to tell me anything about yesterday. One of my colleagues in

Adelaide has picked it up.' She ran her fingers through her hair and took another sip of water.

Her mouth felt like she'd been open-mouth breathing for the past month.

She heard Courtney sigh. 'I'm worried about you. All you do is talk shop these days. Ever since Will died. It's like you don't want to let anyone get close.'

'Don't be stupid. Jack and I are close.' Not knowing what else to do, Zara got up and paced the floor, up and back, her head pounding as she listened to Courtney talk. She didn't agree with one thing her friend was saying.

'And look at last night . . .'

'Court, I've got to go. I need to follow up on this story. I'll catch you later, okay?' Pressing the disconnect button, Zara sat down and dropped her face to the desk, letting her phone fall to the floor. She stayed like that until her phone buzzed with a text message.

I saw you come home late last night, are you okay?

A carefully worded text from Kim. Great. She would have seen Jesse come inside then.

Suddenly, all she wanted to do was run far away from Barker. Far away from where her brother had died, from his memory and all the feelings and emotions that went with his death. She didn't want to feel anything anymore.

Instead, she got up and went to have a shower. She wanted to wash away last night and avoid the thoughts of Jack and how she was going to have to tell him what she'd done before the rest of the town did.

117

That was a conversation she wasn't looking forward to.

Her phone rang again but she ignored it as she stepped under the hot water and let the hard needle-like spray hit her face.

The need to yell and scream was intense. Instead, a few tears trickled down her face and mingled with the water.

'Why?' she whispered, leaning her head against the tiles and closing her eyes. The image of Will lying in his bed, gaunt and pale. The shallow breathing before there was nothing. The feel of her mother's hand on her shoulder, telling her Will was gone. The coffin at the front of the church, surrounded by his footy club friends. These thoughts followed her everywhere.

No point in standing under the water if the memories were going to come in there with her. She turned off the taps and got out, wrapping herself in a towel and going to find her phone to see who had called.

Dave's name with two missed calls was on her screen.

Forgetting about her headache, she hit redial and dropped the towel as she ran for her notebook.

'Hi, Zara.'

She could tell he was in the car.

'Hi, Dave. How are you?'

Zara heard the blinker tick down the line.

'Fine. Just wanted to give you the heads up that Essie Carter was arrested last night for possession of narcotics.'

Was it her imagination or was Dave being short with her? Kim would have told him what she'd seen last night, Zara had no doubt. Her breathing picked up slightly.

'Yes, I heard.'

They both breathed into a long silence.

'How'd you hear?'

'Colleague in Adelaide picked up the story last night.' It was her turn to pause. 'Do you have anything else I can use, that she won't have?'

'No. I don't.'

'Right.'

'Zara, I apologise for the way I spoke to you yesterday. I want you to understand . . . the reason I didn't tell you anything was because I don't want Essie to come back to Barker and have everyone talking about her. She'll find the homecoming difficult enough without gossip raging around her.'

'I wouldn't have filed the story until you told me I could. As it is, now I have no control over what the *Farming Telegraph* will print and what the other journo will write.'

'I understand that.'

'You'll tell me when there's more to tell, then?'

'We're going to have to see how this plays out.' He went on to tell her about the arraignment. 'All of this is off the record, you understand? Once I've heard back about the charge and if there was the opportunity of bail, then I'll know a bit more.'

'Right. Well, thanks, Dave.' Zara took the phone away from her ear and was about to press the button to hang up when Dave spoke again.

'Are you all right, Zara?'

'What? Of course. Why wouldn't I be?'

119

The sound of the blinker again.

'No reason,' Dave finally said. 'I was just checking.' He disconnected the call and Zara stared at the words she'd written until they blurred in front of her.

❧

Taking a deep breath, Zara knocked on Jack's door. She knew he was home because the blind in the front window was open. Above all else, Jack was a creature of habit. He would close all the blinds before he went to work and open them when he came home. She knew the pot plant at the front of the house would have been watered, and whatever he was having for dinner would be sitting on the kitchen sink either defrosting or getting to room temperature so he could cook it.

Jack would have showered and be dressed in jeans and jumper, with the heater on.

Before Zara had time to prepare her opening line, the door opened and Jack stood in front of her, dressed exactly as she'd known he would be. His blond hair was still damp from the shower, and it curled at the base of his neck.

Zara fought the urge to reach up and twist it around her finger. Jack was a good head taller than she was and was blessed with boyish good looks. Dave joked that he still looked like he'd just come out of the academy, even though he'd been on the beat for six years.

'Hi,' she said, swallowing hard.

Jack leaned against the door frame and looked at her. 'Hi.'

'Sorry about last night,' she said, looking him in the eye.

'Had a good time?'

'Yeah. Late. Actually, I'm not sure what time I got home. Had a few too many wines.'

Jack just looked at her.

'Can I come in?'

Moving away from the door, he stepped inside, leaving her to follow. With another deep breath, Zara went up the steps.

'Do you want a wine, or are you off it tonight?' Jack asked. He made no move to kiss her.

He knows, she thought. *He's heard already.*

'I'll have a wine. Hair of the dog and all that. What are you having for dinner?' Following him through the passageway, she thought she could smell chicken.

'Kim popped over with a chicken pasta dish. Thought I might need something home cooked and filling since it's been so cold.'

A trickle of dread dripped into Zara's stomach.

'I spent a bit of time talking to Jesse last night,' she blurted out.

'I know. You said that was who you were with before you hung up on me.' He opened the fridge and got out a beer and a bottle of wine.

'We had quite a few down there.'

Not looking at her, Jack poured the wine and handed the glass to her.

'He walked me home. I was pissed, Jack. Really pissed and he wanted to make sure I got home okay.'

Jack stopped opening his beer, his hand still wrapped around the lid. 'Did something happen?'

Zara immediately shook her head, holding eye contact. 'No. Absolutely not. I kept falling over and he wanted to . . .'

'Yeah, make sure you got home safely. You said that.'

'I don't know why I drank so much.'

Leaning against the bench, Jack took a long swallow of his drink. 'Because you were pissed off at not getting any information out of Dave? And, at a guess, you were pissed off that you couldn't ask me anything.'

'Well,' Zara said uncomfortably, 'I wasn't happy about what happened with Dave. But I know I can't ask you anything.'

'He said you fairly got stuck into him. That's not like you.'

'He fairly got stuck into me,' Zara snapped, guilt-ridden anger welling up in her again as she thought about Dave's cutting words. 'I didn't even catch the story in the end, Jack! Liz in Adelaide got it. Dave could have told me, and I wouldn't have printed anything until I had his go ahead.' Her voice rose at the injustice.

'Is that all you care about? The story? What about your friendship with Dave, your relationship with me?' He put his beer down heavily. 'Didn't any of that cross your mind when you gave Dave a mouthful or you hung up on me last night? When you ran off to bury your head in work and wine?'

Trying to control her temper, Zara clenched her teeth. 'I'm not saying I don't care about that, Jack, but you know as well as I do that I've got a job to do.'

Taking a step towards her, Jack glared at her. 'I backed you up yesterday. Told Dave he should've known you were just doing your job. Then you blow me off and get drunk with some shearer who then walks you home. Tell me how I'm supposed to be happy with that situation.'

'I'm not expecting you to be happy. That's why I'm here, telling you what I did.' She took a breath as his other words filtered through to her. 'You backed me up?'

'Of course I did. That's what partners do for each other.' He turned away and opened the microwave door as it beeped. 'When they're not out getting drunk with another bloke.'

Zara stared at his back. Embarrassed, she didn't know what to say except, 'I'm sorry, Jack.'

'I'm sorry too. And I'm worried about you.'

'Why?'

'Because you're not yourself,' he sounded exasperated. 'You're distant, all caught up in work. You rarely talk about anything else anymore.'

'That's not true,' she said sharply, putting the glass on the bench. 'Have you looked at yourself lately? God, you've got all stuffy and uptight.' She crossed her arms, hugging herself, immediately regretting her words. Neither of her accusations was true, but she'd had to deflect his words.

'I think you'd better go.'

Looking down at the floor, she didn't answer.

'I mean it, Zara. I don't want to talk to you now. Just go.'

'Sorry,' she said again as she let herself out into the cold weather, which somehow seemed a whole lot warmer than Jack's house.

Chapter 12

1980

'Here we are.' Evie pushed open the door and reached inside for the switch. Light flooded the narrow hallway and Evie stepped aside to let Rose in. She held one baby in her arms and the other was in a borrowed pram that Evie was pushing.

Anticipation flooded through Rose. A house! Her own little house.

The time in the hospital had been full of doctors and nurses, and cloudy thoughts. Once she was out of danger, she'd begun to enjoy that she wasn't moving seemingly every other day, the bed was comfortable and there was a shower in her room, which she didn't have to share with anyone.

It was easy to walk from the bed to the two cradles that had been set up next to each other, and there was a large armchair for her to sit and feed the babies before she put them down again to sleep. Rose liked the stability of the hospital and the fact that she was going to stay in Barker for a while.

The house Evie was lending her smelled musty, like it had been closed up for some time, but that didn't bother her. An open window would sort that out soon enough. She stepped inside and looked up at the high ceiling and smiled. She could see this being a home, even though there was cleaning and painting to do. Off to the side was a kitchen, and as her footsteps echoed around the empty hall and she walked further in, she could see one bedroom opposite the kitchen and another two further down. The back opened to a small sunroom that ran the length of the house and had louvred windows along the wall.

'It's beautiful,' she whispered, turning to face Evie, who was standing behind her, a half smile on her face. 'Thank you.'

'You should all be comfortable here,' Evie said, looking down at the baby girl asleep in the pram. 'Won't you, Bridget?'

Rose smiled as she looked down at Alroy in her arms. She'd received Ian's letter a week ago and had named his twins as he'd asked. A tribute to his Irish heritage, he'd said.

'Yes, more than comfortable.'

'Better than the Kingswood!'

Rose laughed. 'For a home, absolutely!' She turned around, the smile still on her face and a little bubble of excitement starting through her. 'I'm so grateful, Evie. Thank you. And I don't have to worry about furniture because it's all here. How come . . .'

'It was my sister's. She went overseas, to Canada, about three years ago.' Her voice faltered. 'She was on a sight-seeing trip when the bus went over the edge of a cliff.'

Rose watched her swallow and turn away, running her fingers along the wall as she walked towards the kitchen.

'Everyone on the bus was killed.'

Following her, Rose wasn't sure what to say. She ached to reach out and hug the kind woman she'd only met the month before and who was now offering her safety and security. A home. The home of her dead sister.

'I'm sorry.' Her words sounded so inadequate for the enormity of the story.

'Cassie would love to have you here.' She stopped next to the kitchen table and touched the wooden top lightly, a sad smile on her face. 'She was always gathering up orphans and people who needed help and bringing them here. You would've fitted right in.' Evie swallowed a couple of times before speaking again. 'Now, I've turned the fridge on and checked all the kitchen utensils. I've cooked two casseroles so you won't have to worry about food for a couple of days, while you're getting settled.

'Everything you need should be here. Stewie and I went to the shed earlier today and found the meat-safe cot we used for our kids. Come this way.' Evie indicated towards the front of the house.

Leaning into the pram, Evie picked Bridget up and she snuggled her into her chest. 'Aren't you precious? she whispered. Turning to Rose, she said, 'We've given it a bit of a tidy up, so the cot should do for the bubs. They can sleep in there together for the time being. I've got my feelers out for another one. I like these types of cots. Keeps the kids safe from mozzies and flies. Out on the stations, the mums used them so snakes couldn't get in with the babies.'

'What?' Rose looked at her aghast, then across at the white cot, which was up against the wall. She could see where it got its name: it looked like an old meat safe on its side—a wooden frame, with fly wire inside to let the air flow through and keep out any nasties.

'Oh, yeah, those houses out in the bush, they had dirt floors and cracks in the walls and under the doors. Snakes were a daily part of life. Along with the flies and mozzies. The kids were tucked up nice and safe in these things.' She patted the top of the cot affectionately.

'Sounds scary,' Rose said, thinking about her two precious babies.

'Could be,' Evie answered in her practical way, patting Bridget's back. 'There's also a rocker—I know it's old and could do with a clean-up, but you'll have time to do that in the next week or so. I'm trying to find one that might carry twins, but I'm not having much luck at the moment. It's easy to find things for one baby, but two, well, that's a little more difficult.'

'I'm so grateful,' Rose said again.

'Tomorrow, once you're unpacked and settled in, we can go down to the church op shop and see what clothes we can find for the babies. And I'm going to Port Augusta next week, so you can come with me if you like and buy some nappies and so on. There're some things you just have to have new. Or, if that's too hard with both of them, just give me a list and I'll get them for you.'

'I've got a little bit of money,' Rose said. 'That would be lovely. I can give you some towards fuel and a bit of rent.'

Evie waved her hand away. 'I'd be going anyway, and the house is sitting empty. It's beneficial having you in here because the house will be looked after.' She turned and headed towards the front door. 'I've got to get on. I'll let you unpack. If you need anything, just yell; I'm only a couple of blocks away. The corner store is that way.' She pointed north. 'They have a good range of fresh fruit and veggies, and the butcher's shop has nice meat. The truck comes in with fresh produce every Tuesday, so that's the best time to shop. If you like, only get what you need for now and we can do a bigger shop in Port Augusta when we go.'

Rose walked Evie to the entrance.

'One more thing,' Evie said as Rose opened the front door with her free hand. 'Don't forget to make that doctor's appointment with Ben Hooper. He's a nice bloke and will take you under his wing. We need to make sure those bubs are happy and you're upright!' She smiled as she touched Rose's arm. 'You've had a bit of a going-over with the blood transfusions and emergency caesarean. He's going to need to keep a good eye on you.'

'I can't tell you how much this means.' She wanted to give Evie a hug but wasn't sure if she should.

Evie didn't give her a choice, pulling her into a quick cuddle which made both babies squirm as they were squashed together. 'You'll be right here, Rose. Barker will look out for you. See you later.' She gently placed Bridget in Rose's free arm. Alroy was in the other and Rose jiggled them both gently until they were comfortable.

'See you later.'

Rose watched her new friend walk down the path and open the front gate, then shut it behind her with a click. She wanted to hug herself! Jump with joy! Run around and throw open every cupboard door and look at everything all at once. But she didn't have the energy, and she had two babies in her arms.

Evie had been right when she said Rose had been through the mill. It had taken four weeks for her to recover enough to leave hospital, and to ensure the babies were healthy and strong. Four weeks of constant blood tests and monitoring. Not just for her but for the bubs as well. Four weeks of visits from Evie, and one from Ali, but never from Ian. Her jaw clenched at that thought.

He'd sent messages. Letters. But he hadn't come in to see them, to meet his children.

Still, Rose reminded herself, she had a house! A base for her children and Ian when he came.

And she had a new friend.

'Can you believe it?' she whispered to the baby in each arm, as she looked around in wonder. 'We're home.'

❧

It was dark when Bridget cried out for a feed. Rose had fallen asleep in the chair, overlooking the cot that held both children. Even after four weeks, she found it hard to believe she was a mum of two littlies.

Picking up the crying child, she undid her bra and latched Bridget onto her breast. Greedily the baby sucked at the nipple and Rose felt instant relief as the milk left her. Her breasts had nearly doubled in size since her milk had come in. Evie had managed to find her some maternity bras; they were ill-fitting but workable, and matron had plied her with cabbage leaves to stop the heat and help ease the ache.

I smell like a Sunday lunch at Grandma's—steamed cabbage, she thought with a smile.

In the pale glow of the passage light Rose had left on, she pulled out Ian's last letter, delivered by Ali. She almost knew the words by heart now.

Sweet Rosie, nothing is the same without you here. My bed is empty and I miss your warmth next to me. Your smile.

The shed is nearly finished. Maybe another week. The boss ended up with five hundred more sheep than he thought he had. I don't know how that happens when someone should be keeping records. Still, I'm not complaining. More money for us when I've finished.

How are you and the babies?

Ali told me you're getting stronger by the day. It won't be too much longer before I can get in to see for myself. She also said that the babies both have red hair! Such good Irish stock.

Sweet Rosie, I must away to sharpen all the gear for shearing tomorrow. It's been a hard shed. The wethers are strong and there is much dirt in the wool, which blunts the cutters more quickly than normal.

I've prickles all through my hands from the burrs the sheep have picked up as they've been sleeping or grazing. Still, I've loved it and can't wait to get back on the road again.

Not long until I can see you all.

My heart, Ian

Rose had tried to write back saying exactly that—she didn't want to get back on the road again—but the words hadn't come and the babies had needed bathing, changing and feeding, so the letter had remained unfinished on the kitchen table.

'Can't wait to get back on the road again,' Rose said quietly, letting her head fall back against the wooden frame of the rocking chair. 'But, Ian, I don't want that.'

She looked down at her daughter and saw she had fallen asleep. Her rosebud mouth was open, and ginger eyelashes brushed her cheeks as she slept. The thought of loading the children up every few weeks was more than Rose could bear.

'No, Ian, I don't want that.' Standing up, she placed the baby back into the cot next to her brother and stood there looking at them both, her heart full of love. 'We can't do that.'

Chapter 13

Ian threw the last of his gear into the back of the Kingswood and slammed the boot shut. A puff of dust rose into the air and he shooed away the flies that were gathering around his face.

'See you at the pub tonight?' Kiz asked as rolled a smoke and offered it to Ian.

He took it, knowing it would be his last one for a while, almost certain that Rose wouldn't let him smoke around the kids.

'Yeah, I'll be there,' Ian said.

Muzza let out a whoop. 'Good to know that the ball and chain won't stop ya. We're heading there as soon as we get to town. Get rid of some of this dust in my throat.'

'I've got to visit the kids first, though. I want to at least see if they look like me!'

'God, another two of you, Paddy. The world isn't ready

for that. Anyway, she should've brought them out to see you. You've been working, makin' sure they've got money.'

'Yeah,' Kiz said. 'Don't forget they're your kids too, mate. She's not got the right to keep them from you.'

Ian wanted to explain that even if Rose had a car and could drive, she couldn't have brought them out anyway; they'd all only just come out of hospital. Four weeks in there would be enough to make any person insane. He was sure that Rose would be sick of being stuck in one spot, and desperate to get back on the road again.

'I'm goin' to get my pay. Catch you boys in town.'

As he walked towards the house, he heard the slamming car doors and shouts of the men who were excited to be heading to the closest pub. He'd left getting his pay until last because he wanted to be alone to thank the family who'd helped his own, without jeers and taunts from the other blokes.

He knocked on the office door.

'Come.'

'G'day, boss.' Ian stuck his head around the door before he entered.

'Ah, Ian, I bet you're looking forward to getting to town tonight. See the new babies.'

'Yes, sir, that I am.' He nodded. 'Just wanted to thank you . . .'

Ross waved his hand, brushing away his thanks. 'Not necessary, Ian. Anything we could do to help.'

'Well, I appreciate it.'

'You'll be looking for your money.' Ross leaned across the desk and picked up an envelope. 'Thank you for your service here. I know you realise that we managed to finish earlier than we would have if you'd gone in to see the family. We appreciate your sacrifice.' He tapped the envelope in his hand before passing it towards Ian. 'There's a little bonus in there for you, and I'll ask you not to tell the other blokes about it. And I've made the cheque out to cash, so you can head straight to the bank and get the money. There will be things that Rose and the babies will need urgently, I assume.'

Ian took the envelope, which was thicker than any pay cheque he'd ever received. He itched to look inside.

'See you next year, boss, and thanks again.'

'You will. With your two littlies running around, I'm sure.' Ross nodded and turned back to his paperwork.

Outside, Ian headed back to his car, the envelope burning a hole in his pocket. He looked up at the blue sky and felt a touch of excitement at the thought of being in town tonight. A few drinks at the pub, and the chance to see the new bubs. And he'd be back in the same bed as Rose and could relieve a bit of the tension that had been building up. Yes, tonight was going to be a good night.

He said goodbye to Dougie, who was still packing. 'Thanks for your wise words,' he said, shaking the older man's hand.

'I hope you'll heed them.'

'Do my best. See you at the next shed.' He nodded, got in the car and drove away, a cloud of dust following him.

❧

Rose washed the cup in soapy water, before rinsing it and placing it on the drain. She glanced down at the babies who were lying on their backs on the shaggy rug which had come with the house. Bridget was cooing, her eyes wide open, looking at her mother; Alroy was asleep.

The last week had been a jumble of feeding, crying and sleeping. And the nappies—so many dirty nappies to change, soak and wash. The babies didn't nap at the same time, so Rose hadn't been able to rest when they were sleeping, as Evie had suggested. Instead, she'd been snatching cat naps while sitting in the rocking chair feeding them. Nights had been a blur of sleepwalking to the bedroom to feed. Alroy was colicky and no amount of gripe water would settle him.

She'd been frightened that if she went to sleep her large breasts might suffocate the twins as they were feeding, but even though she tried hard to stay awake, more often than not she felt her head rolling forward, before jerking it upright and checking they were still suckling.

Rose had pulled the plug as she finished washing the dishes and was reaching for a tea-towel when a loud knock at the door echoed through the house. She jumped and the sleeping Alroy woke, his cry loud and high-pitched. Bridget's eyes widened and she looked startled, before starting to cry as well.

'Oh, no!' She dried her hands on the tea-towel and bent down. Putting her hand on both their bellies, she rocked them gently from side to side, hushing them. 'It's okay. Just a knock at the door, shush.' In a louder voice she called out, 'Hold on.'

But the babies didn't stop, seeming instead to feed off each other, so Rose went to open the door before whomever it was knocked loudly again.

The crying followed her, making her want to cover her ears. Their screams certainly were enough to drive any mother to drink, as Evie had said to her yesterday. Rose had been quick to agree. This mothering thing was hard, especially without Ian here to help.

'I'm coming,' she called out again.

Swinging the door open, her face broke into a smile. Ian was standing on the doorstep, cap in hand and holding a single rose.

He held it out to her. 'A rose for a rose,' he said.

'You've finished!' A large smile broke over her face.

Ian took a step towards her and pulled her to him. 'I've finished, sweet Rosie. My Lord, you're a sight for sore eyes, I tell you.' Letting her go, he peered in behind her. 'What is that noise?'

'Your children!' Rose felt giddy with excitement that her husband was finally here.

'Do they always sound like that?' A look of fear crossed his face.

'They're pretty noisy. Come on, follow me. Alroy's got colic, so his tummy hurts a lot of the time. Bridget has a good set of lungs on her too.'

In the kitchen, she bent down and picked up her daughter. 'Here you go, little one, meet your daddy.'

The baby opened her mouth and screamed even louder.

'No, no,' Ian said backing away. 'That's okay, you hold her.' He glanced down at the other baby, whose face was red and scrunched up as he roared. 'Hello, down there. You're a noisy little mite too.'

'Hold her, Ian. Or pick up Alroy. Neither of them bite, they're just noisy.' She jiggled the baby up and down. 'It's time for their feed anyway. Can you bring him?' She went to the babies' room and sat in the rocking chair, unlatching her bra. Instantly Bridget's cries stopped, and the sucking noises started.

The only cries now came from the kitchen.

'There, there, little one,' she hushed. 'Ian?'

He appeared at the doorway, looking flustered. 'I don't really know . . .'

Rose saw a look of revulsion cross his face when he realised what she was doing.

'What's wrong?'

Seeming to recover himself, Ian said, 'I don't really know how to pick him up.'

'You can't break them,' she said, repeating what Evie had told her the first day she'd come to visit in the hospital. 'They're a lot tougher than you think they are.'

'And he won't stop squawking.'

'He's hungry. Bring him to me, and I'll stop him.'

Pursing his lips, Ian went back out again and Rose smiled to herself. *Funny man*, she thought. Using her feet to push off in a gentle rocking motion, she heard the screaming increase. 'You'll get the hang of them quickly enough,' she called out. Realising that her daughter had fallen asleep again, she put her in the cot and quickly walked out to see how Ian was getting on.

Bent over the baby, he was trying to get his hands underneath the baby's back. Rose stood in the doorway and watched.

Getting a grip, Ian stood up, his arms outstretched, but holding the child. He looked so uncomfortable she wanted to laugh.

'Try this way,' she said, going to them. Cradling Alroy's head, she slipped her hand along his back until the child was nestled in the crook of her arm, supporting his head. Latching him onto the other nipple, she walked back into the nursery and sat down again.

'You wait,' she said. 'Bridget here will start again in a minute. You'll need to pick her up and put her over your shoulder.'

'What for?'

Rose noticed he averted his eyes from her and the suckling child.

'She'll need burping. The air in her tummy hurts her otherwise.'

'Right.' He looked around. 'You gave them the names I wanted?'

Rose glanced up at him. 'Of course.'

He looked around the room. 'Nice place. You like it?'

'I love this house. Evie has been so good to us.'

A flicker of darkness crossed Ian's face at the mention of Evie. 'She likes to interfere. I saw that from the moment I met her.'

'Oh, no, Ian, she doesn't. She just cares. I wouldn't have managed without . . .'

Bridget started to cry, drawing her knees up to her chest and letting them back out again.

'Can you burp her?' Rose said, then watched as he stared down at the small baby as if she were something foreign.

'Ah . . .'

'She'll stop once you get the pain out of her tummy.'

'You've managed all this time.' Ian turned away.

She fixed him with a frown.

'Ian Kelly, these are your children. You can help while you're here.'

Ian's eyes didn't stop moving around, falling everywhere except her. He moved forward and awkwardly picked the baby up, as Rose had shown him earlier.

'Tell me about the shed,' Rose said, trying to find a safe subject. 'It ended up all right?'

He nodded. 'Boss was really good to me. Got a bonus and all. Speaking of that, I've put three hundred quid on the kitchen table. Guess you'll be needing that.'

'That's fantastic.' Rose felt relieved knowing there was more money. Even with her frugalness she was down to the last hundred dollars.

'I . . .'

Right on cue, Bridget let out a long loud burp and Ian jumped, then laughed. 'She's got her father's genes there.'

Even with the laughter, Rose could see he wasn't comfortable, but at least he wasn't as frightened as he'd been a couple of minutes ago, although he still wouldn't meet her eyes.

～

Finally both babies were asleep and Rose made Ian a cup of tea. They sat opposite each other, and it was clear to Rose that neither of them really knew what to say.

Ian looked worn and his eyes were bloodshot. Rose suspected he'd been giving the rum a hammering while he'd been alone, and she detected the faint whiff of cigarette smoke on his clothes. He still was the handsome Irishman she'd fallen in love with, but there was an air of defiance in his stare, something she hadn't seen before.

'You got a bonus?' Rose grasped onto something he'd already said.

'A hundred quid. I'm going to shout the bar with it tonight.' He took a sip of tea. Glancing around, he said, 'You've got this set up nicely, sweet Rose, but I guess you'll be pleased to get back on the road again.'

Rose stilled and then took a careful sip of her tea. 'Leave?' she asked. What she really wanted to say was, *'How dare you spend that obscene amount of money at the pub! That could keep us in food for nearly a month.'*

But if it were a choice between spending the money and facing the fact that Ian wanted to leave, then she'd have to deal with the leaving and let the money slide.

'When we head off. I know you'll be wanting to get back out to the sheds after all this time in one place.'

Placing the cup gently on the table, she took a breath. 'Actually, Ian, I don't want to leave. The bubs and I, we're settled here and just in the few days I've been home from hospital, I've realised how hard taking them on the road would be.'

'What do you mean?' He frowned as if he didn't understand.

'I mean I want to stay here.' She looked at him steadily and saw him glance at her chest, and another look of disgust pass across his face. She looked down and saw excess milk leaking out through her shirt. 'One thing I know,' she said lightly, grabbing a tissue, 'is that I'm a good cow! Haven't had any trouble in feeding them both since my milk came in.' She gave a laugh and looked at Ian, but he wasn't following suit. In fact, he was again looking in every other direction other than her.

'Right,' Ian said.

'I have a lot of milk,' she clarified. Suddenly she realised the problem. Ian had always loved her breasts and now there were two babies at them. Maybe he hadn't thought about that part and it was confronting for him.

Shuffling in his chair, Ian said, 'I have a shed in northern New South Wales in a week. We're going to need to leave in two days if we're going to get there on time.'

Rose shook her head. 'Ian, you've seen what it's like in the short time you've been here. These babies aren't going to be easy to take on the road. In fact, they'll be nigh on impossible. Can you imagine driving a twelve-hour day with them screaming in the back? We'd all go insane.'

'What do you suggest, then? I go without you?'

Rose was quiet for a long time. Then she said, 'Yes.'

Chapter 14

2020

Three days after Essie was taken to Adelaide, Joan unlocked the police station door as the clock hands were dead on nine and twelve. Kim watched her from across the street, her hands tucked into her coat and her nose hidden under the bright pink scarf wrapped around her neck.

She'd just walked Paris to school, where a curious mother had asked about Essie. It wasn't the first time and she knew the questions would continue to come. Essie had been involved with Paris's schooling—helping in the classroom, walking her to and from school every day and, even though she was in her sixties, Essie had been on the P&C. The parents were concerned about her.

Over years of fostering, Kim had become skilled at deflecting queries with smiles and questions of her own.

Distraction was always a good tactic, she'd discovered—what mother didn't want to talk about her own child?

The cold wind was blowing down the street, lifting the leaves and tossing them together, sending them dancing down the pavement around her feet. With a purposeful step forward, she started towards the police station.

'Morning, Joan.' Kim peered in the door and glanced around before entering properly. 'Dave's not here, is he?'

'Haven't seen him yet. I thought you'd know where he was.'

'No, he left without telling me where he was going this morning,' she lied. Kim knew Dave was on his way to Adelaide. 'Oh well, I'll have to make do with Jack.'

'He's out the back; you know the way. Didn't you bring anything for us for smoko this morning?' Joan asked with a smile.

'Sorry, I was in a bit of a rush when I left. I didn't think. I've just come back from walking Paris to school.' She usually brought freshly baked pies or biscuits and Dave would always joke he could smell her coming.

Not today. She had other things on her mind.

Swallowing her nerves, she gave Joan a smile as she walked behind her towards the offices. 'I'll bring something tomorrow. Paris and I made chocolate-chip biscuits and banana cake a couple of nights ago, so there's enough to go around.'

'How is the poor little thing?' Joan's face sobered.

'She's a bit confused, but okay. School will be a great diversion and she'll be with her friends.' She pointed towards Jack's office. 'I'll just catch Jack.'

Joan nodded and started to open the mail on her desk.

Kim tapped quietly on the office door and heard Jack call out, 'Come in.'

'Hi, Jack, just me.' She pushed open the door and stepped inside. 'Gosh, it's cold out there. I think it gets colder every winter.'

'There's a good reason I'm in the office this morning. I could've been out doing licence and speed checks, but I think I'll let everyone get to where they need to go without stopping them. Too cold. Got a mountain of paperwork to get through anyway.'

'I think I saw all the carnies packing up and shifting out today. You might have found some of their vehicles weren't up to scratch!' Kim pulled out a chair and sat down.

'I did a bit of a run through there last night. They knew we were around. And those guys travel all the time. They know what the rules and regs are.'

'How's Zara?' She still couldn't get past the image of a strange man following Zara into her house.

Jack picked up a pen, twirling it between his fingers, avoiding her eyes.

'I haven't seen her for a couple of days. She was itching to write this story about Essie.' He changed position and tapped his pen on the desk, the way Dave did when he was worried about something. 'We had a bit of an argument.'

'Oh, no.' Kim looked at him, ready to listen.

'Sometimes I wonder if we're really suited. She's always off chasing the story and I'm chasing the crims. I don't know, she's obsessed with work at the moment.' He shrugged and looked despondent. 'She's not really acting like herself.'

'Like you can get when you're obsessed with work?' Kim gave him a wry look.

'Yeah, I know I can be too, but not like this.' He stopped. 'Anyway. That's not why you came to see me. What can I do for you?'

'Jack, you *are* suited,' Kim said firmly, hoping her words were true. 'Of course you are! A little argument isn't a reason to throw all of this away. Couples argue all the time.'

Throwing the pen down, Jack shrugged his shoulders. 'I know you're right, but this is the first time we've been through this type of thing—I know the answers she wants, and we both know I can't give them to her. Then she goes off and gets drunk with some other bloke because she's pissed off.'

'Ah. Well, we all make mistakes. You'll navigate your way through, Jack. You guys have always had something pretty special.'

Jack smiled, and Kim saw he was looking at the photo of Zara on his desk. 'Yeah, you're right. We do. I should call her. Maybe I'm the one being stubborn.' He refocused and then cocked his head to one side with a questioning look on his face. 'To what do I owe the pleasure today?'

A shiver of anxiety ran through Kim. 'I know Dave's gone to Adelaide to sit in on the bail hearing. He wanted to be there to reassure Essie if she doesn't get it. Have you heard anything from him?'

Jack slowly sat back in his chair and looked at her steadily.

'Only that she doesn't have the money to cover the fifty thousand needed.'

'I have it.' The words burst from Kim in a rush.

Touching his two pointer fingers together, Jack continued to look at her without saying anything. He didn't have to. Kim could see the question there.

'I've got the fifty thousand,' she said, more quietly this time.

'And you've talked to Dave about this?'

'No.'

Jack's eyebrows shot up. 'You're kidding me?'

'No.' Kim opened her handbag and brought out the title of her investment house in Adelaide. 'You can take this. It's worth more than Essie needs, but it will get her out of there.'

'Kim . . .'

She held up her hand. 'No, Jack, don't try to talk me out of this. I'm a really good judge of character and I know she didn't do this. I've known Essie since I was a kid. She's been through so much, what with Melissa and having to care for Paris. She needs help and I'm able to give it.'

'You're wrong, Kim.' Jack broke in over the top of her. 'She did do it. She accepted a parcel with the narcotics in it. I saw it with my own eyes. Essie did do this.'

Leaning forward in her chair, Kim shook her head. 'That's not what I meant,' she said earnestly. 'Essie's doing this for a reason, whatever that is. You and Dave need to look into whatever is making her do something so out of character, but she wouldn't willingly have accepted that parcel.'

Standing up, Jack paced the floor. 'There's a conflict of interest.'

'How?' Kim stood too and challenged him.

'Because the arresting officer is your husband!'

'No, he's not. It was the AFP who arrested her and took her away. Dave just assisted in the raid.'

'Jesus!' Jack ran his hands through his hair and kept pacing. 'Talk about a couple arguing. That's what you'll be doing when he gets home.'

Kim stayed quiet, letting him think through the situation. She wasn't going to change her mind, no matter what he threw at her.

'Are you sure?' He stopped in front of her, his hands on his hips.

'Yes.'

'Why? There's got to be a reason behind this.'

Kim shook her head. 'No reason. I can see that someone badly needs help—help I can give. Give me the papers to sign, Jack. Let's get Essie home and Paris back with her grandmother before the system upsets another little girl's life.'

'I'd rather you talked to Dave about this.'

Giving her low throaty laugh, Kim said, 'What, so he can have the same reaction as you? Look, Jack, let me worry about Dave. I've thought this through and there's no changing my mind. Let's just get on with it. I've got to get home and do some washing for Paris; try to get it dry before she comes home from school.' She sat in the chair and waited.

'Have you thought about what this might do to Dave?'

'Nothing,' she snorted. 'He's not involved in this at all.'

Jack sat down heavily and sighed, but from the look on his face, she knew she'd won.

Just for good measure she added, 'Jack, this is coming from me. Kim Burrows. Not David Burrows. There won't be any blowback.'

'I'm not so sure about that, but I can see I'm not going to change your mind.' He drew out a form from his desk and began filling in the details. 'But by hell, Kim, make sure you tell Dave before he gets to Adelaide. Don't let him walk into a shit fight when he gets down there.'

'I'll ring him once you've emailed the documents through. Maybe he'll be able to bring her home with him.' Kim smiled at the thought, but Jack didn't smile with her.

Half an hour later, Kim walked out of the Barker police station knowing plans were in motion to get Essie home. She dialled Dave's number as she walked down the street, back towards her house. A strong gust of wind blew her scarf off her shoulder and she grabbed at it.

'You've reached Dave Burrows from the Barker Police . . .'

'Damn.' As she finished fighting with her scarf she said into the phone, 'Dave, it's me. Can you give me a call?'

She looked at the time as she ended the call: ten-thirty. Dave wouldn't be in Adelaide yet, but he'd be close. Another trickle of anxiety ran through her. Jack was right—she really needed to tell him before he got there.

Debating whether she should call again, she kept walking against the wind, her head down. Thankfully, her house was just around the corner.

Her phone rang and she snatched it up without looking at the screen. 'Dave?'

'Hello? Is that Kim Burrows?'

Kim took the phone away from her ear and looked at the caller ID.

Unknown. Damn. Not Dave.

'Yes,' she said, putting the phone back to her ear.

'Oh, good.' The relief in the woman's voice was clear. 'You run Catering Angels, don't you? My father has had a fall and is in hospital. I need someone to cook for my mum while he's there.'

'Sure,' Kim answered. 'Can you give me some details?' As she spoke, she heard the ding of a message coming in. Taking the phone away from her ear again, she saw it was from Dave. 'Actually, look, I'm just out in the street, in this shocking wind. Can you give me five minutes and I'll call you back once I get inside?'

'No problems. I'll wait to hear from you.'

Kim hung up and went straight to her call register, to hit Dave's number. As she did, Dave's name flashed up on her screen again, this time a text message:

Hi honey, hope everything is okay. Just got to courts in Adelaide, so won't be able to talk. Ring you on the way home.

'Shit!' Her stomach clenched as she read the words.

Kim put the phone back in her handbag and felt around for her keys. She knew that she couldn't explain adequately what she'd done in a text message, and so Dave was now walking into a situation that she'd caused. The bravado Kim had felt when convincing Jack slid away, replaced by nausea.

Chapter 15

Zara was outside the courthouse in Adelaide when she saw Dave walk up the steps. She knew she wasn't supposed to be there, but the pull of the story had been too strong.

She'd texted Lachie to let him know she was going to the hearing. *Whatever is going on here is bigger than just her, I'm sure of it. I'm going down.*

Have you spoken to those pollies?

Not yet. I'll get you that story in time.

She could imagine Lachie shaking his head but knew he wouldn't stop her. Anyway, she had to do something to stop thinking about Jack.

For days her fingers had hovered over her phone, wanting to call him. Then she would put the phone away; she couldn't bear a rejection on top of everything else, even though she probably deserved it.

Cars raced by, their tyres hissing on the wet streets. Under the balcony of the courthouse, Zara watched people hurry inside. Some were dressed in suits, carrying briefcases or pulling trollies with cardboard boxes full of files for the case they were defending or prosecuting. Others were dressed casually, fidgeting, smoking; some had headphones in and bounced in time to music no one else could hear. Everyone in the building was there for a trial in some way.

Policemen and women came and went in their uniforms, giving evidence against criminals, Zara presumed, while the security guards checked the bags through the security scanner as everyone walked through.

Zara sipped her coffee, wondering about her plan of attack. Getting inside wasn't a problem; everyone, so long as they passed security, could walk through the front doors. She had covered trials here before and knew the layout; the issue would be finding Essie's bail hearing and not letting Dave see her until she was ready.

She watched Dave flash his badge at security and empty his pockets of his phone and other bits and pieces into the tray and then walk through the scanner.

Zara followed at a distance and waited until he was out of sight before grabbing her bag from the conveyer and hoisting it onto her shoulder.

She couldn't see him amid the throng of people milling around outside the many courtroom doors lining the corridor. She quickly pushed through, trying to see Dave's tall frame in front of her. As she rounded a corner, she saw him, straightening his suit and about to walk through a courtroom door. She saw his arm move forward to push the door when a man stepped up and brought his arm down on Dave's.

Zara took a sharp breath and pushed herself against the wall to hide herself. This was the man she'd seen in the Barker police station, she was sure, and he looked furious.

Zara shifted forward a little while remaining close to the wall, trying to hear what they were saying. It didn't take much because the man was speaking loudly—not loudly enough to bring security, but not far off.

'You've got a bleeding heart, Dave,' Zara heard the man say. 'A Red Cross sticker on your arm.'

'What the fuck?' Dave stepped back and glared at the man. 'What are you doing?'

'Like hell you don't know. I can't believe you've let her do this.'

'I've got no idea what you're talking about.' Dave rounded on the man and towered over him. The fury radiating from him would have been enough to make most people walk away, but not this bloke. He took a step closer.

Zara thought about getting her camera out but decided against it. Her heart was beating fast; she knew she was seeing something newsworthy, but there were too many problems with this.

'See, this is the whole reason we wouldn't tell you whose door we were going to knock on. The small-town syndrome. Too many of you know each other, like each other, drink together, and you'll protect each other. Just. Like. Your. Wife. Is. Doing.' With every word the man hit Dave's chest with a sheaf of papers.

'What the fuck are you talking about, Simms?'

'We wanted to oppose bail. In fact, we tried to. Never mind all the evidence we have against Essie Carter. Three packages being delivered to her address. The fact she's not providing any assistance in the investigation, which is a clear sign of guilt in my experience, and let's not forget the fact she is a flight risk.' The man stood in front of Dave, his arms crossed.

'A flight risk? You've got no idea what you're saying. Where's she going to go other than home?'

'Yeah, a flight risk. The only thing keeping that woman in Barker is her granddaughter. She has no one else. We can't even track the daughter down—she's probably dead in a pauper's grave if your story is anything to go by.' He took a breath. 'But it turns out, despite everything we've got, someone decided to put up bail anyway.'

Zara could see that Dave wanted to smile but was too angry. 'Well, that's good news as far as I'm concerned. Her age should have mitigated anything the judge imposed on her anyway. Obviously, I missed the good news. Nice you were here to give it to me.'

Simms took another step forward and poked Dave in the chest again. 'Yeah, great that she's got bail.' He let the words hang and Zara could see confusion cross Dave's face.

'Look here, Simms, I don't know what you're implying, but—'

'Take a look at the paperwork, Burrows. I'm sure you'll recognise the signature and the address of the asset put up for bail.' The paperwork was slapped across Dave's chest and left there until Dave put his hand up and took it.

Zara watched as he took his glasses out of his pocket and read the paperwork, horror crossing his face before it was quickly masked again.

'So,' he shrugged, 'what's that got to do with me? If you did your research, Simms, you'd see that house is my wife's. Not mine. It has nothing to do with me.'

Simms gave a tight-lipped smile. 'Maybe not, but you live with the woman who set bail. Surely you talk at night?'

Dave said nothing.

'Or perhaps you don't. Since you don't seem to know about this.' He gave a taunting grimace 'See, I feel that everyone in that police station is a little too close to people they shouldn't be. Like that constable of yours and the journalist.'

There was silence, and trepidation ran through Zara.

'Oh, you think we didn't know?' Simms taunted. 'We do more research before we make an arrest than you could ever imagine. I know when you take a shit!'

Dave shrugged. 'And so you might, but I told you earlier there was more to this case than what you were seeing. More than the package of drugs. Kim obviously thinks so too. That's why she would have done this. She's her own person and I never—hear me on this, Simms—*never* tell her what to do or influence her in any way.'

'You'll hear more about this, Burrows. It's completely against all the ethics we as coppers stand for.'

Dave laughed. 'I don't see how. I don't own that house. It's not my signature on the bail papers. Nothing leads back to me. Good luck in proving otherwise.'

People kept pushing past Zara, obstructing her view. She knew there was no way Dave would want her seeing or hearing any of this, but she took another few steps closer anyway. She had to get the full story. By this point she wasn't worried about being seen. Simms and Dave were so intent on each other, she knew they wouldn't see anyone else. She was sure that if they could have grabbed each other by the throat, they would have.

Surprisingly, Simms laughed and took a couple of steps back. He narrowed his eyes. 'No, perhaps not. But I guess when I tell the judge that the person who signed the bail paperwork is your wife *and* is currently looking after the accused's granddaughter in your house . . .' He shrugged. 'Hmm, who knows what the judge will think of that.'

'I'd imagine not much. Everything is above board, which I'm starting to think is more than I can say for you and your boys, Simms. Your reaction to Essie's bail has told me you know there's more to this too. Which means—' Zara watched Dave get in Simms's face '—maybe Jack and I will have to investigate this case a little more.'

Zara's heart leaped as Dave smiled at Simms and drew himself up to his full height.

'You just make sure you let me know if you've got a problem with us looking into Essie's case, Simms, because if you do, I'm sure there's no issue with what my wife has done.'

Dave touched his finger to his forehead in a salute and, with another smile, side-stepped around Simms and walked towards Zara.

'Shit!' Zara tried to press back into the crowd and disappear, but she needn't have worried; Dave stormed past her without a word or a look.

Breathing a sigh of relief, she turned back to see Simms glowering at Dave's retreating figure. She toyed with the idea of asking him for a quote, but after seeing the fury on Dave's face as he walked by, she decided to follow him instead.

Dave was outside now, his phone jammed to his ear.

'How could you do that without talking to me?' Dave roared. 'We always talk about everything!'

There was silence while, Zara assumed, Kim put her case forward, then Dave spoke again.

'We'll talk about this when I get home, but what you've done has put me in the spotlight. It's one thing to care for Essie's granddaughter but another completely to post bail. You and I know that you've done this off your own back. And Jack knows and Joan knows. But the people higher up, the commissioner, my boss, they don't! They'll think I sanctioned it.'

Zara listened to his outburst with ever-increasing concern. He needed to calm down—he was an older bloke and she had a sudden vision of him dropping on the spot from a heart attack. She was sure her appearance wouldn't help, though, so for now she stayed where she was.

'Kim, let's talk about this when I get home.'

He shoved the phone into his pocket. Zara watched as he bought a bottle of water from the deli over the road and found a bench and sat down. Opening the top, he took a few sips.

His chest was heaving and he wiped his brow. A few minutes later, seeming to have himself under control, he ran his fingers through his hair and glanced around before walking away from the courthouse.

All Zara could do was watch.

Chapter 16

1980

Kiz slammed another beer down.

'Here we go boys, drink up. Only twenty minutes until closing time. Should be able to get another couple in before then.'

'Thanking you, Kiz,' Ian said, raising his glass.

'Here's to your kids, Paddy,' Muzza said, raising his glass as well. That had been their toast for every drink that evening. 'What time are you heading off in the morning?' he asked, wiping the froth from his mouth.

'Get up and get going, I guess,' Ian answered. 'Not much point in hanging around with Rose and the kids if they're not coming with me. I'm pretty keen to get a move on anyway.'

He took a drink and felt Kiz's hand on his shoulder. 'She would have only slowed you down, you know, Paddy. Best you leave her here.'

Ian wanted to agree with him, but he didn't. He wanted Rose alongside him as they drove. They both loved passing the time and kilometres singing the Irish songs he'd taught her. She told him Australian folk stories and he told her Irish ones.

To be sure, this afternoon had showed him that the kids could be a pain, there was no doubting that, and he wasn't sure how he would handle their incessant screaming.

He'd had visions of coming to the house and being met with smiles and giggles from his son, not crying and them each feeding from his Rose.

When he'd seen his daughter sucking on Rose's nipple, the feeling of disgust had taken him by surprise. Ian had always loved Rose's breasts, and to see a child at them had made him never want to touch them again. He wasn't sure he wanted anything to do with her body at all.

'I hear you,' Ian said.

'You know what I reckon?' Muzza said. He swayed a little as he leaned forward, his eyes glazed.

'Nah, what?' Ian said.

'I reckon your missus is just selfish. Yeah? I mean, they're your kids too. Why wouldn't she go with you so you get to see 'em grow up. If you're on the road and in and out of sheds, you're never gonna see them. I think she should be going with yer.'

Ian nodded and held up his beer. 'True,' he agreed.

'Mate, doesn't matter. Maybe it is best if they stay here until they're a bit older. Shit, you should have heard the noise coming out of there when I turned up today. Got a good set of lungs on them both.'

The barman leaned over the counter. 'Never had anything to do with kids before, by the sound of it? You have a new baby, huh?'

Ian nodded. 'Twins.'

'Ah, your missus is the one Evie put up in her sister's house, just down the road?'

'That'd be her.'

'Kind lady, Evie.'

'Not sure about that,' Ian said, sipping his drink. 'Not good at minding her own beeswax. If it weren't for her, Rosie and the kids would have to come with me.'

'Well, if you don't mind me saying, lad, you shouldn't be taking her on the road with you. I don't know where you're going next, but she should be in a house, letting those two bubs settle into their skin. Babies take a bit to settle down.'

'Got a few, have you?'

The barman stood up tall and proud, with a large smile on his face. 'I've got seven. Three boys and four girls.'

'Good Catholics, then?' Ian asked. 'Just like my family.'

Kiz and Muzza howled with laughter.

'Maybe they haven't got a TV!'

'You can take the piss all you want,' the barman said, 'but there's nothing better than looking at a child and seeing your own eyes reflected back at you. And as they grow up, they bring a lot of joy and laughter to the place. My eldest, now he's in year seven at school and he comes in here after he's finished and helps me wash the glasses and get ready for the evening. It's our time together. Teaching him a work ethic, but he's also hanging out with his old man and I get to hear everything that's going on in his world. And you know what that makes me?'

'A mug,' Muzza said, waving his empty glass around. 'One more round, Pop.'

The barman pulled the first pint and put it on the bar, then selected a second glass.

'Not a mug. A privileged man.'

Through hazy thoughts, Ian wondered if he would ever have a relationship like that with his son. He hadn't with his own father. They'd been close enough, but not best mates like some of the boys at school.

He'd been closer to his granddad, Alroy.

Alroy Kelly been a wild-looking man—tall and strong, with flame-red hair. He didn't know why, but Ian had always remembered his rough hands running over his own red head when he was little, saying Alroy was a good name for a red-haired child. And now Ian had an Alroy he could be close to, if Rose would let him.

'A privileged man?' Muzza scoffed. 'Sounds like a lot of mollycoddling to me. What happened to tossing them out into the sheep yards and making them work?'

The barman smiled. 'If you haven't noticed, there aren't a lot of sheep yards in a pub, and my boy works, it's just that he's spending time with me when he does.'

'I'd like that,' Ian suddenly said. 'To be able to teach my young man a few things. My granddad did that for me and I remember how much I enjoyed that time with him.'

'There you go,' the barman nodded. 'You've got a sensible head on your shoulders. Children never ask to be born and so we have a responsibility to give them the best life we can.' He nodded with a smile.

Kiz turned to Ian. 'You gone soft in the head or something?'

Ian looked down at his empty glass. 'Nah, must be needing another drink.' He brushed off Kiz's comments. Geez, it was hard to be a masculine shearer and have a family. He was beginning to realise that his two mates were always going to put the family down, but he loved these two blokes almost as much as his sweet Rose. Could you love kids you'd never spent any time with yet? he wondered. Probably not, so maybe that's why he hadn't felt anything except horror when he'd walked into that house.

'There's no denying the baby stage is hard,' Ian's new friend told him.

'Let's change the bloody subject!' Kiz said, taking another drink. 'We don't care about any of this shit.'

'What stage is nice?' Ian asked.

'My favourite? About twelve months. They're beginning to walk and interact with things around them. Not so reliant on mum and they recognise you with a big smile. There's other good stages, but I always like that one. They're starting to become their own little person. Like I said, when they're really young, they take a bit to settle down.'

'There you go, Paddy,' Muzza said, slapping Ian's shoulder. 'Head off, live the good life and turn back up again in twelve months. I reckon that's the best plan I've heard!'

'Boys, I'm sorry to cut you short, but you're going to have to finish up now. Closing time.'

'Mate, you didn't give us the last-drinks call.'

'Reckon you've all had enough, don't you? And you.' He pointed at Ian. 'You'd be best to leave them if you're going to another shearing shed. Only a father without a conscience would take babes on the road. Now be off with you all.'

❧

Ian climbed into bed beside Rose. He wanted to put his arm around her and pull her to him, but he couldn't forget her sitting in the chair with a child at her breast.

She was breathing evenly, as she did when she slept, and the house was blessedly quiet.

'Rose,' he whispered. 'Sweet Rosie?'

Nothing.

He put his arm over her hip and pulled her to him.

She felt different. Soft rolls of flesh under his hands, as he explored her body. He couldn't bring himself to go higher, and he could feel she was wearing a bra anyway.

Rose muttered something and pushed his hand away.

'Come on, Rose, I'm going tomorrow,' he whispered against her hair. 'I don't know when I'll be able to see you again.'

Rose rolled towards him. 'I can't yet, Ian.'

'What do you mean you can't?'

'The doctor told me I can't for six weeks. It's only been five.'

'Five, six, won't make any difference.' He put his hands back on her waist and tried to slip them lower.

'No.' She pushed his hands away. 'I don't want to.'

'Well, suck me, then. I won't have to go anywhere near you. Or did the doctor say you can't do that too?' The drink was making him mean and he knew it, but he was so close to her and his body had responded the way it always did when he was near her, wanting her.

'No, Ian. The babies are due to be fed in an hour, I really need to sleep so I can get up for them. You've got no idea how tiring this all is. Please let me go back to sleep. And you stink like beer.' She rolled away and curled up on her side of the bed.

Ian frowned. 'Why are you feeding them in the middle of the night?'

'Because they're hungry. They don't have three meals a day, you know. Like a lamb, they need to feed lots and often. You would've known that if you'd been here.'

Ian sat up. 'Are you going to go on about that again?'

'You never came!' she cried. 'I almost died and you never came to see us!' Rose pulled the blankets around her tightly and shifted further away from him.

'I was earning money for us.'

'You were staying where it was safe. I thought I meant something to you, but I mustn't.' Her voice broke.

He wordlessly tried to put his arms over her, but she wouldn't let him.

'I . . . I don't know what to say,' he said. 'You know I love you. I've told you.'

'But you didn't come.'

'Geez.' Ian got out of bed and started to pace the floor. 'What do you want from me? I was out there trying to earn a living for us and you've got your knickers in a twist 'cause I didn't turn up at the hospital. I know you've had a hard time of it, but you're better now.'

Rose was quiet, and Ian was sure her tears had stopped. Thank goodness for that. He didn't like it when women cried. He remembered his grandmother used to do it all the time, when Alroy came home and she found out he'd spent the shopping money on the trots.

'I love you, sweet Rosie,' Ian said, hoping she was listening. 'I really do. I'm sorry I didn't come to see you and the bubs. I guess I thought it was better to stay where I was.' He sat down on her side of the bed and put his hand on her waist again. This time she didn't pull away.

'Are you sure you won't come with me? I'd like it if you did.' He felt Rose shake her head.

'No, Ian. I'm not strong enough to go with you. I'm still recovering and the doctor said I should rest as much as I can.'

'What do you do during the day?'

'The whole day is taken up with nappies and feeding and washing! And that's the real truth of it.'

The silence stretched out into the darkness.

From the back room, there was a little noise, like a snuffle, then a loud, high-pitched wail.

'There we go,' Rose said. 'He's a little early tonight. Your son is always the hungriest of the two.' She pushed the bed covers back and got up.

'Alroy.'

'Yes, Alroy.'

'Do you like that name?'

'I do. Alroy and Bridget. Lovely.'

The wailing increased and Rose started out the door.

'You're really not coming?' Ian asked as she disappeared down the hall.

'No, I'm not.'

Letting out a sigh, Ian got back into his side of the bed and pulled up the covers. He was on his own. The feeling was strange and exhilarating at the same time. And sad. Very sad.

The crying stopped and Ian imagined Rose sitting in the chair with Alroy at her breast.

'My sweet Rosie won't be alongside me,' he muttered, trying to get comfortable in the soft bed. 'I'll send money to you when I can.' His eyes flicked shut.

Chapter 17

1981

Rose put the iron down and went to check on the twins. They were in their cots—one each now. It had turned out that Bridget didn't like sharing, and she'd kept kicking and biting Alroy when he was next to her.

Both children were asleep, and Rose let out a thankful sigh. It had been a long, hard twelve months, but Dr Hooper said she and the kids were finally on the other side. She had found more energy as the months passed, even as the kids needed more from her with every day that went by.

Rose reached into the cot and stroked Bridget's ginger hair, then turned to do the same with Alroy. She watched him stretch and withdrew her hand. It was easier not to wake the babies, as much as all she wanted to do was pick them up and cuddle them, feel their soft cheeks against hers, feel love from them, rather than the emptiness and loneliness that came to her every evening when she sat down to have dinner alone and then crawled into the empty bed.

Surely, he'll be home soon, she thought. The last letter had been brief on details: *Sweet Rosie, I'm heading your way. Hopefully, I won't take too long, but I have one small shed on the way to you. How are the bubs? How are you?*

The trouble was, his letters had no return address, so she had no way to answer. The last letter had reached her three weeks after the post date; Ian could turn up at any time.

Sneaking out of the room, hoping she hadn't woken Alroy, she went back to work.

The few dollars that Ian had sent early on hadn't amounted to enough to pay the power and water, let alone feed the children and her, and it had arrived haphazardly, never to be relied on, so she had sought other income.

Evie had suggested she take in ironing, which she had; ten dollars per basket. She managed to get about ten baskets done a week. Then the cleaning of the two churches came up. Fifty dollars a week, which seemed like a fortune to Rose. A fortune, yes, but no matter how she scrimped and saved, there never seemed to be much left at the end of every week.

But she managed. Over the year, she'd found cheap fabric and bought a second-hand sewing machine. Sewing while the children were asleep, she made curtains and clothes for them and herself. She'd relied on the church op shop for things she couldn't make, like the sipper cups and children's utensils, and occasionally Evie brought her a packet of flower seeds.

Rose was happiest when her fingers were deep in the dark, rich soil of her garden. She loved pottering while the children rolled on the lawn and gurgled to her; grateful to not only have a solid base but to Evie for providing one.

Her little family didn't go out much; Rose found it difficult with the two babies together, so she usually waited until Evie was available to look after one of them and Rose would take the other with her for a quick dash to the shop or to clean the churches.

Every night, as she said her prayers, she asked God to keep Ian safe, to bring him home to her. And she thanked God for Evie. She wouldn't have coped without Evie.

Folding the pair of shorts she'd just ironed, she placed them in the basket and picked up a shirt. Glancing at the clock, she realised there was only half an hour before Mrs Foster came to pick up the ironing; she'd have to get a wriggle on and hope the kids didn't wake up early.

She sprayed starch onto the collar, then pushed the iron over the shirt, sending a whoosh of steam into her face. Ironing was therapeutic to Rose, and she often got through a whole basket without realising she'd finished. As she worked she would plan what flowers she would plant next, in which spot, daydreaming about Ian sitting on the lawn, underneath the tree, playing with the kids and then snuggling up in bed with her while the children slept.

Rose grabbed a coathanger for the shirt. Two more items to go and she was done.

Alroy made a cooing sound, and Rose knew he was awake. He would be okay in his cot for a while, playing with the activity centre Evie had bought. The telephone dial and the bell were Alroy's favourite parts, while Bridget liked the mirror on hers. She kept trying to eat her reflection.

Rose finished the ironing and put the basket on the kitchen table ready for Mrs Foster, then went to peer into the kids' room.

Just as she'd suspected, Alroy was sitting in front of his activity centre, hitting the ball, which was spinning in a blur of yellow and blue. Rose leaned against the door and watched him, a smile on her face. The likeness between Alroy and Ian was uncanny—down to their lop-sided smile and their eyes. Bridget looked more like Rose—finer features and a cute button nose. But they both had fiery red hair and occasionally the temper to match.

A knock sounded on the front door and Rose pushed herself away to answer it. Mrs Foster was always on time.

On the way past the kitchen, she picked up the basket, propping it on her hip, and pulled the door open, a smile on her face.

Mrs Foster wasn't there.

Ian was—with a large grin on his face and his arms outstretched.

'Hello, my sweet Rosie! Aren't you a sight for sore eyes?'

Rose opened her mouth but couldn't speak. Finally, after all this time, here he was ... and a feeling of resentment flared throughout her body, taking her by surprise.

'Cat got your tongue?' Ian asked, leaning forward to kiss her.

'You're back,' she managed.

'In the flesh. Aren't you going to invite me in?' He gave her a quizzical look. 'What have you got there?' He indicated the basket.

'Oh.' Rose looked down as if she had forgotten she was holding it. 'Ironing. For Mrs Foster.'

'You've taken in ironing?'

'Yes.' She stood back so Ian could come inside. 'I had to. There wasn't enough money.'

'That's all about to change, my love.' Ian bounced into the room and folded her into his arms. 'Ah, my sweet Rosie, how I've missed you.' Letting her go, he asked, 'Now, where's my boy?'

Rose pointed to the end bedroom and followed as Ian went in.

'Hello, *mo stór*,' Ian said softly.

Rose watched as he looked down into the cot and a smile spread across his face. 'My, my, aren't you a good-looking young man. Must take after your father!' He reached down and touched Alroy's fist, and the boy screwed up his face as if he were about to scream.

Rose swooped in and picked him up, holding her fingers to her lips. 'Don't wake up Bridget,' she whispered. Beckoning Ian out of the room, she went into the garden and put Alroy on the lawn.

Outside, the soft breeze calmed Rose and she smiled at Ian. 'It's good to see you. I've missed you.'

'And I have missed you.' He gathered her into his arms again and kissed the top of her head.

'How long are you here for?'

'Long enough to pack you all up and take you with me. I've got a shed over out on the Nullarbor. A big one! Nearly two months' worth and I'm on my way there now. Thought I'd pick you up and we could keep going across to Perth once I'm done there. Get some more work on the way, then head north. I've heard there're big sheds up there. Ones that aren't having the same problems as out near Broken Hill—better conditions.' His face darkened. 'Those bloody cockies over in New South Wales, they're trying to stuff things up for us. Bringing other shearers out from New Zealand. They've got different gear to us—wider combs so they're shearing more sheep than we can.'

'What does that mean?' Rose asked, sitting on the grass next to Alroy.

'Well, our combs and cutters are 'bout this wide.' He held out his thumb and pointer finger to show the width. 'And theirs are like this.' He widened his fingers about half an inch. 'When they're shearing they cover more of the sheep and get the wool off faster than we can with our combs. Upsets the whole shed; the rousies and classers aren't getting paid as much either because the sheds are finishing sooner. It's a debacle.' Ian frowned. 'Let's not talk about that. Tell me, how are you and the kids? Isn't he a little beauty?' Hooking his hands under Alroy's arms, he pulled him onto his lap and bounced him up and down.

'Alroy usually cries when anyone he doesn't know picks him up,' Rose said.

'He knows his dad when he sees him, don't you, young man?'

Cooing, Alroy reached up to touch Ian's face, putting his hands on his lips. Ian made a smacking sound and Rose looked away.

The old resentment flooded through her again. She'd been here, with the kids, scrimping and saving for a year—and he turns up, unannounced, telling her they're leaving.

'I don't want to go to Western Australia,' she blurted out. 'I'm happy here. I've made a home for these two and we're settled, Ian. I've got friends who help out when I need a break. If you want to go, then do, but please don't ask me to. The thought of travelling from shed to shed with these two is too much.' She looked up and saw the look of surprise on his face. 'Honestly, you haven't been here, so you don't know how much work goes into having babies. The washing and feeding and sleeping.' Rose looked at him in despair. 'Please don't ask me to go,' she repeated, twisting her wedding ring.

Ian looked at her, then down at her finger. 'But if you don't come I won't get to see the kids grow up.' He paused. 'Don't you want to be with me anymore? Have you met someone else?' A flicker of rage crossed his face and he carefully put Alroy on the ground and moved to sit next to Rose, taking her hand. 'Is there something you want to tell me?'

'What? No! No, Ian, that's got nothing to do with what I'm talking about. I've missed you and I'm glad you're here. But I don't want to travel all the time anymore. No more. You've got no idea how hard our old lifestyle would be with these two in tow. The thought just frightens me.'

She closed her eyes and shuddered, before drawing in a deep breath. 'In time the kids will need to go to school and then they really won't be able to be pulled and pushed all over the country.'

'I don't understand.' He was watching her, then put his hand up to her face. 'If you still love me, why wouldn't you want to be with me?'

'I haven't once said I don't want to be with you. Stay here for a week and you will see. Kids aren't playthings you can just put in the car and drive with. They'll slow you down; stops for changing nappies, a feed. You know they still cry? Can you imagine driving thousands of kilometres with a screaming baby in the back?' Tears pricked her eyes.

'Well, if you feel so strongly, Rose, I won't ask you.' He glanced at the boy, who had rolled onto his stomach and was now picking at the lawn. 'The kids . . .'

'You haven't been here for the past year,' Rose said bravely. 'You've missed a lot of their growing up anyway.' She paused. 'You don't have to go, you know. Would you . . . Would you think about staying around here? Getting a job on a farm? Please?'

Ian shook his head immediately. 'You know that's not what I like doing. I don't stay in one spot.'

Rose looked at him sadly. 'Guess we're at a stalemate, then.' She paused. 'Can I ask you something? Did you miss us at all?' The expression that passed over Ian's face told her everything she needed to know. She got up. 'I'm going to check on Bridget. It's odd she hasn't woken up yet.'

Disappearing into the house, she put her fist up against her mouth and leaned against the wall, trying to stop the sobs that wanted to rip from her. He hadn't missed her and she'd be naive to think he hadn't had other women. Maybe it was better to tell him their relationship was over.

Breathing hard to get back in control, she wiped her eyes and went in to see Bridget. Placing her hand on her head, Rose frowned. Bridget was hot to touch.

'Bridget?' She shook her a little and then reached in and picked her up. 'Bridget?'

The baby didn't open her eyes and Rose could tell now she had a fever.

'Ian,' she called, the panic plain in her voice. 'Ian? I have to take Bridget to the hospital.'

He appeared in the doorway. 'What's wrong?'

'She's got a temperature and she's not waking up. Can you stay with Alroy?'

Ian looked down at the baby in her arms and nodded. 'Best you get on, then,' he said. 'We can finish talking about this later.'

Chapter 18

2020

Dave slammed the car door, hard. He'd stewed all the way home from Adelaide, and he still wasn't sure what he was more furious about: the fact that Kim hadn't told him what was going on, or that she'd bailed Essie.

'What the fuck was she thinking?' he muttered as he stomped up the pathway.

The door opened and Kim stood there, a look of defiance on her face. He shook his head, pushing past.

'I did the right thing,' Kim said, following him inside.

'And how do you arrive at that conclusion?' Dave walked down the passage and put his briefcase on the kitchen bench before turning to face her. Blood thudded in his temples.

'Calm down, Dave. Please. You know Essie needed help.'

'She would've got all the help she needed from me *in the right capacity*.'

'You would have left her in jail?'

'Not necessarily. I was going to her bail hearing so I could speak on her behalf if I had to. Then, if she wasn't given bail, I was going to be there to reassure her everything would be all right.' He took a breath. 'Next thing I know, I'm being abused by the AFP and they're the ones telling me that my wife—*my wife*—had given the surety. How the fuck do you expect me to calm down when I'm informed about something so important as this by the arresting officer!'

Sitting at the breakfast bar, Dave tapped his fingers on the bench and looked at Kim, who had her back to him now.

'How could you not discuss this with me?' he asked. 'And why you thought it was okay to raise bail for Essie and not even let me know you had beggars belief.'

'I tried. That's when you sent the text saying you were at court and couldn't talk. I did try, Dave.'

'No, you didn't. You tried *after the fact*. After you'd been in to see Jack and signed the papers, but not before. You didn't give me an opportunity to tell you how your actions might affect me and my job.' He got up and went to the fridge, grabbing a beer. 'To get shown up by those plastics.' He shook his head in disgust.

Kim turned around, fury on her face. 'Is that what you're worried about?' she hissed. 'The fact that they knew before you did?'

'No! That wasn't ideal, but it looks like I was party to what you did, when I wasn't. And it'll cause me problems.'

'If it does, I'm sorry for that, but you knew who I was when you married me, David Burrows,' Kim shot back at him. 'I'm my own person. I make decisions without being swayed by what people think or tell me. Essie needs help. So does that little girl! How could you think I'd let an old lady languish in the cells? Surely you know me better than that. God knows what could have happened to her in there already. She's not strong! And Paris needs her here.'

'But this wasn't the way to do it,' Dave argued. 'I can't help—'

Dave's mobile phone rang. Angrily, he took it out of his pocket and looked at the screen. 'Shit,' he muttered. 'I've got to take this.' He didn't look at Kim as he answered. 'Detective Dave Burrows.'

He paused, then pounded his fist softly on the bench. 'Yes.'

Pause.

'Yes. Okay.'

Pause.

'Yes, sir. See you tomorrow, sir.' Deflated, Dave put the phone gently down on the bench.

'Dave?'

'That's wrecked that.'

Kim's tone was fearful. 'What?'

'That was the Assistant Commissioner. I have to go and see him tomorrow.'

'Oh, no, Dave. I never meant . . .'

Dave took a sip of his drink and shook his head. 'Fuck,' he whispered, looking at the kitchen counter.

Kim put her hand on his shoulder and squeezed gently. A few moments later, he put his hand on top of hers and swung around to look at her.

'For God's sake, next time something like this comes up, talk to me about what you're going to do first, okay?'

Kim nodded, her face full of concern. 'I'm sorry. I just wanted to help Essie.'

'I know.' He sighed. 'I probably knew deep down you were going to pull something like this. To bail Essie is just the sort of thing you'd do.' Dave looked up at her. 'And that's the sort of thing that made me want to marry you.' He stood and drew her into a hug.

Dave pulled his car up at the police station, the humiliation of the Assistant Commissioner's words still stinging after the four-hour drive back from Adelaide.

His sat tapping his fingers on the steering wheel, then reached over and rifled through the glove box to see if he could find any mints. Actually, what he was doing was delaying seeing Jack. He'd already texted Kim with the news.

'Just rip the bandaid off, Burrows,' he muttered to himself.

The wind tried to tear the car door from his hands as he got out, but he held on tightly, retrieving his briefcase and wallet.

'You're back,' Jack said from behind him.

Turning around, Dave nodded. 'Well, that's stating the obvious,' he said with a grin.

'How'd you go?'

'Come inside first. It's bloody cold. What's happened here today?'

'Not too much. Did a highway patrol out near Port Augusta. Got a couple speeding and one with mobile-phone use. A P-plater texting. Know how I got her?'

'How?' Dave pushed open the door, nodded to Joan and headed towards his office, Jack following.

'She was on the wrong side of the road coming around a corner.'

'They never learn, do they? What'd you say to her?'

'That I really didn't want to be informing her parents that she'd been involved in a fatality, which is what it would have been if I hadn't been watching and on my game. Unless I'd been killed too.'

'And the response?'

'"I wasn't texting."'

Dave shook his head and closed his eyes. 'They think we're stupid sometimes—as if we haven't heard every excuse in the book. Did you give her a ticket?'

'Sure did. Said I had the authority to look at her phone and I'd be able to see at what time any text message had been sent or if she'd been texting in the last five minutes, which would have been while she was driving. Funnily enough she didn't give me any trouble after that.'

'Good job.' Dave sat down heavily, and Jack did the same, looking at him expectantly. 'Well, I'm out,' he said.

Jack reared back in his chair. 'What do you mean "out"?'

'I can't have anything to do with the Essie Carter case. Or anything to do with her at all. Can't even be seen to be talking to her.'

Relaxing, Jack sank back into his chair opposite Dave. 'I thought you meant you were out of the force.'

'Oh, don't worry, Simms would like to see that happen.' Dave leaned forward and put his elbows on his desk. 'He's put in a report on me. Said I interfered with his arrest right from the beginning. Can't see what's in front of my face. You know, the sob-story bullshit he went on with when he was here. Twisted my words, et cetera, et cetera.' He waved his hand as if he didn't care. 'Oh, and let's not forget he thinks I'm past it.'

'What did the AC say to you?'

'Formally instructed me to stay away from everything to do with the case. And to keep Kim away from anything like this again. Nothing I wasn't expecting. A bit of a rap over the knuckles. But I'm not going to be able to help Essie in any way.' He rubbed his hand over his chin and gave a heavy sigh. 'And that gives me the shits because there must be a reason Essie has done what she's done. There is no way she'd take possession of drugs by choice.'

Jack was silent.

'I wonder where Melissa got to after you pulled her out of that car and saved her life,' he finally asked.

Dave shook his head. 'No idea. But Essie did say she was frightened to talk to anyone. That should have raised my antenna in regards to Melissa. I stuffed that up.' He paused.

'I should have tried to find Melissa, but now I can't do anything.'

'You didn't know this was going to happen.'

'You're right there. Anyway, going back to the AC, he said a few more things you might be interested in.'

Jack looked at him expectantly.

'Well, he agrees with me. What sixty-plus woman with no priors would be importing drugs without a reason? Something isn't sitting right with him either, and we all know as coppers we have to trust our gut and then find the evidence to back that feeling up.' He ran his hand through his hair. 'It's a pain in the arse, because we still can't do anything, even knowing he agrees with us.'

Jack frowned and jiggled a knee up and down. 'If you and I and the AC see it, why can't the Feds see it?'

'All they're interested in is a conviction. They don't care about causal triggers. Just statistics. They've made an arrest and that'll go towards making them look good.'

'That's fucked.'

'That's the plastics.' Dave shrugged. 'And, look, it's not just me who's been warned off. It's both of us.'

'Why?' Jack looked incensed. 'I haven't done anything.'

'Guilt by association. That's the way it is, mate. We're going to have to run with it.'

'I wonder if the darling daughter might be black-mailing her mother into buying the drugs for her,' Jack said thoughtfully.

Giving a ghost of a smile, Dave said, 'Now, Jack, you're beginning to sound like me.'

Jack laughed. 'Don't think that's a bad thing,' he said.

'Well, I guess a rap over the knuckles is better than being booted off altogether. Anyway, I've got an idea.'

'You've always got ideas, Dave. What is it?'

'I think I should set up a meeting with Zara.'

'What the hell? What for?' His tone was high with shock.

'We can't give Essie the help she needs. If we're seen to be involved, the boss will cut us off at the knees. But Zara's an investigative journo and can look into this as a public-interest story.'

Jack watched him before speaking. 'That doesn't sound like you.'

'I know. Desperate times call for desperate measures. I just don't see any other way of helping Essie—I can't even be in the same room as her.'

Jack nodded his understanding, then rubbed his head as if he had a headache.

'I'm not sure how Zara and I are going at the moment,' he said quietly.

'Yeah, Kim told me what she saw the other night.'

'Oh yeah.' Jack fiddled with the ruler on his desk but didn't look at Dave.

'Just because you think something doesn't mean that the first conclusion is the right one. Look at all the cases we solve. If you love someone you've got to trust them.'

'Yeah, good idea. Just like you and Kim,' Jack bristled.

Dave harrumphed. 'Touché.'

Chapter 19

Jack opened up the *Farming Telegraph* and flicked through the first couple of pages, past stories about seeding rates and fertiliser applications, past the barley price and the planned inquiry for the egg industry. Scanning for stories written by Zara was a habit he'd picked up when they first got together.

Early on in their relationship, Jack had told Zara that he'd never been much of a reader or a writer. 'Only writing I do is the reports I have to,' he'd told her over dinner. 'And I read fishing magazines.'

'Do you fish?'

'Nope.'

She'd laughed at him that night and told him he was weird, but in a nice way. He still remembered how she'd leaned forward and kissed him, her long hair tickling his arm.

How had something so good gone so wrong in a matter of days, he wondered. Still, looking back, he was sure Zara had started to change about six months after Will died. Her face had always been open, a smile ready, but as time had gone on her frown became permanent and the laughter stopped. Unless she'd had a bit to drink. And that was the other unusual thing: she was drinking much more than Jack had ever known her to.

Work was really all she focused on. Kim had mentioned something to him about it a few months back, but Jack had dismissed her concerns, because Zara hadn't said anything. He was sure she would have talked to him if there was something wrong.

Flicking the page over, a shiver of horror ran through his body.

There was Zara's name under the story about Jesse. Not just her name, but a photo of her and Jesse together. Jesse had his arm around Zara's shoulders.

Jack wanted to slam the paper shut, but some morbid fascination took over him. He leaned forward.

Zara was smiling up at Jesse as he stood in front of the shearing shed and looked straight at the camera. What was Zara even doing in the photo? She was the journalist, not the subject of the story and, as far as he knew, she'd never worked with a photographer before. Had she asked someone to take a photograph of them together?

The next photo was of Zara and Jesse crouched over a wether, sweat dripping from his forehead and glistening on his arms. The creamy wool was piled on the board and the look on the sheep's face was one of confusion, while it waited for the haircut to finish.

Jack turned his attention to Zara. Her smile was wide and she was leaning in towards Jesse.

Shaking his head, Jack couldn't think. What he was seeing didn't make any sense. Who took the photo? He felt as if an invisible hand was squeezing his heart.

Turning his attention to the story, he read.

> Jesse Barnett has travelled the length and breadth of this land since he was sixteen years old. There wouldn't be many people who have seen as many sights as he has.
>
> He's breathed the agricultural industry since he was born: life started for Jesse on the wide outback plains of Wilcannia on Palcarinya Station. Here he was taught through School of the Air, alongside the other children on the station, but his real education came on the land . . .

He didn't get any further before throwing down the magazine in disgust.

'Hey, what's got your goat?' Dave said, looking up from his desk.

'Nothing,' Jack snapped.

'Sure doesn't look like it.'

'I just need to go and see Zara about something.' He picked the paper up and put it under his arm.

'Maybe ask her to come and see me when she's got a spare moment.'

'You're really going to go ahead with that idea?'

'Yeah, I thought about it overnight.' Dave nodded. 'But you're not to have anything to do with what I'm doing. Just ask her to come and see me, then get the hell out of there. You guys not talking might be a good thing once this starts to play out.'

Jack nodded. 'Fine.'

❧

Dialling Zara's number, Jack listened to the ring tone, before putting the car into gear and turning on to the main street.

'Hey,' Zara answered the phone.

Jack's heart rate kicked up a notch. Her voice was so familiar, it made him want to go to her and touch her.

'Hey, what are you up to?' He struggled to keep his tone even.

'Just about to head out to interview the boss of the Port Augusta grain handlers. The forecast for the harvest is due to come out today.'

'Right.'

Silence hummed between them. 'Have you got time for a chat before you go?'

'If you want. I'm still at home.'

Jack flicked his blinker on and did a U-turn. 'I'm coming now. I'll be there in two minutes.' He jabbed at the disconnect button and ran his hand nervously through his hair. How was he supposed to start this conversation?

Butterflies flickered through his stomach as he waved to Kim, who was just coming out her front door as he pulled into Zara's driveway.

Zara was standing in the doorway. Jack took a breath, looking at her. She was gorgeous, and he couldn't stop the white-hot anger that flooded through him at the thought of the photo.

He picked up the *Farming Telegraph* and glanced over his shoulder as he got out of the car. Kim had retreated quickly back inside.

'Hi,' Zara said.

Jack swallowed. 'Hi.'

'Coming in?'

'Yes.'

Zara pushed the door open wider and walked towards her office.

Jack followed her, tapping the *Farming Telegraph* on his palm.

Leaning against her desk, she watched him, not smiling. He could tell she was waiting for him to start. He opened his mouth, intending to ask quietly about the photo. What came out instead was pent-up fury and hurt.

'What the fuck is this story?' He threw the newspaper on her desk, and opened it to the photo.

'That's the story I did on Jesse.' Zara crossed her arms.

'I can see that. I wasn't really interested in the story. More the photo. Seen it?'

Giving a ghost of a smile, she nodded. 'It's my story, of course I've seen it.'

'Looks like you've got stars in your eyes.'

'Oh, for God's sake, Jack, you're jealous over a photo? That's my job—to get people to talk, and if it means I play nice and smile or buy them a few drinks, then that's what I do.'

'Yeah, do they all get to take you home afterwards?' He was breathing heavily now, blood thumping in his ears.

Zara looked down. 'I told you, nothing happened.'

'But this photo looks like you wanted it to.'

'Don't be stupid, Jack! I love you. If you remember, I came straight to you and told you the next morning. I got drunk, and he made sure I got home okay. End of story.'

Now it was his turn to be quiet. The anger simmering in his stomach meant he had to stop talking because he might say something he shouldn't. And really, if Dave's plan was going to get put into motion, he shouldn't even be here.

He changed the subject.

'Dave wants to see you.' He turned away from her and started towards the door.

'Oh, yeah, what have I done now?'

'What?' He turned back to see her looking at him, the defiance in her face. That comment was so un-Zara like.

'Pissed him off again, have I? Surely not, I haven't been near the police station, or him.'

Frustration trickled through him. 'God, you're angry. All I know is he asked if I could ask you to go and see him.'

'What about us? I thought we were talking about us.'

'No, I don't think I want to talk about us now.'

'Why not?' she challenged. 'I've already told you everything and you're the one who told me to leave the other night. Ball's in your court.'

'I think we both need a bit of time to calm down, a bit of air. Zara, you've changed and I'm just not sure what's going on with you, so let's leave it until you've been to see Dave and you hear what he wants.' He paused and gave her a sad smile. 'We'll deal with us when the time's right. But,' he looked at her steadily, 'if you want any type of relationship with Dave on a professional level, you need to go and see him.'

Her defiance changed to curiosity. 'Why can't you tell me?'

'Oh, Zara!' His frustration was clear. 'Didn't you just hear me? Go and see Dave.'

'Hang on, before I go and do that, I want to know where *we* are. And don't give me that crap about now not being the right time. If you're angry with what I did, then you should say so.'

'I don't know what I am, and I really don't want to have this conversation now. I've got to get on. See you later.'

'What's that supposed to mean? You're too busy to talk about us? Aren't we more important?'

'Look, all I'm going to say is that not talking at the moment might be mutually beneficial.' He held up his hand. 'I'm not saying anything more, so don't bother asking me.'

He left the house and quickly moved to his car. As he opened the door he looked back and saw Zara standing in the doorway, tears on her cheeks.

He started the car and reversed out before he could race back in there to give her a hug and whisper in her ear that he loved her, to tell her it didn't matter about the photo or the fact Jesse had walked her home and that he really did believe nothing had happened.

He just couldn't escape the nagging feeling that Zara had changed, maybe forever.

Chapter 20

Kim waited in the car until the bus pulled into the stop and the doors sprang open. The driver got out and opened up the underneath to get out the bags, while two young girls in school uniforms followed.

Their mothers were there waiting and Kim recognised the girls as locals who attended boarding school, home for the weekend.

She smiled as the girls hugged their mums, chatting about the homework they had and life at school.

Looking into the bus, she saw Essie holding on tightly to the back of the seats as she slowly made her way to the front.

'Come on, Paris,' she said, opening the door. 'I can see your grandma coming.'

'She's nearly here?'

The excitement in her voice broke Kim's heart. None of this should have ever happened.

As Essie's first foot hit the ground, Paris ran from Kim and threw her arms around her grandmother.

'Granny! I've missed you. Where have you been? How come you've been gone so long?'

'Oh, my darling girl.' Essie's voice broke as she put her arms around the little girl and hugged her tightly.

Kim pointed to a bag on the ground. 'This one yours?' she asked, and Essie nodded, mouthing *thank you*.

'Come on, darling, let's get home, shall we?' Essie held out her arms to Kim. 'Oh, my goodness, Kim, thank you. Thank you.' The older woman's voice caught again. 'You can't know how grateful I am to you and Dave.'

Kim hugged her. 'There was no way I wasn't going to help, Essie,' she said quietly.

'Help do what?' Paris asked.

'It's grown-up talk, darling,' Essie said as they made their way to the car. 'Did I tell you how pleased I am to see you?' She took a firm hold of Paris's hand. 'I am very, *very* glad to see you. How has school been?'

'Okay. My friends have been asking where you've been. Why were you away for so long, Granny?' Paris queried again as they climbed into the car. 'Did the police take a long time to ask questions?'

Kim smiled and answered before Essie could. 'Yes, they took far too long.'

She glanced over at Essie and saw tears in her eyes, which made anger well up inside her. She reached across to take her friend's hand. 'It's going to be okay,' she said. 'You're home and safe now.' Looking in the rear-vision mirror she saw that Paris was looking out of the window, distracted now. 'Was it awful?' she whispered to Essie.

Essie nodded. 'You've got no idea.'

❧

Pulling up at the house, Essie sighed. 'The old place has never looked so good.'

Kim laughed. 'There's no place like home, that's for sure.'

Putting the key in the lock, Essie pushed the faded blue door open and put her bag on the floor. 'Yes,' she said, looking around, 'no place like it.'

Paris ran through to the kitchen and Kim followed, hoisting shopping bags onto the bench. 'I've made a few meals for you and got all the essentials, so you won't have to go anywhere for a couple of days if you don't feel like it.'

'Did you bring the chocolate cake I helped make, Kim?' Paris asked. 'I made a chocolate cake, Granny. Kim let me mix it with a wooden spoon, then I got to eat the mixture.'

'Did you? Was it yummy?'

'It was the best!'

Essie laughed, but Kim heard the sob behind it.

'Paris, can you run out to the car and bring your school bag in please, honey?' Kim asked.

When the little girl had gone, Kim turned to Essie and drew her into a hug. 'I know you've been through a lot, Essie. You make sure you come and talk to me any time. About anything. There's always space at my kitchen table for you when you need it.'

'I don't know what I would've done if you hadn't posted the bail . . .' Her voice trailed off.

'You needed to be back with Paris as soon as possible.' Kim's voice was gentle.

'I hope I haven't caused you any problems, financially. You're so kind, Kim.'

'It was my pleasure. Like I said, Paris needed you back.'

Essie filled the kettle and took a cup out of the cupboard. 'Do you want one?'

'Yeah, that would be nice.'

Kim could see the act of doing something normal was calming for Essie.

'I really want to go and see Dave, to thank him as well. Will he be at the station tomorrow?'

Paris came flying through the door. 'I get to sleep in my bed tonight!'

The two women laughed.

'Yes, you do,' Essie said. 'Now, go and unpack your bag. Put your dirty clothes in the basket and then you can come and cut me a piece of that cake you made.'

'Okay, Granny.'

When the kitchen was quiet and Essie had put a cup of tea in front of Kim, she spoke. 'Essie, nothing is wrong, but I need to tell you something.'

Essie's head shot up and her eyes showed fear.

'What is it?'

'Dave can't come and see you, and you can't go and see him,' Kim answered carefully.

'Why? Is it because you posted bail? Oh, no. I'm so sorry.'

Kim covered Essie's hand with her own.

'Dave's in some trouble and I've caused him a lot of embarrassment because I posted your bail. As a detective's wife, doing something like that isn't a conflict of interest, but the way it happened made the Assistant Commissioner call him in for a talk. They're not allowing him to have anything to do with you until this case is over. So, if you want to come and see me, just call first to make sure Dave isn't home.'

Essie had her hand over her mouth.

'Don't worry, Essie. It's fine, we can work around it, but I'm going to ask that you don't contact him. You know that we're here to help but if you need to talk, come to me, not Dave.'

'He hasn't lost his job?'

'Oh, no! Not at all. In fact, I think he's out patrolling as we speak. He knew I was coming to pick you up. Me seeing you, or helping you, isn't a problem.'

Paris came running back into the kitchen and threw her arms around Essie. 'I've done it all, Granny.'

'Good girl. Now, where's that cake? You'd better cut us all a piece of that and tell me about what you've done at school while I've been gone.'

Paris looked at Kim.

'Ah, it's in the esky in the boot. I'll go and get it. That esky will be far too heavy for you, young lady!'

'I've got muscles,' Paris said, putting her arms in a position to show off her biceps.

'I know you do. The way you stirred that mixture, your muscles were very clear! But I don't know that even you can carry this. Sit and tell Granny about school while I go and bring it inside.'

She got up and went out the door, pausing to look at the photos on the wall. Essie's wedding photo was in the middle, surrounded in an oval by others. Mr Clippers was dressed in a suit and Essie was in a modest white dress, holding a sprig of roses. The background showed greenery, perhaps a park. They were smiling at each other, not looking at the camera. To the left, Paris's baby photos took pride of place, then one each year, tracking her growth. In the first school photo, Paris had her hair pulled back in a tight ponytail, and the next one showed a gap where her front tooth should have been.

To the right, there were two photos of a young woman. Kim could see the resemblance to Paris and assumed this was Essie's daughter.

'Where's the cake, Kim?' Paris called.

'Coming right up.'

Out at the car, Kim popped the boot and got out the esky. She'd been right, it was heavy. Inside it were over a week's worth of meals that Kim had cooked, then frozen, along with two cakes and three batches of biscuits. Essie wouldn't have to worry about Paris's recess and lunches for a little while.

'Hello.'

A woman dressed in a tracksuit jogged past and Kim smiled at her.

'Cold day,' she said.

'That's what makes the running good. Keeps me warm,' she puffed back.

Kim watched her go, wondering who she was. Maybe a tourist at the caravan park.

Picking up the esky, she took it back inside, where Paris was still talking as fast as she could. Kim handed Paris the container with the cake inside and started to put the meals in the freezer.

'Here we go.'

'You're so kind, Kim. This is all a bit overwhelming.'

'Here, Granny.' Paris held out the cake.

'Well, well, that looks yummy. That icing is . . . bright.'

Kim laughed. 'We had fun with red food colouring, didn't we? Your granddaughter seemed to think it was your favourite colour.'

'And she'd be right. I love red roses and any red flower, don't I, darling?'

'Granny's got a whole garden bed just full of red flowers.'

'Does she? Now she's got a red cake too.'

Kim sat back down and pointed to the photos on the wall. 'That's your daughter?'

'Yes, that's Melissa,' she said quietly.

'How's she going?'

'She's fine, as far as I know.' Essie took another bite of the cake. 'Paris, darling, can you take your cake outside and play out there for a little while? Kim and I need to have some grown-up talk.'

Paris frowned. 'Why can't I hear it?'

'Because it's adult conversation,' Essie answered. 'Go on with you now.'

Paris stomped through the kitchen and down the hallway, before slamming the door on the way out.

'Little miss,' Essie muttered. 'Anyone would think she was a teenager already.'

'You've done a beautiful job in raising her, Essie. Her manners are impeccable and she loved helping out.'

'Having a young one around when I'm on the wrong side of sixty—well, it's been a bit of a struggle. But when life doesn't give you any options, you do what you have to. I'd do anything for my family.'

'Well, she adores you.'

'It's the teenage bit that worries me. I'm frightened I'm too old to raise her. I've already had a go at caring for a teenager and I didn't do so well on that front. And these days? Well, what do I know about mobile phones and the internet? Not much. How am I supposed to guide her through that time?'

'You've got a few years before you have to worry. I'm sure you'll have all the support you need when the time comes.' Kim gave a smile. 'Where is Melissa now? Does she ever contact you?'

'I haven't heard from her since she discharged herself from the hospital.' Tears glistened in her eyes again. 'I keep hoping that I'll hear from her one day. That I'll pick up the phone and it will be her voice on the other end.' She was silent for a few moments. 'I pray for her every day. I'm sure if she had ... died, I would have heard.' Her voice trailed off, her pain hanging in the air. 'Someone would have found me. Told me. Wouldn't they?'

The thought of having a child in the morgue, unclaimed, must haunt her daily, Kim thought. She took a sip of her tea as the silence lengthened.

Finally, Essie looked up. 'Kim, there's something I need to get off my chest. Like I said, you've been so kind, it's only fair you know the truth.'

Kim's heart started to race and she put down her cup. 'I'd be happy to listen.'

Essie followed suit and seemed to square her shoulders before she lifted her head and stared straight at Kim. 'I had to—'

The shrill sound of the phone made them both jump and Essie slumped down. 'Darn it all.'

'Leave it, if you like.' Kim didn't want the momentum broken.

'Better answer the call, just in case. Hello?'

Kim watched as Essie suddenly turned away from her and hunched her shoulders. Her heart ached for the woman who obviously lived in daily hope that every phone call would bring news of her daughter.

'Yes, of course, I understand.' She put the phone down, her hand shaking, but kept her back to Kim.

Kim stood up and went to her. 'What is it, Essie? What's wrong?'

Essie didn't answer but went to the window. Kim stood behind her, looking out onto the empty street.

Reaching out, Essie yanked the curtains closed and turned around, leaning against the bench, her hand covering her heart.

'Essie?'

She shook her head and went back to the table. Grasping Kim's hand, she said, 'I need to ask you to leave now, Kim. Please don't ask any questions. I can't talk to you. Just go.' She walked to the front door and held it open for Kim.

Staring, Kim said, 'What just happened, Essie? Who's frightening you? I want to help you—haven't I shown that?'

There wasn't any answer and there didn't seem to be a choice, so Kim picked up her handbag and walked out the door.

'You know where I am when you need me,' she said quietly. 'Say goodbye to Paris.'

Again, Essie didn't answer; she just shut the door and left Kim standing outside, wondering what had terrified Essie so badly.

Chapter 21

Dave came in the front door, a spring in his step. Tonight, they didn't have Paris for the first time in a few days. He wouldn't have to watch what he said, or make sure he was fully dressed when he walked out in the morning. His home was his castle, and Dave liked it when it was only him and Kim there.

'Hi, honey,' he said, dropping a kiss on Kim's head. She was sitting at the kitchen bench, a glass of wine in front of her, looking out the window.

'Hi,' she said softly, not looking over.

Dave paused. 'Something wrong?'

'Yeah, I think there is.' Kim took a sip of wine and turned towards him as he took a beer from the fridge. 'I met Essie off the bus today, like I told you I was going to,' Kim said.

'How is she?'

'Shaken, scared but glad to be home. Dave,' Kim said, leaning forward, 'I thought she was going to talk. She told me I deserved to know the truth, but then a phone call came through and she wouldn't. Kicked me out of the house before I could say boo!'

'Is that right?' Dave took the top off his beer and had a long sip. 'How long did the phone call last?'

'A minute. Tops.'

'Did she say anything?'

'Yeah, something about "I understand", but I couldn't tell you exactly. I wasn't paying attention until she hung up. Do you think someone is watching her here in Barker? I mean, how could they even have known she was home? We didn't know when she was coming until she rang this morning.'

Dave walked over to her and swung the seat around until she faced him. Brushing her hair back from her face, he looked down at her, seeing the concern in her eyes. He kissed her lips, each cheek and each eye, before resting his lips on her forehead.

'Don't worry. I've got an idea, and I'm working on it. We'll make sure we get to the bottom of whatever's going on.'

Kim leaned back and looked at him. 'David Burrows, what are you doing? You've been told to stay away from this.'

'I know and I can't tell you what my plan is.'

'Mr Mysterious.'

Dave could see that she was trying to be flippant, but his beautiful wife was worried.

'It's better this way, Kim. You have to trust me.'

Kim closed her eyes and shook her head, then took another sip of wine. 'It's a good thing I do.'

Dave sat next to her and squeezed her leg. 'Have you seen Zara?'

'No. Oh, that's right!' Kim turned to him with a look of glee in her eyes. 'But what I did see was Jack going to talk to her late this afternoon. I was just about to go and pick up Essie and he parked in her driveway. I hightailed it back inside because I didn't want him thinking I was watching them or anything.'

Dave grinned. 'Nothing like a bit of gossip to get you excited.'

'It's not gossip—I'm *hoping* they've worked it out.'

'Well, that's all up to them, isn't it? I did have a bit of a chat to Jack today, but I don't know how much went in. Anyway, leave them to their own devices. It won't surprise me if this takes a little bit to work out.' He took a sip of beer. 'I need to go and see Zara before I head off in the morning.'

'Now who's interfering?' Kim raised an eyebrow at him, and he cocked one back before raising his beer in a salute to her.

❧

It was seven in the morning when Dave's phone beeped with a text message.

Jack said you wanted to see me. What time suits?

Getting the voice-to-text app up, Dave spoke into the phone. *I can come to you in half an hour?*

Okay.

Kim came out of the shower, towelling her hair dry. 'You on the move already?'

Dave told her what he was doing, before giving her a kiss. 'Hey, by the way—' he patted her on the bum '—you're an incredible lover,' he whispered. 'I never get sick of making love to you.'

Pursing her lips into a pout, Kim kissed him back. 'That's lucky because the feeling's mutual.'

Dave raced through breakfast and then walked across the street to knock on Zara's door.

He heard her footsteps on the wooden floorboards and the door creaked open. 'Good morning,' she said, squinting in the sunlight.

'Good morning to you,' Dave walked in without being invited. 'Have you got the coffee pot on?'

'I thought you would've brought one with you, since you're so fussy about coffee.' Zara turned away and Dave got the distinct impression she was pissed off.

'You've got a machine. Thought I'd test it out.' He leaned against the kitchen bench as Zara filled the coffee maker with water and put the milk on to froth. Dave could see she was burning to ask questions but wouldn't give him the pleasure.

One stubborn bloke, one stubborn girl.

Silence filled the kitchen until Zara handed him a cup of coffee and stood back, her arms crossed, and looked at him.

'So, what can I do for you?'

'Feeling a little prickly this morning, Zara?' Dave asked.

'You've been pretty prickly with me the last few times I've seen you.'

'It's not personal.'

'I'm sure this visit isn't personal either.'

Dave looked at her and a thought started in the back of his mind. *When did Zara become so cynical?* he wondered. She always used to be smiling. Will's death had hit her hard, of course, but there was something more.

'Okay, okay.' He took a sip of his coffee and put it on the bench. 'I've told you from the start that when I have something for you, I'll let you know.'

'Yep.'

The one-word answer reminded Dave of his first wife, Melinda. Her one-word answers were sharp enough to sink a submarine. Zara's could have too.

'Jack would have told you we've been formally advised not to have anything to do with the investigation regarding Essie Carter.'

'All Jack said was I had to come and see you.'

Nodding, Dave picked up his mug again and took another sip. 'This is good coffee, Zara. Really good.'

'Yep.'

Dave sighed. 'Right. The reason he couldn't tell you much is because I hadn't given him the information. I'm protecting him. Like I said, we've been instructed not to have anything more to do with the investigation and so to look out for Jack I won't involve him in anything further to do with Essie. If it all goes pear-shaped . . . well, I'm close to retirement. Jack's not and I refuse to jeopardise his career.'

'You're talking in riddles.'

'Let me ask you: Do you think Essie would have willingly received those drugs?'

Zara shrugged. 'Who knows? Stranger things have happened.'

'Okay, well, since now you're the one being obtuse and I'm here with an olive branch, I'll answer the question. No. She detested drugs. I know this for a fact. Now, again, do you think she would have willingly received drugs?'

'No.' Zara looked at the floor.

'Okay, so we're on the same page. She didn't do it willingly. Now if I were able to, I'd do some background work on this case. Find out where Essie's daughter is, see if she's still on the gear, try to trace it back to why Essie received those drugs.' Dave paused, until Zara looked back up at him. 'But you see, I can't. I'm off the case.'

Narrowing her eyes, Zara asked, 'What are you involving me in? What are you involving Jack in?'

'That's my point—I'm not involving Jack in anything. If you want to participate in this it's your choice. But I think you'll want to.' He paused to look at her levelly before saying deliberately, 'If anyone finds out I'm even speaking to you about this investigation, I'll lose my job.'

'I don't get it, Dave. Why are you doing this? You're anti journalists and now you're turning into a source?'

'I strongly believe Essie is being manipulated, blackmailed even. As an investigative journalist you have the licence to do just that, investigate.' He took a piece of paper from his pocket and waved it at her. 'We only speak face to face. Don't come into the police station, don't ring me. Or Jack either, unless you're discussing personal issues. As hard as it may be, maybe you and Jack need to put your relationship on hold for a bit, because the last thing we need is the AFP implying he's involved. I know you'll understand that.'

He was taken aback when he saw tears on Zara's cheeks.

'I don't even know if we've got a relationship anymore.'

'Ah.' Dave looked at her, wanting to give her a hug, but knowing he couldn't. 'Are you okay, Zara? I can't help feeling there's something going on with you.'

'What? Nothing. I'm fine.' She swallowed and refocused. 'What can you tell me? What am I looking for?'

Ah, there we have it. Back on safe ground with work. Not wanting to feel anything. I reckon I know what's going on, he thought before answering her questions.

'I haven't got anything concrete, but I firmly suspect that Essie's involvement is connected to her daughter.'

'You alluded to that earlier. But why? You must have something to back it up.'

'Do you remember I pulled her out of a car when she OD'd?'

Zara shook her head. 'No, I wasn't here then, but I've heard the story.'

'Melissa was a recovering heroin addict and she came back here to escape that lifestyle. Paris was a year old. Unfortunately, one of Melissa's previous associates followed her here and got her back on drugs.

211

'The cowardly bastard didn't even bother to call an ambo when she OD'd, he just left her there. Before I could interview her at the hospital, she discharged herself and disappeared. We don't know where she is. I made some enquiries not long after she left, but it was as if she'd vanished off the face of the Earth. But I don't think that's the case. You know why?'

'Because she's the common thread here. She's an addict, and there's heroin being delivered to her mother's place.'

By the excitement on Zara's face, Dave knew he had her.

'You're spot on. Either she's blackmailing her mum so the drugs can be collected from the house or someone is using her to manipulate Essie.'

'You want me to do your work.' A statement not a question. 'You can't do it, so you want me to.'

Dave shook his head. 'No, Zara. I want you to do *your* work. You can keep doing airy-fairy stories for the *Farming Telegraph* or you can do some balls-to-the-wall, hard-core investigative journalism. I know that's what you really like doing. That's what you're good at.' He paused before throwing out the last bit of bait. 'Who knows, at the end of it, there might be a really good story here. An award-winning story.'

Zara walked to the window, her arms crossed and her brow a little furrowed. Dave knew she was thinking hard. After what seemed like an eternity, she spun around on her heel and stared at him. 'What do you want me to do?'

'Just your job. Find out about Essie's family—her daughter. I can't do this for you, and you can't use my name. If it gets back that I'm talking to you, I'm done. That's why Jack can't have any involvement. I'm not fucking around, you hear?'

'Yeah, I understand.' She grabbed a notepad from the bench and plucked a pen from next to the phone. 'What's the daughter's name? Melissa?'

'Melissa Carter, born 23 January 1980. Not sure where, but I think it was down south. You'll know how to find what you need to with that.'

'Down south as in South Australia?'

'Yeah, but that isn't concrete. I'm going on memory, from what Essie told me a few years ago and of course I can't check the police records.'

'Right.' Zara scribbled a few more notes down and looked over at Dave. He could see her fingers were itching and suppressed a smile. This investigation was now underway.

'I'll leave you to it,' Dave said, swallowing the last mouthful of coffee.

'Wait, that piece of paper. What's on it?'

'Nothing. Just a bit of enticement.' He grinned at her. 'Hey, before I go, I just want to say when this is over you and Jack need to work things out. You're good for each other.'

'Yeah, well, that's his call,' Zara replied dismissively.

'Actually, Zara, it's mostly yours.' He fished out a card from his wallet and handed it over. 'Give this woman a call. I think you'll find she can help you.'

'A psychologist?' She didn't hide her contempt as she tossed the card onto the coffee table.

'Yeah, who specialises in post-traumatic stress disorder.' He paused. 'When did you last sleep through the night?'

Zara looked down.

'Yeah, thought so. Nightmares? Thinking about Will's funeral, or when he died, all the time? Maybe the car accident when your dad was killed?'

She still didn't answer.

'Zara, it's easier to get help now than it will be in four or five or even twenty years' time. Don't push the people who love you away because you're struggling. Okay?'

He patted her shoulder and left the house.

Chapter 22

Zara had spent the morning googling, but she hadn't got far. Essie had lived a quiet life in a quiet country town. She didn't have a Facebook page or Twitter account.

The closest Essie had ever come to fame was when she'd had her photo taken for the local paper, the *Barker Times*—which had gone the way a lot of regional newspapers and didn't exist anymore. On an historical website, Zara had found a copy of the *Barker Times* that showed a young Essie smiling into the camera, holding a bunch of prize-winning red roses at the Barker Show.

Zara had pored over the photo, trying to find some hint of who Essie had been before she'd become mother to Melissa and grandmother to Paris—but there were no clues.

Then she'd researched birth announcements for Melissa Carter. She'd come up with thirty-two hits in South Australia among the more than four hundred Australia-wide, but none of them matched the limited information that Zara had of the family. By the time she'd rubbed her tired eyes and stretched just after lunch, she knew she would have to go to the source herself—Essie—and she would have to make her approach carefully.

Now, as Zara sat in her car parked near the school, the bell sounded and the laughs and squeals from the younger children reached her above the whistle of the ever-present cold wind. She watched as the kids ran out into the school yard, excited to be free for another day. Most of them were wrapped in thick jumpers and beanies, but she noticed a few of the older boys were too cool for that and were mooching along in short-sleeved shirts, their backpacks swung over their shoulders.

Cars were lined up next to the netball courts, ahead of the buses ready to carry the farm kids home.

From her vehicle, Zara looked at each child. She knew a lot of the kids at the school, more the older ones. She had never met Paris, though; indeed she had only met Essie once. She knew her by sight, of course; knew that she arranged the flowers at the church and volunteered for Meals on Wheels during the week, but Zara and Essie had only had one conversation, many years ago. If Essie even knew who Zara was, she would be surprised.

Zara spotted Essie as the older woman stepped out of her car and walked over towards the throng of kids, a large smile on her face.

A little girl with brown curly hair and a red beanie ran across calling out, 'Granny!'

There we are, Zara thought, smiling to herself when Essie bent down to hug her granddaughter.

Zara could see that Paris talked constantly as she walked alongside her grandmother, her school bag on her shoulders almost tipping her backwards in the wind.

A couple of other mothers took one look at Essie and directed their children away from her, the distrust clear on their faces. The women were gathered in a clutch, their heads close, occasionally glancing towards Essie and shaking their heads.

Zara watched Essie's face crumble, but then focus on Paris and pull her shoulders back and smile.

Today was only Essie's second day home and already the community's suspicion of her was evident. Suddenly Zara saw Dave's point. The parents of Barker wouldn't want Essie around if there was even a hint of her being a drug dealer. They would be frightened and keep their children away. She would be ostracised.

The older woman opened the car door and Zara watched as Paris climbed in, beaming up at Essie, still talking.

Thinking back to her own childhood, she tried to remember what she had understood at the age of six. Would she have comprehended the cruel taunts of children repeating things they'd heard their parents say about her family, or would she have been confused? Paris didn't look either sad or confused. Just thrilled to be with her grandmother.

A friend who was a teacher had told her once she'd been in a classroom during news time and one little boy had told the class how his father had drunk 'five beers and weed in the corner of the kitchen, like the puppy does'. The teacher had tried not to laugh, especially when she realised the dad was the local physio.

'What's said in the classroom, stays in the classroom,' she'd said. 'But you can never stop the kids from saying anything, no matter how often you tell them not to talk. They don't have a filter!'

The full force of what could happen to Essie hit Zara and she realised that she felt the same way as Dave and Kim; she had to help her.

There was no way she could approach Essie at the school with so many eyes watching. Then and there she made a promise to Essie—one Essie would never hear. *I'll follow this story to the end and clear your name. We will get the person who's causing all this grief. They'll be locked away, for you and for Paris.*

Zara watched the car leave and then started her own, following as Essie drove down the main street and then turned into the road to the oval.

'Beauty,' Zara said. 'Nettie practice maybe?' It would be a perfect chance for Zara to approach Essie. Paris would be busy on the court and if the other mums' reactions were anything to go by, there wouldn't be too many people lining up to talk to Essie.

Seeing eight cars parked around the netball courts, and two other little girls throwing a ball to each other, she realised she was right, so she swung the car in and parked next to the footy ground.

The grandstand lay empty, as did the playground, but there was a lone car that Zara didn't recognise parked near the goal sticks and, on the oval, a woman dressed in lycra and a long-sleeved T-shirt jogging near the edge.

Zara shuddered as her eyes landed on the scoreboard.

The footy club had named the scoreboard in honour of Will. His name was now emblazoned across the top, reminding everyone, every time they went to the grounds, that Will was dead. He wasn't going to run onto the footy oval ever again. He wasn't going to come in through the door, laughing.

Will would never celebrate his engagement, never kiss his bride, never give their mum grandchildren or Zara nieces or nephews.

She dragged air into her lungs, trying to catch the breath that seemed to have disappeared. Her breaths were short and sharp and she couldn't control them, just as she couldn't control the dots that were appearing in front of her eyes.

'Stop it,' she told herself. 'Stop it. It's just his name. It doesn't mean anything.'

Yes, it does, her brain told her. *Will isn't here anymore. His ashes are in the creek, being tossed around by the wind. There's probably not even anything of him left where we scattered him now. There's nothing of him left . . .*

'No,' Zara moaned, clenching her fists together.

She was hit with another blast of cold air, and as quickly as the panic attack had started, it left her body. Turning away from the scoreboard so she didn't have to see his name, Zara dug through the back of the car to find her sneakers and put them on.

Rearranging her thoughts so Will wasn't foremost in her mind, she wondered how best to play this. Accidentally bumping into Essie was going to be hard to pull off at the netball court.

'Wing it like you always do,' she told herself. Putting her head down against the wind, she started towards the netball courts, just as the girl running the edge of the oval jogged past. She flicked her hand in acknowledgement and wiped the sweat from her brow.

Zara frowned, wondering who she was and why she was training in the bitter wind on a Wednesday afternoon.

'Zara!' A familiar car sidled to a halt alongside her. 'What are you doing here?'

'Hi, Jackie,' Zara said to her neighbour from three doors down. 'Hello, Miss Tori, are you here for nettie training?'

'Zara, come and watch me play?' Tori said, putting her head out the window.

'Oh, no, you don't,' Jackie said. 'Zara is busy. Looks like she was about to go for a run. I didn't know you trained, Zara.'

Looking down at her tracksuit pants and runners, she didn't want to say she just couldn't be bothered getting dressed up today. Side-stepping the question, she answered: 'I'd love to come and watch you play for a bit. Who's in your team?'

'There're seven of us—all the girls from grade one.'

'Well, then, I'd better come over, hadn't I? I tell you what, you go on and I'll be there shortly.' To Jackie she said, 'Are you staying? We haven't caught up for a while.'

'Nope, this is just a drop and run. I've got to get back to work.'

'Do you want me to bring Tori home? I'm going that way, obviously.'

'Would you? I'd really appreciate that.'

'No worries. I'll be able to watch you play, Miss Tori,' Zara told the child. 'I'll see you later, Jackie.'

Zara turned away and closed her eyes. She saw her brother's coffin being carried out by the boys from the footy club, heard her mum's soft sobs.

Maybe Dave was right, she thought. *There is something wrong with me.* She'd put all these feelings down as grief— the times she'd snapped at Jack or woken sweat-laden from a nightmare.

She wondered if her mum had the same problems. If Lynda did, she never talked about them. Her mum hadn't called her back since asking her and Jack out to Rowberry Glen for dinner. Zara would have to phone her. Perhaps she could ask the question then. She really didn't want to though. Displaying weakness was something Zara despised and, by asking, that's exactly what she was doing.

Gathering herself, she looked towards the netball courts. Essie's car was still there. The elderly woman was sitting alone on a bench away from the other mums, watching the girls run up and down the court. Zara felt her heart go out to Essie. It appeared everyone was avoiding her.

She headed over to the courts. Pushing open the wire-framed gate, she nodded to a few of the other mums who were calling out encouragement from the sidelines, and stood watching Tori for a minute.

Tori saw her and gave a big wave. Zara waved back and then casually walked over to Essie.

'Can I sit here?' she asked. 'Doesn't seem like there're many other places.'

'Of course, you're more than welcome,' Essie said.

'Nothing like netball practice in the middle of winter,' Zara laughed, pulling her coat tightly around her as she sat down.

'You're right there. That wind chills to the bones. Thankfully it's not raining.'

'That *is* a bonus,' Zara agreed.

They were quiet for a moment, then Zara asked, 'Which one is yours?'

Essie pointed to Paris, who was next to Tori, bobbing up and down with warm-up squats. 'Paris is my granddaughter.'

'Oh, she's next to Tori, my neighbour. That's why I'm here, she asked me to come and watch.' The perfect excuse. 'I've heard Tori talk about Paris. They must be friends.'

'Yes, they often play together.'

'So, you're on the grandma delivery round? That must be nice to spend some time with her.'

Essie's mouth tightened. 'Paris lives with me. Her mum left her with me years ago.'

'Oh. I'm sorry.' Zara was quiet, not liking that she wasn't being wholly truthful. 'I'm Zara Ellison.'

'Essie Carter.'

'Sounds like you have a challenging life. A child should always have their mother, but the next best thing is a loving grandmother and you're clearly that.'

Giving a small smile, Essie nodded. 'That's really nice of you to say. We've certainly had some tricky times, but we've adjusted.' She looked at Paris fondly. 'I don't think I could be without her now.' She looked over at Zara. 'Do you live in Barker? I don't think I've seen you around.'

'I was living in Adelaide for work. Came back last year when my brother was sick.' As she said the words, Zara felt her heart rate kick up a notch. 'He, uh, he died.'

'Oh, are you Lynda Ellison's daughter? I heard about your brother. I don't know your family but I'm sorry for your loss.'

'Yep, that was Will.' She paused. 'Life is a funny thing, isn't it? I've lost Will and you've gained a granddaughter. Was Paris born in Barker? Or did she come here to live with you?'

'Oh, no, Port Augusta, where her mother was living at the time. Wasn't very far away for me to go and visit. But they were staying with me in Barker when my daughter ran off, leaving Paris behind. Worst day of my life.' She paused. 'Almost.'

'Well, I think you're doing an amazing thing by raising her. She's lucky to have you.'

'You're very kind.'

Sitting there in comfortable silence, Zara looked over at the other mothers. Some of them had their arms crossed, looking at Essie, but Essie seemed to take no notice. Rather, she called out encouraging comments from the sideline.

'Great pass!'

'Good try. Throw a little higher next time.'

Zara ran back over what she knew about Essie. Certainly, the conversation they had just had didn't suggest she was a drug-running mule. She must have gone through hell when Melissa had overdosed, but, Zara reflected, she wouldn't have had time to dwell on it because she had Paris to look after.

The sound of a sharp whistle brought Zara back to the present and she realised training was nearly over.

The girls were now all lined up on the court for a mock match. Tori was playing Centre, and Paris was in the Wing Attack position.

As Paris ran forward and planted a foot to take the throw from Tori, she spun around and faced Zara just for a moment. Zara felt a jolt as she watched the girl. She'd seen a similar face before, she was sure of it. She searched her memory but couldn't come up with anyone. Who did Paris remind her of?

'Your granddaughter looks very familiar. Have you got any other family in Barker?'

Everyone broke into claps and they both looked over at the netball court, where Tori and Paris's team had scored a goal. Zara clapped along with them.

'She's the spitting image of her mother. Melissa grew up and went to school here. She's older than you, I'd say.'

'Oh, really?' Zara turned to look at Essie. 'What was her name? Maybe I know her.'

'Melissa Carter.'

Zara pretended to think about the time she'd spent at school in Barker, then shook her head. 'Not a familiar name. How old is she?'

'Forty. I don't know where that time has gone.'

'Oh, yeah. She's a bit older. Maybe I've just seen her around when she's visited.'

'Right-oh, girls, that's it for today,' the coach called.

'Gosh, where's that hour gone?' Zara asked as she stood up. 'It was nice talking to you. I hope to see you around again.'

Paris and Tori ran up to them.

'Zara, did you see me?' Tori said. 'I helped Corrina get a goal, because I threw the ball to her.'

Grinning, Zara nodded. 'I did. You're a little legend!' She glanced at Paris. 'Hi, Paris, I'm Zara. You looked like you were having fun on the court.' Zara committed the little girl's face to memory. She was positive she knew it and was determined to figure out how.

'I was.' She turned to Essie. 'It's freezing. Can we go home?'

'Of course we can. We'll see you later.'

They said their goodbyes, and Zara led Tori to her car, the little girl talking the whole time.

Chapter 23

Flicking through old school magazines, Zara searched for Melissa Carter's face or name in its pages. The school library had proved a good source of the old yearbooks, and Zara narrowed her search to the eighties. She'd calculated that Melissa must have been born in 1980, to make her forty now.

Back at home, she had poured herself a glass of wine and lit the gas heater on the front porch, where she would be sheltered from the wind, and started to look through them.

The first two were lying on the swing seat alongside her and there were another two to go. So far, she'd found nothing to indicate Melissa had attended the school. She wasn't in any class photos and didn't have any work published on her year-group pages. Zara reasoned she could've been absent on the days the photos had been taken.

'Where are you?' Zara muttered.

The sound of a car driving sedately down the road caught her attention and she looked up just as it passed. The vehicle continued to the end of the street, where it did a U-turn and came back along. The investigative reporter in Zara made her get up and move to the edge of the alcove to look out. Had someone missed turning into a house, or was it something more?

As the car came back, it slowed right down and Zara saw the flash of a camera from inside the car just as it drew level with her house. Fear ran through her body and she backed away from the entrance and behind the wall, where she couldn't be seen.

When the engine noise faded, Zara ran out to the edge of the pavement, staying in the shadows, to try to see the numberplate. The car drove through the pale dome of the street light, and another flicker of fear ran through her and her face flushed hot. It was the same vehicle she'd seen parked at the oval during Tori's netball practice.

An interstate numberplate that she couldn't read taunted her as the red glowing tail-lights disappeared around the corner.

Holy fuck, she thought.

She grabbed her wine and journals and raced inside, slamming the door behind her and turning the lock. Letting the magazines fall onto the couch, she put her glass down and checked the back door and all the windows and drew the curtains.

Flicking off the lights in the front room, she leaned against the wall for a minute, trying to calm herself. She'd been in scary situations before, but none that really could have threatened her life. If this had anything to do with the Essie Carter case and the drugs, Zara knew that whoever was threatening Essie wouldn't think twice about killing her to avoid being exposed.

Zara took her mobile phone from her pocket and flicked her finger over the screen, getting Jack's number up in case she needed to call him, and crept to the window. Opening the curtains a crack, she stared out. No one would be able to look into the house, but she would be able to make out whomever was outside.

The street was quiet.

Across the road she could see Dave and Kim's lights behind their closed blinds; their dark shadows moved behind them.

Normally, Zara wouldn't have thought twice about racing over there to ask for help, but there was nothing to ask for at this point. Plus, Dave's words kept playing in her ears.

'Don't ring me . . .'

Why? she thought. *What's this about? Essie? It has to be.*

Grabbing a piece of paper, she wrote down the afternoon's activities.

School pick-up. Was the car there?
Netball. Observed the car parked on the footy oval.
Girl running/training.
Watched Tori and Paris train. Didn't move.

Took Tori home. Saw the car still parked on oval.
Woman not sighted.
Same type of vehicle drove past my house at . . .

She checked her watch: *6.50 p.m.*

Closing her eyes, she tried to remember if she'd seen the vehicle at school pick-up. In her mind's eye she heard the noise and saw the kids swarming around. The school buses and cars . . .

Damn it! I wasn't looking for it, so I can't remember.

What was the driver looking for? The obvious answer was Essie. Could they be watching her, and because they saw Zara talking to Essie they had followed her too?

Zara went back to stand at the window, realising with relief that, finally, the wind had dropped. The stillness was now only broken by the occasional drop of rain. She looked upwards. Maybe the heavens would open tonight.

Listening hard, the sound of an engine reached her. Racing into her office, she grabbed her camera and opened the back door, sliding herself quietly along the wall, watching.

There it was again. Driving slowly along the road. This time it pulled to the side of the road and cut the lights. As Zara watched, the window slid down, and a camera's zoom lens appeared through the crack.

Click, click, click.

Pause.

Click, click, click.

Pause.

The driver took still more photos of Zara's house.

In turn, Zara raised her camera and tried to zoom in on the numberplate.

'Shit.' No luck, but glancing down the road, she realised the streetlight would be throwing light towards where the car was parked. Stealing around the back and along the other side fence, Zara held her breath as she crept into the garden bed and settled behind a geranium bush before peering out.

As she blinked to get her eyes accustomed to the soft light, she heard the car start up again and slowly start to drive off. Whoever was stalking her was pretty amateurish. Starting an engine on a calm night, in a country town, where strange vehicles were always noticed, was nothing short of crazy. Almost like they wanted to be caught.

Glancing across at Dave's house, it didn't seem like the blinds had moved at all; maybe he hadn't heard the car's engine or noticed there was something strange happening.

The light illuminated the numberplate, and Zara quickly raised her camera to her eye and zoomed in.

Click.

She ducked down as the car swung around and the headlights flashed across where she was crouching.

This time it was anger more than fear that ran through her. This was bullshit! What she wanted to do was race out into the middle of the road and demand the car stop. Make them tell her what this was all about.

Deep down, she already knew. Whatever Essie was caught up in must be big.

After waiting until the car had driven by, she got up and ran back inside.

Checking the display screen on the camera, she smiled. Yes! *YNE-807.*

Turning on her computer, she tried googling the number-plate, hoping to find a name on the registration. Nothing, but the ACT numberplate check website came up in the top hits, so she clicked on the link.

All ACT numberplates start with Y, she read. Finding the search bar, she entered the plate and waited while the database search went to work.

Numberplate not found.

'What? Of course it is!' she snapped. Hitting the keyboard with extra force, she typed the letters and numbers in again, checking the photo on her camera screen against what she'd already typed. A match.

Number not found.

Going out into she kitchen she poured herself another wine. All plates had to be registered.

She really needed Dave.

Shit, shit, I can't ring him, she thought. *But he needs to know this.*

Another mouthful of wine and she wrote the number-plate on a piece of paper and unlocked her front door. Slipping outside, she checked the street before ducking across, avoiding the lights.

The gate into the back yard was closed so Bob, the old dog Dave and Kim had inherited from an elderly farmer, couldn't get out.

She opened the latch and froze as the hinges let out a loud screech.

Standing still for a moment, she waited, listening. Nothing but silence and the occasional drop of rain.

She left the gate ajar, knowing Bob would be inside the warmth, and went in, debating whether to knock on the back door. No, he'd told her not to contact him. Somehow, Zara had to get him outside of his own accord. He wouldn't want Kim knowing anything about this.

Looking around, she saw the path that led out to the veggie patch . . . made of little white pebbles. Picking up a couple, she tossed them towards the roof. A loud bang echoed through the empty night.

Nothing.

Zara tried again.

Nothing.

Third time lucky? She tossed the pebbles onto the roof.

This time the door swung open and Dave stood there, silhouetted in the frame.

'Who's there?' he called out.

'Dave?' Zara whispered in the loudest low voice she could manage.

Dave took a step down from the door and walked out into the darkness. 'I'm the police,' he called.

'It's me! Zara.'

Silence. 'Zara?' This time Dave's voice was low too. 'What are you doing here?'

'I think someone is watching Essie.'

Walking to the side of the house where no light reached, he motioned for Zara to follow him.

'What's going on?'

Summarising exactly what had happened that afternoon, she finished with: 'I've got the numberplate. Can you do anything with it?'

'Give it to me. I'll try, but I don't know—if it comes back to the people who are sending the drugs to her place and Simms knows who they are, there'll be a flag on the plate.'

Zara held out the piece of paper, and Dave reached out to take it. 'Have you kept a record of the plate?'

'Yeah, I've got a photo of the car too.'

Dave paused. 'Kim said something similar happened when she was with Essie yesterday.'

Listening as he described the phone call and subsequent fear from Essie, Zara nodded. 'It's the people with the drugs for sure,' she said.

'Like I tell Jack—never assume anything, but I'd say you're right. You're going to have to be careful. Especially if they're taking photos of your house. They're probably trying to work out who you are. Won't take much, your name's all over the web.'

Zara nodded.

'I'll keep an eye out too. Let you know if I see anything suspicious. If this gets too hot, you'll need to pull out and I'll go back to the AC and talk to him, tell him what we know.'

'It'll be fine. Hopefully, it won't take me long to get the info I need and we can make sure Essie is okay.'

Dave nodded, then paused. 'Why'd you chuck rocks on my roof?'

Zara laughed a little. 'I didn't know how to get your attention. You said not to contact you. I felt like a teenager rocking someone's roof!'

Dave gave a laugh. 'That's exactly what Kim said.'

The rain got a little heavier and Zara looked up at the sky, feeling the cold drops on her face. 'That's a welcome relief.'

'Isn't it just. Been a while between fronts.'

'Well, I'll get back to it. Do a bit of googling. Start pounding the pavement in the morning. See what else I can find.'

Dave turned to go back inside. 'You'd better make this the code if you need me. Chuck rocks on my roof.' He gave her funny smile. 'You're good at hurling rocks, from what I can see.'

Laughing quietly, Zara moved towards the gate. 'Have you seen Jack?'

'He's fine, Zara. Did you think about that counselling service?'

She nodded, then realised he wouldn't be able to see her as she'd moved too far away. 'Yeah. I know you're right. I'll do something about it once I've finished with this story.'

'Don't leave it too long.'

Chapter 24

Back in the house, Zara re-checked all the locks and then opened her laptop.

Googling Melissa Carter didn't get her any further than her search of birth announcements—there were a few Facebook pages, five Twitter accounts and nine people with the same name on Instagram. None seemed to be the Melissa Carter she was looking for. She knew there were other private accounts she couldn't see, but all the public social media websites were a dead end.

What she did find was a newspaper story in the Port Augusta *Transcontinental* under the Police Reports. Dated 25 July 2012. Eight years ago. Well and truly before Paris was born.

> Local woman Melissa Carter will appear in the Port Augusta court today charged with the supply of illicit drugs in the town.

Port Augusta police say that they received a tip-off
from a member of the public and, on further investigation, search warrants were issued for a house on
Chapman Street.

Police say Ms Carter, aged 32, was not in possession of the drugs at the time of arrest.

Zara read on through the links that Google had thrown
up, but there didn't appear to be any other information—
nothing about whether Melissa Carter had been convicted
or acquitted.

She tried different wording—*Local woman overdoses
in Barker*—and found something:

Fatal drug overdoses are on the rise in rural areas,
and Barker is no exception. Last night, a woman was
found in her car and only through the quick thinking
of the local policeman was her life saved.

There was a photo of the car, an ambulance, and Dave
and the body of a woman being stretchered away.

Nothing useful.

Flicking back to the Google search results, she clicked
on another link. This time it was about a man in Port Pirie
who had overdosed.

He had died. As had the woman in the next article—she
was from Port Pirie too, but according to police reports
their deaths were unrelated.

Three deaths in a 300-kilometre radius. Zara checked

the dates of the newspaper reports. They were all within two days of each other.

Frowning, she clicked back and went to a different newspaper report, titled '*Bad batch*':

> Police in Port Augusta and Port Pirie have today confirmed the spate of drug-related deaths were caused by a contaminated batch of drugs. Although police are still awaiting toxicology tests on two of the victims, three others have been confirmed to be intravenous drug users who injected heroin.
>
> A 23-year-old man in Port Augusta was found unconscious in Jewel Nightclub toilets, while a 35-year-old woman was found dead in her home by relatives.

Zara rubbed her tired eyes and considered the connection. Victims of contaminated drugs. Someone had to have supplied these people. Would the same person have supplied Melissa? The stretch wasn't that big considering the towns were close together. Was this the person now stalking Essie? And now possibly Zara too?

Looking at her watch, she decided it wasn't too late to call Lachie. He picked up on the first ring.

'How goes?' he asked. Zara could hear the noise of the newsroom in the background.

'You still at work?'

'Sure am. It's deadline day, or had you forgotten?'

'Of course it is! Sorry, you'll be flat strap.'

'How's that story on the pollies coming along?'

'I'll have it to you next week.'

'Don't forget. I know it's only a filler, but I want it.'

'You'll get your story, Lachie.'

She paused as Lachie yelled to someone, 'It's in your inbox! . . . Sorry,' he continued.

'I'm wondering if you've got any contacts who'd have a line into the heroin trade?'

'What the hell for?'

She knew she had Lachie's attention now. She imagined him sitting straight up at his desk, his eyes wide, patting his tie down as he spoke.

'If you do, I need to see if we can get a lead on a woman called Melissa Carter.'

'And who's she when she's at home?'

'If I knew that, I wouldn't be asking you for help. But she's Essie Carter's daughter. I think there's a link between her and why Essie is, or was, receiving drugs through the post.'

'Zara, Zara, Zara, I told you—this is a granny story. Why are you still looking into it?'

'It's more than a public-interest story. You've got a sixty-plus-year-old woman importing heroin into Barker four hours north of Adelaide in the Flinders Ranges where there isn't a population large enough to warrant what she was caught with. She's looking after the six-year-old grand-daughter, who her daughter abandoned after she nearly OD'd in the back streets. Doesn't that raise a few flags with you?'

'What does your pet policeman have to say about this?'

Zara heard him take the phone away from his ear and yell again. 'Send it through and I'll mock it up.' Smiling, she imagined him waving his hand towards whomever he was talking to, commanding them to send through their story *right now*.

She waited until she knew she had his attention before speaking again. 'Nothing. Jack and Dave have been warned off any further investigations. Officially.'

Silence. Then, 'Why?' The word was drawn out slowly.

'Dave's wife posted bail for Essie Carter. He took some flak for it.'

'You're kidding me?'

'No, there's a story there in itself.'

'Make sure you get that one too,' he said, giving Zara the green light to go ahead with the piece. 'I'll put in some calls to a few blokes I knew back when I worked the night shift at *The Advertiser* and see what I can find out.'

'Thanks, Lachie.'

'Great piece on the shearer, by the way.'

'I was going to talk to you about that. Why the hell did you use that photo? Jack went off his tree.'

Lachie laughed. 'Surely not? That was a great pic.' He paused. 'Trouble in paradise?'

Not wanting to answer, Zara stayed silent. The rising anger in her chest had come from nowhere. Suddenly all she wanted to do was yell at Lachie. She'd never felt like doing that in her life.

'I just don't know why you used that photo. I didn't send it in to be used.'

'That photo was the best one we had. The others you took were okay, but that one told a story.'

'Well, it caused me trouble. Check with me next time.'

'Okay, well, moving on . . . Let me make some calls. I'll see what I can find out.'

'Thanks, Lachie.' The anger subsided and she hung up the phone feeling exhausted. Craving uninterrupted sleep, she stretched out on the couch, her computer propped up on her knees as she wrote a few notes:

WHAT I KNOW

Package arrived in mail—Essie collected.

Essie charged with receiving narcotics—taken by AFP to Adelaide.

Kim bailed Essie.

Essie frightened by a phone call.

Strange car at oval where Essie was taking Paris to netball.

I spoke with Essie at netball.

Same car drives past my house—numberplate YNE-807.

Essie Carter: Long-time resident of Barker. Looking after granddaughter. Receiving illicit drugs. Daughter drug addict.

Melissa Carter: Born and schooled in Barker. Drug addict. Left daughter behind.

Paris Carter: Born in Port Augusta. Lives and schooled in Barker.

She tapped her keyboard, thinking. What was the best way to track down Melissa? Maybe through Paris.

Perhaps the girl's father knew where Melissa was.

She logged into Trove and put in Paris's name and the town name.

Scrolling through the hits, she saw a headline: '*The Five Faces of the Heroin Epidemic*', dated the same time as Melissa Carter's first overdose. *Look at these faces and remember them,* the opinion article started.

> Because if you don't, these faces will be forgotten in time, and they should never be.
>
> Last week, South Australia had its worst recorded spate of overdoses from contaminated drugs being sold across the state. The destruction caused by the batch of heroin has reached outside of Adelaide, all the way north to Port Augusta and south to Mount Gambier. Scores of people have been found unconscious, keeping the ambulance service and hospitals busy. Thankfully there have been only five deaths, but that is still five too many.
>
> These are senseless deaths, unnecessary deaths.
>
> Jeremy Gunner, 18, Head Prefect at Mount Gambier High School, was found dead last week in his car. His school principal spoke publicly of his achievements and the many things he could have accomplished throughout his life. His family declined to speak to the media.
>
> Holly McKay, 25, went out with her friends to a nightclub on Hindley Street. Her body was discovered

by a street cleaner the following morning. Holly had, three weeks previously, been promoted to associate with her legal firm. She leaves behind a husband, Frank. 'I wasn't aware that Holly was taking drugs. My heart is broken. I want to track down the bastards who sold the shit to her.'

Grant Beacon's body was found in the parklands across from his home in Bentley. The 28-year-old was a known drug user, as was his partner, Kelly-Ann Hare, but he had been attending a rehab clinic in an attempt to break the habit.

Ryan Kipling, 32, had become a new father only six months before his body was found in his bed by his partner, Melissa Carter. His daughter, Paris, will now never know her father and his partner will never grow old alongside the man she told me was 'the only reason life was worth living'.

Finally, 22-year-old Carrie Plain had her life cut short by heroin. Her family told me she was 'the one most likely to go places' in her class at high school. She'd finished at the top of her class and was studying medicine.

These five faces should never be forgotten. These people are dead because someone brought drugs into their lives. Someone brought drugs into our state and our cities.

These five faces represent families who now have to bear the trauma of pain.

I'm sure some of you will write into the paper and tell me I'm wrong. That these five, plus all the others who have taken these drugs, chose to take heroin—and, yes, you would be right. They had their own free will, but if the drugs weren't here in the first place, no one would have the choice to take them.

It's the drug producers and dealers who are a blight on our society. They have knowingly declared war on our community, on our young people, and for this they should be given a life sentence. As the families of these five people have been given.

Zara blinked, then checked the dates, noting that Melissa had come back to Barker to get off the gear eight months after Ryan's death. Why hadn't the Department for Child Protection taken Paris away from her before, if she was using with a baby in the house?

She added Ryan Kipling to her notes, but there were still only a few links she could make with the information she had. Everything came back to two simple facts: Essie Carter had a drug-addicted daughter, and Essie Carter was being mailed drugs. They had to be connected.

The question was whether Essie was receiving them and passing them on to Melissa, or was it something else?

Frustrated, Zara got up and paced the floor. None of this was helping her get any closer to finding Melissa, and Zara was now certain that to find the answers, that was what she needed to do.

Chapter 25

1981

Ian sat at the bar and rocked the pusher with his foot.

There was nothing to this parenting thing, he decided as he sipped his beer. Rosie must have been exaggerating when she said it was hard and the twins wouldn't travel well. Alroy hadn't cried once in the four hours he'd been at the pub. In fact, he'd slept for most of it. Even the barman, whom Ian had taken to calling Pop because he kept offering unsolicited advice, had commented how good he was.

'I thought he would've needed a feed by now,' he'd said two hours in, as he'd put a beer down for Ian. Ian remembered him from his last time here with Kiz and Muzza. In fact, it had been Kiz who had given him the name Pop. The bloke with too many kids and too many opinions.

Soon afterwards, a couple of cute girls had come up and cooed over Alroy and spent ten or fifteen minutes talking with him. Ian had played up to them, being the doting dad while the barman frowned at him from behind the bar.

Alroy had let out a couple of squawks and cries when one of the girls had picked him up, but quickly nestled into her chest and fallen back to sleep.

'See, he knows a good spot when he sees it,' Ian said with a grin, nodding towards the girls' breasts. 'Buy you a drink?'

'Thanks, but no. We're on our way out the door,' the girl had said as she gently laid Alroy back in the pram.

Now, the barman put down the glass he was polishing and took a step towards Ian. 'Don't you think it's time to go home?' he asked. 'It's nearly ten o'clock. I'm sure your wife will be wondering where you are. Where the baby is.'

'Nah,' Ian took a sip of his beer. 'I'll have another one, mate.' He waggled the empty glass. 'She's off doing something at the hospital.'

'Maybe you should be with her?'

The man still hadn't drawn his beer.

'I think she'll be managing just fine, thanks Pop. Rosie has done this all by herself for the past twelve months.' He looked down at the sleeping child. 'Tells me it's a hard job. It doesn't seem to be.'

Ian noticed the barman shake his head as he lifted a clean glass and held it to the beer tap.

'What's your name, mate?' Ian asked. 'Don't suppose I should call you Pop all the time. Sounds like you are, though. Giving all this advice about being a parent when I haven't asked for it. You did that last time I came in too.'

'Bruce.'

'Well, Bruce, I tell you, I've been here all of a day and I've hardly seen the wife. All caught up with these ones. No time for me. Don't think she was even that pleased to see me.' He raised his glass to Bruce. 'Cheers. Don't reckon she's going to come away with me either.' Sighing, he looked down into his beer. 'Never really thought life would pan out this way. Thought we'd get our little family on the road together and set off to the next shed.'

'Children can be needy,' Bruce replied, 'especially when they're as little as yours and can't do anything for themselves.' He stepped away and poured a beer for another customer, while Ian looked down at Alroy. 'Be hard not to have a proper base.'

'But families did that in the Depression, didn't they? All on the road together. Some of them even walked to the next job, rather than driving. I've got a car, so they'd be comfortable.' He scratched his head and leaned back, looking at the ceiling.

'If you want my advice, cobber,' Bruce said, 'then you'll stay here. Find a job on a farm. Or a shearing team that sticks around. You'd have the best of both worlds—the shearing and the time with the boys, and watching your kids grow up. If you keep up with this flitting here, there and everywhere, your kids won't know you when you come home. How long has it been since you left here? Twelve months?'

'That's what you told me last time I was here, that when they were twelve months was one of the nicest times with the kids, so here I am. Fronted up and ready to be a dad.'

Bruce looked at him and shook his head. 'I think you've got the wrong end of the stick.'

'You still spending time with your boy behind the bar?'

'Sure am, and I wouldn't want it any other way. I wouldn't like it if I didn't get to see him every day. Boys and their fathers have a special bond and I'm making sure ours is unbreakable.'

'What about your other kids?'

'I spend time with them too.'

Looking at Alroy again, Ian saw his button nose peeking out above the blanket that was snuggled up to his chin, and his mouth moving in a sucking motion while he slept. Ian felt something stir inside him, but he didn't know what it was. A bubble. A warm feeling in his stomach, like he'd had too many whiskeys.

Leaning forward, he pulled the blanket back and looked carefully at the child's face. He thought he could see traces of his grandfather and his mother—he only had photos to show him what she had looked like, but Alroy's chin was pointy, like hers had been. The fine ginger hair was the same colour as his own. He couldn't stop himself; he reached out and stroked the hair. It was soft and downy, almost like the lambs' wool he shore, but not as dense.

Startling at the touch, Alroy's eyes flew open and he looked at Ian. He opened his mouth to scream, but instinctively Ian put his hand on the boy's stomach and rocked him gently from side to side as he'd seen Rosie do earlier.

'Now then,' he whispered.

Alroy's mouth closed and he looked at Ian and let out a noise that sounded like a giggle. In an instant, Ian saw his own eyes reflected in his son's. Green. Bright.

My son, he marvelled. *I have a son. What do you think about that, Granddad? I can't believe it either.*

'Reckon we might be up for last drinks,' Bruce said as he closed the cash register and dimmed the lights in the bar.

'I'll have one more,' Ian said, tearing his eyes away from the pram.

'Where's your next shed?'

'Heading out to the Nullarbor first thing in the morning.'

'And your family? What are you going to do about them?'

Ian shrugged. 'Rose made it pretty clear she wasn't coming. I'm still hoping to talk her around.'

Bruce shook his head again. 'Haven't you heard a word I've said?'

'Oh, yeah, I have, mate, but I'm not made to put down roots. Guess if that means I have to give up seeing my kids grow up, then so be it.' Alroy started to grizzle, which in seconds became a full-blown cry.

'Reckon your boy doesn't like the sound of that,' Bruce said. 'Can't say I blame him.'

'Maybe not,' Ian said as he picked Alroy up and jiggled him around until he quietened.

'Looks like he needs a feed to me.'

Glancing at the screwed-up face on his shoulder, Ian remembered seeing a tin and two bottles on the bench in the kitchen.

'Well then, I'd better get home and give him something to eat.' Popping Alroy back in the pram, he nodded to Bruce. 'See you round.'

'Take care, cobber. Look after your family.'

The cold night air made Ian stop and tuck Alroy's blanket around his little body before he walked quickly back to the house.

Inside, he picked up the tin and tried to ignore Alroy's cries while he read the instructions.

'Shush there, little mate,' he hushed as he boiled the kettle and rolled the pram with his foot. Grabbing the measuring spoon next to the tin he put in the amount of formula needed, then mixed it up with the hot water, before pouring it into the bottle.

He bent down and gave the milk to Alroy, who grabbed at it greedily. Ian helped guide it to his mouth where he took two sucks, then screamed loudly and threw it away.

'What?' Ian asked in surprise. 'Isn't that what you want?' He picked the bottle up and tried to put it in Alroy's mouth again, but the screaming continued, his little face growing red with exertion.

As Ian held the bottle, he realised it was very hot. Too hot for a little mouth, he assumed. He poured in cold water and gave it a shake, then gently held it out to the screaming baby, who this time gulped at the milk and settled quickly, sucking hard.

Ian watched him for a moment, before smiling. 'Well then, lad, I managed that all right, didn't I?' He opened the fridge, pleased with himself, and rummaged around for something to eat.

There was ham and cheese, so he made a sandwich and watched Alroy as he continued to drink.

Moments later, the bottle was empty and Alroy was crying again.

'You want more? Surely not.' He picked him up. 'Maybe I need to burp you again,' he said quietly, remembering what he'd had to do the first time he'd seen the babies a year ago. He tapped Alroy's back a few times but nothing happened.

Ian walked around the kitchen holding the squirming child until he heard a loud fart and felt heat under his hand. He looked at Alroy in horror.

'Ah, have you done what I think you've done?'

The crying stopped and Ian held him at arm's length, regarding him with a turned-up nose. 'Well, my boy, I didn't think about that. Guess we'd better fix you up somehow.' Still holding him out, he went into the bedroom and found some nappies.

Lying Alroy on the floor, Ian gingerly undid the all-in-one suit and looked at the cloth nappy beneath it. He took a breath and tried to undo the safety pins, his large sausage-like fingers struggling with the fiddly-ness of them.

'What's all this about, then?' he asked, as he put them aside and opened the nappy. Trying not to gag, he looked around for something to wipe Alroy's bottom with but didn't know what to use.

'Best way to fix this,' he said, looking at Alroy. 'The garden hose.'

Outside, he switched on the verandah light, placed Alroy on the grass and looked around for a tap.

Alroy, happy with the unexpected turn of events, chatted in a language Ian didn't understand, then giggled loudly. 'Wonder where your mum is,' Ian said as he turned the tap on and squirted it towards Alroy.

With a loud scream of shock, Alroy started to cry, but Ian didn't stop until he was clean.

'Yeah, it's a bit chilly there, lad, I know. But better than having shit all over you.' He took him back inside and dressed him again, not knowing whether the nappy he put on was going to hold anything or not. Alroy was still sniffling.

'Tell you what, my lad, let's go for a drive. That'll distract you.' He gathered up a few items and then picked up Alroy. He glanced around the kitchen before he turned off the light and shut the door behind them.

Chapter 26

2020

After the rain the night before and during the morning, Zara opened the door to a calm, blue-sky day. The familiar chill of the icy air still bit at her cheeks as she walked, but it was pleasant without the wind.

She walked along the pavement, her hands tucked tightly into the pockets of her Driza-Bone coat, her hair whipping around her face. She avoided the small puddles so her jeans and leather boots didn't get wet, all the while keeping an eye out for the car that had cased her place last night, and for Essie.

And for Jack.

The main street was quiet. Although all the shops were open, only a few cars were parked diagonally in front of them.

Waving to a couple outside the supermarket, she kept going until she passed the school-zone sign, reminding drivers to keep to a slower speed.

Large dew drops fell from the trees along the front fence of the school, and the buses were lined up, six in a row ready to depart in different directions around the council boundaries.

School was just about to be dismissed for the day, and Zara wanted to be in place to see if the strange car was there. If it was, she could be almost certain Essie was being followed. The next question was: by whom? Dave had indicated he thought it was the drug dealers, but exactly who were they?

Zara leaned against a tree and put her sunglasses on. Glancing around, she recognised most the cars parked to pick the kids up. Janine Docker from out on Nymbina Road—the school bus didn't go past her front gate. Mrs Parker—she was picking up her grandchildren. Down the side street, Zara saw a circle of town mums leaning against their cars and talking. Nothing strange here.

Essie was parked a few metres away from the other vehicles and stayed in the car. It seemed to Zara as if she were reading the paper while she waited.

As the bell sounded and the children ran into the playground, Zara saw Essie get out of her car and walk over, just as she had the day before.

And, as had happened the day before, the other mothers turned away from the older woman. They put their heads together and whispered, all the while watching Essie and Paris as they made their way to their car.

Zara watched them drive away in the direction of the oval. Surely not netball training again today? Regardless, she knew it was time to come clean and talk to Essie openly.

❧

The carpark and oval were empty, and Essie was sitting on the bench watching Paris play on the swings in the playground, when Zara sat next to her.

'Hi, Essie. How are you today?'

'Hello, love, out for some exercise? Such a good thing to do for the soul.'

Zara laughed. 'I'd like to say yes, but I can't. I did need to clear my head though, so I thought a walk was in order.'

A movement caught her eye and Zara turned quickly to look at the oval. Who would be there without a car?

A figure in the distance was running around the edge of the oval. Squinting, Zara tried to work out if it was the same woman; she was too far away to tell for certain, but Zara thought it was.

Zara leaned in towards Essie. 'Essie, every time you come here, is there a woman exercising?'

Glancing over, Essie smiled. 'Oh, yes, for about the last three months, she's here. Doesn't talk, though. I have to say, she's not very friendly. I tried to chat with her once, asking if she was training for an event. She answered my questions but couldn't get away from me quick enough.' She paused. 'You know, the funny thing is that I never see her around town.' Essie shrugged. 'Still, I hadn't met you before either. Barker is small, but not so small that we know everyone, especially people out of our generation.'

Zara's mind whirred as she processed Essie's words, then she slowly asked, 'Do you come at the same time every day?'

'Yes, straight after school. Sometimes Paris has friends with her and sometimes not. I like to give her a dose of fresh air before we head home. My garden, even though it's lovely, is not very big.'

Pulling out her phone, Zara zoomed in, hoping the extra magnification would help, and it did. The woman was now walking with her hands on her hips, shaking her legs as if she were nearly finished her workout.

Same woman. Without a doubt.

Click.

Zara looked at the photo to see if it was clear enough to show Dave. Grainy, but the woman's features showed.

'Who are you?' Essie asked in a tentative voice. 'Why are you doing that?'

Confused, Zara looked over at her. 'What? I'm Zara.'

'I know, but *who* are you?' Her voice was laden with meaning.

'Oh.' She put down her phone and looked at Essie. 'I work for the *Farming Telegraph*,' she admitted.

'A journalist?' Essie snatched her handbag and got up, calling to Paris. 'Come on, darling, we have to go.'

'No, wait! Don't go. I'm a journo, but I also freelance— I feel something's not right with your case and I want to help you. Find out who is really behind the drugs, so you can clear your name and not be hassled anymore.'

Essie rounded on Zara, her cheeks red.

Zara thought she was going to yell at her, her eyes were so furious, but instead Essie regarded her for a moment, then raised her head high. 'Well, young lady, I would appreciate it if you'd stay away from me and my granddaughter. We have nothing to say to you.' She went to Paris, who was sliding down the slippery dip and bent down to whisper in her ear. Then she took her granddaughter's hand and walked towards the car, not looking at Zara.

Zara knew there was no point in trying to persuade her to talk now. Instead, she sat on the bench and waited until the woman on the oval had finished her stretches, watching to see where she would go.

Setting off at a quick pace, the woman headed towards the street, about five minutes after Essie left, but turned in the opposite direction to Essie's home.

Zara let out a sigh. Perhaps she was on the wrong track.

Twenty-four hours later, Zara was in the pub. Hopper had the fire roaring and there were two customers sitting close, warming their hands.

Overnight, a cold front had roared up from the south, bringing heavy grey clouds and a curtain of drizzle. The warmth of the flames was welcome, even though it stung her cheeks.

'How's it all going?' she asked, leaning on the bar and picking up a coaster, which she twisted around in her fingers.

'Slow. The weather's keeping everyone away.'

'Yeah, you haven't even got your regular in.' She nodded to a stool that was usually kept warm by an old gambler.

'He's in hospital. Got gout.'

Zara chuckled. 'Don't suppose that's surprising.'

'What are you working on?'

Leaning in, Zara said, 'Well, that's why I'm here. You know Essie Carter?'

'Sure do. Been here longer than I have.'

'What do you know about her?'

Hopper made a groaning noise as he sighed. 'What type of things do you want to know? Always been a bit of a strange old duck. Keeps to herself mostly. Don't think she's ever set foot through my pub door.

'Her husband used to cut everyone's hair in town and he kept to himself too. Used to come and have a beer every Friday night after he'd closed the shop, then head home for tea. You could set your watch by him. Five-fifteen and he'd order a schooner of bitter, sit right over there.' He pointed to the window. 'Never really spoke to anyone. I always thought he must've got sick of people talking to him during the day.'

'Did she ever get involved in anything strange. Illegal?'

'What?' His voice rose like his eyebrows. 'They were both involved in the church.'

'I don't know that that counts them out,' Zara said.

'Oh.' Hopper's voice held meaning. 'Yeah, point taken. Hmm. I'm trying to think who would be able to tell you more. I don't know if she was born in Barker, or moved here later. She's just always been part of the furniture.' He paused. 'This was before my time but I know back in the early seventies and eighties the butter factory used to go hell for leather and the trains would be constantly going, taking the grain away. Some people living in the cities couldn't get jobs, so they came to places they could. Maybe she was one of them? A lot of people moved on when the boom stopped, and the town got quiet. After the butter factory shut, and the trains stopped running because the grain dried up.'

'Can you think of anyone else who would know about her?' She glanced over her shoulder as the door opened. A customer came in and sat at the other end of the bar, in front of the TV showing the horse races.

'In for a punt, Lucky?' Hopper said to him as he went to pull a beer.

'Got a tip for race five,' he said, looking down at the newspaper he had put on the counter. Zara could see red rings marked around some of the races.

Zara got up. 'I'd better go. Thanks for your help.'

'Let me think about who else could know anything. I'll give you a call.'

'Cheers, Hopper.'

Outside, Zara dialled Lachie's number as she walked.

'Zara, any news?' Lachie greeted her call.

'I was hoping you'd have some for me.'

'Not yet. I made a few calls after I spoke to you but haven't had any luck yet.'

Her call waiting beeped and she took it away from her ear to check. Hopper.

'I'll call you back, Lachie,' she said and disconnected without giving him time to say goodbye. 'That was quick,' she greeted Hopper.

'I had a thought. Don't know why I didn't remember when I was talking to you. Have you come across Old Ted Leeson?'

Zara paused for a moment. 'Don't think I have.'

'Well, he's a real old timer, I help him out occasionally. Maybe go and see him out at Two Mile Creek.'

Zara frowned. 'Where's Two Mile Creek? I've never heard of it. Is there a community out there?'

'Nope, just old Ted. You'll need to head out towards the old railway bridge. Count three gum trees from the bridge and you'll see a narrow two-wheel track. Follow that down until you see his camp. Ted's been down there since they closed the train line.'

'But there isn't a station out there.' Zara was confused. She was local and neither Old Ted Leeson nor Two Mile Creek were ringing any bells with her.

'Nope.'

'So, why's he living out there?'

'Ted doesn't really like people. Prefers his own company. Once he got booted from the trains, he got the shits with society and wanted to be alone. Set his humpy up next to the spring. Surely you know there's permanent water in places around here?'

'Oh, yeah, I knew that, but I've never heard of anyone living on them. I know some of the cameleers back in the early days used to camp on them.'

'Yep, they did, and a couple of springs were on stock routes, so the drovers would camp on them with their cattle as well.'

Zara stopped walking and dug out her notebook. She leaned it against a fence and started taking notes—the droving story would be good to follow up once this one with Essie was finished. 'Okay, so the third tree from the bridge?'

'That's the one. Ted doesn't drive anymore, so I do a run out there every fortnight when he gets his government cheque. Pick him up and bring him into town. He buys his supplies and then I take him back. I'm scared I'll go out there one week and find him dead and fly blown.'

Zara wrinkled her nose at the thought, although she knew that it wasn't an uncommon end for people in isolated areas.

'Now, when you head out to see him, don't go too early—after mid-morning, but before afternoon smoko. Let him get a couple of drinks in first, but don't go out after smoko 'cause you won't get anything out of him. You'll have to judge it pretty well.'

'Okay. Sounds like a character. When are you due to go and visit Ted again?'

'Not for another week. Next Thursday.'

'Right. No point in trying to go together, then. I was thinking an introduction might be helpful if he doesn't like people turning up uninvited and asking questions.'

'You'll be right. Take a bottle of rum with you and make sure you tell him I sent you. Once he's got a couple of drinks into him, I promise you he'll be fine. If he gets a bit aggro, then offer him the bottle.'

'Okey dokey. Brilliant. Thanks, Hopper. Talk to you soon.'

She disconnected then dialled Lachie back again. 'Sorry, just needed to talk to someone,' she said.

'Good intel, I hope?'

'I'm getting there. Slow going. You said you hadn't found a line yet?'

'Nah. Put some feelers out for you, though. You got anything?'

'Just some names. Could you get someone to look into them?'

'Shoot.'

'I came across an article listing five people who died in South Australia from a contaminated batch of heroin.'

'What are the names?'

Zara gave them to him. 'Now, the interesting thing about this is that one of the names—Ryan Kipling—is linked back to Melissa Carter. He's the father of her child.'

She could hear Lachie's fingers fly across the keyboard.

'Right,' he muttered. 'I'm flicking you some information on email. Shit, this is only five or so years ago.'

'That's right.'

'I don't know why I don't remember this,' Lachie said. 'Deaths across Australia, four in Melbourne, three in Brisbane. Plus more in other states. Saying it was due to a batch of contaminated heroin coming in. No arrests. Not even any leads on who brought it in.'

'Got to be a link here, wouldn't you think? The same people who imported would distribute it Australia-wide?'

'Depending on who, but, yes. If it's one of the drug families, then, absolutely. What I don't understand, Zara, is what link you're seeing to Essie Carter here. You've got Melissa's partner deceased from an OD and her daughter who's missing—if she hasn't been heard of since she took off five years ago, then there's every chance she ended up dead on the streets and in a morgue with a Jane Doe tag on her toe.'

'I hear you, but there's something telling me that's not right. I think the daughter's still alive—and nearby. Maybe she's getting Essie to take possession of the drugs for her. Perhaps she's on the streets working as a prostitute.'

'Why would Essie get the drugs for her if she's on the street? Melissa would have access to anything she wants out there.'

Zara was silent, her brain whirling. 'I know,' she said finally. 'That's the part that doesn't make sense. All I know is, Essie is protecting someone and that person is the key to finding out why she accepted the drugs. It would make sense for her to look out for her daughter.'

'Or someone blackmailing her to keep her daughter safe?' Lachie suggested. 'Shit, that's been done a million times over.'

'Yeah, that's another option. Or—' She broke off. 'Or, what about if whomever it is has threatened Paris's safety?'

It was Lachie's turn to be silent.

'Well, that would be a mongrel act. But I guess that's been done before too.'

Zara put her notepad back into her bag and looked down the street. Butterflies ran through her stomach as she saw Jack's car pull out from the police station and head towards her. As he drove past, she raised her hand to wave to him.

Jack looked as if he wanted to ignore her, but before he passed her by he gave a small wave, without smiling. Zara felt a hot flush of humiliation rush through her.

'You still there?' Lachie asked.

'What? Oh, yeah.'

'You know, when I was reporting on the streets I was always told that druggies return to their roots. Where would Melissa's roots be?'

'She grew up in Barker.'

'Okay, and she's not there?'

'Not a chance.'

'If she's alive—and I say "if" because there's still a high chance she's not with us anymore—she's not going to be too far away. That's my guess, anyway. Which is what you just said. Probably one of the bigger centres. Port Augusta or Port Pirie. Somewhere like that.'

'Adelaide, if she's prostituting herself?'

'Not necessarily. They've got pros in the smaller towns too, you know.'

'Thanks for the tip. I'll keep on with it.'

'I'll do some digging too.'

They rang off and Zara put her hand to her head as she thought about Jack. She dug her purse out and looked at the business card Dave had given her. She stood on the pavement turning it over and over in her hand.

Chapter 27

'Um, yes, hello. Could I make an appointment, please?' Zara's heart was thumping and she felt sweat on her brow despite the chill in the air.

After she'd seen Jack, she'd known she didn't have a choice—she wanted their relationship to work, and to do that, she had to fix herself. They'd been together since just after Will died; as time had gone on, and they'd talked, become closer, Zara had realised that she'd never had a relationship like the one she shared with Jack. They talked late into the night, by phone, about anything and everything. They texted during the day, laughed on her verandah. She'd cheered him on while he played footy and they'd started having dinner parties with their friends.

They'd even talked about moving in together.

Then Zara had started to pull away. Close down. Because if both her dad and her brother could be taken from her, then surely Jack could too. She didn't want to feel the pain of losing someone she loved ever again.

But was the alternative to feel this empty for the rest of her life? Wasn't Jack worth taking a punt on?

The only way to make their love work was for her to deal with the grief that plagued her constantly. She had to let go of the pain and find a way to think about Will and see things that reminded her of him without having a panic attack. To stop the nightmares and flashbacks. To stop thinking she could lose Jack as well.

The first step was admitting she might be suffering from PTSD. She'd googled the symptoms after Dave had spoken to her, but she didn't want to believe it.

Everyone went through grief, she told herself again and again—everyone had someone they love die.

But she hadn't lost just Will. Her father had died only a few short years before her brother, and it had been Zara who'd found his car upside-down on the road near their property, Rowberry Glen.

Mum lost her husband and her son, and she's managing okay, she silently berated herself.

But then there were the symptoms, right in front of her: *re-experiencing trauma through intrusive, distressing recollections of the event, through flashbacks and nightmares.* Well, that was certainly true. Most nights she woke having seen her father upended in his ute and Will's coffin being carried out of the church. Sometimes it wasn't Will in the coffin—it was Jack. Sometimes it wasn't her dad hanging upside-down in the ute—it was Jack. She would wake, expecting there to be tears on her cheeks, but she didn't feel anything: *emotional numbness*, another symptom. Her avoidance of the footy field and the farm because they were reminders.

Recently, she'd found her mind drifting as she wrote; she couldn't concentrate, just as she tossed and turned in bed and snapped at people when she didn't mean to.

There were more severe symptoms as she read on, but the ones that had caught her attention were those she recognised in herself, thanks to Dave's comment. If he hadn't pointed them out to her, she doubted she would have realised there was anything wrong.

Although she had known that her behaviour the night she'd gone to the bar with Jesse was out of character. Again, a flush of humiliation washed over her as she thought about that night. Thank God Jesse was a gentleman. Someone different could have taken advantage of her and there would have been nothing she could have done about it.

'Hello, are you there?' the receptionist asked, pulling Zara away from her thoughts.

'Yes, sorry. What was the date?'

'We have one in two weeks' time. Wednesday at 2 p.m. Have you been here before?'

'No.' Zara put the call on speaker and looked at her diary. She had a meeting with Lachie in Adelaide that day. 'Is there another time sooner?' she asked.

'No, and this appointment is the last one we have until . . . hmm, another two months. Dr Connelly is very busy.'

Zara didn't want to miss that meeting with Lachie and she was about to say no, when she realised she was running away from all this again. 'That will be fine, thank you.'

She tapped the date and time into her phone and hung up. She knew she'd taken a big step forward, but the sense of relief she'd expected wasn't there. In fact, there was nothing inside her. Except a need to hear Jack's voice. To tell him what she'd done. And why. For him. For her. For them.

As the countryside passed by on the way to Old Ted Leeson's humpy, Zara saw tractors seeding into paddocks that had enjoyed rain over the past few days. When she'd spoken to her mum the previous night, Lynda had told her Rowberry Glen had had fifty millimetres of rain—the biggest fall in three years. The spiderwebs were being dusted off the tractor, and the grain that Will had put into the silos for seed three years ago was about to be sown.

Zara had tears in her eyes by the time she'd hung up. The relief in her mother's voice was obvious, and she knew that, between Lynda and the young workman, the seeding would get done quickly and efficiently.

However, the thought of Will being there, three years ago, sitting behind the steering wheel of the tractor was enough to give Zara a panic attack. She'd had to walk the edges of the room, breathing slowly to ward it off.

Her mother had been so excited, Zara didn't want to burst her happiness by talking about the counsellor's appointment or, for that matter, about Jack. Other than finding love with Will's doctor, James, Lynda's reasons to smile had been few and far between.

Barker hadn't received anything like the rain that had fallen at Rowberry Glen—just the misty showers she'd felt the night the strange car had driven past her house. The falls hadn't been widespread, but the lucky farmers under the drenching were now busy.

The rich red dirt was being turned over and the smell of moist soil and diesel fumes filled the air. Zara breathed it in deeply, remembering the times she'd sat alongside her father as he'd seeded wheat into the ground. How they'd watched it germinate and grow into plants as tall as her thighs, then turn from the rich green to golden and finally the header would be serviced and prepared for harvest.

Zara found a smile playing on her lips amid the sadness as she watched a red tractor turn a sharp corner and line up again go back. Gone were the days of seeding around the fence line in an ever-decreasing circle. Now they were all on tram lines. Every tractor had a GPS to keep the driver on the correct line. Her dad had said they were creating 'steering wheel attendants' rather than farmers who knew how to drive a seeder and fix something if it went wrong. It was the computers that drove the machines now and the mechanics who drove from the closest dealership to fix them.

'Can't hold back the times, Dad,' she'd said.

Her smile faded as she remembered his smile and laughter.

She saw the sixty-kilometre sign for the tiny town of Torrica and slowed down as the anger started, bubbling in her chest until it screamed to be released. Hitting the steering wheel with her hand, she cried out. There was no one to hear her.

'Why?' she yelled, brushing the falling tears away. 'Why was it both of you?'

Pulling over in the parking bay at the edge of town, she ranted and cried until she had nothing left.

The occasional car passed her, but she didn't take any notice. Some of the people in this town would know her car and others would probably think she was on the phone. Leaning her head against the cold window, she continued to cry, but not with the intensity of before. Tears trickled down her cheeks but she didn't wipe them away.

Emptiness swarmed through her like a cold wave. Emptiness, loneliness, fear. Then nothing.

She jumped as there was a knock on the window. Looking out, she saw Jack standing there in his uniform. Drained and tired, she wiped her face. She didn't want him to know she'd been crying—that would show weakness—but there didn't seem a choice.

Zara wound the window down. 'What are you doing here?'

'Had a call out. Why are you parked up here? Are you . . . You've been crying. What's wrong?' He opened the door and squatted down, holding her hand.

She looked at the concern on his face and tried to speak. 'Nothing. Just . . .' Everything she was feeling, or not feeling, was too hard to explain.

'Talk to me, Zara. Tell me.' He reached forward and put his hand against her cheek. 'Don't you know I want to help? I want to be here for you?' He stroked his thumb along her cheekbone.

Jack's kindness and love brought the tears again. 'I don't know,' she whispered. 'All the memories, they keep coming back up. I don't . . .'

He moved his hand and ran his thumb under her eye to get rid of the tears and then pulled her to him.

Zara pulled back. 'I can't be seen talking to you.'

'I know.'

'Dave thinks . . . um, Dave said . . .' She broke eye contact with him and looked at the ground.

Jack waited.

'Dave thinks I've got something wrong with my head. Post-traumatic stress disorder.'

Relief spread over Jack's face. 'That makes sense,' he said. 'It really does. You've been through a lot over the past few years. And you've had pressure from work too. All that's bound to have some sort of lasting effect on you.'

'But it's weak . . .'

Jack shook his head. 'Don't let me hear you say that. It's not true. You've had trauma.' He continued to hold her hand and look at her steadily.

Feeling his strength flow into her, she began to relax. She sniffed and took her hand away to reach for a tissue. Jack wasn't having any of that, though, and he put his hand on her knee and continued to stroke her in long,

271

calming motions. Finally she put her hand over his and closed her eyes.

'I've made an appointment. To talk to someone.' Her sentences were sharp and jerky.

'There's no shame in talking, if that's what you're thinking, Zara. Plenty of people have counsellors.'

She nodded and resisted the urge to rest her head on his shoulder. Jack was so solid and steady and reliable. And loving.

'When's the appointment?'

'In a couple of weeks. I decided . . . I thought . . .' She took a breath and tried again. 'I want things to work out between us, Jack, and I know it's me who's causing the problems.'

He shook his head and grasped her hand tightly. 'It's not all you. I haven't reacted well either. Let's start again, hey? Make sure we talk through everything this time. If there isn't any communication, then we've got problems. Just like we have now.'

Pulling away, Zara looked at him. 'But what if I can't be fixed?' Her eyes darted around as she felt the fear trickle through her stomach. Maybe she was beyond help.

Jack opened his mouth to speak, then shut it again.

'Jack?'

'I was going to say of course you can be, but I guess we won't know anything until you see the doc. Let's take it one step at a time.'

'I've got to go,' Zara said, pulling away. She'd needed an affirmation she would be well again, not more doubt. 'I don't want to talk about it anymore.'

'That's my point, Zara!' Jack sounded frustrated as he reached for her again, but she moved away. 'You don't talk and then we get into this situation where the smallest things blow up because we haven't said how we're feeling. If we can't talk, there's not a lot of hope for us.'

'You might be better off without me.' As she said the words, she heard Dave's voice. *If it all goes pear-shaped ... well, I'm close to retirement. Jack's not and I refuse to jeopardise his career.*

A look of shock crossed his face and he retorted quickly, 'I don't agree with that at all.'

'We're not supposed to be talking. Dave told me that explicitly.' Zara made to close the door. 'We *shouldn't* be talking.' That wasn't strictly true. Dave had suggested it but the words gave her an out now.

'Zara ...'

'No, Jack, it's better this way. Honestly. I'd better go.'

Jack stepped away from the car. 'Fine. Go on, then. I'll talk to you later.'

Zara slammed the door shut and started the engine, before pulling back out onto the road.

Blood pounded in her head as the regret started immediately. She put her foot over the brake then changed her mind and pushed the accelerator down and drove through Torrica towards Old Ted's camp. *Bloody hell, you fucked that up again, Zara,* she thought furiously. *Why couldn't you talk to him?*

Stay away from him, a little voice inside her head told her. *He'll only leave you too.*

Taking a deep breath, Zara counted the trees from the bridge and saw the road that Hopper had told her about. Old Ted should be at the end of it, and she hoped two things: that he wasn't dead, and that he'd had enough to drink to be sociable.

Tentatively, she drove down the track, the overhanging tree branches scratching the roof of the car. As she drove deeper into the valley, trees shaded the grey sky and purple stones crunched under her tyres.

A humpy came into sight—a tin shed with a tarpaulin stretched out the front acting as a verandah. A fire with a kettle on the coals smoked and there was a yellow-coloured dog lying next to it.

He heard the engine and started to bark, but he was chained, so Zara wasn't worried as she turned off the engine and stepped out to a round of barking and whining. The dog strained at the end of the chain, trying to get to her. She looked at him, trying to work out if he was friendly. Deciding he was, she spoke gently to him.

'It's okay, I'm friendly. Where's your master?' Raising her voice, she called out, 'Hello? Ted, are you home?'

No answer. The barking bounced off the walls of the valley, echoing in surround sound. The dog mustn't see a lot of people, Zara decided; he was very excited, standing on his hind legs, his tongue lolling out the side as he encouraged her to come and pat him.

She looked around, hoping to catch a glimpse of the old man coming out of the bush. There was nothing; only trees and bushes, whose leaves held raindrops that occasionally shook loose when a puff of wind swept through.

If Ted's anywhere nearby, he'll come back just on account of the noise, she thought.

'It's all right, mate,' she said to the dog, going a little closer and holding out her hand so he could smell her. 'I'm not going to hurt you.' The dog wagged his tail and slumped back down, whining. 'Ah, there you go, all bark and no bite. Good to know.' She looked around and saw a well-worn path leading away from the camp.

Glad she'd worn her normal winter uniform of jeans and a heavy jacket, along with her Rossi work boots instead of her good R.M. Williams, she started towards the track, calling out, 'Ted? Hopper from the pub sent me.'

'Is that right?' A voice behind her made her jump. He must have been at the camp the whole time. Slowly turning, she looked at a short man whose grey beard was almost down to the middle of his chest. His worn jeans and short-sleeved shirt hung from a thin frame but his eyes were alert and curious. Not the eyes of someone who drank as much as Hopper had implied. She wanted to ask if he was cold, but he didn't appear to be concerned about the weather.

'Yes, he did.'

'And you are?'

'Zara Ellison from the *Farming Telegraph*.'

Ted's eyebrows suddenly combined with his hair. 'What brings you to the middle of nowhere wanting to talk to a hermit?'

'Can we sit down?' A gust of wind brought down fat raindrops from the trees above. They were cold on her scalp.

'Course. Sorry, don't know where my manners are. Been a long time since I entertained a lady.'

They walked over to the camp and Ted brought out two camp chairs from the humpy. He unfolded them and put them next to the fire.

'Cup of tea?'

'That would be nice,' Zara answered, leaning forward to pat the dog. 'What's his name?'

'Deefer.' Ted got out two cups and lifted the kettle from the fire. The tea was strong and black. 'Sugar?'

'Yes, please. Why Deefer?'

'D for dog. Or Dickhead. Depending on the day.' Ted spoke as if she were silly, and Zara gave a laugh.

'Makes sense.'

He handed her the cup and indicated for her to sit down. 'So, what's this all about?'

'I'm working on a story and Hopper thought you might be able to help me. There's a woman in town named Essie Carter.' She went on to tell him why she was following the story. 'I'm trying to find out a little more about her so we can help her with this horrible situation.'

Ted leaned back in his camp chair. 'Now that's a name I haven't heard for a long time.' He was quiet for a moment. 'Let me think. I vaguely remember her. I was still working on the railway and I remember her catching the train to Port Augusta. Always seemed distant. Unreachable.' He stared into the fire, and Zara could see him sifting through memories. 'Reckon she turned up quite out of the blue. No one really knew why she settled here. Wasn't born here or had any family or anything. Bit like a drifter who'd decided to put down some roots.'

'Do you remember if she worked anywhere or had kids?'

'She kept to herself a lot. Was seen out with a kid. There were rumours, though . . . I can't remember exactly what. Without spending a bit of time thinking, that's about all I can tell you.'

Zara took a sip of her tea. 'That's helpful,' she said.

'Sometimes things come back to me after a while, but I need time. My brain isn't as good as it used to be.'

'I can come back and see you in a few days' time in case you think of anything else?'

Ted nodded slowly. 'Yeah, you could. Or I'll find you when I come in to pick up my groceries.'

'Hopper will know where to find me.' She looked around. 'You must like living out here by yourself.'

'I do. There is nothing about society that makes me want to live in a town. My company and that of Deefer is enough. Occasionally Hopper brings news of things that are going on in town, so I'm not completely alone.'

'How long have you lived here?' She caught sight of a basin on a table, behind a tree. Next to it was a grubby piece of soap.

'Must be nearly thirty years.'

Zara looked back and took in the deep lines around his eyes and his dirty hands. His arms were strong and muscular and held a deep tan, which matched the colour of his skin around his eyes.

There was a wood saw leaning against the tin hut and she surmised he must cut his own wood, which kept him strong.

'I used to be the station master, but the company gave my job away, then shut the lines down.' He spat in the dirt, showing his disgust. 'I didn't trust anyone after that. I gave 'em the best years of my life and they repaid with what? Nothing. Not even a decent payout.'

'You never married?'

Ted's look became distant. 'I loved a girl once. But I didn't know how to hold onto her.'

Chapter 28

'Message for you, Dave.' Joan waved a piece of paper at him as he walked in. 'You won't believe who it's from.'

'Oh, yeah? Sounds interesting. Who?'

'Jerry Simms.'

Dave stopped. 'What does he want now?'

'Not sure, he just said to ring.'

Dave took the number and looked at it, before folding the paper and putting it in his pocket. 'Joan, what's your take on this Essie Carter situation?' he asked, pulling out a chair and sitting next to her.

Joan turned to look at him. 'You've never asked my opinion before.'

'You know her, probably better than Kim and I do. You go to church with her. And she's your age. Is there anything you can think of that would make *you* take possession of drugs?'

Joan sighed and put her pen behind her ear and clicked to save the document she was working on. 'We've been praying for her, the congregation—our church has shrunk so much we don't have a preacher anymore to lead us, so we've been doing the best we can.'

Dave nodded. 'It certainly was sad to see Pastor White move on.'

'So few of us, and so few prayers,' Joan said softly. She raised her eyes to look at Dave. 'But as for something that would make me do what Essie's done? I can't think of anything. We did talk about it. Trying to understand. None of us parents thought we would traffic drugs to give to our children.' She shrugged. 'I just can't think of anything that would make any of us do it.'

Dave nodded slowly. 'Blackmail?' he asked.

Joan shook her head. 'I guess we're all of the belief that if anything like that happened to us, the law would protect us. All of us at church would come to you.' She frowned and picked at the hem of her cardigan. 'See, that's what's got us all confused. Essie knows you. She's comfortable with you. We don't understand why she didn't ring you in the first place. We're such a small town and all of Barker knows how invested you are in us. She could have stopped all of this before it started.'

'You're right,' Dave said. 'You really are, but some people think there isn't an option—that what's held over them is too big for them to come to the police. I think that's what has happened here and that's why I'm trying to work out what could have made her make the wrong call.'

Joan paused and looked at Dave. 'Do you remember

the case in Queensland where a mother sold drugs to get a better life for her children?'

Dave pursed his lips. 'Not off the top of my head.'

'Not sure how long ago it was, but I remember it because I was horrified but at the same time I could understand why she'd done it. I think the story was on one of the Sunday night programs.' Joan took a sip of her tea from the cup alongside her, and continued. 'This woman was a victim of domestic violence for years and she finally left the relationship. But the husband was a lawyer and managed to get the child-support payments reduced to a minimum, which left her with virtually nothing.'

'An all too common story,' Dave said. 'And it can happen the other way round where the men are left with nothing.'

'Yes, that's true. Anyhow, her son was gifted and she couldn't afford the fees for the private school he'd been going to when they'd been married. The scholarships for the year had been allocated and he was about to be asked to leave.

'Somehow the mother managed to get hold of some drugs and sell them, and that was how she paid the school fees. She kept doing it until the police caught her. It was how she paid her rent, put food on the table for the kids and gave them the few little extras she'd never otherwise be able to afford. Didn't matter that she was trying to improve her children's lives, the judge still put her in jail.'

'I bet the media reported her as a "great mother",' Dave said and then rubbed his hands over his head, sighing at the same time. 'Yeah, it's such a hard one. I can understand why she did it, but how many other kids' lives did she stuff up because they were taking the drugs she sold.'

'I wonder if that's where Essie has got into trouble?'

Dave stared at her. 'What? As in, she was running out of money to look after Paris?'

'Well, I'm not sure if that would be the exact reason, but maybe there is a situation like that, which is worth considering.'

Getting up, he smiled. 'Thanks, Joan, I'm sure you're on the right track.'

He went into his office and started up his computer, just as Jack came in with Kim behind him. The station suddenly smelled of freshly baked pastry.

'Meals on Wheels has arrived,' Kim called out. 'Hello, Joan.'

Dave heard Kim and Joan talking in reception as Jack hung his coat up in the office.

'I don't know what sort they are, but it's some type of pie,' he said to Dave in a hushed tone.

'If the meat defrosting on the sink this morning was anything to go by, they'll be chicken,' Dave said with a grin.

'Be still my beating heart.'

'God, you're dramatic about food.' Dave shook his head, still smiling.

'Only Kim's.'

'Should I be jealous?'

Jack laughed. 'I'd love for Kim to come and live with me and cook the way she does for you, but I reckon I'd barely be able to stand two weeks after she moved in.'

Chuckling, Dave put his hands on Kim's waist and gave her an affectionate squeeze as she came into the office and put the pies on the desk.

'Those smell amazing,' he said. 'I think you have a not-so-secret admirer. Only for your cooking, though.'

'Yeah, nothing untoward,' Jack added.

'I'm flattered.' Kim gave a chuckle. 'They're chicken.'

Dave threw an *I told you so* look at Jack, who pointed his finger at him acknowledging he'd been right.

'While you two are here,' Dave said, helping himself to a pie, 'I want to quiz you. I've just talked to Joan, and she came up with a thought about why Essie might have done what she did. Sit down, honey.' He pulled a chair out for Kim and slid the container across to Jack, who helped himself and bit in immediately.

'Whoa,' he fanned his mouth and Kim laughed again as steam came out of it.

'They've just come out of the oven. You're worse than a kid sometimes, Jack.'

'Can't help it,' he said. 'No one cooks like you do.'

'Spoken like a true bachelor.'

'He's not really,' Dave said, frowning at Kim.

'How *is* Zara?' Kim asked, blatantly ignoring Dave's warning glance.

'Can't talk with my mouth full,' Jack mumbled.

'Um, as I was saying . . .' Dave said pointedly, trying to get their attention.

'What would have made Essie do this?' Kim asked. She shook her head. 'I wish I knew. What was Joan's thought?'

Dave told them both and then clicked his mouse to bring up his internet browser.

'I don't think it's because she's short of money,' Kim said.

'Well, she's certainly never indicated that to me.'

'I agree,' Jack said. 'More likely some type of blackmail.'

'We can't dismiss anything yet,' Dave said. 'Now, what sort of blackmail would be enough for a sixty-plus woman to risk going to jail and leaving her granddaughter without someone to care for her?'

'Dave?' Joan called out from the front office. 'Jerry Simms is on the phone for you.'

'Again?' He looked at Kim and Jack. 'I'd better take this. It's the second time he's tried to call. I ignored the first one.' He got up and went into another office and pressed the flashing red light.

'Burrows?'

'Simms.'

There was silence that neither was prepared to break.

Finally, Dave said, 'How can I help you?'

'I'm hoping you can assist me with some local knowledge.'

Harrumphing, Dave stayed silent, wondering what could have been so important to make this man—who clearly thought Dave was past his use-by date—call asking for help.

'Let me make this clear, Burrows, I'm not enjoying having to phone you, but you're probably the only one who can give me the information I need.'

'Good thing I don't hold grudges,' Dave said. 'What do you need to know?'

'Has there ever been any inkling of drug families in the Flinders Ranges?'

'Loaded question. By "drug families", do you mean living here or just supplying here?'

'I'd suggest living with perhaps a small amount of supply.'

Dave thought back through the cases he'd been involved in over the past five years. 'Just here in Barker or across the Flinders?' he finally asked.

'Across your area. I've checked the system and records and haven't found anything, but I thought you might know more.'

'Look, Simms, there's nothing that I know about. Certainly nothing I've investigated. If there is a drug family living here or in surrounding areas, I haven't heard of them. There hasn't been any increase in crime or drug use that I'm aware of in my area and I believe I would know if there was.'

'How?'

Dave rolled his eyes. 'For one, despite what you think of me, I know if there are changes in my patch. Two, I have an open-door policy and if there were any young adults with changed habits or parent with concerns, I'm sure I would have heard from them. Three, before the arrest of Essie Carter, there hadn't been any increase in crime or other indicators that there is a drug problem in Barker.'

'Right. What about new people moving into the area? I'm sure someone from a drug family isn't going to knock on the door of the Barker cop-shop and announce they've moved in.'

Dave paused. He really wanted to punch Simms. His arrogant, demeaning attitude made Dave really not want to help him. But that wasn't the oath he took when he joined the force.

'There is a woman who has been in Barker about three months. She's staying in the caravan park as far as I'm aware and spends a lot of time running. Training for some sort of event. And I believe she could be keeping an eye on Essie.'

'You were told to stay away from the investigation.' The words came like bullets from a machine gun.

'And I have. That information has come to light recently and through a source that had nothing to do with me.'

'Got a name?'

'No, but I can get one, if you'd like me to.'

'No, you stay out of it. Anyone else?'

'Not that I'm aware of. Simms, I'm not the gatekeeper into Barker.'

'But according to your boss, Steve, you know everything that goes on within a couple of hundred kilometres of the town.'

A surge of pleasure washed over Dave at the professional recognition. 'I'd like to think so.'

'Right. Thanks for your help.'

Simms hung up before Dave could say, *You're welcome.* Dave sat staring at the wall, thinking through the information he'd just been given.

Drug families. That would be in line with their thoughts about blackmail.

He got up and went back into the shared office and looked at the empty chair where Kim had been.

'What'd he want?' Jack asked.

'Let's think about this. Let's say there was a drug family in town—not Barker, it's too small, but say, somewhere like Port Pirie or Port Augusta. There would be a reason they've moved there. To keep out of sight, to stay under the cops' radar . . . A living arrangement like that would be strategic. Small country towns wouldn't normally suit their business.'

'Hmm.' Jack bit into his second pie.

'Why do you suppose they would be living here, and which town would you choose?'

'Good question. The why? Is there a supply here? Coming in through the ports maybe?'

Dave nodded slowly. 'Or the post?'

Jack shook his head immediately. 'The amount Essie got was minimal. It wouldn't be enough to make someone shift up here. What makes you think someone has?'

'Well, I'm not sure. In fact, my knowledge of what's going on in this area wouldn't indicate to me that anyone like that has moved in, but, like I said to Simms, I'm not a gatekeeper. He wanted to know if there had ever been any drug families living here.'

'Ever? Not right now?'

'No,' Dave said slowly. 'Not necessarily right now, which again doesn't make any sense.' He thought back to when Melissa had been in Barker. Even then he'd been sure she'd brought her supply with her rather than buying it anywhere nearby. Then her so-called boyfriend had turned up with a bit more, but he'd been a run-of-the-mill street junkie, nothing more.

'Wish I could get on the computer and start looking,' Dave said, staring in frustration at the screen.

Chapter 29

'Found her,' Lachie said down the phone.

'What do you mean? Melissa?'

'Yep. My contact came through. She's in Port Augusta.'

'You're kidding? So close. On the streets?' Zara asked, fishing around for her notepad just as her phone pinged with a text message.

Jack. *Can we catch up?*

She stared at the message, not hearing Lachie's voice as he kept talking.

'Zara?'

'What? Oh, sorry.' She put the phone up to her ear so she wouldn't see another message come through and tried to focus on Lachie's answer.

'Strangely enough, no. My contact says she's been clean for a while. Working in a halfway house there. Helping other junkies. I've got to say, I'm very surprised.'

'You're telling me! I really thought she'd still be on the gear. That puts a bit of a hole in my theory that Essie was taking the drugs for her.'

'Not really. She could be on-selling to the people in the halfway house.'

'No way! That would completely defeat the purpose of her being there.'

Zara could tell he was sceptical from his silence.

'Stranger things have happened,' Lachie finally said.

'Are you sure it's her? How do you know?'

'My bloke is never wrong. You'll have to trust me on this. I'll text you the details.'

'Right-oh, I'll head down there now.'

Her phone dinged with the message from Lachie and she read it while he was on speaker. 'Got it,' she said. 'Thanks, Lachie. I just know this is going to be a good story, and we've got to get to the bottom of all this for Essie's sake.'

'You're not getting involved are you?' Lachie's tone indicated he knew she was.

'Not at all.' Zara put on her most professional voice. 'This is a story about righting a wrong.'

'Keep it that way, Zara,' Lachie warned. 'I don't want you taking risks or making mistakes because you're too invested.'

'Have I ever done that?'

'No, but you're not quite yourself at the moment. Just keep that wall up, okay?'

Zara put the phone down and stared at the desk. Could everyone read her like a book?

❧

Zara wound her way through the deep gorge of Horrocks Pass on her way to Port Augusta. The towering hills rose above her and she marvelled at how the gum trees grew so straight on the steep sides of the hills.

'Turn right at the T-junction,' the voice of Karen, the navigator, told her.

'Yes, yes, I know that. I really only need your help when I get to town.'

Zara went over in her mind how she was going to approach Melissa. Her heart had been beating extra fast since she'd received Lachie's text, and now she had the feeling that she was on the homeward stretch. If she could only get Melissa to talk . . .

Or Dave. Dave would have had some ideas about how to approach her. It had crossed Zara's mind that a visit out of the blue could put Melissa on a backwards trajectory, and that wasn't something she wanted to be the cause of.

That was if Melissa would even talk to her. Zara expected some resistance—obviously, Melissa hadn't wanted to be found, otherwise she would be in contact with Essie. And Paris.

Zara entered the eighty-kilometre zone of Port Augusta and followed the directions, winding her way through the back streets until she heard the GPS say: 'Turn right at Cooper Street and the destination is on your left.'

Slowing the car, Zara looked across the street to a

nondescript house. The paint was peeling from the window-sills and the lawn was overgrown.

She wasn't sure what she had expected to see, but not this. A tidy, sterile environment maybe. To her, this looked more like a users' house than somewhere they came to get clean.

Checking the address Lachie had texted her and then her location, she concluded it was the house she was looking for. Taking a deep breath, she got out of the car, locked it and walked across the street.

A sign on the door told Zara to ring the bell.

Chimes echoed inside the house and after a few moments the door squeaked open and a woman in her sixties peered out. She was thin and frumpy, dressed in a large print dress. Her skin and eyes were clear, though she seemed drawn and tired.

'Yes?'

'Hello, I'm looking for Melissa.'

'Melissa?'

'Yes, is she around?'

'Who's asking?'

'I'm Zara. I just need a few words with her.'

The woman assessed her for a moment, then the door swung open. 'Come in.' She tried to smile, showing blackened and cracked teeth.

Resisting the urge to shudder, Zara smiled back and stepped over the threshold.

'Thanks.'

Inside, she looked around. There were three people sitting on an old, drab couch that looked as if it had once been red but was now a dull rose colour.

One of the women turned and looked over at Zara. She was, Zara judged, in her thirties, wearing a stained white shirt and jeans. Her face was covered in sores and her eyes were dim and lifeless. The other two stared at a TV, though they didn't seem to be taking in what was on the screen. From behind, Zara could see they had greasy hair and one had large pimples covering the back of his neck.

She'd heard that users always had bad skin, but what she was looking at was something else.

As she surveyed the room, she realised it was dimly lit, with a couple of pot plants in each corner. A bookshelf with a few books was against one wall and the other had a vending machine full of chips and chocolate bars. The floor was clean, but the amenities were old and worn out. Everything about the place had seen much better days.

'You want to see Melissa?' the older woman asked.

'Yes, if I could.' Zara had to pull her gaze away from the people on the couch, but just as she was about to, the younger woman turned at the sound of their voices and Zara sucked in her breath. Her eyes were dead, face covered in sores and she was dangerously gaunt.

The woman who had opened the door spoke again and Zara refocused. 'Come this way.'

'Is Melissa here?' she asked.

'I'm Melissa. Who are you?' She opened the door to an office and led Zara inside.

'You're Melissa?' She couldn't keep the surprise out of her voice. 'Melissa Carter?' She looked at the woman, who Zara would have sworn was older. Her hair was ragged and grey, her face bony, eyes protruding.

'Too many years on the gear does this to you,' she said, sitting at her desk. 'I know I'm not an oil painting. Anyway, I've told you who I am, it's your turn now.'

'I'm Zara Ellison. I live in Barker.'

Melissa stood straight back up again. 'I don't want to talk to you.'

Zara reacted quickly, trying to keep her in the room. 'Please, just hear me out.'

'I don't want anything to do with that town. It's a bad place for me.'

'It's about your daughter,' Zara got out. 'Paris.'

Melissa stopped and looked at her. Her fingers traced the scars on her arms and she looked uncertain. 'Paris?'

'Yes, and your mum.'

'Are they okay?' Melissa sounded frightened and Zara caught glimpses of Essie in her face.

'Paris is fine,' she said soothingly. 'But Essie, well, she's got a few problems and she could probably do with your help.'

'Can she still look after my daughter?'

'For now,' Zara said. 'But honestly, Melissa, I can't guarantee how much longer she will be able to.'

Melissa sank into her chair again, almost disappearing behind the mounds of paperwork. Taking in the office for the first time, Zara saw that it was tired and old, just as everything in the house seemed to be. She removed a pile of papers from another chair and sat down, looking at Melissa, who appeared to have suddenly aged another five years.

'What's wrong with Mum?'

'She's been charged with importing heroin.'

Melissa looked as if she'd been slapped in the face. 'What? No! That's not possible. Why would she do that? She hates drugs. She hated what they did to me.'

'I'm sorry, Melissa. But, yes, she's already been to court and was bailed. Her trial will be coming up soon. If she goes to prison, she won't be able to care for Paris, who will probably end up a ward of the state.'

'No. That can't be.' Melissa stared pleadingly at Zara. 'Who's looking after Paris now?'

'While Essie was in custody, Kim Burrows was. She's a foster carer.' Zara paused. 'She was the one who posted bail for your mum.'

'Dave's wife? Is that who you mean?'

'Yes.'

Melissa shook her head. 'This doesn't make sense. Mum taking drugs. She's so anti-drugs . . .' Her voice trailed off and she shook her head as her knee jiggled up and down.

'Look, we all know that. That's why I'm here. To see if we can work out what's going on. Originally, Dave thought she was doing it for you, but from what I can see you're clean. Is that right?'

'Yeah, I have been for eighteen months.' Melissa looked up, clearly proud of her achievement. 'It's a special kind of hell, when you're going through the withdrawals and trying to get clean. Took me three weeks to be able to go out in public again. I'd lie in bed feeling like I had a bad flu, headaches, sweating. I'd tell myself I'd be okay because I had to get through this so I could go and see Paris again. She was the only thing that kept me focused.

'That's why I discharged myself from the hospital after Dave saved me. I didn't want Mum to see me like that. When I saw her again, I wanted to be able to look her in the eye and say I was clean and I'd come through the other side.

'Mum buying drugs is crazy. Totally not right.'

'How come you aren't home looking after Paris now, then?' Zara asked gently. 'Looks like you've done a wonderful job caring for these people here. That's what you do, isn't it?'

Nodding, Melissa smiled again, showing her terrible teeth. Zara wanted to run away at the grizzly sight, but she stayed where she was. This woman had worked hard to get better, and Zara wasn't backing down from the game now.

'Because I can't do that to Mum and Paris again. I promised myself I'd never put them through what I did five years ago. They're better off without me. Every day I fight the demons within me not to take a hit. Not to go and find a dealer to get some smack.' She rubbed her arms with jerky movements. 'Working here keeps me in reality, reminds me never to go back there again. Dealing with the bureaucrats keeps my mind busy. I'm always chasing extra funding and helping new clients who walk through the door. That's why

I let you in. I thought you must have someone who needed help and heard about us. If I wasn't doing this, I'd . . . Well, I'm not sure.' She breathed in deeply through her nose and Zara could keenly feel the desperation of a woman who badly wanted to be well, but had to continually fight to stay that way. 'How was Mum getting the drugs?'

'They were being posted to her.'

Melissa sat still and Zara felt a change in the air.

Suddenly, Melissa catapulted out of her seat and thumped her fist into her hand. 'That bastard!' she spat.

Zara pulled back a little, suddenly alert. 'What do you mean?'

Melissa looked up, anger blazing in her eyes. 'We had a guy in here eighteen months ago. Tried to blackmail me into receiving drugs through the mail. I said no, I wouldn't be a part of it, but by then I'd already been hooking up with him and he knew about Paris and Mum. Sounds like he's found her and is blackmailing her. I know he's done it to others.'

The familiar rush of adrenalin coursed through Zara. Now they were getting somewhere. 'Can you tell me about that guy?'

'Not really, he was only here a few weeks. There're strict rules about us being involved with the clients. He wasn't a client, but he said he'd had trouble with drugs before and needed a place to crash. I had a spare room and said it was fine. I always need money to keep this place going, you see. He paid for three weeks up front. I wasn't about to say no.

'Course it only took a couple of days and he'd wormed his way in—he's very charismatic.' She shrugged. 'Then when I said no, I had to ask him to leave because I couldn't have him bringing drugs here, he would have undone all the good work with everyone.' She spread her arms out. 'Everyone who lives in the house is clean, but really fragile. One slip and they could be back on the dark side again, so we won't allow anything that could cause that. It's not rocket science. He did get really angry when I asked him to leave. Threatened me, but I didn't take much notice of what he said. I've been threatened lots and no one has ever made good on it.'

'What was his threat?'

'Just that he'd make sure I'd pay. But maybe he meant my family would.'

Zara's heart went out to Melissa. Her thin frame seemed to shrink even more, with each little piece of the puzzle she told.

'I wonder why your mum hasn't said anything. She's refusing to cooperate with the police.'

'Who knows. If it *is* Spritz, then maybe he's got her brainwashed. Thinking he'll do something to me if she doesn't take them. That's how he gets control over people. Tells them he'll hurt their family. Maybe she thinks she's protecting me and Paris.' Twiddling her thumbs and unable to stay still, she kept talking. 'He's not a very nice person. And I can't go back to Barker and see them, I'm too fragile. But I'll do anything to help Mum. Just tell me what you need me to do.'

Zara thought quickly. Dave would want her to get anything that might help. Everything that Melissa could tell her would be of use. She got out her notepad and looked at Melissa.

'The best thing you can do is to talk to me, Melissa. This man—you said his name was Spritz? Tell me everything you know about him.'

Chapter 30

'You've come up with the goods, my man,' she told Lachie when he answered.

'What'd you get?'

'Some good info, but I need to see Dave about it. I'm still not sure how I'm going to handle this.' She paused. 'Melissa is definitely clean but still fighting to stay that way.' She filled him in, ending with: 'What can you tell me about a bloke whose street name is Spritz? Have you heard of him?'

'Zara, it's been nearly fifteen years since I was on the street gig. Got a real name?'

'Melissa isn't sure, but she thought it was something like Esperitzo.'

'That sounds like a pork-and-cheese name. Tell me again?'

'Pork and cheese?'

'Yeah, Portuguese. That's what we used to call them back when I was out there. Probably politically incorrect now.'

'Right. Esperitzo was what she thought.'

'Yeah, right. See, there're many Spritzes around. But if I remember correctly, back in my day there was a big drug family headed up by Manuel Esperitzo. Guessing they might be related.' He paused. 'If that's the case, then you're dead on the money—this will be huge. Imports, distribution, the works. You name it, they did it when it came to drugs. This would be why the AFP is involved. I'll see what I can find out. You'll have to be discreet, Zara. You're playing with dangerous people here. They'll stop at nothing if they think you're about to bring them down. I knew a bloke, used to be one of my snitches; they got wind he'd been talking to the coppers, and he disappeared. Word on the street was they put him in a cage full of rats and let them eat him. So, don't get in the mix and get yourself killed. Or worse. If this is run by them, they won't think twice about eliminating a journo.'

Zara shuddered. 'Oh my God!'

'Exactly,' Lachie said. 'Be careful.'

A rush of fear ran through her. 'Would they put people on Essie to monitor her movements?'

'Sure. If they thought she might talk.'

Zara told him about the strange vehicle and the woman seen running each day.

'Hmm. I reckon they're already in Barker. You're right, you're going to need to talk to your friendly policeman about this. Find out the best way to handle it. It'll be tricky if he's been warned off. By hell, Zara, be careful. This is bigger than even you hoped for.'

'I will.' She hung up and sat contemplating what Lachie had just told her. Visions of a man in a cage, shrieking with terror as rats bit and tore at his flesh came to her. Looking over her shoulder she quickly started the engine and put the car into gear and drove home, watching her rear-vision mirror the whole way.

❧

Zara was going through her phone messages and stopped at Jack's.

Can we catch up?

She tapped the phone against her chin as she thought. Maybe it would be easier not to see him until all this was over. She certainly didn't want to put him in any danger. But then she thought about the last time she saw him, on the roadside as she broke down in tears, and remembered how good she'd felt when he'd pulled her against his chest.

Trying not to think too much, she sent back her answer: *Am out of town at the moment. I'll call you when I get back.* Her fingers hovered above the keys, wanting to say something more, something to bridge the gap between them, but she decided against it and hit send.

Not strictly true, but she'd only just got home, and it was close to 9 p.m. She still had to get dinner and speak to Dave. She would call Jack tomorrow, if Dave said that was okay.

The second hand inched towards 10 p.m. and Zara slipped out of her house as it ticked over the hour and the clock hand hit the twelve.

Walking in the shadows, she opened the back gate and picked up a handful of rocks, before hurling them at his roof. This time it only took two throws to get him outside.

'Lachie and I found Melissa,' she told him as they huddled around the side of the house. 'And you won't believe what she's doing. It's a long and involved story.'

'Hit me with it,' Dave said, putting his hands underneath his armpits for warmth.

She filled him in on everything she'd found out that day.

'So, this Spritz, he was her dealer, pimping her out for a while in Port Augusta. She'd known him for a while—longer than she first claimed.

'Spritz was Ryan Kipling's supplier for a few years and sold him the drugs that killed him. Long and short of the story: Spritz was worried that Melissa was going to grass him. She took Ryan's death really hard and wanted revenge.

'He knew she'd been on the gear before, but both she and Ryan had got off it before they conceived Paris, and Melissa hadn't realised that Ryan was using again.

'Spritz came to Barker once Melissa had moved back here. He said he wanted to rekindle the relationship they'd had before Ryan. He spiked her drink and then injected her—and that's when you found her. Sounds like he was worried she would turn him into the authorities.'

'Fuck,' said Dave. 'What a tosser.'

'Melissa said it took her a long time after that to break away from him. She's been clean for eighteen months, but he turned up at the halfway house she's working at and they shacked up again. That was when he asked about having drugs sent through the mail to her. Not to Essie. To Melissa.

'Sounds like this is how he works. Befriends a former user and asks them to take delivery of the drugs. Of course, he doesn't want a user to get them because there's every chance they'd take off with the drugs.'

'They'd only do that once,' Dave muttered. 'And this fits in with the phone call I had from the AFP today asking if I knew if there had ever been any drug families living in the Flinders region. This Spritz obviously was in the area, even if only for a few weeks.'

A shower of rain came through and the wind tossed the leaves of the tree against the house, while Zara continued with her story.

'She's really proud that she managed to get away from him and get clean.'

'So she should be.'

'But,' Zara held up her finger, 'Melissa never thought he'd use her mother to access the drugs. She thought if she got herself clean, he wouldn't have anything to hold over either her mum or her.'

'I suspect he's threatened either Melissa or Essie's life. That's how those lowlifes work.' Anger filtered through his voice. 'If someone threatened to kill your daughter, well, that would be enough to make you agree to receive a parcel of drugs.'

'Yeah,' Zara said. 'That makes a lot of sense. He's very charming, Melissa said, so he could have easily wooed Essie, then hit her with what he actually wanted once she trusted him. But the family isn't that charming. Lachie told me about a source he had—they killed him by letting rats eat him alive.'

'I've heard similar stories. They're ruthless.' He looked to the sky as a sliver of moonlight shone through the clouds. 'He could've got to her that way, for sure.' He was quiet. 'Or there's another possibility. He mightn't have done either. He could have threatened Paris right from the start. I could see how that would work. Both women would be pliable if that had happened. He could have said he'd get her into the sex trade or sell her organs.'

Zara blanched. 'God almighty.'

'Yeah, we're dealing with the dregs of society here. Look at the rat story. Okay, anything else you've got for me?'

'Lachie's looking into whether Spritz is related to Manuel Esperitzo.'

Dave nodded. 'They're an old and established drug family and I'm certain the family tree will end up back at Manuel. Really, I should be contacting the AC and seeking permission for Jack to talk to Melissa, but let's see what Lachie comes back with first. The more evidence we get that this Spritz is connected to Esperitzo, the better chance I'll have of making that happen.'

'No worries. Have you seen that car around town yet? And the woman—the runner?'

'Funny you should ask. I pulled her over today. You're never going to believe this.'

'What?'

'We were wrong. It's not the pimp following Essie, it's the Feds.'

Zara slumped a little. 'Oh my God, you won't believe how happy I am to hear that. I was convinced it was Spritz and his gang by the time I left Melissa today. I guess the Feds are hoping the dealer is going to contact Essie?'

'Spot on the money. My guess is they're watching me as well. Making sure I don't contact her.' He shrugged. 'Let 'em watch. They won't find anything.'

Zara narrowed her eyes as she thought back over the past few days. 'So, why are they driving past my place and taking photos?'

'They'll be watching you but, the thing is, there's only one of them here, so you're in the clear, just so long as you keep moving. Doesn't appear to me that we're the main interest. It's mostly Essie, but if you're close by, they'll watch you too.'

'Sneaky buggers.'

'That's the Feds.'

'Actually, they're really bad at tailing people.'

Dave laughed softly. 'Sometimes out in the open is the best way to hide. If people see them, they won't give them a second thought.'

'Hang on, that doesn't make sense.'

'Which bit?'

'What about the phone call to Essie? If it was the Feds, they must have known Kim was with her to ring right then.'

Dave nodded. 'I'm not convinced that phone call was from them, and it was just lucky timing on the caller's behalf. I reckon it was a reminder from Spritz, to keep her quiet.'

'Can you put a trace on her phone? Actually, why wouldn't the Feds put a trace on her phone?'

'They may have,' Dave said, glancing up as the drizzle became heavier. 'I wouldn't be able to find that out because I'm not supposed to have anything to do with this, remember.'

'Here comes the rain,' Zara sang, putting her hood up. 'I'm heading off. Speak to you soon, if I need to.'

'Stay safe.'

❧

The next morning Zara waited until after school drop-off and then knocked on Essie's door.

Zara had never taken much notice of Essie's house but, as she stood listening to the bell chime fade, she could see the garden was beautifully neat, as was every part of the house, except the front door. The paint was peeling in sections and the blue was so faded that it was barely recognisable.

That's weird. If everything else is so tidy, why is the door like this?

The door opened and as Essie saw Zara, she tried to close it quickly.

'I can't talk to you,' she said.

'I've spoken to Melissa,' Zara told her.

The door stopped closing and Essie looked out from behind it, her face hungry for information. 'Really?'

'Yes. Can I come in?'

Essie glanced around. 'I don't know . . .'

'Please. I won't stay long. What I do know, though, is you won't have to live like this much longer.'

Not saying anything, Essie held the door open and let her in. 'Is Melissa okay? I mean, is she . . .'

'Yes, she is. Melissa is clean.' Zara smiled at the older woman. 'I spent a few hours with her yesterday. She's trying to get herself healthy enough to come back into your life but she's really worried that she's going to cave and disappoint you again.'

'Where is—'

Zara shook her head. 'I can't tell you that yet, but what I can say is that she's running a halfway house for other people who are trying to stay away from drugs too. She's doing it as a reminder to make sure she doesn't slip back into that way of life again.'

'Oh God, thank you.' Essie dropped her head in her hands and started to cry. 'I thought they had her.'

'No, they haven't. She's safe and she's got support where she is. But Melissa is just too fragile to come back here at the moment. I'm sure it won't be long.'

'She needs to come home,' Essie sobbed. 'I can help her.'

'Not yet, Essie. Gently does it. If she slips up, knowing she's put you through hell again could be enough for her to never get back on track. Let's go and sit down.' She guided Essie into the kitchen and looked around for a packet of tissues. Grabbing them from the bench, she put them on the table in front of Essie.

Then she sat and rubbed Essie's back, while she cried herself out.

When she calmed down, Zara put a glass of water in front of her and took a breath. 'Essie, I know you might not want to answer this question, but I really need you to. Can you tell me anything about the person who approached you about collecting the drugs?'

Essie shook her head, while wiping tears away. 'Paris.'

Chapter 31

You've got a visitor in the pub.

Zara read the message from Hopper and frowned. She didn't have time to talk to anyone at the moment; she was flat-out researching the Manuel Esperitzo cartel. The little Dave had told her wasn't enough for her story. She needed history, names, similar cases.

What she'd found was horrifying.

The Esperitzo family had infiltrated Australia in the early 1990s. The patriarch, Manuel, was from Portugal, just as Lachie had suggested. He had five sons, who each ran a section of the business. They were involved in international drug trafficking, money laundering and organised crime across the world, but their links into Australia were strong.

The third most powerful Portuguese syndicate in the world, behind the José and Miguel families, Esperitzo was responsible for importing and distributing nearly fifty tonnes of heroin and large amounts of cocaine over the past five years and was currently the most active drug family in Australia. Zara was well aware that if they found out she was investigating them, her life wouldn't go on much longer. And the same was true for Essie, Melissa, Paris and Dave, and of course Kim and Jack.

Shutting her computer and heading to the pub, she kept her eyes peeled for anything suspicious. Barker was quiet today. Even the Feds' car had disappeared.

Pushing open the door, she saw Ted Leeson sitting at the bar, a rum in front of him.

'Ah, here she is,' Hopper said. And to Zara, 'He's come in just to see you. He never comes to town without me, so he must have some good news to share with you.'

Zara smiled and sat on a stool. 'How are you, Ted?'

The old man looked at her blearily over the rim of his drink. 'Don't drink much when I'm out there on my own,' he slurred. 'But I gotta get the guts to come into town. That's what this is. Dutch courage.'

'I appreciate you coming in. Can I have a lemon squash, Hopper?' she asked. To Ted she said, 'Can I buy you a steak for lunch?'

'Well, now, I haven't had a steak for years. I'd like that.'

'Come on. Let's head into the dining room then. Two steaks, thanks, Hopper.'

'Comin' up.'

Zara guided Ted through the bar and out to the empty dining room set with tablecloths and cutlery. The room was cold; no fire going. Not many people ate lunch in the pub during the week.

'How's Deefer?'

'Good as gold. Good watchdog, that one. Barked like a bastard when you turned up, didn't he?'

'Sure did. I thought if you were around you'd hear the noise and come back.'

'Just wanted to check who you were before I showed myself. Sometimes I get people creeping around out there, seeing what they can pinch.'

'Well, I'm glad you decided to come out and talk to me.' She played with the salt shaker, twirling it around in her fingers. 'Did you remember some information about Essie?' she asked.

Ted brandished his glass around in the air, looking pleased with himself. 'That I did. That I did.'

Putting her elbows on the table, Zara looked at him expectantly.

'Well, the barbershop man she was married to, he wasn't her first husband, I don't think.'

Zara pricked up her ears. 'Really?'

'I'm sure she had a fella before that. Now, whether they were married or not, I couldn't be sure.'

'Did this other man work with you on the railways?'

'Nah, nah, nothing like that.' He waved his now-empty glass around. 'Can't quite recall . . .'

'Would you like another drink?'

'That'd be grand.'

Zara took the glass and went back into the front bar. 'Same again, Hopper, please.'

'I might lighten the load this time,' Hopper said. 'Maybe just a single shot rather than a double.'

'Good idea. I don't think he'll notice.' She leaned in towards Hopper and lowered her voice. 'How much weight should I give whatever he tells me? He's pretty far gone.'

'I'd listen to him and see if you can verify the story somehow. He's usually pretty spot on, but this is going back a while.'

'He hadn't been drinking when I went out there.'

Hopper nodded. 'Sometimes he's on the wagon and sometimes not. Depends on what week you get him. Guess you got a good day. I know that he has to have a few before coming to town.' He handed her the drink. 'But whatever he wants to tell you must have been important enough for him to make the trip to Barker without me. Long way to hitchhike.'

'Okay, I'll listen up. Thanks.' She raised the glass towards him and he gave her a smile.

'Get along and get your story, Zara.'

Zara put the drink in front of Ted and sat down again.

'Thank you kindly, young lady. Oh, and look at this. Here's lunch.' He leaned back and let the chef put the steaks down in front of them both and grinned. 'Fit for a king. Thank you, sir.'

He picked up his knife and fork, cut through the steak and popped a piece into his mouth, chewing with his eyes closed. Finally, he opened them. 'That, missy, is a beautiful piece of beef.'

'So, back to Essie . . .' Zara prompted.

'Ah, yes. See, this is all so long ago, I'm trying to remember if I've got everything right and I'm not mixing two different stories together.'

'Yeah, sure is a while ago. Did you remember how Essie came to live in Barker?'

'She was friendly with the service-station owner. Her and . . . whatever-her-name-was used to go to church together.'

'Did you know Essie's first bloke?'

'Don't think I ever did.' He took another bite.

'Do you know what he did?'

'Reckon he was a bit of a drifter from all accounts. Drank a lot at the pub. A man's man sort of fella. I got some recollection that he was a bit of a womaniser too. Used to go away a lot and leave her by herself. He'd be away for months at a time and you can't tell me he was faithful to her while he was gone. A man has needs, you know.'

Zara took a sip of her lemon squash and popped a chip into her mouth, after dragging it through the gravy. She arranged her thoughts. 'Where do you think he used to go?'

'Well, I don't rightly know, but I think he was a shearer.'

'So, he would have been going to sheds all around the country?'

Ted nodded enthusiastically. 'Yeah, yeah, that's what he did, I'm sure.'

'Okay.' She scraped her fork around the mushroom sauce and ate another piece of steak, hoping Ted had more to tell her.

314

'What was it like for shearers back then?'

'A hard life, missy, a hard life. Always on the road, one shed following onto the next. It would have been tricky to take a woman on the road with him, that's for sure. Not surprised she settled here and didn't move on.

'Lots of fights as the wide-comb dispute came in. See, shearers got pretty upset when the blokes from across the ditch came over and started using shearing gear that was larger than ours.' Ted took another sip of his drink, lost in memories. 'It was a nasty episode. Union blokes bashed the shearers who were using the wider gear. It was really all about pay and conditions. Pay and conditions.'

'Turbulent times.' Zara paused. 'You seem to know a lot about it.'

'You couldn't miss the debate. The blokes would talk all about it at the pub and I'd listen.' He lapsed into silence.

Trying to bring the conversation back to Essie, Zara cleared her throat and asked, 'Was this shearer Melissa's father?'

Ted sat up straight and put his knife and fork down. 'Well, now, here's the clincher. When Essie arrived in Barker, she was pregnant, so I'd have to say yes, that was a possibility. I know she had the child because one of my mates used to work at the hospital and he heard her screaming the house down, when she was having her.

'"Ted," he said, "Ted, I really thought someone was murdering that poor girl. When I finished up that day I had to go straight to the pub and have myself a drink."'

Zara wanted to smile at the absurd story but couldn't. Her gut was telling her that Ted knew exactly what he was talking about and he was working up to something.

'Right.'

'I reckon he was their dad, for sure.'

'*Their* dad? Has Melissa got a sibling?'

'I don't rightly know.' He wagged his finger at her. 'I know she was only ever seen with one child. Someone said she had twins. She screamed enough in labour for that to be the case, but she was only ever seen out and about with one. A little girl. Can't remember what her name was.'

'Melissa?'

Ted screwed up his eyes thinking. Then shook his head. 'Like I've said, it was a long time ago. I can't rightly remember ... There was talk that one child died during the labour.' He paused, his face gloomy. 'Sad that. Pushed the husband over the edge and he disappeared.'

Chapter 32

Dave left home at daybreak, hoping to catch the Assistant Commissioner before he went into his daily meetings. He was now standing in the large office, the walls adorned with many awards.

'Sir, please, I'd really like your permission for Jack to speak to Melissa Carter.'

The Assistant Commissioner steepled his fingers. He was sitting in his large plush chair and hadn't taken his eyes off Dave since he'd sat down. 'Why are you even here, Burrows? I instructed you to stay away from this case.'

Nodding, Dave said, 'I know, sir, but I wouldn't be any good at my job if I did that when I knew the Feds were on the wrong track. I'm not saying Essie didn't receive the drugs. That was never my argument. What I knew was—'

'There was more to the story, yes, yes, you're sounding like a broken record, Burrows.' He stared at Dave. 'Tell me what you know.'

'My source . . .'

'Who is?'

Dave merely raised an eyebrow. 'My source,' he continued, 'has named Melissa's supplier as "Spritz". I think we both know who that leads back to. And what I've believed the whole way along was that the supplier, this Spritz, was threatening either the daughter or granddaughter's life. My source has managed to get Melissa to trust her. Sir, if we could bring Jack in to get the information officially then we could take it to the Feds. You know as well as I do, they aren't following this angle any further. Essie is only a pawn to them, expendable, but from the information I have, I believe we could put a lot of drug dealing to bed if we follow this through. Save a lot of lives. I'm sure you would get the credit for giving the Feds the intel, sir.'

The Assistant Commissioner stiffened. 'I police for the greater good of the community, not accolades.'

'Sir,' Dave replied evenly.

'And questioning the Feds is not something we do lightly, in case you've forgotten, Burrows.' He sat back, and sighed. 'Tell me what you're thinking.'

Dave, pleased the reprimand was over, stood up and paced the floor. 'What are we looking at here? We have a woman being threatened by a family known for their involvement with not only drugs but money laundering and organised crime. We have her daughter, who has named a son of this family, and a granddaughter who could be in danger. If we can convince Melissa Carter to wear a wire, we might be able to shut down the drug-dealing circle and take a lot of drugs off the streets.'

The Assistant Commissioner was listening with his eyes closed and nodded at each point that Dave made. When the narration was finished, he opened his eyes and made a few notes. Then he moved from his desk to stand toe to toe with Dave. 'You're not just out to get Simms since he embarrassed you with his complaints?'

'Can't say I was happy. I'm neither corrupt nor complacent about the importation of drugs. I think that's how Simms worded the complaint, wasn't it? As far as I can see, they were just trying to embarrass the SA police and me. But, no, this isn't about humiliating the Feds in turn by doing their job for them.'

The Assistant Commissioner raised his eyebrows.

'I've told everyone from the start, what we were seeing with Essie wasn't what was going on behind the scenes. From the outset, there was more to this story. My source has confirmed that this is true.' Dave looked at his boss. 'I'm sure you can understand what I'm saying, sir.'

The Assistant Commissioner shook his head. 'God, Burrows, you do this all the time. I told you to stay away from this case and yet you went around me and got information I can't ignore. You're a pain in the arse.'

'I haven't contacted Melissa Carter in person. My source has.'

'That's splitting hairs and you know it. If I didn't know better, I'd say you put whomever your source is up to this.'

Dave didn't say anything.

The silence stretched out in the office, until finally the Assistant Commissioner sighed and spread his hands in a defeated attitude. 'Burrows, I'm uncomfortable with this but I'm willing to give you some leeway. But—' he looked Dave in the eye '—you cannot, *cannot*, have anything to do with this.'

'Yes, sir, I appreciate that. My colleague Jack Higgins will make the approach.'

'You seem to forget we're dealing with the Feds here, and they don't like to be embarrassed. If you fuck this up, Dave, I won't be able to protect you. It might be the end of your career.'

❧

Jack knocked on the door of the halfway-house and waited, as Zara had instructed.

Finally, it cracked open and Jack found himself staring at the thin pale face of a man. His eyes were bloodshot and Jack could smell him from where he stood.

'What the fuck do you want, copper?'

'G'day. Here to see Melissa.'

The man turned away, not opening the door any wider. 'There's a pig to see you, Melissa. You want me to let him in?'

'Has he got a warrant?'

He stuck his head into the gap in the doorway. 'Got a warrant?'

'Nah, mate, I'm just here for a friendly chat. No warrant needed. Tell her I'm a friend of Zara's.'

Melissa appeared at the door. Jack was prepared for the way she looked, because Zara had briefed him when they'd met with Dave to discuss the way forward.

'What can I do you for?' Melissa asked, shooing away the man who had been guarding the door.

'You said you'd do anything to help your mother. I'm here about that. Can we talk?'

Chewing her fingernails, Melissa shook her head, looked behind her and stepped outside. 'I've thought about it. I know how crazy-arse that man can be. It's too dangerous.'

'How dangerous is it to Essie and Paris?' Jack said evenly.

'Won't be dangerous if you just let them continue on the way they have been.' She glanced around again. 'Look, he might be watching, so you should go.'

Jack put a hand on her arm but she wrenched it away. 'Get the fuck away from me.'

'Sorry, sorry.' He made a calming gesture. 'I didn't mean to upset you. We can't turn a blind eye to what's going on with Essie and the drugs. The Australian Federal Police are involved, and they won't let it drop. Could we please go inside and chat about this?'

'No. You need to go.'

'We really need your help. Don't you want to take this bastard down so he can't kill any more people?'

Melissa moved from foot to foot. She was jumpy and agitated.

'We know he sold Ryan the bad batch of heroin. He's responsible for Ryan's death, Melissa.'

Melissa turned back to the house. 'If you get my family hurt, I'll . . . I'll . . .' She swallowed hard and stomped inside, throwing open the door to her office. 'Shut the door behind you.'

'Thank you,' Jack said, quietly closing the door. 'I understand how frightening this must be for you.'

'You've got no idea.'

'What if I told you that he'd threatened Essie with kidnapping Paris and getting her hooked on heroin? Would that change your mind about helping us?' Jack leaned forward, holding his breath. That was the last card he had up his sleeve.

His reaction when Dave had told him was pure hatred for a person who could even think of such a thing. No wonder Essie had been so frightened.

'Fuck off,' Melissa leaned back in her chair. 'I know you're lying.'

'Why would you think that?'

''Cause you're a copper, and you blokes don't always tell the truth. Who would do that to a little kid?'

'A person who has everything to lose and needs to keep people quiet. What I'm telling you, Melissa, is a true story. And let me tell you something else. Your great friend, Dave Burrows, who saved your life? Remember him?'

Melissa nodded.

'Well, he's putting his whole career on the line to help you, and Essie and Paris. The only way to clear your mum's name is to prove she was being blackmailed.'

Silence stretched out between them as Melissa's eyes darted around, weighing up what she'd been told.

'What would I need to do?'

'You'd wear a wire and face Spritz. Get him to talk.'

Melissa reared back as if she'd been slapped. 'No way. No fucking way! Do you know what he did to me?' Melissa burst into tears. 'I was clean. Doing real well and he came and found me. Spiked my drink then injected me. Made me dependent on him again. I don't want to see that bastard ever again.'

'We'll be right there, Melissa,' Jack looked into her eyes, willing her to believe him. 'We won't let that happen again. I promise you.'

She kept shaking her head. 'No. Please, no.'

'Think of Paris. Think how you would feel if he got his hands on her. If she was hooked on drugs.'

'That's emotional blackmail.'

'Look, Dave and I will be right in the van alongside you. We'll have visual and audio contact. We can talk to you through the earpiece. We thought a local cafe would be the best place; out in the open with lots of other people around. We'll have the Special Tasks and Rescue team ready and waiting to take him down when we've got what we need.'

'What if he searches me?'

'He's not going to do that in public. We'll have every plan we can in place so you will be safe.'

Rubbing her palms along her legs, Melissa seemed a little calmer. 'Did he really say he'd do that to Paris?'

'That's what Essie told Zara when we finally got her to talk. I've come straight from her house in Barker to see you. Zara is with Essie and Paris now, and we'll be taking them to a safe house very soon.'

'So, he reckons he can kill Ryan and my little girl too?'

Jack nodded. 'And the hundreds of others he's sold heroin to. You could be instrumental in bringing him down.'

'I don't know.' She paused and scratched at her arms again, before she stood up and paced to the window.

It seemed to Jack she was unable to stay still.

She spoke in a low voice and Jack strained to hear her. 'I'm sorry, I didn't catch that.'

Melissa turned around and faced him. 'Okay,' she said. 'I'll do it. Let's get the bastard.'

Chapter 33

Zara looked at the photos hanging on Essie's wall. The one of a young Melissa intrigued her.

'Do you promise that Melissa will be okay?' Essie wrung her hands as she sat at the kitchen table. Dave was across from her.

'We'll do our best to keep her safe, Essie. Now, can I get you to pack a bag? We really need to get a move on.'

'But what if he works out I'm not here anymore and he finds Melissa before all this takes place?'

'We're doing our best to make sure that doesn't happen. We've got a very experienced team on their way from Adelaide to help out with the operation and they'll help protect Melissa.' He wished he could promise that Melissa would be okay, but he'd been involved with operations where things had gone wrong and, despite their best efforts, people had died. Dave's memories were littered with loved

ones yelling, 'You promised!' He'd stopped making promises a long time ago.

'Essie,' Zara said, 'I think I've said before . . .'

'Grandma?' Paris came in and looked at the many people
in the kitchen. Her eyes were wide and questioning.

'Ah, sweetie, come here.' Essie held out her hands and
gathered her granddaughter to her as if she would never
let her go. 'It's going to be okay.'

'What is?' her granddaughter asked.

'Essie,' Zara tried again, 'that photo of Melissa—I've
said before, she looks familiar. Do you have any other
relatives around Barker?'

The older lady shook her head. 'No. For such a long
time, it was just Melissa and me. Then I met Mr Clippers
and he became my family. Then this beautiful one came
along.' She stroked her hand over Paris's hair and hushed
her as she tried to speak again.

'Where were you from before you came to Barker?'

Dave interrupted. 'Zara, we don't have time for this,
we really have to get going.'

'Okay, sorry.' She got up and went to the door, looking
for Kim. She was running late. Together, they were going
to pack up the most important things in the house, while
Dave and Jack got Essie and Paris safely to Adelaide. Kim
had gone to find boxes. Essie had been told it was unlikely
she could ever return to Barker.

Zara's heart had felt like it would break when Essie's
tears started after hearing that.

Dave now took charge. 'Right, gather what you need. Let's get on the road.'

'Where are we going?' Paris asked.

'I'm taking you to a special house in Adelaide.'

'Why?'

Dave raised his eyebrows and Zara could see he wished Kim was there to help him with the persistent questions. 'Because . . .'

Zara turned back to the kitchen. 'It's a little holiday,' she improvised. 'Have you been on a holiday before?'

Paris shook her head.

'Come on, then, I'll help you pack your bag.' She held out her hand to the little girl. 'Can you show me where your room is?'

'Yep, this way.'

'What about this?' Essie asked, getting up and opening the fridge door. 'I have lots of food still in here.'

'Kim's on her way to clean the fridge out and pack your important things.' Dave stood. 'Come on, we need to get a move on. Is your bag packed, Essie?'

'No, I'll do it now.'

'Don't worry about Paris,' Zara called out. 'I'll help her. Now, where will I find a suitcase for you?'

'In the passageway cupboard,' Essie answered before Paris could.

Paris ran to the storage cupboard and yanked open the door. 'Here you are,' she said, pulling out an old battered suitcase.

'Great, let's get packing! Have you got a favourite dress you want to take?'

She followed Paris into her bedroom and laid the case on the bed, before going through the chest of drawers and pulling out the essentials to pack.

'Can you get me your toothbrush and hairbrush from the bathroom?'

Paris bounced off and Zara grabbed another bundle of clothes and folded them. As she placed them in the suitcase, she felt something hard in the storage part of the lid. Frowning, she felt along until her fingers touched a hard, square box. She brought the box out and looked at it, knowing instinctively that this held something very important to Essie.

Glancing over her shoulder to make sure no one was watching, she tried to open the lid, but it was stuck. She frowned and tipped it over to see if she could wedge a fingernail into the joint. That didn't work. Giving the box a shake, it sounded like papers rustling inside.

Curiosity got the better of her and she turned to look for a knife.

'You ready yet?' Dave called.

'Not yet,' she answered.

Quickly, Zara put the box in her handbag and went to find Paris. On her way to the bathroom she passed another bedroom. She opened the door, thinking Paris might be in there getting more clothes, but she wasn't.

Zara drew in a breath. She'd never seen a bedroom like this; the furniture was from a different era, as were the curtains and carpet. In the dim light, she could see a fine layer of dust covering everything: the rocking chair, the wardrobe, the dresser.

And the two cots. Goosebumps spread across her skin.

Taking a step inside, she looked into both cots—they were neatly made, with a teddy bear in each. To Zara, the room looked lost in time, as if something had happened here that meant the children wouldn't ever come back.

Her mind flew back to what Ted had told her. *She was only ever seen with one child. Someone said she had twins.*

Who would have two cots in one bedroom, if they only had one baby? Her mind raced over everything Ted had told her. He remembered Essie catching the train to Port Augusta. She was friends with ladies from the church. What else did Essie get up to in her spare time?

'Come on!' Dave's voice was hurried. 'It's time to go.'

Quickly and quietly, Zara shut the door and turned back to Paris's bedroom.

'Where have you got to, Paris? We're not finished packing yet.'

Paris came out of Essie's room, with Essie behind her. 'I've got what I want,' she said to Zara.

Essie was looking worried. She carried a small suitcase—one that looked like it had seen better days—and handed it to Dave.

'Can you zip yours up, Paris?' Zara asked, dragging her thoughts away from the two cots. To Dave she said, 'On the bed in there.' She nodded to Paris's bedroom.

Dave looked at Essie. 'Do you have your identification documents? Birth certificates, passports?'

'Oh, I . . .'

'Don't worry,' Dave said. 'Zara and Kim can get them after we leave.'

'In my desk,' Essie waved towards the sunroom at the end of the house.

'Yep, leave it with me,' Zara said. 'Is there anything special that you want to make sure we pack?'

Essie paused, her eyes straying towards the tightly shut door of the room lost in time. 'No,' she said quietly, and put her head down and followed Dave out of the house.

Zara stood in the doorway, her arms crossed, watching as Dave made sure they were safely in the car. Conflicting emotions ran through her as she looked at Essie, peering out the car window, looking at her home of so many years. Essie's life had turned upside-down so quickly.

Dave surveyed the road, then turned back to Zara and took a couple of steps towards her, his face focused, but with a small smile.

'Better get out of here. You good?'

'Yep, no problems here.'

'You've done a great job. Well done.'

'We're not over and done with yet. And considering you're not supposed to have anything to do with this case, you seem to have wormed your way in!' Zara grinned at him. She wanted to laugh, but the whole situation felt too surreal and tense for anything as frivolous as that. 'Dave, in the house, there's a nursery—an old one—with two cots in it. Don't you think that's strange?'

'Two cots?'

'She's only got one child—Melissa. The old bloke I talked to said he remembered there was talk that Essie had twins, but she was only ever seen with one, so no one was ever sure. Maybe there's something more to this than we realise?'

'I haven't got time to think about that now. Let's focus on what we know, which is that Melissa has a connection to Spritz and now he's connected to Essie. Okay?'

'Okay.' Zara understood. This was an older mystery and it wasn't going anywhere. There would be time for talking about it later.

'Don't know where Kim has got to.' He looked around as if hoping she would materialise as he said her name. 'She's taking longer than I thought.' A worried look crossed his face. 'I'll just check in with her before I leave.'

'I'm sure she won't be too far away,' Zara said, walking out onto the footpath to look down the road. A trickle of fear ran through her stomach.

'Hi, honey,' she heard Dave say and relaxed instantly. 'Yeah, we're just about to leave.'

Pause.

'I'll let her know. Be safe. I love you.'

Zara turned back to Dave, feeling like she had intruded on a private conversation.

'She'll be here in five. You get going as quick as you can, once you've packed everything, okay? Keep an eye on the rear-vision mirror at all times and don't stop for anyone unless they are coppers with flashing lights. Got that?'

Zara nodded.

'Okay, I'm out of here. I'll let you know when Melissa will be talking to Spritz. Keep your eyes open, okay?'

'Drive safe,' she said. She was about to turn to go back into the house when she stopped. Dave was getting into the car. 'Give my love to Jack.'

Dave glanced up. It was the first time Zara had mentioned anything personal regarding Jack, and they both knew how significant this was considering what Jack was about to do. 'I will.'

Back inside, Zara headed straight for the nursery and pushed the door open. As she stood still in the middle of the room looking around, a tremor ran through her and the hairs on her arms stood up. She couldn't put her finger on what the feeling was in this room, other than that at a certain point time had simply stopped.

She opened the wardrobe and found a christening dress. Only one. Not two, as she would have expected if there had been twins.

The dresser drawers were empty, and Zara couldn't find anything else that might indicate what had happened in this room.

A loud knock sounded through the house and Zara froze. She looked around for something to defend herself with, if she needed to, and sagged with relief as she heard Kim's voice. 'Yoo-hoo! I'm here. Sorry I took so long.'

Zara left the room, shutting the door behind her, glad to be out in the light. Dave was right—this was a mystery for another day.

'Hi! You gave me a fright.'

'Sorry, that's why I called out.' Kim came in carrying an esky. 'So they're gone?' She screwed her face up in disappointment. 'Bugger, I wanted to give them both a hug.'

'They left about five minutes ago. Dave was practically carrying them out the door.'

'Damn. The phone rang just as I was about to leave. How were they?'

'Paris was confused and Essie was pretty sad, but she didn't seem frightened. Just sad she was leaving.'

'I'm finding it hard to believe this has escalated so quickly. How are you holding up?'

'You and me both.' Zara paused, thinking about the question. 'I think I'm okay. Good to have something to keep me busy. What about you?'

'Yeah . . .' Kim's voice trailed off and she looked sad. 'I worry for Essie and Paris. This will be such an upheaval— Essie is older and it's hard to make friends in new places. Paris won't have her friends.' She let out a deep sigh. 'Well, nothing we can do about that now. Let's do the practical things. You take the fridge, I'll check the pantry.' Before she opened the pantry she took Zara by the arms. 'Jack will be okay, you know,' she said, then folded her into a hug.

'I hope so. And Dave too.'

Both women were silent as they thought about the enormity of what was happening.

'Best get on,' Kim finally said.

Opening the fridge, Zara began to pull out the perishables and put them on the kitchen table. What was it like, she wondered, when people were shifted out even more quickly than Essie and Paris? They had had a few hours' notice at least. Who came in behind the people who had five minutes to get out of their house? How would they remember to take everything important—photos, letters, things that had sentimental value? She thought about the box she'd found—Essie hadn't said she wanted it, but Zara was sure that box held something important.

'Remind me to get their birth certificates before I leave,' Zara said.

Kim nodded, just as the phone started to ring.

The two women looked at each other. Zara noticed Kim's hands had started to shake and she'd gone pale. Zara felt like her breath had been taken away. The reality of Essie's situation and why she'd agreed to accept the drug deliveries was much clearer to Zara now than it had ever been. Terror did strange things to you.

'Do we answer it?' Zara asked, moving towards the noise.

Kim shook her head. 'No. If it's anything to do with Spritz or his family, better that they think she's just out of the house rather than having a stranger answer the call.'

'But I bet they know her movements down pat, so they're going to expect her to be here.'

'Mightn't even be them. Come on.' The urgency in Kim's voice escalated. 'Let's get this done and get out of here.'

Zara went down into the sunroom and opened the old-fashioned desk in the corner. Twisting the key, she slid the lid up and looked around, trying to see where the important documents could be kept.

The phone rang again.

Spurred into urgency, Zara pulled open the drawer and glanced through the headings of the files. 'Bank Statements, Invoices . . .' she muttered, flicking through quickly. 'Manuals, Church Roster . . . Damn it, where are they?'

Slowing down, she went back through the records again.

Right at the back of the filing drawer she found a white envelope marked 'Birth Certificates'. She pulled it out and breathed a sigh of relief. 'Got them,' she called. Glancing around the desk, she made sure there was nothing Essie might need. She saw a cheque book and scooped that up, along with a photo of Paris.

As Zara took the photo, she saw that behind it was a black-and-white picture. It was Essie—a much younger Essie—with a man Zara didn't recognise. They were smiling at the camera outside what looked like a church building or registry office.

Grabbing it, she stuck that in the envelope too and ran out of the office.

'Good to go?'

'Yep.' Kim lifted the esky and started to walk out. She stopped and glanced around before saying thoughtfully, 'I wonder if Essie had any idea what was going to happen when she was first contacted.'

'I wouldn't have thought so,' Zara said.

'This is all just so sad.'

Kim walked out, switching the light off as she went, and Zara pulled the door closed behind them, making sure it was locked.

Chapter 34

Melissa fidgeted up and down and side to side, as the technician tested the sound on the microphone.

'Don't jiggle if you can avoid it,' he said. 'Your necklace is banging against the mic.'

Jack saw her reach up and tuck the necklace back inside her shirt.

'Could we take it off?' he asked.

'No!' The word ripped from Melissa. 'No, I need this. Ryan gave it to me. I always wear it when I need a bit of courage.'

'Fine,' the technician answered. 'Let me see if I can adjust it.'

Melissa unbuttoned the first three buttons of her shirt and let the man change the position of the mic from the top of her bra to the bottom.

'Say something,' he instructed.

'One, two, three.'

'That's better.'

She tucked her shirt back into her jeans and looked over at Jack.

'I'm only doing this for Ryan. And for Mum and Paris. The pain and emptiness I felt when Ryan died . . .' She shrugged. 'Life felt so meaningless, even with Paris there. The drugs, they made me feel . . . I don't know. Better. But I know they're not the answer. I know I can't bring Ryan back.' Her head snapped up. 'You're going to be here?' she asked for the umpteenth time.

'We sure are. Dave, and our friend here working the sound, and me. We'll be in the van. But we've got coppers all over the place. Dave has organised the STAR team to be here. They specialise in taking down armed and violent offenders, so you'll be in safe hands. In addition to that we have six undercover officers, also from Adelaide. They arrived about three hours ago and are now stationed all over the shopping centre. All in plain clothes. You're going to be well looked after.' He pointed to a small TV screen. 'See that woman there, sitting drinking coffee? She's one of us. And that bloke there, standing and talking on his phone? Again, he's one of us. If something goes pear-shaped, we're right there to help you.'

Leaning in, Jack looked at the TV screen closely. The meeting had been set in a coffee shop in a shopping centre. They'd been in the day before and wired the back booth, in case Spritz decided he wanted to search Melissa. The likelihood of that was low, in a public place, but they weren't taking any chances.

'Are you right with your story?' Jack asked. 'You contacted him to see if you could pick up where you left off when he was staying at the halfway house.'

Melissa nodded. 'Yeah. To get back together with him.' She looked disgusted as she said it. 'Like that's ever going to happen.'

The van door opened and Dave was silhouetted in the doorframe.

Melissa gasped and her hand flew to her mouth.

'It's okay,' Jack said quickly, realising she couldn't see him clearly with the sun behind him. 'It's only Dave.'

'Hello, Melissa,' he said straightaway. 'It's good to see you.'

'Right. Um, hi.' She shook her hands as if trying to get rid of the tremors in her fingers.

Melissa didn't seem capable of saying much else.

'Now, you need to relax,' Jack told her, glancing at Dave. 'If he sees that you're really nervous, he might get up and leave, thinking something isn't right. Can you take a few deep breaths for me?'

As she started to, the sound man went over to a panel covered in buttons and pushed a few. 'Testing again. Count to ten, please,' he instructed.

'One, two, three . . .'

Adjusting the levels as Melissa continued to count, he listened with the headset on and then gave a thumbs up. 'All good.'

'Great,' Dave said and sat down. 'Come and sit here, Melissa. You've got ten minutes before you need to go in. How are you feeling?'

'How the fuck do you think I'm feeling? I can't believe you talked me into this.' Her eyes had dark circles under them, and Dave suspected she hadn't slept since she'd agreed to wear the wire.

She'd made an effort with her appearance, under Jack's instruction, wearing a nice shirt and pair of jeans, but no matter how nice the clothes were, she couldn't hide the fact that she was a recovering heroin addict. The deep lines in her face and heavy lids made her seem so much older than she was.

'You're doing great. Do you remember how we're going to play this?' Dave asked.

She nodded. 'I've got to get him to admit that he threatened Mum and Paris.'

'That's right.'

'Once we've talked about getting back together, then I tell him I'm in need of a hit and we go from there.'

Jack nodded. 'See? I know you feel scared, but you're all over it. Have you got any questions for me?'

She shook her head.

Dave leaned closer to Melissa and held out a pen. 'This has got a camera in the end of it. If you can somehow position it in your pocket, so this part here—' he tapped the lid '—is facing Spritz we'll get some video footage of him too.'

'Won't you be able to see him on there?' she pointed to the screens.

'Yeah, we will, but this will be a closer shot.'

Melissa nodded her understanding.

'Okay, time to go.'

Swallowing, Melissa teared up. 'Can you tell Mum—' She took a breath. 'If something goes wrong, can you tell Mum I'm sorry?'

Dave put his hand on her arm. 'Nothing is going wrong. Thank you for doing this. There are going to be so many families you'll never even know who'll be helped by this. And Ryan would thank you if he were here too.'

'Bastard,' she whispered and straightened up, before shaking her hair out. 'Okay. I'm ready.'

Dave and Jack were glued to the screens as they watched Melissa order a hot chocolate and muffin and then walk across the cafe floor and slide into the booth.

'Her hands are shaking,' Jack observed.

'That will give credence to the idea that she wants a hit.'

They were silent, both watching for the perp to appear.

'Got a copy, Two?' Dave asked into the headphones. They saw the woman sitting at the table nod, then raise her hand to her ear as if she were scratching an itch.

'Roger.'

'Four?' Dave asked.

'Roger.'

He turned to the technician. 'You got ears for the STAR team?'

The man flicked a few buttons and nodded.

'STAR Six, got a copy?'

'Roger, boss. In position and waiting for your command.'

Jack watched as Dave drew in a few deep breaths. *Okay*, he told himself. *Here we go*.

The door opened and they all turned around, then shot to their feet.

'Sir,' Dave said as the Assistant Commissioner entered. 'We weren't expecting you.'

'By hell, Burrows,' he shook his head, 'trouble seems to follow you. I'm sitting in on this so I know exactly what goes down. If you fuck it up, understand, you'll be finished.'

Jack looked at Dave, who was nodding. 'Yes, sir.'

'HQ, got eyes on a man who matches the description.' A loud voice came through the headsets and Dave instantly turned his back on the AC, who was signalling for the technician to give him a set of headphones.

'Entering the shopping centre at the western end.'

'Here.' Jack pointed to the screen and moved to the side so the Assistant Commissioner could see.

'Melissa?' Dave said calmly. 'He's about two minutes from you. I'm watching him walk past EB Games and now Books Galore.'

They all heard a shuddering breath. 'Okay.'

'On the countdown into the cafe. Five, four, three, two . . . He's just entered the cafe.'

Melissa didn't answer.

They watched as Spritz pushed his sunglasses to the top of his head and sauntered over, an arrogant smile on his face. His jeans were faded, his shirt light blue and the heavy fabric jacket, grey. Nothing that would make him stand out in a crowd. Except perhaps the way he walked. Jaunty and egotistical.

Spritz leaned down to kiss her cheek and said, 'I knew you'd be back. Can't get enough of me?'

Melissa smiled but it was forced.

He slid into the booth and beckoned to the waitress. 'Black coffee, thanks.' Turning back to her, they watched as he looked her up and down. 'You're looking good. Being clean suits you.'

'I need to make a bit of money,' Melissa said.

Dave and Jack glanced at each other then back at the screen. This wasn't the script.

'Do you? What have you got in mind?'

'I'll do what you asked me to do when you were here last.'

'Clever girl,' Dave muttered.

'And what was that? I don't remember asking anything.'

'Don't tell him,' Jack said. 'Get him to say it.'

'But I want a cut of the profits.'

'Is that right?' They fell silent as the waitress brought the hot chocolate and coffee. 'Thanks, love.'

Spritz took two sugars from the jar and ripped the tops off, before stirring them into his drink. Then he leaned forward.

'What do you want a part of, Melissa? Sorry, I don't remember having a conversation with you about anything.'

'You know what I'm talking about.' Melissa leaned forward too and looked him straight in the eye. 'Please. I'm desperate.'

'I'm not sure. I mean, you said no last time. What's happened to make you change your mind.'

Her hands were still shaking when she lifted the cup to her mouth. 'Nothing.'

'I don't think I believe that.'

'Spritz, please. Tell me what I have to do.'

He regarded her, then leaned back and tapped the table. 'Not until you tell me why the change of heart.'

'I told you. I need money.'

'For what?'

'My little girl. She needs to go to a different school when she gets a bit older. I want to do that for her. Mum won't be able to afford it.'

'You been speaking to your family?'

Melissa shook her head. 'It was her birthday last week and I just got thinking about later, that's all. The halfway house doesn't pay much.'

'Careful,' Dave warned, but he didn't see Melissa respond to his voice.

'What about something else?' Spritz said, his voice changing. 'You've turned out pretty good since you've got off the gear. Don't really even look like you've had a kid. I might be able to get you into one of the family's stables instead. You've put a few pounds on around your tits, which is helpful. I could get that sorted for you, bitch.'

'No, Spritz, I don't want to go on the game. That'll just lead me back to the drugs and I don't want to do that. Worked too hard and long to get clean. I'd rather the other way.'

Spritz leaned back and hooked his elbow over the back of the chair, a cruel smile on his lips.

'I wouldn't be telling me what your options are, love. As I see it, you're a half-fucked druggie without options. Selling your arse on the street will earn you money. Take it or leave it.'

'Hold on,' Dave said to Jack. 'She's getting angry. Get everyone on alert.'

'I can't go that low again,' Melissa said, her tone cold. 'Look, you asked me before you left if I would do some work for you. You know, receiving packages. I'm here saying I will.'

'Yeah, well, I got that sorted. Got myself a few people who were happy to earn some bucks from collecting and passing the stuff on. And they just do it out of the goodness of their heart. So, why should I let you in now? Everything is working pretty well without you.'

'Come on, Spritz, you and me? We've always been mates, you know.' She leaned forward, running her fingers through her hair. 'I know you've always had a thing for me. I won't go on the streets for you, but maybe we can work something out on a personal level?'

Dave drew in a breath as he watched a lustful expression cross Spritz's face. He licked his lips and leaned over the table to cup Melissa's breast.

'Yeah, a bit of weight has done you good, bitch,' he said, staring at her chest.

Melissa drew her shoulders back and pushed her breasts into his hands. 'I need some sort of guarantee that you'll help me.'

Spritz's thumbs felt their way across her nipples. Dave wondered how she could stand to let him touch her. He knew how much she hated this man; Melissa was a great actress.

'I'll give you a guarantee: you do what I want and I'll cut you into my supply chain. You don't, and I'll cut your fucking throat and dump you in the river where all good whores end up.'

'Come on. I need to know I'll get something for my kid.'

Spritz gave a cold smile. 'Don't worry about your mum and the kid. I've got them taken care of.'

Fury crossed Melissa's face and she reared back. 'What the fuck do you mean?'

'Oh, come on, you've taken your nice titties away. Bring them back over here where I can reach them, while I tell you a bedtime story.'

'What have you done to them?'

Dave held his breath.

'When you declined my kind offer I made your mother an offer she couldn't refuse. She collects my packages and sends them on without question and I let you live and that brat of yours doesn't get hooked on meth.' He smiled. 'It all works rather well.'

Melissa half rose. 'You bastard,' she hissed.

'Got him,' said Dave.

'Good to go?' asked Jack.

'No, just wait a minute. See what else he offers up.'

'Burrows,' the Assistant Commissioner warned, 'go in now while everything is still okay.'

'Just hold a minute,' Dave held up his hand.

'Business is business, bitch. You made the choice not to have me in the halfway house, so I took the next option. Believe me, some old nan with a grandkid in the back of nowhere is a far better mule than some strung-out ex-whore like you. Worked pretty well until the Feds got wind of it.'

'What do you mean, "the Feds"?'

'They caught poor old Essie with a delivery last month. She's been smart enough to keep her mouth shut and I don't think she'll ever say anything. She knows how far and wide my family is spread and I made it clear that anything from her to the police will see that kid of yours selling her arse on the street by the time she's eight. And she'll be hooked because I will have made her that way.'

'Don't get angry. Stay focused.' Dave said into her earpiece and pushed his own mic away from his mouth, indicating to the technician to shut it off for the moment. 'Get the STAR team up on audio,' he instructed. 'And get a fucking ambulance too.'

A flick of the switch and a nod indicated he was clear to talk.

'Stand by, boys,' he told them.

On the video screen, Melissa raised her hand and slapped Spritz across the cheek.

Instantly, Spritz threw himself across the table and grabbed Melissa by the throat and squeezed hard.

'That's disrespectful, bitch.'

'Go, go, go, boys!' Dave shouted to the STAR team.

Spritz pushed Melissa against the wall, as a waitress yelled out, 'Hey!'

'Remember you came to me and I offered you a way out. But I don't do business with people who disrespect me. I'm gonna make your kid wish she'd never been born.'

Dave, Jack, the Assistant Commissioner and technician all leaned towards the screen and watched as five men dressed in black gear and bulletproof vests raced in through the cafe door, towards the back booth, and grabbed hold of Spritz's jacket, pulling him off Melissa. Jack heard Spritz say, 'What the fuck?'

'Get on the floor! Get on the floor!'

Spritz looked up at Melissa. 'You fucking whore, you set me up?'

The men sat on Spritz's back, forcing his face against the floor and pulling his hands behind his back.

Melissa sagged against the back of the booth, crying and gasping for breath. Somehow, she managed to slide out of the booth until she was standing over him. 'Don't ever threaten a mama lion's cub,' she said. 'You'll always come off second best.' Her knees buckled and one of the STAR team caught her and led her out.

Jack stared at the screen, a grin spreading over his face. 'Go Melissa,' he said.

'Secured,' the voice of the STAR commander came through and Dave leaned back, sighing with relief. He wiped his forehead with his hanky and grinned. 'That girl has got some guts. Get the ambos to her as quickly as you can.'

The Assistant Commissioner stood up and held out his hand. 'Well done, Burrows. Good to see that went without a hitch.'

'Yes, sir.'

'And the family? Are they all safe? There will be repercussions from this. The Esperitzo family won't take this lying down. From the research we've done we know he's Manuel's golden boy.'

'If he's the best they've got, then they're fucked anyway,' Jack said. 'What type of criminal would spill the beans like that, out in the open and so quickly.'

The Assistant Commissioner looked at him. 'Son, if you want a bit of advice, don't turn out like Burrows here. He rides too close to the wind too often, and you're sounding like him now.' He turned to leave the van. 'Make sure that girl and her family are looked after.'

'We will. The mother and granddaughter are at a safe house as we speak. I dropped them there this morning.'

The Assistant Commissioner stared at Dave and shook his head, before walking out.

Jack and Dave looked at each other before letting out their breath.

'Good job, Jack,' Dave said.

'No, mate, that's for you.' He held out his hand. 'And for the record: despite what the AC says, when I grow up I want to be just like you.'

Chapter 35

Jack opened the door to the safe house and ushered Melissa inside. Dave brought up the rear, making sure no one was watching them.

The house was quiet and Dave frowned.

'Essie?' he called out. 'You here?'

No answer.

Dave and Jack exchanged glances. Dave grabbed Melissa's arm and pulled her behind him. 'Clear the house,' he said to Jack.

As Jack got out his gun, Melissa gasped. 'What's going on?'

'Shh,' Dave instructed, his tone hard. 'Kim and Zara should be here by now too,' he said in a low voice.

Jack crept along the wall to the open door and looked in.

'Clear,' he nodded and continued through the rest of the house.

Dave got out his mobile phone and dialled Kim's number.

He listened as it switched straight to voicemail, then he tried Zara's, with the same result.

'House is clear,' Jack said, coming back into the hallway.

'They're not here?'

'No.'

'What's going on?' Melissa looked from one to the other. 'Where are they?'

'Watch Melissa,' Dave said to Jack, ignoring her questions. 'Keep your eyes open.' He walked outside and looked around, his phone to his ear again.

'Simms. It's Burrows,' he said.

'Hear you had a take down. Well done.' Simms didn't sound as if he meant it.

'Where are Essie and Paris Carter?'

'What do you mean?' Simms sounded alert. 'I organised the house and you took them there.'

'Yeah, I did. They're not here now, and neither are Kim and Zara. They should've been. Kim texted when they left Barker over five hours ago. Everyone should be here, tucked in safely.' His voice rose with concern. 'Where are your boys? I thought they were watching them.'

'They were. They are. I'll make a call.'

The line went dead.

'Fuck,' Dave said, running his hands over his hair. What could have happened here? He went back inside and carefully examined the door. The lock didn't look forced.

'Check the rest of the house for signs of a break-in,' he said to Jack.

'Shit, surely they haven't got to them?' Jack asked.

'I don't fucking know. You can see the house is empty as well as I can. I instructed them not to go anywhere. Kim and Zara should be here too.'

Jack looked at Dave without expression. 'No.'

'Come on, look.'

'Where's Mum and Paris?' Melissa asked, coming into the lounge room. She was scratching nervously at her arm.

'I don't know,' Dave answered honestly.

He pulled on a pair of gloves and ran his fingers along the window sills, looking for an entry point. Nothing.

His phone rang.

'Yes?'

'They were watching them but got called off by someone. I don't know how this has happened.'

'You're kidding me? I swear, if they're in any trouble . . .' Dave snapped. 'How could you have fucked this up?'

'I'm bringing the agents in now to find out what's going on. I'll send you as many guys as you need to find them.'

'You wanna hope it's not too late when we do, Simms. And you thought *I* was fucking past it.' Dave took a breath and tried to push his anger and fear away. 'Kim and Zara, they haven't arrived either. Get someone to check the cameras along the main drag to Adelaide. Find out where they were last seen on the road. Is there CCTV around this area?'

Dave heard the keyboard clicking as Simms brought up the information.

'Cameras on the corner of the street just below where you are. I'll pull the footage. What's the numberplate I'm looking for on the road?'

Dave reeled it off. 'I'm bringing Melissa in to you,' he said finally. 'She needs to be safe and out of the investigation.'

'I'll make arrangements for her.'

Without answering, Dave hung up.

Frowning, he turned to find Jack and saw Melissa watching him. 'Spritz's family have got them, haven't they?' said Melissa, as the colour drained from Jack's face. 'I've done all this for nothing.'

'We don't know that, Melissa,' Dave answered, going to her. It took every ounce of self-control he had not to let his personal feelings take over. He had to maintain his copper's dissociation from the case. He couldn't worry about Kim and Zara as a husband and friend, only as a detective. He kept his voice calm and steady. 'We can't make assumptions; we have to go with evidence. There is no evidence here to suggest they've been kidnapped. The house hasn't been broken into and I haven't found any sign of forced entry.

'Yes, obviously their disappearance could have something to do with the family because word on the street travels fast and they would know by now that we have Spritz in custody.

'But let's get you to the AFP office where you'll be safe, and then Jack and I can get on the case and find them. I'm hoping it's just a small thing, like Essie hasn't understood the seriousness of the situation and they've gone for a walk.' He patted her shoulder. 'Come on, let's get you in the car and over to Simms. Now.'

❧

In the conference room, Simms brought up images of Kim's car.

Dave and Jack watched as a white van drove in front of them on a corner and skewed in front of Kim's Toyota Kluger, forcing her to a stop.

Two men jumped from the van and opened the driver's and passenger's doors simultaneously, dragging Kim and Zara from their seats and piling them into the back of the van.

One man got in the back with them and the other ran to the driver's seat and pulled away, the van fishtailing as it sped off.

'A report was made by the next car passing and the locals have been out there assessing the scene since. That was—' Simms glanced at his paperwork '—four hours ago.'

Dave's fists were clenched alongside his body. 'Four-hour head start.' He felt sick, watching Kim fight the man who was dragging her away. A sidelong glance at Jack told him that he was feeling the same about Zara. 'I don't know how this could've happened, Simms. I swear, if anything happens to them . . .'

'We're on it now. I've traced the van to the last lot of cameras, which is here.' He brought up another live camera feed on an intersection in the city. 'They passed through here about two hours ago, which works timing-wise from where they were abducted.

'Now, if you look at this . . .' He clicked to another screen: a white, nondescript van was parked outside the safe house where Dave and Jack had just been.

'I didn't think there was a camera there.'

'One was installed prior to Mrs Carter and her granddaughter arriving.' He paused and looked down. 'I wasn't made aware of it until after your call came through.'

'Communication working well in the Feds department then,' Jack snapped, showing Dave just how on edge he was.

Simms ignored his outburst and clicked across to another screen. 'We don't have footage of Mrs Carter and Paris being taken as the camera was disabled, but we do have a van matching this description leaving the tunnel and going through the same intersection half an hour ahead of the other van.

'This road leads to an industrial area down on the wharf and I am certain that's where they've all been taken.' He turned to Dave. 'Now, you said that Mrs Carter told you that Spritz had threatened Paris?'

'Yes. That he would drug her and inject her with heroin or meth or something to get her addicted. He also threatened that, and more, in the interaction with Melissa. Told Melissa he'd make Paris wish she'd never been born.'

'We've found that the Esperitzo family owns a warehouse down there. I suspect that's where they're being held.'

Jack started towards the door. 'What are we waiting for then?'

'Jack!' Dave snapped. 'Wait.'

'We have men there now.' Simms changed screens again, and this time the TV showed a live feed of men dressed in full protective gear, rifles held up and all wearing earpieces. He turned to Dave and Jack. 'We don't have eyes inside,' he warned them. 'We're making an educated guess and with the urgency of the situation and four people's lives in danger, we're hoping that nothing goes wrong.'

'What the fuck?' Jack yelled. 'You're putting them all in worse danger!'

Dave put a heavy hand on Jack's shoulder and made him look at him. 'There'll be a reason. Stop and listen.' He glared at Simms now. 'There'd better be a damn good reason. My wife is in there. And a six-year-old child. You'll never work again if something goes wrong with this sting.'

Simms was pale but holding his ground. 'Yesterday morning a notification came through from the Interpol comms system I-24/7.'

Dave took an involuntary step towards Simms. 'Interpol?'

Nodding, Simms continued, his eyes on the screen. 'The Esperitzo family has just been proved to have links to child smuggling. There is a boat arriving this week that we believe transports children.'

Silence.

All three men now had their eyes on the screen. Dave's heart was beating much quicker than he would have liked. If child smuggling was the game, he knew that Kim, Zara and Essie would be murdered. Without a doubt. They would try to protect Paris and would go down in the process.

Oh, Kim, he thought. *You're my world*. His breathing quickened as the tinny voice of the commander came through the speaker.

'Ready? Two min,' he said.

Affirmative replies came from six or seven different people. Dave couldn't tell. Glancing at Jack, he saw his partner was wide-eyed, staring at the screen, pale. Helpless. He walked over to him and put an arm around his shoulders.

'Trust,' he muttered quietly.

'On my command. Three, two, one, go, go, go!'

The doors of the warehouse flew open and the men ran into the large open empty shed.

The men in the office were watching from the commander's point of view, a video on his helmet. 'Left, left,' he puffed as they now followed a narrow passage that ran along the edge of the corrugated iron wall. 'Down.'

Dave struggled to keep up with the commands as they were whispered into the microphones.

They came to a door that was shut.

'Jesus,' Jack said.

The door was flung open.

Dave heard the clink of a stun grenade being thrown and hitting the cement floor.

Loud bangs and a small amount of smoke went up, meant to disorientate whoever was inside.

A male voice yelled and was quickly quietened.

'Here.'

'I've got one.'

'Three here. Plus another two.'

'Get 'em outside.'

Dave couldn't see what was happening. The commander was facing away from his team, watching their backs while they dragged the people out.

'Need three ambulances,' a muffled voice said.

Jack and Dave were glued to the screen. The sound of a gun-shot ripped through the office and there was another round of yelling. Dave couldn't make out what they were saying.

The smoke began to dispel and then came the call: 'Clear!'

Dave hadn't realised he was holding his breath until he dragged in a breath.

'Four packages safe. Drugged and bound, but safe. Ambulances for checks, thanks.'

Simms turned to Dave and Jack, relief on his face. 'We'll get you to the hospital now.'

Chapter 36

'Mum?' Melissa dropped her handbag and ran to Essie, who was sitting on the hospital bed.

At the sound of her voice, Essie turned and looked at her daughter. 'Melissa, darling . . .' She got up and held open her arms.

'Paris?' Melissa asked.

'She's okay. The doctors are with her at the moment. She was drugged, but she's coming out of it. I have to wait for them to clear me.'

At that moment, a nurse entered. 'I can take you to her now,' she said with a smile.

Together the two women followed her to a ward where Paris lay in a bed. Her dark hair was strewn across the pillow and her little face was pale. The monitors around her beeped quietly.

'She's fine,' the nurse said encouragingly. 'Paris will wake up very soon—she's a tough little kid.'

'Thank you,' Melissa said, as she stared at the daughter she hadn't seen for five years. 'Oh, Mum, she's beautiful.'

'She looks just like you did when you were her age,' Essie said as she sat alongside her grandchild and took the small hand in hers.

Paris's eyes flickered open. 'Hello, darling girl,' Essie said, leaning towards her.

'Granny!' Her voice was high and frightened.

'Shh, shh, it's over now.'

Paris looked towards Melissa, then looked back at her grandmother. 'Who's that?' she whispered.

'This is someone very special, darling. Do you remember all the photos I showed you of your mum? Well, this is her. This is Melissa, your mother.'

❧

In the next room, Dave held Kim tightly to him. He kissed her forehead over and over. 'I thought I'd lost you,' he said quietly.

'I was so scared, I didn't know what to think,' she said. 'I tried to get them just to take me and to leave the others behind.'

Dave felt his chest constrict. Of course she would have done that, without a second thought.

'They won't get away with it. Simms knows who they are. They'll be on the run now. You're safe.'

'The others? Where's Paris?'

'Everyone's okay. Once the drugs wear off, there won't be any physical consequences.' He was silent and they looked at each other, both knowing that the psychological trauma would be harder for everyone to get through.

'Hopefully, Paris is young enough for this not to affect her for the rest of her life. Maybe she'll forget, in time.'

'She may well do.' He looked carefully at Kim. 'How about you?'

Kim gave a watery smile. 'Give it time and I'll be okay. I've got you to help me.'

'You sure do, honey. I'll do everything you need me to.'

'I know.' She leaned into him harder and Dave pressed his lips to her forehead again. They stayed like that for a long time.

❧

Jack held Zara as if he would never let her go. He couldn't speak, just tried to show how much she meant to him, by holding her close.

'Well, that's the most exciting story I've ever been involved in,' Zara said, trying to make light of what had just happened. She rubbed the bruised skin on her elbow where she had been dragged from the car.

'Not one I ever want you to be involved in again,' Jack whispered.

Zara shuddered. 'No. Me neither,' she said quietly.

'What did they do to you?'

'Honestly? I don't remember much once we were taken out of the van. Just that they put hoods over our heads and marched us into where you found us. I'm not sure what they gave us, but whatever it was made me really sleepy.

I don't remember anything until the cops came crashing through the doors.'

'Weren't you frightened?'

Zara turned to face him. 'Frightened? More than you could imagine.' She paused. 'I'm sorry, Jack. Sorry for everything. When they kidnapped us all I could think about was seeing you again. I was so scared that I wasn't ever going to be able to tell you I love you.' She stopped and tried to swallow the lump in her throat. 'And I do, you know. I love you.'

Jack smoothed her hair back from her forehead and kissed her. 'I love you,' he said.

❧

Two days later, after everyone had been released from hospital, Jack and Dave watched Melissa, Essie and Paris play on the lawn through the windows of the safe house.

'This is part of the job that gives me so much satisfaction,' Dave whispered to Jack. 'Changing people's lives for the better.'

'The best part,' Jack agreed.

Essie looked up and saw them standing there. She said something to Paris, pointing at the window, then came inside. As she walked towards them her arms were outstretched, and Dave could see tears on her cheeks.

'Thank you,' she said. 'Thank you for believing in me.'

Jack and Dave nodded, because neither of them had words.

Essie's mobile phone rang and she went to answer it, smiling.

'Zara, how nice . . .' She broke off and listened. 'I'll have to ask. Hold on.' Taking the phone away from her ear, she said to Dave, 'Zara needs to come here. She's got urgent news.'

Dave held his hand out for the phone.

'What's up?' Listening, he glanced at Melissa, then at Essie. 'Okay, get the copper at the front gate to let you in. I'll authorise it.'

He gave the phone back to Essie and went to the front door to open it.

Jack followed. 'What's going on?' He glanced back at the happy family and kept his voice low.

'Your girlfriend is a dog with a bone, that's what.' But there was a smile in Dave's voice as he said it.

Jack looked at him. 'I'm not sure if that's a good or a bad thing.'

'In this case, I think it's good. Here she is. Hi, Zara,' he said as she appeared, walking up the driveway.

'Hi, Dave.' She looked over at Jack. 'Hey, you.'

Jack leaned forward and kissed her. 'I've missed you.'

'Me too. But I'm not finished work yet. Hold on to your hat because you're going to love this story. Can I come in?'

Dave and Jack stood back to let her enter and Zara went to Essie. 'It's lovely to see you so happy. Hello, Melissa.'

Everyone was inside now. Melissa had Paris on her lap and the child gave a squeal of delight when she saw Zara. She slipped down and ran to her.

'This is my mum,' Paris said, jumping up and down. 'I've only seen photos of her before!'

363

'How wonderful you get to see her in real life!' Zara said. 'Can we all sit down?'

Essie looked at her. 'What's going on?'

'Come on, over here,' Zara pointed to the chairs at the kitchen table. 'We can all fit around here as this is going to take some time.' She took a breath as they all sat, and Jack watched as she looked over at him. He wished he knew what she was about to say.

'Essie, when this all started, and you wouldn't talk to me, I started researching you. I was trying to find information on Melissa so I could track her down and find out what was going on with the drugs.'

'What are drugs?' Paris asked.

Essie turned to her. 'Darling, this is an adult conversation. Can you please go into your room and I'll call you when you can come out.'

Paris pouted. 'But . . .'

Melissa rose. 'I'll go with her.'

Zara shook her head. 'No, you need to hear this too.'

Paris let out a theatrical sigh. 'Okay, I'll goooo.'

They all smiled as she flounced out of the room.

Zara started her story again. 'You may remember that I said Paris reminded me of someone and I've been trying to work out who it was. I couldn't place it, but faces are what I'm good at, so I kept thinking and researching and watching.' She kept her tone even. 'I looked through the school yearbooks and, Melissa, you weren't in any that I had.'

Melissa shook her head. 'No, I was never good enough at school to have any of my work published in the magazines.

And I always seemed to be sick when the school photos were taken, wasn't I, Mum?'

'Yes, you were. They took them in August, if I remember correctly, and you always had a cold that turned into bronchitis. Every year without fail.'

'That explains that then,' Zara said.

Everyone was looking at her, waiting.

Essie suddenly seemed uneasy and looked down at the floor.

'Then Hopper put me on to a bloke who lives in a humpy down on the railway line. Ted, his name is. He gave me some interesting information on you. Said that a long time ago there was talk that you had twins, but everyone only ever saw you with one baby, so people either assumed one had died, or that the rumour was untrue.'

Jack saw Essie move her hands to her throat as if she were stopping herself from speaking.

Melissa's face showed her confusion. 'What?' She looked over at Essie. 'Twins? That can't be right. You always told me I was an only child.'

Essie nodded. 'Yes, I had twins. A boy and a girl.' Her voice seemed stilted, as if she had to force the words out of her body.

'But . . . I don't understand.' Melissa regarded Essie curiously. 'Where are they?'

Essie's eyes welled up. 'You're the twin girl, Melissa. Your brother—' She let out a little sob. 'I don't know where he is. I think he's dead.'

'No.' Melissa blinked a couple of times and put her hand over her mouth. 'That can't be right. You would have said something.'

Essie didn't seem to be able to answer her daughter, breathing deeply before she turned to Zara. 'How did you find out? Essie wasn't even my name then.' She paused. 'Well, it was, but I never went by it.'

'First of all, I saw the name on your suitcase. Rose Kelly.'

A ghost of a smile appeared as everyone watched her memories crowd in. 'Yes, Ian always called me Rose. That wasn't my name—it's Essie—but he said I was his Irish rose. I loved that the name made me feel wild and romantic and free. All the things I was craving when I left home.' Sadness crossed her face. 'But after he'd gone, I couldn't bear anyone to call me Rose, so I started correcting everyone. Telling them my name was Essie so I didn't have to feel so desolate every time someone called me Rosie.'

'Oh, Essie, I'm so sorry,' Zara said, sympathy on her face. She waited before starting again in her steady, soothing voice. 'Then I saw the birth certificates when I was helping get you ready for this move. Two of them. Bridget Melissa and Alroy Ian. Both had the same birthday. And the box of black-and-white photos I found when I was helping Paris pack. You and two babies sitting on the back lawn of your house.' She waited for Essie to take over.

'I went to the hospital one night,' Essie said. She looked over at Melissa. 'You both were still only tiny—twelve months old. Ian had just come home from working away for a year, shearing. You were sick. Had a fever and I didn't know what to do, so I took you to the hospital. It was a tricky time. I'd spent the previous two years following him from shed to shed, and part of the lifestyle had been wonderful, exotic—I was seeing things I'd never seen before.' She paused and looked at them all. 'And part of it was nothing but hard work. That afternoon, before you'd become sick, I'd told him I wouldn't go on the road with him anymore. You couldn't understand what it was like, having never done it. He was a shearer and we were chasing sheds all time. Never staying one place more than three weeks.

'I had liked the travel to begin with. We had fun. Oh, he was a rascal, your father.' Her face took on a faraway look. 'Such a tease. He'd make me laugh even when I was angry. He worked so hard, Ian did. But he played hard too.

'Then I got pregnant and all that changed. I didn't want to move around anymore, but he still did.

'After a chance meeting I moved into the house we live in now and I've never left. I always thought he might come back, but he never did.'

'And he left with your son?' Zara asked quietly.

'Ah,' Essie swallowed a few times and looked down. Her hands were picking at the hem of her cardigan. 'Well . . . I never . . .' Then she looked up, her face a world of pain. 'Yes. Yes, he did. I came back from the hospital and Ian was gone. Alroy was gone too. There was a note saying not to worry. They'd be okay and that if I wasn't going to get back on the road, then he had no choice but to get going with Alroy. "One for you and one for me," he said.' Essie's voice quavered.

Melissa shot up, her eyes wild. 'What? Is that even legal? How could he do that?' She stopped and then sat down. 'Oh my God,' she said quietly. 'I've got a brother I don't even remember. How does . . . how does that even happen? Oh, Mum.' Melissa reached out to clasp Essie's hand.

'I never went to the police. Just got on with life. What could I do? Nothing. I didn't know where they'd gone,' Essie said.

'The police would have helped,' Jack broke in.

Essie shook her head. 'No. Ian would have known how to disappear. Headed up to some shed in the back of beyond. He would have been hard to find. Even my friend Evie said not to chase him. She thought looking after a little boy would be too much for Ian and he'd bring him back. But he never did.

'From then on I made sure no one ever called us Rose or Bridget. I didn't want any reminders of Ian and our lives together, it was too painful. I never forgot Alroy, and in later years I did try to find him—I used newspapers and searched for his name. It was so distinctive.' A little sob escaped her. 'Ian must've changed it, or he died, because I've never been able to find either of them.' Frowning, she looked at Zara. 'What's this family resemblance you talk about? You've only met Melissa twice and never Ian. But you've said for some time you thought Paris looks like someone you know.'

Zara nodded and smiled, before getting her phone out and sending a text message. Turning back to the others, she said, 'Melissa, I knew when I saw you; it was something about your eyes. I'd seen someone recently with a gold patch under the iris just the way you have. It took me ages to remember who it was.'

A knock sounded, and Essie went pale. 'No?'

Grinning, Zara got up. 'Yes. I found him.'

Looking ready to faint, Essie followed Zara to the door.

'I always kept my door blue, in case he ever came home,' Essie said, more to herself than anyone else. 'I thought he might remember.'

Everyone in the room was standing in anticipation.

The door opened, and Jesse Barnett stood there.

'Oh my God, Alroy, you look just like him!' Essie flew across the distance between them.

Alroy opened his arms and held her tightly, all the while looking at Melissa in fascination. She had her hand over her mouth, and tears running down her cheeks.

'Hello, Mum,' he said in a gruff voice. 'Been a while. Dad changed my name.'

Epilogue

Courtney passed Zara a wine then filled her plate with the salads set out on the bench.

Tye and Jack were standing at the barbecue talking about the impending footy grand final with Dave and James, while Kim and Zara's mother Lynda sat chatting at the kitchen table.

'You good?' Courtney asked Zara.

She nodded, taking a sip of the wine and looking around contentedly at the people in her house.

'Tell me about today,' Courtney said.

Zara's mind flew back to the counsellor's office. She and Jack had gone together and he'd waited outside for her appointment to finish. She put her drink down and practised the strategy Helen had given her when she didn't want to talk about something. A couple of deeper breaths than normal, then organise the words in her mind.

'It was good. She asked all the normal questions, you know, did I sleep through the night and what did I dream about? I felt like I should be lying on a couch, to begin with, but she made me really comfortable—and I don't feel like I am going mad—' Zara paused '—which I thought I was. All the dreams and stuff.'

Jack came over and put his hand on her shoulder, dropping a kiss on her head. 'This is a good thing,' he said.

Zara looked up at him, her hand going up to cover his. 'I know,' she answered simply. Turning her head, she looked at Dave, who had sat down next to Kim. 'Thank you.'

He nodded. 'All in a day's work!'

Lynda jumped up. 'I've got something for you,' she said, before going to her bag. She drew out a photograph and handed the frame to Zara. 'Maybe seeing them every day will help.'

Reaching out, Zara felt goosebumps prickle her skin as she looked at her brother's smiling face and then at her dad's. They both looked back at her from the creek on Rowberry Glen. Her dad was in the driver's seat of his old ute and Will was on the back.

She traced the outlines of their faces and swallowed hard. Helen had made her sit with the uncomfortable feeling of grief for a few minutes earlier that day, so now she recognised the feeling and understood it was okay to feel this way. To feel the emptiness and sadness. In time, it would lessen. Talking would help too and never forgetting them. But right now, she felt like she had two men who were protecting her from a higher realm.

'It's beautiful. Thanks, Mum,' Zara said, setting the picture gently on the table. 'I'm so glad you're all here. Thank you for caring so much about me—I'm sure there were times when you wondered what was going on, but now we know. Getting better will take time, but I'm up for the challenge if you guys are alongside me.'

Jack raised his beer, toasting her. 'We wouldn't be anywhere else.'

'Hear, hear,' Dave and James said together as Kim leaned over and squeezed her hand.

'Of course we are.'

Zara's phone buzzed.

Just got your article on the granny story, and I'm happy to admit I was wrong. Now get on with the politician story please. Lachie.

Acknowledgements

The biggest thank yous and love go to:

Everyone from A&U, but mostly Tom, Annette, Christa and Sarah. Laura, looking forward to working with you on this book.

Gaby Naher, from Left Bank Literary.

DB.

Rochelle and Hayden. Rocket and Jack.

Carolyn, Heather, Robyn, Kelly (even though you don't read), Lauren and Graham, Ewin, Jan and Pete, Chrissy, Bev, Lee and Paul and Al.

Mum, Dad, Nicholas, Ellie, Elijah and Chloe.

Tanya.

Everyone who reads these books.

As always, it's hard to find the words to thank everyone. You have my heart and I have yours.

I know our world has changed so much since I wrote to you all last. I'm wishing you health and safety and hope you find a little bit of escapism within these pages—written when life was normal.

With love,
  Fleur x

OUT IN NOVEMBER 2021

Deception Creek

FLEUR McDONALD

Emma Cameron, a recently divorced farmer and a local in Barker, runs Deception Creek, the farm that three generations of her family have owned before her. Every day Emma pushes herself hard on the land, hoping to make ten-year-old memories of a terrible car accident disappear. And now there are more recent nightmares of an ex-husband who refuses to understand how much the farm means to Emma.

When criminal Joel Hammond is released from jail and heads home to Barker, Detective Dave Burrows and his officer Senior Sergeant Jack Higgins are on high alert. Joel has a long and sorry history with many of the townsfolk and they are not keen to see him home to stay.

Not all of the Barker locals want to see Joel run out of town though. Some even harbour doubts about Joel's conviction. The town finds itself split down the middle, families pitted against each other with devastating outcomes.

ISBN 978 1 76087 882 5

PROLOGUE

2011

'I've told you, Alice, I haven't touched anything! What can I do to make you believe me?' Kyle's voice was pleading as he looked over at his wife, but she wouldn't return his gaze.

Her arms were crossed tightly across her chest as she stared out the car window at the Mount Gambier country. The paddocks of tall grass rippling in the wind were passing at a hundred and ten kilometres an hour.

'Alice?'

This time she turned to him, her blue eyes flat and cold, no trace of their usual sparkle.

Kyle drew a breath as he remembered the words from his mother: *Never get between a Sharpe and their money, son. There's some truth in their last name.*

'You've been skimming money from the bank accounts,' Alice snapped. 'Dad told me all about it.'

At a glance, Kyle could see heat flooding her cheeks. She was fuming, and he knew he had two options: he could deny all knowledge, calmly and quietly, or he could get angry.

'Look in my briefcase. The statements are there, along with all the reconciliations. There's nothing amiss. Oliver's got this wrong.' His words were firm and quiet, but anger pulsed through him as he said his father-in-law's name.

Oliver Sharpe was an interfering, obnoxious man who thought he knew better than everyone about everything, and Kyle didn't like or trust him one bit. He had only ever seen the old man's aggression aimed at others, but now here it was, coming at him. He shouldn't have been surprised.

'I don't believe you. Dad doesn't make mistakes like this.' She shifted in her seat to look straight at him. 'A hundred grand? In six months? The whole time we've been married!'

'And as a senior accounts officer I'd like to think I don't make mistakes either. If you believe him,' Kyle snapped, pushing his foot down on the accelerator, 'why are you here with me, going to the accountant? There must be some doubt in your mind.' He rearranged his face and voice, with difficulty. 'I'd hope there's doubt in your mind. After all, I *am* your husband—I'd like to think you trust me.' The hurt was real.

'Do you think I *want* this to be true?' Her voice held an accusation, while her long fingernails tapped on the edge of the window. 'No, I *want* to go to the accountant, I *want* to hear that this is all a big misunderstanding. I *want* to go home. I *want* things to be the way they were when we brought you into the business.' She paused. 'The trouble is, I don't think that's going to happen.'

Gripping the steering wheel tighter, Kyle could see all his hard work, the long hours on the tractor, the countless times he'd bitten his tongue to get on Oliver's good side, being snatched away by opinion of a person he didn't even know. The accountant was paid by Oliver—if he wanted Kyle out of the business, that's exactly what would happen.

Everything was going wrong. His whole life was coming to a grinding halt over a stupid misunderstanding.

'Kyle, slow down!'

'What?'

Alice's voice broke through the waves of anger that were overtaking Kyle's mind.

'You're going too fast. Look!' His wife nodded frantically towards the speedo.

He looked down. One hundred and twenty.

Lifting his foot slightly, the ute slowed. Kyle dragged in a deep breath. 'Look, Alice . . .'

'No, Kyle, I don't want to talk about it.' She held up her hand in a stop sign. 'I want to get to Foster and Foster and see what Hannah has to tell me.'

'Oh yeah? And what about what *I* want? I'm your husband, don't I get a say in any of this?' The red-hot angry words shot out of him before he could stop them.

'I don't think you're in a position to have a say.'

His knuckles were white. This wasn't how it was supposed to go. Glancing in the rear-view mirror, he saw a vehicle coming up behind them, the indicator on as if they were going to overtake. His eyes flicked back to the landscape ahead; large, fat-trunked trees lined the road leading to the corner not far ahead.

The morning was foggy and dew was glistening in the pale light as the sun tried to force its rays through the heavy, lead-grey cloud.

The white Nissan X-Trail pulled out.

'Really?'

There was no way the driver behind should be passing on this stretch of road. Kyle's instinct was to lift his foot from the accelerator, but he didn't. Instead, he pushed it down harder and felt the ute jump away as the turbo kicked in.

'What are you doing now?' Alice's tone was a mix of exasperation and angst.

'This bloke needs a lesson on how to drive.'

'Kyle! Don't.'

Clearly the driver realised there was a problem, because he pulled back in behind Kyle.

'Shouldn't try to pass when there's a corner coming up, idiot,' he muttered, once again glancing to the front.

On the wide, sweeping bend was a large tree and on the other side, Kyle knew, the road opened up into a long stretch of bitumen, where the guy behind would be able to pass. Kyle pushed his foot down a bit harder.

'Kyle, stop it. Slow down. Please.' This time there was fear in his wife's voice. 'Don't be stupid.'

He ignored her, his eyes flicking between the road ahead and the ute behind them. The Nissan was still in the left lane. Good. He took a couple of breaths.

'This is crazy, Kyle,' Alice said softly. 'Come on, slow down.'

'How about you grab all the information from the back seat and look at it, Alice. I haven't done anything wrong.' Lifting his foot, the vehicle slowed.

Alice cast a worried look towards him. 'Okay.' She twisted around in the seat and reached behind her.

'Every cent is accounted for.' He watched her in the mirror as she did as he asked.

Not able to reach, Alice undid her seatbelt, grabbed the paperwork and sat back down in one quick, fluid motion.

'You'll see *now*,' Kyle said, the word coming from him more loudly than intended.

'It's not going to matter what I think,' she said tightly, as she studied the reconciliations. 'If Dad has found something amiss . . .'

'But I haven't stolen anything!' He banged the steering wheel hard with his fist, and the ute jumped away as he pushed his foot down once more. 'I haven't!' His face was warm from the anger that was radiating through him, and his fist throbbed a little from hitting the wheel.

She looked up from the printed pages.

'Kyle!'

'What?' The word snapped out of him.

'The corner! It's . . .' His wife reached out to yank his arm but didn't connect, because with one quick movement, Kyle had pulled the steering wheel to the left, throwing the ute to the side. A wheel hit a pothole and the ute bounced, throwing them together, and Alice's arm bounded off Kyle's as he held the wheel.

A loud, high-pitched shriek emerged from Alice, just as the left-hand side nose of the ute hit the gum tree.

Glass shattered.

Metal tore.

Alice's squeal stopped instantly as Kyle's head hit the steering wheel.

CHAPTER 1

2021

Dave climbed out of the police-issue vehicle and looked at the house.

A loose sheet of tin lifted in the breeze, and the verandah sagged at one end. Deep cracks ran through the cement path leading to the front steps, and black ants ran busily in and out of the crevices.

Derelict and uninhabited, Dave thought. *Lonely.*

Ducking under the overgrown bougainvillea bush and taking the few steps to the door, Dave raised his hand to knock on the splintered wood.

The noise echoed around the large stone house. Then, nothing.

'You in there, Joel? It's Dave Burrows, Barker Police.' Moving over to the dirty windows, he cupped his hands to peer inside, but all he could see in the darkness was a lone couch with a throw sheet over it and screwed-up newspapers scattered across the floor.

He walked along the verandah, his boots grinding in the dirt, looking in each window.

Nothing.

'Joel Hammond? I'm here to check in on you. Make sure you understand your parole conditions. Dave Burrows from Barker Police,' he called again.

'Oh yeah? Why's that?'

At the corner of the house, a small, wiry man with shaggy hair stood with a shovel in his hand.

Dave smiled. 'Joel Hammond?'

'Yeah.'

'Good to meet you. I'm Dave Burrows—'

'From Barker Police. Yeah, I heard. What can I do you for?'

'I got a note from my colleagues in Adelaide, saying you were being released and heading back up this way. Thought I'd pop in and say g'day. Let you know if you need anything, I'm around.'

Joel didn't answer, he just stared at Dave and lifted the shovel up and down and dug it into the dirt, in the same spot.

'You got back out here all right?'

'Yeah.'

'And no trouble?'

'Look, I don't know what you know, or what you've been told, but I'm not here to cause trouble. Or take it from anyone else. I've just come back home.' Joel glanced around and leaned the shovel against the house. He took a couple of steps towards Dave before he spoke again.

'Not that there's anyone here to make it a home anymore. But I've done my time. I just want to get on with things without any interference from anyone.' He paused and looked steadily at Dave. 'I've already lost nine years of my life for a crime I didn't commit, so how about you get on your white horse and fuck off to where you came from. I don't need anybody's help.'

Dave had to give it to the man, he sounded sincere, if not angry. 'Look, I understand your mistrust of the police. And, sure thing, I'll head off now, but I'm here to keep the peace in Barker, and if you get hassled, I want to know. Like you said, you've done your time. I'm not saying it's going to happen, but it's only fair you know, there've been a few rumblings around the place.

'The Douglas family knew you were coming back, and the brothers—well, Steve—were stirring up a bit of trouble at the pub last Friday night. I just wanted you to know. Look, I'll leave you my details. Any problems, just get in contact.' Dave nodded and dug in his wallet for his card, before holding it out to the man. 'And just a reminder— don't forget to report in once a week at the station. That way I won't have to come looking for you.'

Joel Hammond didn't move, so Dave placed the card on the nearest windowsill and turned away.

'How'd you go?' Jack asked from behind the mountain of paperwork on his desk at the police station.

'Pretty stand-offish,' Dave said as he took his jacket off and hung it behind the door. 'I can understand why, though—the bloke's just spent nine years in jail. I'd be the last person he'd want to see. Might've thought I was coming to give him a hard time.'

'He should've been pleased at the heads up, especially if Steve Douglas wants to make trouble.'

'I bet he hoped he'd just slip back under the radar. The fact the town knows already and it's hardly been twenty-four hours isn't a good sign.'

'Don't know why you'd be surprised that word Joel is back has spread so quickly. This is Barker we're talking about here.' Jack took a piece of paper and signed the bottom. 'Did you find out anything more about him?'

Shaking his head, Dave sat down and wiggled the mouse next to his computer to wake the screen. 'He didn't offer anything except that he was innocent.'

'Of fraud? A crim saying they're innocent? Gosh, there's a surprise!' Jack's tone was as dry as the paint on the walls.

'Who's innocent of fraud?' Kim stood in the doorway holding a plastic cake carrier. 'Joel Hammond?'

Both men broke into a grin and Jack got up quickly to take the container from her.

'Smoko on wheels. Cheers, Kim,' Jack said as he lifted the lid. 'Look, Dave. Chocolate mud cake.'

'One of my faves.' Dave stepped over and put his arm around his wife, and dropped a kiss on her head. 'Thanks, honey.'

'You're welcome,' Kim said as she sat in Dave's chair. 'Were you talking about Joel?'

'Hmm,' Dave nodded. 'I went and saw him today. Community policing and all that.'

'Such a shame. He was a nice boy at school.'

Dave glanced at Joel Hammond's file, open on his desk. 'How did you know him at school?' he asked. 'You wouldn't have been there together.'

Kim shook her head. 'No, not in the same year, but I was a prefect in Year 12 and he was in primary school then. I can't remember what year, but he was a little-y. Big brown eyes and freckles. A bit of a clown. Always teasing and playing jokes. Then as he grew up, he used to come into the roadhouse all the time. Just a genuine, nice guy. Quietly spoken and polite.'

'Who defrauded his employer,' Jack said around the cake in his mouth. 'This is really good, Kim.'

Kim raised a shoulder. 'Hmm, well, that was what the jury decided, wasn't it?'

'You think there was some doubt? What makes you say that?' Dave frowned a little as he looked at her.

'Answering a question with a question. So typical of you, Dave! And what can I say?' Kim chided. 'I wasn't on the jury, so I don't have all the evidence or the information they would have had.'

Raising his eyebrows at his wife, he gave a slight shake of his head. 'That's my girl, always making sure that everyone gets a fair hearing!'

She cut a piece of the cake and handed it to him with a sunny smile. 'Seriously, though,' she continued, 'I found it hard to believe—I never thought there was a reason for him to do it.'

'Do what exactly?' Jack asked. 'I wasn't here then, so I only know what I've read on the file—that's he defrauded his employer to the tune of two hundred and fifty thousand by getting cheques signed and depositing them in his own bank account.'

'Yeah,' said Dave, 'it was back in the days before EFT was used. The stock and wool cheques would be piled up on the desk of the finance manager and he'd go through and sign each cheque. He didn't know who or what he was signing for—he trusted the people below him. And think about this: it was a large stock firm with heaps of cheques being written. He might've had to sign two or three hundred cheques a day. Joel put the cheques with his name on them in the middle of the pile and the finance manager signed away.' Dave shook his head. 'It's so easy and obvious now to see how it all happened, but he got away with it for a couple of years.'

'Hold on,' Jack said. 'Joel was put away for defrauding a company, not the Douglas family. What's their connection to all this?'

'Ah well, that's another story,' Kim said, making herself comfortable on the chair in between the two desks. 'Joel was dating Maggie Douglas when they were teenagers. Max and Paula were quite strict with their daughter. Well, the boys too, but not as much. There were a few times the three Douglas boys went out and got drunk and caused havoc around the town, and I didn't hear of any repercussions.

'Now let's remember that Max Douglas is the minister at the Baptist church. But there has always been a difference in the way the boys were disciplined to how Maggie was.

'The story is that Maggie slipped out the window one night to meet Joel. They went to the grain silos on the edge of town. You know how there're ladders to climb up the side? Well, they were climbing to the top when she slipped and fell. She was only sixteen, so quite a while ago now.' Kim paused. 'The first thing the parents knew about it was the police knocking on their door. They thought she was tucked up in bed, when in reality she was in the morgue at the hospital.

'Joel was already being questioned, because he'd raised the alarm. He was completely innocent of what happened, but the family made it so hard for him, he had to leave town.' Kim gave a sad smile. 'The whole incident was horrible for everyone.'

Jack's eyes narrowed. 'How did the coppers know for sure he didn't have something to do with her fall?'

'I don't know, Jack.' Kim fixed him with a look a mother might give her insolent child. 'But they must have been certain, because there weren't any charges laid. Nothing more than a tragic accident. But the family couldn't understand why he was walking away when they'd lost their daughter.' She paused. 'I can't remember if Joel was even at the top of the silos as Maggie went up. It's a long time ago now. I wasn't involved with either of the families, except when they came into the roadhouse, so I only heard what was on the street and there was plenty of talk, let me tell you.' She shrugged. 'You know me, I don't take any notice of gossip unless I know it to be true.'

'What did the Douglases do to make it so difficult for Joel to stay?' Jack pressed.

'Honestly, I can't remember all the details. I just know that he left town and went to work in Adelaide, then the next thing I read was that he was on trial for fraud.'

There was silence then, as Jack leaned forwards to cut himself another piece of cake. 'That's all pretty terrible,' he said finally.

'The Douglases never recovered from Maggie's death,' Kim said. 'As you wouldn't from the death of a child.' She stopped for a moment and took a breath, and Dave knew she was remembering her sister, whose only son had been murdered. It was the first case Dave had investigated in Barker, the reason he'd come here to live.

Graham had been run over by a stampeding mob of cattle. Trampled to death. The police were never able to prove Dave's theory, but he was sure that the cattle had been spooked by men Graham owed money to. Perhaps they'd cracked a whip or let out a yell—however they'd done it, they'd been clever and covered their tracks. It was the one murder he had never been able to solve.

Graham's parents had become shells of the people they once were, and eventually they sold the farm and moved away, no longer able to bear being on the land where their son died.

The only good thing to come out of that case was that Dave and Kim had reconnected years—decades—after their short-lived teenage summer romance. A summer romance neither of them had ever forgotten, despite their lives taking them in different directions.

Dave reached out and touched Kim's arm as he remembered walking into the roadhouse and seeing her for the first time in more than ten years. Her hundred-watt smile had been enough to make him fall head over heels in love with her again. If he'd ever fallen out of love with her; he doubted he had.

'So, all that aside,' she said, glancing at him, 'my question would be why would he have wanted to steal that money? His family was comfortable. He never wanted for anything when he was growing up. He always drove the nicest cars and dressed in fashionable clothes when he came back here. Not that he came home often. But people ran into him in the city and he used to meet his parents halfway, in Clare, instead of coming to Barker.' Kim frowned. 'It must have been so hard for him, not being able to come back to his family home. But he did it for the sake of the Douglas family, I think, to stay out of their way. I imagine he didn't want to be the reminder of what they'd lost.'

'Where was he working?' Jack asked.

Dave picked up the file and tossed it towards him. 'Have a read, if you want. It's only a personnel file, nothing about the investigation in there. We can order that if need be. But he was in Adelaide at the head office of Stockomatic. Like Elders and Nutrien today, but a smaller company. They went bankrupt a few years ago.' Dave leaned back in his chair, putting his hands behind his head.

'I'm not surprised, given the way their finance manager checked things,' Jack scoffed.

'His mum and dad were lovely people,' Kim said. 'Generous. Always used to donate at the annual P and C fundraiser and to the church, and Verity always gave whatever food she had left over from the market garden to the old folks home at the hospital. But they never wanted any recognition. They're both dead now.'

'Wait on,' Jack said. 'Joel hasn't got any family here? There's no one at all left? Why would he come back?'

Kim shook her head. 'From what I know he's alone in the world now. His parents died . . . oh, must be four or five years ago, and they didn't have any other children. Poor Joel was still in prison when they passed. I remember there was talk about him not being at the funeral. The father went first, then she did. Only six or eight months apart. Dave, you must remember that?' She looked at him. 'Billy and Verity Hammond.'

Dave nodded slightly before turning to Jack. 'Often people who get out of jail go back to what's familiar. The house he's in is where he grew up; it would feel safe to him. After being in prison all that time, safety would be very important to Joel.' To Kim, he said, 'I remember them vaguely. I never had anything to do with them really—they must've been law-abiding citizens.'

Dave gave her a gentle wink and Kim's smile was sad as she answered.

'They were. Very much so. That's why Joel being caught up with a fraud charge doesn't make any sense to me.'

Dave harrumphed. 'Why does anyone do anything? I've met enough crims to know they don't need to come from—' he used his fingers to act as quotation marks '—a "bad" family to break the law. If the court convicted him, then it was proved beyond reasonable doubt. That's all I know. What I don't want to happen here is the town taking revenge against a bloke who's done his time in jail and was cleared of any wrongdoing in an accident.' He shook his head. 'Some people just seem to have horrible luck, don't they? I mean, look at this case. His girlfriend dead and he ends up in jail—two completely different situations.'

'Yeah, you're right,' Kim said, standing up. 'Anyhow, I've got other meals to cook for Catering Angels. Poor old Mrs Hunter had a fall and her daughter called asking me to cook up a week's worth of meals for her, so I'd best get on.'

'Barker's own meals on wheels,' Dave said with a gentle smile. 'Okey-doke, honey. I'll see you at home.'

Kim looked at Dave. 'Maybe I'll drop some food off to Joel.'

Not able to help himself, Dave laughed. 'Of course, you will. I never doubted it.'

Jack looked up from the file he'd been flicking through and waited until Kim left.

'Nine years,' he said.

'Nine years, what?' Dave asked, reaching for another slice of cake.

'Don't you think that's a long time to go away for a white-collar crime?'

Dave stopped chewing. Jack was dead right.

CHAPTER 2

Emma Cameron took a swig of wine and held the glass over her head as she danced. Around her, her friends bumped bodies as they swayed and bounced in time to the music on her verandah.

This was how she forgot the accident. Drinking, partying, working. Blocking out any remnants of the noise: the screams, the tearing metal, the blaring sirens.

This was also how she forgot her divorce.

Jacqui slung an arm around Emma's shoulders and together they belted out 'D-I-V-O-R-C-E' along with Tammy Wynette.

On the verandah, which stretched out into the vastness of the paddock, was a balloon structure: pinks, yellows and oranges interwoven with chiffon and silk. The balloon vagina had been Jacqui's idea. 'It's a divorce party,' she'd said with the usual wicked gleam in her eye. 'You know, the start of a new life. Leave the entertainment with me, I'll fix it!'

Emma had been hesitant, knowing that her friend would turn up with something crazy—and she had. Now, Jacqui was insisting that the two of them, both recent divorcees, be 'rebirthed' by pushing themselves through the balloon vagina.

God almighty, Emma thought. *What is this?*

Through blurry eyes she could see the moon reflecting off the roof of the machinery shed. The noise of their whoops and the music was bouncing off the line of hills behind the house before being swallowed up by the darkness.

'Woo-hoo!' screamed Maddy as she pushed her way through the birth-canal balloons and came out the other side.

Jacqui, who was in charge of the next step—the 'baptism'—grabbed a bottle of champagne and poured it over Maddy's head. The liquid spilled on the cement and splashed up around their feet.

Emma waited her turn, watching the crowd gathered around the front, waiting to welcome the newly rebirthed divorcees into the brand-new scary world of singledom.

Maddy was now dripping with champagne and it was Emma's turn. She set her wine glass down and put her hands out in front as she pushed her way past the rubber-smelling balloons and soft, shiny material. She had tears on her cheeks but she refused to dwell. She was divorced now. She had received the email last week. She and Phil were finally finished.

Thank god. Even though it made her sad. Thank god.

Yesterday her brother had sent her a text message, a meme: *My life didn't go according to plan and that's okay.*

Guessing she might feel like that at some stage in the future, she'd sent back a thumbs up, but the words didn't resonate with her now.

Emma felt hands reaching in to pull her through the final couple of steps of the balloon vagina, and suddenly she emerged into the new world. Raising her arms, she let out a squeal of joy. Or was it pain?

'Yes!'

The three women put their arms around each other while the rest of the party-goers threw confetti and streamers over them.

All three were done. Rebirthed. They were finished with the past and starting anew.

But the other two already had new men in their lives. Emma didn't.

As the women broke apart, someone put another drink in her hand and the music changed to an upbeat nineties song. She was pulled onto the dance floor by a man she'd gone to school with, and she willingly moved in time to the beat and let herself be pushed around the dance floor, all the while looking around. She saw Matt leaning against the wall, beer in hand, talking to a couple of blokes. They locked eyes and he tipped his beer towards her in a form of salute. She smiled and closed her eyes and she twirled around and around. Maybe she'd ask Matt to dance later. He'd always looked like he was light on his feet . . . Especially if there was a cow chasing him!

Maddy handed her another drink as she danced past, and Emma's vision started to get blurry.

Finished. The word kept running through her head. Then another: *Done.*

Yes, they were, and that was good. She and Phil could never have worked. Emma didn't know why she'd thought they could.

But now she was single. Alone. And who was she now that her past life was gone?

The thumping headache made itself known before Emma opened her eyes. Her tongue was stuck to the roof of her mouth, and she didn't want to smell her own rank breath. She could see the sunlight through her closed eyelids, and she threw a hand up to cover her eyes.

'Ugh.' Emma tested parts of her body for pain. Rolling over, but keeping her eyes closed, she reached for the glass of water she always kept alongside her bed. Empty. 'Bugger,' she whispered.

Taking her time, she got up and went to the ensuite and drank straight from the tap, letting the cold water dribble over her tongue before gulping greedily. The headache was throbbing.

Switching the tap off, she rummaged in the vanity drawer for Panadol. Or preferably something stronger. The crumpled packet she found held only one tablet. That would have to do for now. She swallowed it and stuck her head under the tap again, gulping more water before gingerly climbing back into her bed. Pulling the doona around her tightly, she reached down to switch on the electric blanket. Her naked body was freezing as well as hurting.

Closing her eyes again, Emma lay there waiting for the Panadol to kick in, hoping that if she didn't move, the pain might go away.

She couldn't help but think how strange it was—even after eighteen months—to be sleeping alone. Emma had assumed that once Phil left, over time she would get used to the left side of the bed being empty, but she hadn't. Even after all these months she still woke in the middle of the night to silence, and when she stretched her hand out to feel his body and warmth, all it met was a cold, empty sheet.

Hugging the pillow to her, she breathed deeply, trying not to allow the anxiety to overwhelm her. Her stomach felt as if a cold lump had settled at the bottom, and within her heart was a gnawing hurt that didn't stop.

Emma hadn't known that heartache was an actual physical thing until she realised she was going to be divorced at forty. That wasn't how her life was supposed to play out.

She'd wanted children, people to love and care for. A home.

She had a home, but it was empty of everything else. No children. No husband.

A tear leaked out from behind her closed eyes and she frowned gingerly. She needed to stop this right now, otherwise she might never stop crying. There was no place for a pity party when she felt like this, because the sadness would only grow and grow until it threatened to overwhelm her.

When Emma thought about Phil, she knew that some part of her would always love him—but only like a brother. No, not even that. A distant cousin. They hadn't been friends before they were a couple, and they hadn't spent long getting to know each other before they got married . . .

'No!' She said the word loudly, then groaned, her hand flying to the top of her head to hold it. A couple of breaths later, she muttered, much more softly, 'Stop it, Emma. Just stop it.'

Throwing back the covers, and ignoring the pain in her head, she padded out to the kitchen and switched on the kettle.

Her living room was full of half-empty bottles, dirty wine glasses and beer cans. Confetti covered the floor, and in the corner stood the balloon vagina, which at the time had seemed like a fun and crazy thing to do.

Now all it seemed to represent was her loneliness.

She had a vague recollection of the party moving inside as the night had gone on and the damp, cold air settled around them. Maddy had insisted the vagina come inside too.

'In case she gets cold,' she'd said, her face worried, clutching her wine glass.

She couldn't face the clean-up just yet. Instead, she grabbed a glass of water and sucked it down before making herself a strong coffee and walking out onto the verandah, knocking over an empty beer bottle as she went.

'Shit!' Looking around, she saw more bottles scattered. She hoped her girlfriends would come back out this morning to help her clean up. At that thought, another foggy memory sprang into her mind: the bus they'd hired coming to get everyone about 3 a.m., though she was a little fuzzy on the time. What Emma did remember was leaning against the door frame waving everyone goodbye and telling them all how much she loved them.

She was a loving drunk, not a fighting one.

The grey July clouds were scurrying across the sky, as dark and moody as she felt this morning. In contrast, the paddock at the front of the house was green with the barley crop that was just about at the start of jointing mode, when nodules formed at the main stem. Emma called it the untidy stage. The plants were long and straggly, and the leaves fell all over the place, rather than standing strong and tall as they would when they were older.

Sitting in the swinging chair her friends had bought her for Christmas, she gently pushed off with her foot and sipped her coffee. The Panadol must have kicked in a little, she realised, because her head didn't hurt as much as it had half an hour ago.

Looking out across the paddock, she felt a sense of satisfaction. When Phil left, she hadn't been sure she would be able to manage everything. Even though he hadn't worked on the farm, he'd usually been home earlier than she had, so he'd cooked, done the washing and cleaning—all the things she loathed. He certainly had been a good house husband. He'd done the accounts for the farm too, but he'd rarely got his hands dirty. Farming just wasn't his thing, so she had employed Matt and together they had kept the place going.

For a moment she looked at her hands and thought about Phil's. They were white and his fingers long and thin. Inside hands. Ones that had never seen hard work. Whereas her dad's—and Matt's—were tanned and had ingrained dust and grease in the little cracks. They were hands like hers.

Deception Creek had been her father's farm, and his father's before that, and she loved it fiercely. Thankfully, Phil had understood that he didn't have any claim on her heritage. His accountancy work had taken him in to his Barker office every day, while Emma and Matt had worked tirelessly to put the crops in and look after the few cattle they had.

Emma felt a wet nose on her foot and looked down to see her Kelpie, Cash, looking at her with his large brown eyes. It was as if he knew she was hurting.

'What's up there, Cash?' she asked, reaching down to rub his nose. He let out a quiet whine and flopped down under the chair. As she rubbed his belly with her foot, he let out a contented sigh and closed his eyes.

If only all men were as easy to please as Cash.

That had been Phil's problem: farm life was too quiet for him. He'd wanted to spend more time in town—in Adelaide—and a farming lifestyle didn't lend itself to that.

She would never forget their last fight.

'Are you coming with me or not?' he'd asked. 'It's *The Boy from Oz*! I booked the tickets months ago. You said you'd come.'

Emma had shaken her head. 'You didn't tell me the date! And I can't. I've got the seed cleaner coming tomorrow.

I've had it booked since before harvest. I can't cancel on him now, it'll put the rest of his program out with all the other farmers around the place.'

'This is fucked, Emma,' he'd snapped, his eyes bulging as he glared at her. 'This can't go on. You're completely married to the farm. Not me. We never go anywhere together; I might as well be single.' He'd stomped into the bedroom to pack.

The anger that had flared through her had been swift and ferocious. Phil not understanding her business had been a constant theme since they'd married eight years before. He was always getting angry when she couldn't make an event he'd planned—but never told her about. Then he'd go partying in Adelaide without her and posting photos of himself with women she didn't know.

But that wasn't the only thing wrong with their relationship, she'd known that in that final argument. She couldn't remember the last time they'd had sex. He had tried to initiate love-making three or so months earlier, but she'd turned away, having only finished three weeks of seeding that night. Then she'd tried a month later, and he'd turned away. That had been unusual. She'd wondered if he was getting his needs met elsewhere, but she hadn't had the energy to have the conversation.

And without the intimacy of love-making and with the busyness of her work, they'd stopped talking.

Then, as she'd watched him walk away, she'd understood there was nothing between them anymore. As familiar as she was with his face and the landscape of his body, the thought of spending another eight years together was no more appealing than yet another Christmas visit from his parents. Or aphids eating her barley crop.

'Well, maybe you should be single, then.' She'd bitten out the words before she could stop them.

'What?' Phil had stopped midstride and turned to look at her, just as she drew in a gasp of horror.

Had she really said it aloud? She may have thought it often over the past twelve months but she'd never actually said it to Phil's face. Once something like that was said, it couldn't be taken back.

'Nothing. Sorry. I'm just frustrated, that's all. I do want to go with you, I do. But you know as well as I do that there're some things I just can't put off, and this is one of them.'

As Phil had stood looking at her, she'd noticed a myriad of emotions cross his face, but relief had seemed to be the strongest. 'You know what?' he'd finally said. 'You're right. I think we'd be better off apart. You're married to this godforsaken farm, and I have a life to live. I'll pack up and move into town.' He'd glared at her again. 'Maybe you should remember that at some stage you're going to be here alone on Deception Creek, which takes up your whole life, and I bet you'll wish you'd made a different decision.'

By later that afternoon, there had been nothing of his left at the house, and only a cloud of dust hanging in the still air over the driveway to show he'd ever been there.

That had been eighteen months ago.

A small sob escaped her, and Cash lifted his head to look at her.

'It's okay,' she told him. 'I'll be okay. I always am.' She picked up her coffee cup and got off the swing, before heading back inside.

The stench of alcohol hit her, and she wrinkled her nose. The cleaning shouldn't be put off any longer, but instead, Emma went into the office and switched on the computer.

Facebook came up and let her know she was tagged in nine-plus photos. She and Jacqui, clearly drunk, smiling and red-cheeked. The three of them—Maddy, Jacqui and Emma—arms around each other, toasting the newly divorced Emma. Emma emerging reborn from the balloons and Jacqui pouring champagne over her head.

She shook her head. She was forty and acting like a teenager. Her father would probably roll over in his grave if he could see these. Her mother certainly would. She could almost hear her saying *'Now, Emma'* in the disapproving tone Emma remembered so well. Still, she had to admit, when she'd come home to work on the farm ten years ago, her mum's tone had softened towards her, glad that her daughter had come back to where she knew she belonged.

As she scrolled through her timeline, she saw more photos of the night from other friends who'd been there. Everyone had had a good time, there was no doubting it.

As she looked at the picture of her surrounded by pink balloons, an ad flashed into her timeline.

HelloSingles.

A dating site.

She squeezed her eyes shut and let out a breath. When she opened them, the ad was still in front of her.

Against her better judgement, she clicked on the link and was taken through to a page where she could create an account.

'Don't be stupid,' she whispered. 'You're hungover and lonely. Don't do this.'

She shook her head and minimised the screen, got up from her chair, then sat back down again. Her hand hovered over the mouse.

Click.

The website flashed back up.

Click.

Minimised.

The phone rang and she jumped. Looking at the screen, she saw it was Maddy.

'How's the head?' Emma asked her friend.

Maddy groaned. 'I'm too old for this shit.'

'Ha! You're the youngest out of all of us. So, times that by a bit and imagine how the rest of us are feeling.'

Maddy gave a throaty laugh. 'I'm trying not to. The night was awesome though, despite me feeling like crap. My head . . .'

'Yeah, I know. Mine's the same. But you're right, it was a great night. Thanks for everything.'

'Is there much to clean up? I was thinking about coming out to help you, but I don't think I should drive yet.'

Emma walked into the lounge room, then out onto the verandah and looked again. Really there were just a lot of bottles to take to the tip and glasses to wash.

'Nah, don't worry about it. I'll be fine with it.'

Walking through the house, she went into the kitchen and opened the fridge. 'I think I need bacon and eggs for breakfast, though.'

'Good idea. I might head to the cafe and see if they'll cook me a bacon-and-egg burger.'

'Heard from Jacqui?'

'Nah, knowing her she won't be up until later.'

Maddy paused for a moment and Emma could feel there was something big coming.

'Now, look, I know you're not going to like this, but my cousin Paul is coming to visit Mum and Dad for a few days next—'

'No.'

'Hey! You don't even know what I was going to say.' Maddy sounded hurt, but Emma knew better.

'Yes, I do. You were going to play cupid. Just don't, Maddy. I'm fine. Okay?' Her tone was firm.

'But—'

'The answer's no. It's not up for discussion.'

Clearly sensing she wasn't going to get anywhere, Maddy changed the subject. 'What are you going to do once you've cleaned up?'

'Probably go back to bed.' Emma gave a rueful laugh. 'I wish. I've got to get a mob of cattle in for calf marking tomorrow. But I don't need to do that until later. Hopefully I'll feel a bit better by then.'

'Why don't you get Matt to do it? There's a band playing at the pub this afternoon . . .'

'Maddy, if I don't see another glass of wine forever, it won't bother me.'

'Yeah, yeah, yeah, until next time.' She paused. 'Still, I don't think I need any more for a few days.'

Emma couldn't help herself: she giggled, knowing Maddy was right. Over the past year, they'd all said that at some point.

'I'll see how I feel later and text you, okay?'

'Sounds like a plan. Talk to you then.'

They hung up and Emma pulled the bacon and eggs out of the fridge and switched the kettle on again. She thought about Maddy's offer to set her up, and cringed. It just wasn't something she could do. But maybe . . . The singles website popped into her head again. What was the difference between a set-up from a friend and the computer, she wondered.

Nothing, was the answer. But was she really ready for the whole town to know she wanted a partner?

Putting the bacon in the sizzling pan, she went back into the office and brought up the dating website again, looking at it a bit longer this time.